HIDDEN PASSIONS

"You should be frightened, Victoria," Linc whispered huskily against her ear. "I'm half wild Sioux Indian. I take what I want. I could have whatever I wanted from you, but I'll have only this now." He brought his mouth down hard on hers.

In that instant, he realized he'd made a big mistake. The feel of her so close to him sent a shock wave pounding through him. He hadn't expected such a hunger to explode inside him. He suddenly wanted to taste more of her, to feel more of her.

"Savage!" she cried when he finally released her.

Now his fury flared. "That I am. Don't ever forget it." He imprisoned her wrists with one hand and raised his other to touch her face. "But I can be gentle." His fingertips slid down her throat. "And pleasure you in ways I doubt you've ever known . . ."

He brought his mouth down to meet hers again, not harshly as before, but whisper-softly, barely touching her lips. Victoria was motionless in his arms, held captive now by more than just his strength. She couldn't think. She could only feel.

NANCY MOULTON

SAVAGE HEAT

ZEBRA BOOKS
KENSINGTON PUBLISHING CORP.

To Heather Lynne Moulton and Ryan Patrick Moulton,
my pride,
my joy,
my wonderful children.
I love you so very much.
—Mom

ZEBRA BOOKS

are published by

Kensington Publishing Corp.
475 Park Avenue South
New York, NY 10016

First printing: May, 1991

Printed in the United States of America

Chapter One

Wyoming Territory
June, 1880

A dark figure loomed behind her father, arm raised threateningly. A heavy weight crushed her, tearing her breath away. Blood . . .

Victoria Spencer's eyes flew wide open. She jerked upright, gasping, her heart racing wildly. Fearfully, she raked a hand through her blond curls just as rough hands grasped her by the shoulders, shaking her hard.

"Don't act up with this dreaming again, girl!" a stern voice accused.

Confused, Victoria shifted her green eyes around the train car, then to the fifty-year-old woman next to her in the seat.

"You've disturbed my nap, you stupid girl!" Hannah Perkins snapped, her thick, black eyebrows dipping into a harsh frown.

A girl of fifteen with light brown hair leaned across the aisle from her seat on the other side. "Oh, Hannah, please don't scold Victoria. You know she can't help having that awful nightmare about Papa."

"Shut your mouth, Deborah," the older woman ordered, lowering her harsh voice slightly and glancing around. "You're drawing attention to us."

Looking chastised, Deborah shrank back against the brown velvet cushioned seat, saying nothing more.

"The dream always seems so real," Victoria murmured seeing the details of it too clearly in her mind. "I'm lying in bed and I'm so hot. Papa's leaning over me, putting a cool cloth on my forehead. Someone is behind him. Then I feel a heavy weight across my legs. I try to push it away, but I can't. When I draw my hands back, they're covered with blood!" Trembling, she looked down at her upturned palms, expecting to see the terrible sight again, but it wasn't there.

"I'm sick to death of hearing about that absurd dream!" Hannah declared. "You know you were very ill with a fever when your father died of the heart attack, Victoria. He was sick with that weak condition for a long time, just as your sniveling sister Deborah is. This nightmare is a ridiculous nuisance and so are you! How I wish we were back at the estate in London. Traveling through this desolate wilderness in these uncivilized United States is bad enough without having to endure your whining prattle. Now, be quiet, both of you! Bother me again, and your uncle will hear of it—and you *don't* want to arouse his wrath and face another beating! I'm going to join him in the dining car to obtain a glass of lemonade. Don't leave these seats!"

Victoria sighed heavily and turned to look out the open window, glad to be free of Hannah's cruel dictatorial presence for even a little while. Always their conversations about her nightmare were the same. Hannah Perkins never showed sympathy for anyone or anything. She was a hard, cold woman, plump in stature, with graying straight black hair pulled tightly into a braided coil at the top of her head, giving her rounded, lined face a set expression of angry disapproval. Victoria couldn't remember ever seeing her smile. She hated the woman who was companion and maid to her and Deborah. And jailer. There could be no other word to describe the way Hannah kept such close watch on them.

Gazing out the train window, she did have to agree with the servant woman about these United States. This country certainly wasn't like her beloved England. How she longed for the familiar streets and buildings of London, steeped in centuries-old history and traditions. All she could see now was a sprawling desert plain bordered by jagged mountain peaks in the distance. Not a house or road or stream of water touched her view. Not even a tree could be seen. Just spiny cactus, ragged clumps of coarse grass, and parched ground. Shimmering heat waves radiated before her eyes in every direction she looked, matching the stifling heat inside the train car. Dirt, smoke, and cinders from the locomotive's tall black stack blew in through the open window, making the journey even more unbearable.

Oh, to stroll the banks of the Thames River again, Victoria thought longingly. That would be sheer heaven.

"Are you all right, Victoria?" Deborah asked softly, leaning across the aisle once more.

"I wish we were back home. But the nightmares were even worse there." Victoria sighed again. "Five years now since Papa's death, and still the dream haunts me. If only we could be free of Sir Giles. The way he treats us makes me mourn dear Papa every day."

Deborah lowered her eyes. "Uncle Giles says Papa pampered us overmuch."

"That isn't true!" Victoria's green eyes flashed with anger. "Papa loved us with all his heart. And that's far more than I can say for our uncle. But soon he will no longer be our guardian. Only three months remain until my twenty-first birthday, when I'll inherit my share of Papa's estate. Then I'll be in control of my life. I'll take you to Paris or Rome with me, and we'll be free of Sir Giles forever!"

"Oh, Victoria, how I long for that day!" Deborah replied in an eager whisper, reaching out to squeeze her sister's hand.

Linc Masterson folded the copy of the Cheyenne *Daily Leader* newspaper he'd been reading and tucked it down in the crack between the passenger car wall and the cushioned seat. Leaning back, he gazed out the open window next to him, welcoming the sight of the sprawling, treeless grass plain, with its abundance of sweet cactus, low and erect greasewood shrubs, and heavily branched sagebrush. A flash of movement in the distance brought a glimpse of a yellow-brown pronghorn antelope and a surge of excited anticipation. Home. The sun-baked plain with the majestic, purple-black mountain peaks sculpting the horizon painted a heart-tugging, familiar scene that he was only too glad to study. He preferred riding a spirited mustang, fresh-broken from the wild, over this ground, but didn't mind traveling by Union Pacific "iron horse". It would get him to Laramie before dusk, right on schedule. After five years, he was coming home.

Pulling his eyes away from the window, he reached into his shirt pocket for the paper containing the message that was the reason for his return. Unfolding the telegram, he glanced over it again.

> "Lincoln Masterson. Stop.
> Union Pacific Railroad. Stop.
> Cheyenne, Wyoming. Stop.
> Return to ranch. Stop.
> Urgent. Stop.
> Drummond. Stop."

Strange that the telegram had been sent from the town of Rawlins instead of Laramie. The message sounded so like Drumm, though—short, no-nonsense, to the point.

Linc's mood darkened thinking of the older half-brother he hated with a fury so intense it once threatened to destroy them both. His right hand clenched into a fist.

That Drumm inherited the ranch after their father died would never sit well in his memory. It remained a jagged old wound. He clenched his jaw, knowing it would never heal. He'd lived hard and fast these last few years trying to forget all that had happened, but without success.

Something must really be wrong for Drumm to send a telegram like this. *How did he track me to Cheyenne?* he wondered.

Folding the thin telegraph paper in half, he replaced it in

his pocket and forced himself to focus on the interior of the train coach. All the high-backed double seats in front of him were occupied on both sides of the center aisle. Directly across the aisle from him two men in miners' homespun clothes dealt out a hand of poker, tallying with matchsticks. No money appeared on the leather satchel they were using for a flat surface, so he let them keep playing.

Cards once were just a way to pass monotonous traveling time on a train. But slick-handed men of shady reputation discovered that it was easy to fleece the greenhorn travelers found in the confines of a train coach, and many unsuspecting passengers lost all the valuables they carried with them before they reached their destinations. Now gambling for cash violated railroad rules.

The run to Laramie wasn't on his usual work schedule. He'd taken on a special assignment to follow up Drumm's telegram.

His glance traveled to a man who got up from his seat near the front of the car and stood in the aisle. Dressed in laborer's dirty white duck pants and a red shirt, he had unruly brown hair down to his shoulders and a scar curving along his face from the edge of his left eyebrow to the middle of his cheek. Roscoe Ditch. *Long time, no see,* Linc thought, sitting up straighter in his seat.

Ditch reached up to stretch, then turned his back to light a long cigar away from the wind coming in the open windows.

Linc looked for a seat closer to Ditch and spied an empty spot next to a woman wearing a pink bonnet. He couldn't see her face. He hoped no child of hers was sprawled on the cushion next to her.

Pulling the brim of his low-crowned black hat down lower over his eyes to hide his face, he got to his feet and moved quickly up the aisle. When he saw that the seat next to the woman really was empty, he plopped down into it.

Victoria jumped with surprise when he landed next to her. "Oh! What are you doing, sir? You can't sit here. This seat is taken."

"Won't be staying long," he told her sharply, sliding a

glance over her. "Name's Linc Masterson, detective for this here Union Pacific line. I'm watching a suspicious character by the name of Roscoe Ditch to see if he's up to something." Reluctantly, he pulled his eyes away from his lovely seatmate to watch Ditch's movements.

Victoria stared at the man next to her in stunned silence. She'd never seen anyone so ruggedly handsome in all her life. Clean-shaven, he had a square-chiseled jaw and straight nose. A deep cleft dented the middle of his chin. His face was dark-complexioned, more than just sun-bronzed. His blue shirt fit snugly over wide shoulders. Tight denim pants clung to solid-looking legs ending in knee-high black boots. A fancy pearl-handled revolver was holstered to his right thigh.

She suddenly felt very uncomfortable sitting so close to him, but she was certain the uneasiness was caused by her fear that Sir Giles or Hannah would return and find him next to her.

"Is there any danger, sir?" Victoria asked in a nervous whisper, shifting her eyes around to try to determine which person he was watching. When she looked back, the man who'd called himself Linc Masterson was leaning out into the aisle. She couldn't keep from looking at the coal-black hair curling around his ears and hanging low on the back of his neck.

"Don't know yet. He's going outside, maybe just to smoke his cigar." He turned back toward her, frowning slightly and glancing out the window. "We're slowing down."

"Are we nearing Laramie?" Leaning closer to the window, she felt the deceleration of the train but saw no town in view, only the same sun-baked desert wilderness terrain they'd been traveling through all morning.

"No, Laramie's a piece yet." He turned around again to catch sight of Ditch. "Hellfire!" he swore when he saw Ditch leaning over the protective rail at the end of the car.

The squealing sound of hard-applied braking and the hiss of escaping steam from the engine five cars ahead drowned out everything for a few moments. Then the passengers started murmuring and shifting in their seats trying to look out the windows.

"Somethin's blockin' the tracks up ahead!" yelled a teen-aged boy leaning out an open window.

The passengers, including Victoria and Deborah, craned to see what he was talking about.

While everyone else's attention was diverted to the front of the train, Linc stood up and stepped into the aisle.

Victoria sensed his movement. Curious, she quickly shifted to the seat he'd just vacated and leaned out to watch him head toward the back of the train. With surprise, she saw that the express boxcar that had been attached to their passenger coach was now at a standstill about twenty feet down the track. A scar-faced man with a long cigar hanging from his mouth stood outside their car shading his eyes, looking out at the foothills to the south.

Just as Linc arrived at the back door and reached for the handle, a red-haired figure dashed past Victoria with a gun in his hand.

"Watch out!" Victoria screamed, jumping to her feet when he ran up behind Linc.

Too late, Linc turned at her cry. His attacker brought the gun down hard, hitting him on the side of the head. Linc's knees buckled and he slumped to the floor. The assailant swung around, looking fierce as he waved the gun at her and the other passengers.

"You all sit down an' shut up!" he ordered. "This here's a hold-up! Do what we tell you an' nobody else'll git hurt!"

Ditch re-entered the car, a revolver in his hand, too. His ugly face showed a snide grin as he added a nod of agreement to his cohort's threats.

Victoria sank back into the seat, her heart pounding with fear. She glanced across the aisle to where Deborah sat on the edge of her seat, a stricken look on her pale face.

Pulling her eyes away from her sister, Victoria tried to see down the section of the aisle floor where Linc Masterson had fallen. Was he badly hurt, perhaps dead? The shock of such brutality sent a cold shudder down her spine, despite the heat in the train car. She'd heard the loud crack when the cut-throat's gun connected with his skull. If only she could see him, help him somehow. Railroad detectives were supposed to protect the passengers!

She forced her thoughts back to the situation at hand. They must obey the robbers. She prayed no one else would try to stand up to them and be hurt.

While Ditch stood guard with his gun pointing at the passengers, his accomplice walked down the aisle holding his big brown hat upside down for them to drop their valuables into.

"Hurry up with that, you old coot!" Ditch ordered angrily when an elderly man was too slow putting his gold watch into the hat. "Our friends'll be comin' any minute now, an' we'll be takin' on bigger business."

"But robbin' these dumb folks'll give us just a little more'n the others, right, Roscoe?" asked the red-haired outlaw holding the hat.

"Right, Horace, so git what you kin."

They moved down the aisle. When they came to Victoria, Ditch smirked.

"Well now, ain't you the pretty one. I saw you b'fore when you got on the train. Jus' what valuables might you be havin' fer us?" He elbowed the man he'd called Horace and winked. The cigar hung from the corner of his mouth, a curl of smoke rising from the end of it.

"I—I don't have any money," she stammered, feeling her stomach twist in revulsion. He was dirty and showed several days' growth of whiskers on his thick-jowled face. The darkness of the scraggly beard made his long, ugly scar stand out starkly.

"It ain't money I'm thinkin' about," he replied, grinning.

"Take these earrings," she offered quickly, reaching up to her lobes. "They're emeralds and very valuable." She hated to part with the tear-drop-shaped gems set in gilt filagree that had belonged to her deceased mother, but she swiftly unhooked them from her ears and dropped them into the hat. Ditch grabbed her wrist with his free left hand and yanked her up out of the seat.

"Them ain't enough, sweetie. I could use me a kiss or two

from you."

His teeth were blackened at the gums and his breath reeked of tobacco. He tried to pull her closer, but she pushed against his chest.

"*No!*" she cried, and without thinking she reached up, snatched the cigar out of his teeth, and jammed the red-hot end of it into his cheek.

"Yow!" he hollered, dropping his weapon and grabbing for his cheek.

In the same instant, a shot rang out, followed rapidly by a second. Both outlaws jerked and cried out, then crashed to the floor. Deborah screamed, slumping back in her seat. Ditch lay face-down, unmoving. Horace writhed next to him, moaning and clutching a bleeding shoulder.

Victoria stood stock-still in shock, not daring to breathe, her hand to her mouth. Then a baby somewhere in the car started crying at the top of its lungs. Everyone began talking at once. Sir Giles Spencer and Hannah Perkins burst into the car at that moment.

"Victoria! What's happened?" her guardian demanded, a scowl dipping his bushy gray eyebrows.

Her fear lessened not at all as she swung around to face her uncle. "Two men . . ." Her voice died away in horror as she pointed to the outlaws at her feet in the aisle. Then she gingerly stepped over them to go to Deborah's limp form.

Sir Giles squatted his considerable bulk down next to the men. "The scarred one's dead," he announced. "This one's losing a great deal of blood. Who shot them?" He looked around, as did everyone else.

Victoria patted her moaning sister's hand and threw a glance toward the rear of the train car, where Linc Masterson struggled to his feet in the aisle, his gun still smoking in his hand. He staggered forward.

"Damnation! My head's splitting!" he complained, sliding his gun smoothly into the holster at his side. "That was a hell of a stupid thing to do, English, taking on Ditch there the way you did." He sent his cutting words directly at her, reaching out for the back of a seat for support. "He might have shot you on the spot. I should have known Ditch was working with a partner. When I came to after he hit me, I tried to get a bead on both of them, but you were in the way!"

"How was I to know you were trying to do anything?" she defended. "I thought you were dead!" Hot, angry tears welled up in her eyes, but she blinked them back, held by his smoldering dark eyes. "Great heavens, the man's been killed!"

The horrible realization hit her—she'd just seen a man gunned down before her eyes. She started trembling all over. Her knees weakened, causing her to float down to the empty seat next to her sister. She held onto the armrest to steady herself, biting her lower lip to hold back the sobs of shock and fear welling up in her throat.

"Don't start bawling like a newborn calf!" Linc warned with a frown when he saw her lip quivering. "I can't abide a woman getting all wet-eyed on me!"

"I'm not going to cry!" she shot back, then pressed her lips together.

"This country is outrageously uncivilized!" Hannah Perkins exclaimed, looking stern as she shook her head.

Victoria agreed. She glanced down to the weapon in the leather holster at Linc Masterson's side. The detective disregarded Ditch's death and Horace's wounding so easily. His attention was on his bloody fingers, which he'd just drawn away from the side of his head.

Linc clenched his teeth together. His head pounded like a herd of buffalo was stomping over it. But he felt more anger than pain—anger at himself for getting hit. When he'd regained his senses, his vision only cleared at the last second when he'd thrust the Colt Peacemaker up to fire. He'd seen the pretty English gal in the way barely in time to flick his aim a fraction to the right before his reflexes yanked the trigger back. Lucky his brain had been working slower because of the bashing it had taken, or he would have shot her. That thought gouged into his gut. An innocent bystander. The beauty with the lilting accent and eyes deep green as the lush summer grass edging a Laramie mountain stream. She could be lying dead on the floor instead of Roscoe Ditch!

"You're bleeding!" Victoria declared, feeling her stomach grow more unsettled at the sight. "Perhaps I should have a look at your wound." She searched in the side pocket of her pink dress for her lace-edged handkerchief.

Sir Giles stepped up next to her seat. "You'll do nothing of the kind, Victoria! A woman of your stature doesn't tend a common shootist."

She looked at her uncle. "Shootist?"

"A gunman for hire," Sir Giles explained contemptuously. "The conductor said there was a railroad detective on board. In this country, that amounts to a cold-blooded killer paid to shoot people, as you've just seen."

Victoria's mouth dropped open. She saw Linc Masterson's look darken. His sharply arched black brows nearly met at the bridge of his straight nose.

"More riders comin' in!" the teenaged boy shouted suddenly. "Seven or eight of 'em, gallopin' fast!"

Linc leaned down to peer out the window, squinting against the throbbing in his head. He grabbed Horace by the hair, roughly yanking his head back. "The rest of your gang after the payroll gold?"

"Ow! Take it easy!" The outlaw's stubble-whiskered face twisted in a grimace as he clutched his injured shoulder. "Yeah, you got it right. An' they ain't gonna like what you done to me an' Ditch. You kin say yer prayers, detective, 'cuz you can't take 'em all on." His grin had a smug turn to it.

"Don't be too sure of that," Linc stated coldly. He stepped over Ditch's body and hurried back to the seat he'd been sitting in before near the back of the coach. Reaching overhead to the curved wooden luggage rack near the ceiling, he grabbed a long buckskin sheath. Quickly untying the rawhide laces holding the end flap in place, he pulled out a shiny Winchester repeating rifle, then returned to where the outlaws lay. He gazed around at the passengers. "Duck down out of sight!" he ordered. Shifting his eyes to Victoria, he tossed her the empty gun sheath. "Keep this for me, English." Then he was gone, running down the aisle toward the rear of the car.

Startled, Victoria glanced at the buckskin case in her hands, then worriedly looked up at Sir Giles.

"Put that down!" he ordered angrily, snatching at it.

She jerked it out of his reach and slid off the seat to the floor to get below window level. The other passengers did the same, huddling down in the seats and in the aisle. Hannah joined them, kneeling beside a trembling Deborah, who had barely recovered from fainting. Only Sir Giles remained standing, scowling down at Victoria.

Many of the other men in the train car wore guns, but Victoria noticed none of them made any move to assist Masterson.

She clutched the leather sheath to her chest. Why, she didn't know. But it was *his,* and for some reason, she felt safer holding it close, even at the risk of angering Sir Giles. She wanted to see what Linc Masterson was doing, but fear made her keep her head down.

The sound of galloping horses came closer. Suddenly, a shot rang out.

"Hold it right there, boys!" came a shout. "That was just a warning."

Linc Masterson's deep voice. Victoria bobbed up to try to see where he was. She caught a glimpse of the railroad boxcar down the track, but it looked the same as before. No one was outside it. Where was Masterson? Was he going to take on the whole outlaw band by himself?

"Stay down, Victoria!"

Sir Giles again. He'd finally stooped down between the seats and couldn't reach her. So she ignored his command, stretching her neck to see out the window of the rear door. There! She spotted Masterson.

"He's standing on the roof of the boxcar!" she said out loud.

Linc shouted again. "Harvey Trump! I might have known you'd be the one leading these boys down the path of crime and destruction!"

"Linc? You half-breed polecat! I thought you was dead!" A hearty laugh burst through the air. "I don't know what yer talkin' about, son. Why, me an' the boys was jus' plannin' on lightenin' the load of this here fine train. Gold kin be mighty heavy, can't it, boys?" Laughter and calls of agreement followed Trump's words.

"Well, that's real thoughtful of you and the fellas, Harve, but I'm afraid I can't let you do that. Now, throw down your guns and give up peaceable-like, so I don't have to put a bullet from my Winchester here into any of your hides." He raised the weapon to his shoulder.

"What? That almost sounds like lawman talk!" The friendliness vanished from the robber's voice. "You ain't gone soft an' hung on a star, have you, boy?"

"Railroad detective. That makes me the law here and now."

Most of the other passengers had joined Victoria in raising up to window level to peek at the drama unfolding outside. No one spoke. She bit her lower lip and held her breath, fearing what the gang of cutthroats might do next. Linc Masterson was alone, standing tall and broad-shouldered on top of the express car, rifle aimed into the half circle of eight men on horseback.

"This rifle's fixed on you, Harvey," Linc continued. "You'll go down first, so you better consider your next move real careful."

For several long, tense seconds, no one moved or spoke. Harvey Trump stared up at Linc, holding his revolver down at his side. Suddenly, Linc's rifle fired and Trump's hat flew off his head.

"The next one's between the eyes," Linc warned, swiftly cocking the rifle. "Drop the guns *now!*"

"Do what he says, boys! He ain't bluffin'!" Trump shouted, hastily tossing his gun to the ground. Mumbling, the others did the same.

"That's mighty smart, boys," Linc replied. "Now, get down off your horses." He stomped his boot on the roof of the car. "Hillman, open up!"

The double side doors of the boxcar slid open and three men jumped out with rifles poised to shoot.

"You all right, Linc?" one of them shouted over his shoulder.

"Yeah. Collect their guns and get them tied up. There're two others in the last passenger car. I'm going forward to see what's blocking the tracks."

Victoria tried to follow his movements, but he disappeared from sight. The passengers all began talking at once. Deborah lunged across the aisle into Victoria's arms.

"Oh, I was very frightened!" she cried, hugging her sister. "This is all so terrible!"

"There now, it's over," Victoria soothed, stroking her sister's brown hair. While she felt very concerned about Deborah, she couldn't keep from looking out the window to scan the corner of the boxcar. When their rescuer walked into view on the ground again, she felt her stomach lurch. The robbers were no longer a threat to them. Relief must be the reason for the twinge in her middle.

She watched Linc Masterson's handsome profile as he passed the window walking with a jaunty stride, heading for the front of the train, and felt amazed at how courageously, how ruthlessly, he'd faced the whole gang of dangerous outlaws alone.

Chapter Two

To stop the train, Harvey Trump and his gang of outlaws had dynamited a section of foothills near the tracks, causing an avalanche of rock to fall across them. The railroad crew and any willing men passengers now had the difficult job of clearing the rails.

Victoria and Deborah followed Sir Giles and Hannah off the train. Several Negroes unloaded baggage for them to sit on.

"It's hardly cooler out here," Hannah complained, fanning herself with her handkerchief as they stood in the shade cast by the passenger coach. "This desert is an ungodly place."

"Be quiet, woman! Your constant complaining is just as trying as this bloody heat!" Sir Giles spat angrily.

Hannah sent him a black look, but she made no other comment. Not for the first time, Victoria wondered why her uncle kept the stern, sour-faced servant in his employ. He seemed to despise Hannah Perkins as much as she and Deborah did.

"I hope they can clear the rails soon so we can be on our way," Sir Giles continued, running a finger around his high starched collar.

"The process might be facilitated if those men had more help," Victoria offered, looking pointedly at her uncle.

He sent her a disparaging glance. "You aren't suggesting I participate in common laborers' work? Keep your ludicrous opinions to yourself, Victoria. They are of no value or interest to me. A beautiful woman is better seen than heard."

Victoria lowered her eyes, hating her uncle's cutting words. To hide the bristling anger she felt inside, she said nothing more and tried to appear calm and unaffected for Deborah's sake. Whenever she defied Sir Giles' cruel authority, his punishment was swift and painful for her and Deborah. He used her frail younger sister to force her to obedience. They'd felt his wrath often enough, and every incident greatly aggravated Deborah's delicate heart condition. Victoria had learned to curb her rebellion, at least outwardly.

She raised a hand to her forehead to shade her eyes, and made herself study the landscape. Little plant life showed along the rolling land and shallow gulches surrounding the train. She could see only a few wild flowers—bluebells, primrose, prickly pear, yellow gumweed—which added bright dots of color here and there along the desolate plain.

When a brown and gray jack rabbit darted behind a spiny sagebrush covered with gray shreddy bark, she wondered how any animals could survive in such an inhospitable place.

Surreptitiously, she let her eyes drift to the group of men working on the rock pile on the tracks, but she couldn't see Linc Masterson among them. Then she quickly looked away, scolding herself for having such brazen interest in a man like him.

"You have something that belongs to me, English."

She jumped hearing a voice so close at hand. Whirling, she saw Linc standing behind her pointing with his rifle toward his buckskin case. She'd folded it and tucked it under her arm, so her uncle wouldn't see she still had it.

Linc's hat was pulled down low over his forehead, shadowing his handsome features, but she saw them clearly enough. His eyes swept boldly over her.

Feeling unnerved, she swallowed hard and shot a look toward Sir Giles. His glare struck fear in her heart, making her glad for the protection of other people around them, so he couldn't reprimand her in a harsher manner.

Quickly looking back at Linc, she thrust the cover at him, saying nothing, but her pulse raced under his steady gaze.

He slipped it over the Winchester. "Much obliged for keeping it for me. I hope nobody was hurt in that little fracas with the outlaws."

" 'Little fracas'!" Hannah exclaimed. "Why, that was more like the outbreak of a war! It's a wonder we weren't all killed the way the bullets were flying. I must say I'm not very impressed with this wild country. Such violence!"

Linc snorted a laugh. "Nobody's making you stay, lady."

"We'll stay where we please, Masterson!" Sir Giles stated sharply, scowling as he stepped up beside Victoria. "We're just not used to such barbarism. But you are, aren't you? Killing is your way of life. You enjoy it."

Victoria couldn't believe her uncle's brashness. To provoke the American seemed like a very dangerous thing to do.

Linc's cool expression didn't change, but a slight twitch of a muscle in his square jaw revealed that his teeth were clenched. Slowly, he poked the brim of his hat back with his finger. His deep brown eyes took on the glint of two sharp shards of glass as he hooked his thumbs into the top of his gunbelt and looked straight at Sir Giles.

"I do my job, Englishman, using my gun when somebody's of a mind to kill me. A lot of folks are glad to have me on their side when there's trouble. In fact, near as I could tell, you weren't against letting me take care of the outlaws earlier. I don't recollect hearing you volunteer to lend a hand. You stayed in the car with the womenfolk. What's that make you?"

He didn't wait for an answer to his insult, but turned on his heel and strode away toward the men removing the rocks from the tracks.

"Uncivilized lout!" Sir Giles spat when Linc was out of hearing range. "You're to have no further contact with that low-bred brute, do you understand, Victoria?" He grabbed her roughly by the arm.

"Yes, Uncle," she replied, wincing from the pain of his hard grip. While she shrank away from him, she inwardly admired the way Linc had stood up to Sir Giles.

Her eyes darted to Linc's broad back. She should obey her guardian's wishes, for her own safety and Deborah's. But she couldn't stop looking at his tall form walking away from her. He possessed an overwhelming presence, a barely checked energy taut with readiness, like a bowstring pulled back to the limit. Harvey Trump had called him a half-breed. Was he part savage like one of those bloodthirsty renegade American Indians she'd read about in the London newspapers?

The oppressive heat of the afternoon scorched the still air causing shimmering waves to rise from the barren desert ground. Victoria swatted at annoying flies and mosquitoes buzzing around her head, and used her handkerchief to dab at the perspiration beading on her face. Deborah and Sir Giles had gone inside the passenger car seeking shade. Hannah leaned against the side of the train, dozing on a wooden crate.

A young Negro in a railroad uniform passed by Victoria carrying two sloshing buckets of water.

"Is that for the men?" she asked to draw his attention.

Short and well-rounded about the middle, the young man put down the wooden buckets and grinned.

"Yes'm, it shore is. Conductor says they's needin' all ah kin carry to 'em. They's doin' hard work."

"May I help you? It would help pass the time." She leaned down and picked up one of the buckets.

"Oh no, ma'am. Ah don't think that'd be right. It be awful hot out there. You bes' stay here in the shade of the car."

"Please, I'd like to do something. You take the other bucket." She started to walk away.

"Well, all right then. Thank you, ma'am," he said, hurrying to follow her.

"Union Pacific resort to letting passengers haul water?"

Victoria turned and saw Linc Masterson step away from the men breaking up the rocks at the rails. His striking handsomeness stunned her. Her legs went weak and her stomach suddenly knotted when she saw he now had his shirt off. His wide-shouldered upper torso glistened with sweat from wielding a heavy sledge hammer.

Her pulse raced. She felt a hot blush rush up her neck to her face, and she nearly gulped aloud from the shock of seeing him half-naked. Never before had she seen a man in such a state of undress. She had no idea a body could be so muscular, look so powerful. It sent her senses reeling. Well defined bulges along his arm and across his chest flexed when he swung the big hammer up and rested it against his shoulder.

"I—I wanted to help," she said finally, when she managed to find her voice. "Do you wish a drink, Mr. Masterson?"

"Sure, but will that disagreeable old bastard you're traveling with let you work like this, English?"

Her finely arched brow dipped slightly, and she took a step backward as he walked closer. "Please don't call me English. My name is Victoria Spencer. The man you refer to is my uncle and guardian. I don't need his approval to perform an act of Christian service." She spoke boldly, but shot an apprehensive glance back toward the passenger cars, hoping Sir Giles wasn't watching her from a window.

"Why are you afraid of him?"

His blunt question startled her. She swung her head back toward him. "I—I'm not afraid," she stammered the lie. "Here's your drink." Her hand trembled a little as she held the tin ladle out to him and changed the subject. "You were quite brave with those outlaws who tried to rob the train. How is your head injury?"

"I've had worse."

She wished he wouldn't stare at her with those black-lashed brown eyes. They seemed fathoms deep, reflecting a keen and quick intelligence and cunning which took in everything. She lowered her own eyes to try to escape his penetrating gaze, and found herself looking straight at his bare chest. Unwittingly, her glance traced over the thin covering of dark hair to where it ran in a narrow line down his flat belly and disappeared into the top of his low-slung blue denims. Trying to suppress a gasp, she swiftly leaned over to pick up the water bucket from the ground.

"If you've had your drink, Mr. Masterson, I'll go on to the others."

"You better get out of this sun quick-like," he warned. "That little pink bonnet you're wearing won't keep your face from frying crisper than a slab of bacon on a hot griddle. That goes for other places, too." His eyes dropped to low-scooped neckline of her dress.

Shocked and confused, Victoria swiftly raised her hand to the base of her throat, spreading her fingers to cover herself. Not knowing what else to say, she started to turn away.

"Wait." He put his big hand over her much smaller one on the rope handle of the bucket.

The contact with him jolted her reflexes, preventing her from pulling away. His hand seemed to scorch hers.

"I have something for you." He let go to fish in his side pants pocket. Then he held out his hand.

Haltingly, she turned her palm up. Her eyes widened in surprise when she saw what he gave her. Green gems set in gold sparkled in the sunlight.

"My earrings! The outlaw took them. These mean a great deal to me. They belonged to my mother. Oh, thank you, Mr. Masterson!" She almost hugged him. Just in time, she remembered herself, halting so quickly that some of the water sloshed out of the bucket.

Linc watched the delight dance in her eyes that were so like the precious gems she held in her hand. She was a beauty, all right. He liked what he saw, felt a stirring just below his gunbelt, reminding him he hadn't had a woman in a while. But his gals were the she-cat wild kind. This Victoria Spencer hardly fit that breed. She was too skittish, like an untried filly. A jack rabbit could make her jump. Still, there was something about her . . . after all, she'd had the spunk to defy Roscoe Ditch when he'd tried to grab her.

"I could use one more drink of water before you go," he told her, reaching for the ladle.

"Take whatever you want," she offered eagerly, lifting the bucket.

His eyes held hers. "That's a mighty tempting offer."

She blushed to the tips of her ears, realizing what he insinuated. He kept his compelling gaze locked with hers a moment longer, then blinked slowly and looked away. Picking up the tin ladle, he dumped the water in it over his head, sighing with pleasure as it streamed over his face and chest. She jumped when he shook his head and the spray from his thick black hair hit her.

"Hey, ma'am, we could use a little of that water over here!" came a shout.

With confused feelings whirling inside her, Victoria pulled her eyes away from the glistening drops of water sliding down Linc's powerful chest. Clutching the bucket handle harder than she needed to, she backed away, telling herself to stop noticing how handsome Linc Masterson was, how tall and sturdily built. Don't look at that deep cleft in his chiseled chin or his sun-bronzed broad shoulders and chest!

Shocked at her improper thoughts, she hurriedly turned and walked on.

Wiping his hand over his face, Linc watched the graceful sway of Victoria's hips as she moved away, and wondered what very proper British finishing school teacher had taught her to walk like that. Those pale, high-boned cheeks of hers would be sunburned good by nightfall. It would probably make her look prettier! Hellfire, but she could give a man trouble! He knew that in his gut. There was too much wide-eyed innocence and vulnerability about her, not to mention a figure that aroused something downright primal in him.

Shaking his head, he clenched hold of the hammer and returned to the rock pile, glad that they'd be parting company at Laramie. He could imagine her highbrow British reaction if she ever found out he was half Sioux Indian. Then she'd give him that contemptuous, down-the-nose look he'd seen too many times from others. He'd lived with prejudice all his life and hated it, had even killed men over it.

He heard the lilting sound of her accented voice now as she spoke to another man while giving him water. Swinging the hammer ferociously, he pounded the rocks at his feet, determined to ignore her and forget the memory of the happiness he'd seen on her lovely face when he'd handed her the earrings. He didn't need the complication of any woman in his life. Too many other problems plagued his mind.

Dusk streaked the sprawling plain deep crimson before the railroad tracks were finally cleared.

"Get your fireman to stoke her up, Henry!" Linc shouted to the engineer sitting high up in the cab of the diamond stack woodburner locomotive. The man waved in return.

At least the heat's letting up, Linc thought. It had taken a long, hard seven hours to finish the job, but they could still reach Laramie tonight.

With his shirt slung over one shoulder, he headed back toward the express boxcar to check on the prisoners, rolling his head around and flexing back his arm to try to ease the ache in his muscles. Coming to the last of the three passenger coaches, he stopped. Victoria Spencer sat alone on a cloak spread out on the ground. She was asleep, her head resting against her outstretched arm on a travel trunk.

The passengers started boarding on the other side of the coach, so he had a moment to let his eyes slowly roam over

Victoria in the fading light. She no longer wore the pink bonnet. Her long, straight blond hair, held back from her face by a white satin ribbon, was a shade paler than the color of the long lashes resting against her sun-tinged cheeks. Her lips, parted slightly, seemed almost ready for a kiss.

He frowned. Absently, he ran his tongue over his own lips, wondering what her mouth would taste like. That air of innocence he'd sensed about her before seemed to surround her now as she slept, making her very different from most of the women he knew. More like Callamae, his half-sister. Maybe that was why this English gal drew his attention—because she reminded him of Callie. It'd be good to see his older sister again when he reached Laramie. He was reluctant to admit it, but he'd missed her easy laughter and gentle spirit.

He gazed at the beautiful woman at his feet, knowing that behind her closed lids were green eyes created for a poet's pen to describe. Yet their gem-like quality was marred by fear at times. He wondered about that fear and her relationship with the uncle she traveled with as he let his glance slip over her long, slender throat and down to where the gently rounded tops of her breasts showed along the scooped neckline of her pink dress. The alluring fullness of them strained the silky material.

Suddenly, a sound stopped his heart. He stood stockstill, swiftly shifting his eyes over the ground around Victoria. There! At the near corner of the trunk by her bent knee poised the lethal predator, vibrating tail suspended, smooth, tightly coiled body ready to strike.

Linc's Colt cleared the holster faster than the snake could dart out. Two shots shattered the air. Victoria screamed, jerking upright, throwing her hands over her ears.

Linc kicked the dead reptile aside and holstered his smoking revolver, kneeling on one knee to take Victoria into his arms. "It's all right. There was a rattler."

She clung to him, trembling. Pressing against his bare

chest, she raised her head away a little to look up at him. "R-rattler?"

"Rattlesnake. Deadly poisonous and about to have a taste of your leg."

Following where he pointed to the bloody creature, she gasped, pulling her knees in closer under her.

"My God, Victoria, what's happened now?" Sir Giles rushed forward, followed by Hannah and several other passengers.

Linc stood up, drawing Victoria with him.

"There was a terrible snake," she explained shakily, pointing to the ground. "Mr. Masterson killed it."

Giles Spencer frowned as he stepped over to it, prodding it onto a silver-tipped walking stick he carried. "Dead all right." He lifted it high enough for everyone to see. "Clean shots through the head. Bloody fair shooting." He glanced at Linc, but his stern expression didn't lessen. "How do you manage to have these things happen to you, Victoria?" he demanded sharply. "The attention you call to yourself is scandalous!"

Her mouth dropped open in surprise. "I—I don't know, Uncle. I didn't mean to—"

"Nonetheless, you manage to endanger yourself, no matter how closely you're watched!" His disapproving scowl deepened as he grabbed her roughly by the elbow. "Get into the coach with your sister. I'm not letting you out of my sight again!"

Victoria bristled, angry at the unfairness of his accusation. He must be insane to blame her for almost getting bitten by a snake!

Linc frowned, pressing a hand against Sir Giles' shoulder to stop him. "Ease back in the saddle, Englishman. You should be glad she wasn't hurt."

"And bloody grateful to you, I suppose?" Sir Giles glared, hitting Linc's arm away. "Keep to your own affairs, Masterson. Miss Spencer is my responsibility. Stay away from her!"

He turned away abruptly, pulling Victoria along with him. But she hung back to say hurriedly, "Thank you, Mr. Masterson."

Linc bent down to retrieve his shirt from where he'd dropped it on the sandy ground, then stepped back to let the curious passengers surge forward to get a look at the snake. He watched Victoria being pulled up the steps to the passenger car. The rattler wasn't the first snake he'd ever killed, and it likely wouldn't be the last. But the fact that she had almost been its victim unsettled him. Twice in one day her life had been threatened, and by some crazy quirk of fate, he'd been around to help her. Rescuing fair damsels in distress usually wasn't in his line of work, and he didn't want it to be.

Yesterday, he hadn't even known she existed. But he did now. He could still feel where the palms of her hands had pressed against his chest moments ago when he'd held her. The heat from her body lingered there, burning into his flesh.

Chapter Three

Laramie City, Wyoming, was founded in 1868 by the Union Pacific Railroad. Named for French Canadian trapper, Jacques LaRamie, and located on the east bank of the Laramie River, the wild boom town consisted of a transient population during the height of the robust days when the railroad cast its mighty fingers of steel across the breadth of the North American continent. Now, surrounded by jagged-peaked mountains and sprawling arid plains, with its founding days behind it, Laramie thrived as an established railroad terminal with a growing population of nearly six thousand people, catering to cattlemen bent on building empires on the hoof, and homesteaders seeking new frontiers to settle.

The train arrived in town just before midnight. Wearily, Victoria stepped down from the coach to the wooden platform of the station with Deborah and the other passengers. She turned her head to look around and felt a crick in her neck from trying to sleep sitting up in the train seat. Her face and arms were sore from sunburn, but she didn't complain to her sister or to Hannah, who stood close by, guarding them as usual.

The station was illuminated by lanterns hung from wooden posts. The single-story depot needed a new coat of white paint. Pieces of baggage in sundry shapes and sizes and crates of merchandise lined the far end of the platform, awaiting transport. Few railroad personnel were around at the late hour.

Victoria saw Sir Giles walk to the baggage car to see about their trunks. She felt tired and hungry, wanting only the comfort of a soft bed in a half-decent hotel, if that were possible in this rough frontier town. Perhaps with such weariness, she'd be able to sleep without being tormented by the nightmares about her father.

Just then, a man brushed by her. His rumpled, sandy-blond hair and disheveled shirt and pants revealed that he'd just been roused from bed.

"Beggin' yer pardon, ma'am," he said, giving her a nod when he moved past. In his early forties, lanky, with a bushy moustache, he wore a shiny metal badge pinned to the front pocket of his shirt. As he approached the ramp leading up to the boxcar, Linc Masterson appeared in the open doorway.

So that's where you rode, Victoria thought, solving the mystery about why he hadn't returned to his seat in the passenger car for the rest of the trip.

At the sight of him standing tall, with legs apart, her heart began pounding harder, surprising her.

Pushing up the brim of his black hat, Linc stretched out his hand to the lawman. "N. K. Boswell, it's been a long time."

The sheriff grasped his hand, grinning. "Lordy, Linc Masterson. Never thought I'd lay eyes on you agin. We heard tell you was dead, gunned down by Ewing Cooper in Denver for killin' his brother."

"Don't believe all you hear. I was a lawman there for a spell. Shot Neal Cooper in the line of duty when he tried to rob the bank. But Ewing and I haven't settled up on that score yet."

"Is it true Ewing got religion an' he's goin' around claimin' to be a instrument of the Almighty's judgment?"

"You heard right. Reads Bible verses over his victims after he shoots them. But he's preaching in prison now. Got a sentence from a judge who took offense to having the

Reverend Cooper delivering his own brand of justice."

"Well, I hope he got a real long sentence, for your sake, Linc. Cooper's got himself a bad reputation for bein' mean an' quick on the draw. Killed at least a dozen men I know of. Wouldn't want him after me. You as fast as you used to be?"

"I'm still alive. That answer your question? I'm working for the Union Pacific now—detective. Got some guests for your jail. Harvey Trump and his boys. Tried to get the mine payroll shipment. They're tied up inside." He flicked a thumb over his shoulder.

"All right. I'll take care of 'em till the circuit judge kin try 'em. You travelin' on with the train?"

"Nope, be staying a while. The railroad owes me some time off. I might just get a piece of land around here and start ranching again."

"What? Linc Masterson puttin' down roots? Lordy, wonders never do quit. We all thought you was gone for good, answerin' the call of that streak of wild Injun blood in you."

Linc hooked his thumbs in his gunbelt. "I've seen a lot and done a lot, that's certain. Have to tell you a few of the stories about my adventures sometime, like the one with Polly Coleman. Remember her? Saw her in New Orleans. She owns the finest saloon you could ever see. Crystal chandliers, red carpets all over the place, with the prettiest, friendliest bevy of young gals always around, ready to make you happy to lose your money at the gambling tables. Polly and I had quite a reunion."

"Polly Coleman?" The sheriff looked astounded. "Why, she writes her ma every month that she's lookin' after orphaned young'uns at a church mission there!"

Linc grinned. "I didn't see any orphans at the Golden Slipper, N. K., but I sure did see Polly."

The sheriff shook his head. "Well, if that don't beat all git out. By the way, does Drumm know your comin' back?"

Linc's face sobered, creased by a frown. He didn't know yet why Drumm had sent for him, so he decided to keep his reason for returning to himself for the time being.

"No, he doesn't," he answered shortly. "Wouldn't matter if he did. I do as I please."

"Jus' askin'. Don't git your feathers ruffled. But I know the hell you kin raise when you want to, 'specially where your half-brother's concerned. I'm the peace officer here now an'—"

"You want to keep things quiet," Linc finished for him. "I won't start anything. But I have to warn you, I won't sit around whittling if something needs finishing."

"Fair 'nough warnin', Linc, for both of us."

Linc Masterson seemed to be a man of many trades, Victoria thought. Gunfighter, lawman, railroad man, rancher, and what else? Apparently, his talents and interests even included carrying on with a woman who owned a saloon! But then, what else could be expected from a man who drifted around from place to place, making his living with a gun? Then again, he and his gun had saved her life twice today.

She wouldn't think about those frightening experiences. They made her feel grateful to him, and she didn't want to feel that emotion or any other toward him, for when she did, a strange confusion bubbled in her. She should try to forget how strong his powerful arms had felt around her when he'd held her after shooting the snake, and how her senses had reeled just being so close to him then. She should stay away from him and not strain to hear his deep voice or dart a glance at him as he stood talking with the sheriff!

"You want to fill out the paperwork on Harvey an' his gang tonight?" Sheriff Boswell asked. "I'll be needin' some witness statements, too."

Linc shook his head.

"I feel like I bulldogged ornery steers all day. I'll round up some of the passengers to give their statements tomorrow. In fact, the lady over there can verify details. Miss Spencer?"

Victoria swallowed hard and turned, pretending she

hadn't been eavesdropping on their conversation. "Yes, Mr. Masterson?"

"The sheriff here needs your statement about what happened today. Could you come to his office tomorrow morning?"

"She cannot!" Hannah declared tersely, stepping up beside Victoria. "Have someone else do it. Sir Giles wouldn't approve!"

"Now just who might he be, ma'am?" the sheriff asked, cocking an eyebrow. "An' who're you, for that matter?"

"I'm companion and chaperone to Miss Spencer and her sister here." She flipped a hand toward Deborah. "Sir Giles Spencer is their guardian. He's a very wealthy British gentleman with important investments here in your country."

"You know the sort, N. K.," Linc spoke up, a bitter edge punctuating his voice. "High-nosed English with nothing better to do with their money except send it over here to make more out of us. Then they get real bossy-like, trying to tell us how to run our ranches, as if they knew one end of a longhorn doggie from the other."

"Yeah, I reckon I do know the type from what we got around here already," Boswell agreed, his manner growing unfriendly. "They cause a heap of trouble at times. Think they own the world. I know a English feller by the name of Alden Cummings what's took up business with Clint Dandridge. Would you be knowin' him, ma'am?"

Victoria was surprised to hear the name of her uncle's nephew. "Yes, I know him slightly, Sheriff. I didn't realize he was here in your country."

"Well, he is. Real uppity sort. Thinks he's better'n everybody else. But I don't care who he is or who you all are. I'm the law around here, an' everybody settin' foot in my jurisdiction's goin' to abide by what the law says. I'll be takin' your statement at my office tomorrow, ma'am. Bring that sir feller, too, if you want. Be expectin' you b'fore lunch." He turned back to Linc. "Let's have a look-see at Trump an' his boys."

"Why, of all the nerve!" Hannah spouted, straightening her shoulders and lifting her chin. But neither man paid any attention to her huff. The sheriff stepped into the boxcar out of view. Linc's expression was stern as he looked at Victoria and touched a finger to the brim of his hat. Then he, too, turned away.

Victoria tried to ignore the strange sensation that rippled through her from his penetrating gaze, concentrating instead on feeling wicked delight in the sheriff's low opinion of Alden Cummings. And her uncle wouldn't like hearing the lawman's demand to come to his office.

Trying to sound meek, she said, "We'll have to do as the sheriff says, Hannah. We must obey the civil authorities of this country while we're here."

"The decision isn't yours to make, you stupid girl! You have no say about anything," the older woman snapped. "Sir Giles won't like being bothered with such tripe!" She whirled around to look toward the baggage car. "I wish they would hurry with the unloading."

"I hate it when Hannah says such unkind things to you, Victoria," Deborah whispered so the older woman couldn't hear. "I hope Uncle will let you give your statement."

Victoria smiled at her loyal little sister, but said nothing more. Deep inside her, the tiny sparks of anger and resentment flared again. Too many times, Hannah Perkins' abrasive tongue had lashed over her, leaving its sharp cut behind. She pressed her lips together, staring hard into the servant woman's back. She was sick to death of cruel words, threats, and beatings. But she must keep control of her anger and hatred a while longer—until her birthday. Her future and Deborah's depended on the strength of her will.

The disgruntled outlaws filed down the ramp under the watchful eye of Sheriff Boswell, who held his gun on them. When Harvey Trump passed Linc, he stopped.

"I'll git you fer this, Masterson," he ground out, scowling. "Jus' you mark my words."

"I'm shaking in my boots, Harve," Linc replied, smirking.

"Move along."

The outlaws walked on. Linc followed a few steps behind. When he passed Victoria, his eyes flicked to hers once more before he headed toward the baggage car.

Her heart missed a beat when she glimpsed the coldness in his look. Obviously, he included her in his disparaging opinion of Sir Giles and all British people. Well, that was fine with her. She didn't want to be here in these ungodly United States. She didn't like his country or him! How she longed for London, where she at least had a few friends, and the city was familiar and civilized, not crude and untamed like these frontier towns they'd been passing through. And Linc Masterson was just as savage as this land. The sheriff had mentioned his Indian blood. He was a killer, violent and dangerous, clearly a man to avoid!

The next morning, Linc walked up to the sheriff's office from the direction of the livery stable at the same time Victoria approached it escorted by Sir Giles Spencer.

"Miss Spencer," he greeted coolly, touching his hat brim. "Spencer." He looked toward the older man with her, but Sir Giles didn't acknowledge him in any way.

Victoria nodded in return, feeling her face grow warmer from Linc's gaze than it had from walking the short distance from the hotel in the bright sunlight. He wore tight white duck pants and a black leather vest over a tan shirt. The top three buttons of his shirt were unfastened. A red neckerchief was tied around his neck in the wide space that showed his muscular chest, and his gun hung in its holster from his hip. Unexpectedly, the sight of him perched atop the rock pile the day before without a shirt on at all flashed through her mind, quickening her pulse.

"I understand we have you to thank for this gross inconvenience," Sir Giles stated, looking annoyed. "Step aside so we can go into the sheriff's office and get this bothersome business accomplished!"

Linc bristled from the older man's superior-sounding tone. "I'm not partial to dealing with you foreigners. But we have laws around here. You'll have to obey them just like everybody else."

At that moment, two men approached on horseback.

"Sir Giles!" one of them called out, reining in his horse. He dismounted and came forward. "I'm pleased to see you, Uncle. We were just coming to the hotel to find you."

Victoria recognized Alden Cummings standing before her. She hadn't seen him in well over a year, but he looked nearly the same. As he removed his hat and walked over to them with the cocky stride she remembered, she saw he was still thin to the point of gauntness. In his mid-thirties, he was already going bald. Much more of his forehead showed below the line of his straight brown hair than she recalled seeing the last time he'd been in London. His expensively tailored black suit gave him a sinister air.

Sir Giles clasped his outstretched hand. "Alden, my boy, it's good to see you. Victoria, you remember my late wife's nephew, don't you?"

"Of course, she does," Alden answered for her, turning his darting blue eyes in her direction. "How nice to see you again."

His smile showed no warmth. With a shudder she recalled the few social occasions when she'd seen Alden back in England. He usually resided in Paris and only came to London on business occasionally. She hadn't liked him then. He was stern and humorless, reminding her too much of Sir Giles.

"Allow me to introduce your partner, Uncle, Mr. Clinton Dandridge," Alden continued, gesturing toward the tall man who had ridden up with him.

Wide-shouldered, with a stocky, square build, the middle-aged Dandridge was also impeccably dressed. His light gray suit matched the unusual color of his eyes.

"A pleasure to meet you," he said, shaking hands with Sir Giles.

"Dandridge," Sir Giles acknowledged with a nod. "This is my niece, Miss Victoria Spencer."

The cool gray eyes shifted in her direction.

"Ah, Miss Spencer, I've heard a great deal about you. It's a pleasure, indeed, to meet you." He removed his hat and gave her a nod while his gaze swept over her.

Victoria felt uncomfortable under his direct scrutiny and puzzled by the fact that this stranger knew about her.

"Alden has been working for me here in Wyoming for the past year overseeing a profitable investment I've made in Mr. Dandridge's cattle ranch," Sir Giles explained to her.

Dandridge turned his attention to Linc. "Well, I'm surprised to lay eyes on you again. What are you doing in town, Masterson?"

Victoria noted that the question was asked casually enough, but there was a slight overtone of demand in the way the big rancher said the words.

"Business," Linc stated.

"You a friend of the Spencers here?" Dandridge continued.

"Certainly not!" Sir Giles exclaimed, his bushy eyebrows dipping together. "We happened to have the extreme misfortune of traveling on the same train with this gunfighter yesterday when a gang of cutthroats tried to rob it. We must give our statements to the sheriff."

"How distressing for you, Victoria," Alden said in what sounded like a bored tone. He stepped over to her and took hold of her elbow. "You weren't hurt I hope."

"No," she answered, wanting to pull out of his grasp, but she would have to step closer to Linc to do it. That thought kept her standing in the same place.

Dandridge spoke to Linc again. "When you finish your business, come and see me. We'll talk about old times when your pa was still around. Maybe I can interest you in working for me. I could use a good gunhand."

"I don't approve of that idea, Dandridge," Sir Giles spoke up.

Victoria watched Linc through this exchange of conversa tion, wondering why Clinton Dandridge would require the services of a gunfighter. She knew almost nothing about cattle ranching. Did the American need gunmen to shoot the animals for market?

Suddenly, she saw Linc's gaze shift toward the dirt street. Quite a few people walked along the wooden sidewalk and filled the street on horseback and in wagons, but he seemed to be looking straight at a horse and buggy traveling toward them. The fabric top of the vehicle was folded back, revealing a man and a woman riding inside.

"You're new to these parts, Sir Giles," she heard Clinton Dandridge say in a lower voice from slightly behind her. "You'll recall we agreed in our correspondence and through Alden that your interest here would be strictly financial and the actual running of the ranch would be in my hands. Don't question my judgment. Linc Masterson could be an asset in moving our plans forward."

Victoria cocked an eyebrow, looking at her uncle, wondering how he would react to Clinton Dandridge's obvious reprimand. As she expected, he frowned with indignation, but she was surprised when he said nothing more.

At that moment, Linc stepped off the sidewalk into the street directly in the path of the oncoming buggy. The man driving it pulled sharply on the horse's reins, halting the animal. Linc grabbed the roan's harness.

"Lincoln!" exclaimed the beautiful young woman in the vehicle. "My God, Drummond, it's Lincoln! He's alive!" Her face aglow with obvious happiness, she hurriedly stepped down out of the buggy and ran around the horse to hug Linc. She barely came to his shoulder in height.

"Abby."

There was no emotion in Linc's greeting. Victoria saw his handsome features grow hard. He kept his arms down at his sides, making no attempt to return her embrace.

The woman frowned, moving her head to toss a mass of thick chestnut curls showing below the back of her elegant bonnet. Victoria admired her stylish yellow linen dress, which fit her petite figure very becomingly. She also saw that the woman kept her large brown eyes fixed on Linc even when he appeared to ignore her. He gave his attention to the man who still remained in the buggy—a man whose black hair and handsome features were remarkably similar to Linc's, even including the indentation in the chin. But his skin was not as dark, and he appeared to be four or five years older. Victoria felt certain the two men were related. Was this the half-brother she'd heard Sheriff Boswell mention last night?

Linc gave a curt nod toward the man. "Drumm," was all he said.

"What're you doing in town?" the man asked, his obvious displeasure showing in his frowning expression. "You're not welcome here now, any more than you were five years ago. Laramie isn't big enough for both of us."

Victoria saw Linc cock his head slightly. For a moment, he looked puzzled. Then his expression became passive again.

"It's a free country," he replied coldly. "I don't give a damn about any welcome from you."

Clinton Dandridge stepped to the edge of the sidewalk. "Now, boys, let's not be growling at each other in front of the ladies. Abby, you look lovely this morning," he said, smiling at the woman at Linc's side. Then he looked toward the man still in the buggy. "You thought any more about my offer, Drumm?"

"He's still considering it, Clinton," the woman called Abby replied quickly. "Alden, how good it is to see you." She left Linc to step onto the wood plank sidewalk. "Are these the family members you were telling us about?" She smiled at each of them in turn.

Victoria thought her smile sparkled just a little too much. She didn't miss how Alden's eyes steadily watched Mrs. Masterson.

"Yes, Abigail," he replied. "This is Miss Victoria Spencer

and Sir Giles Spencer, my uncle. Victoria, Sir Giles, may I present Mrs. Abigail Masterson. And her husband, Drummond Masterson." He seemed to remember at the last moment to add the man climbing down from the buggy and coming toward them.

Victoria felt the other woman's eyes appraise her coolly. In a moment, she swung her head toward Sir Giles, linking her arm through his.

"Oh, Sir Giles, I've been so anxious to meet you. Alden must bring you out to our ranch. And Miss Spencer, too, of course." She smiled sweetly again, glancing toward Victoria. "We'll have a grand dinner party. We never get the chance to entertain people of quality and refinement here in Laramie. You will come, won't you, sir?" Her long-lashed eyes focused on the older man and blinked slowly.

"How could I resist such a pleasant invitation?" Sir Giles replied, patting her hand and smiling in return. His appreciative look swept over her from head to toe.

"Splendid!" Abby exclaimed. "And you must come, too, Linc. We have so much catching up to do."

Victoria noted the slight change in Abigail Masterson's voice when she spoke to Linc. And the look in her brown eyes said far more than her casual words. She was not a sister-in-law just welcoming home a long-absent relative. Victoria wondered if Abigail Masterson had a past with Linc.

"Since you're doing the asking, Abby, I'll be sure to come to your party," Linc agreed without looking at her. He kept his gaze on Drummond, who brushed by him scowling as he stepped up to the sidewalk to join his wife and shake hands with Sir Giles.

"You all will have to excuse us now," Drummond said, taking hold of his wife's elbow. "We have an appointment at the bank."

"Anything I can help with, Drumm?" Dandridge offered. A smirk curled up one corner of his mouth.

Drummond's expression showed irritation. "Back off,

Clint. I told you I'm not selling. It'll be a cold day in hell before you'll ever own Masterson land!"

He pulled his wife away by the arm. She glared up at him, but he paid no attention to her as he marched her away.

"I see what Alden meant when his correspondence said Masterson's attitude was hostile," Sir Giles stated, turning toward Dandridge.

"He's a stubborn one all right," the rancher replied. "But he'll come around. I haven't exhausted all means of persuasion yet." He looked at Linc. "I'm real interested in those twenty-five thousand acres of your brother's Diamond M ranch. About that job . . ."

"I'll hear you out," Linc answered.

"Good. Come out to my ranch tomorrow. I'll make it worth your while."

Victoria backed out of the open door of the sheriff's office, hoping to slip away unnoticed. The room had become crowded and stifling hot after several railroad officials also arrived to do the follow-up investigation into the attempted robbery of the gold payroll.

She squinted against the bright sunlight, shading her eyes with a hand at her forehead. A steady breeze kept the temperature a little more comfortable outside than the sheriff's office had been.

She valued these few moments alone like precious jewels because she rarely had them. No Hannah Perkins or Sir Giles frowning at her disapprovingly. Not even Deborah claimed her attention, for she was still resting at the hotel from the exhausting train ride. As much as she loved her younger sister and worried over her poor health, she appreciated this brief respite she had from tending her.

Feeling guilty at that thought, she sighed and looked toward the hotel. Deborah would want to see her after she'd taken breakfast in bed. And Sir Giles would expect her to go back to the hotel while he finished with the sheriff. But she longed for just a few more minutes by herself.

"Sneaking away from your watchdog uncle?" a deep voice asked behind her.

She whirled around to face Linc, and her tongue refused to work to answer him. His dark handsomeness left her speechless. His brooding eyes met hers, sending tremors through her. He was so tall and broad-shouldered that he almost completely blocked the doorframe of the sheriff's office behind him. He held his hat in his hand. His shiny black hair glistened in the sunshine.

"I—I wasn't sneaking away," she stammered awkwardly, unnerved that he'd caught her like an errant schoolgirl. Unable to meet his compelling gaze any longer, she looked up the street. "I was merely looking for a—a dressmaker's shop," she finished quickly.

A disdainful smirk touched his lips. "I doubt we have any stores fancy enough to suit your high and mighty tastes."

Her brow dipped as she glared at him. "You have no idea *what* my tastes are, Mr. Masterson. Don't judge me by my uncle. I'm not like him at all."

"Is that so." He took a step closer and lowered his voice. "Might be interesting finding out just what you are all about, English."

He didn't touch her, but his strong masculine virility overwhelmed her, preventing her from moving away from him as she knew she should. She noticed the tiny creases around the edges of his eyes and his sensuous mouth. He was entirely too close to her. His intense look was too confident, even arrogant, as his eyes swept over her. She sensed he was dangerous. She felt frightened without understanding the exact reason. It was caused by more than the distressing fact that he was a part-savage gunfighter, a hired killer. Perhaps her fear stemmed from the sudden realization that in a battle between their wills, she might lose. He could overpower her, not with just physical strength, but with his smoldering eyes and his deep-timbred voice.

She almost collapsed with relief when a young Mexican boy of about age twelve ran up to them and began tugging at Linc's sleeve. Slowly, his gaze shifted from her down to the boy.

"Señor! You are Señor Lincoln Masterson?"

"Si, amigo."

"I have most important message for you, señor, from your brother, Señor Drumm. He give to me one dollar to see you get it."

Linc frowned.

"All right then, let's hear it."

"Señor Drumm say for you to meet with him at midnight tonight at Carbon Timber Town."

"You're sure Señor Drummond Masterson told you this?"

"Oh, si, señor. I am Miguel. Señor Drumm let only me take care of his fine horse when he is in town. He is my amigo. You going to the ghost town to meet him, señor?"

Linc looked puzzled for a moment, then answered.

"Yes. Tell Señor Drumm I'll be there."

"Si, I will. Adios."

The boy turned and ran down the street toward the bank.

"Ah, here you are, Victoria," Alden Cummings said, coming out of the sheriff's office just then, followed by Sir Giles and Clinton Dandridge.

Linc abruptly gave her a farewell nod and turned to walk back inside the building. Though she was surrounded by three other men now, his absence seemed to leave a void.

Feeling annoyed, she realized she wouldn't be able to ask him about Drummond Masterson's strange behavior. The man had appeared openly hostile just a little while ago when he'd first seen Linc. Yet through the Mexican boy, he'd arranged a meeting with him—and at a ghost town! What was the relationship between the two men?

Many questions came to her mind, yet she knew she couldn't ask them of anyone. Linc Masterson's affairs were none of her business, but it was difficult controlling her curiosity.

"Do you think Masterson will help us gain the Diamond M ranch as part of our holdings?" Sir Giles asked Dandridge.

"There's a good chance of it," the rancher answered. "No love's lost between him and Drummond. Never has been either. This whole town knows that. Linc's the bastard son of Holden Masterson by a Sioux Indian squaw who was a servant at the ranch. Drummond's his older half-brother, the son Holden already had by his wife, Eunice. Holden raised the two boys together on the ranch, along with a daughter, Callamae. But he never legally claimed Linc as his son, and when he died a few years back, he left the ranch to Drumm. There was gossip of something going on between Linc and Abby after she married Drumm. Then one day, Linc just disappeared, headed for parts unknown. No one was sorry to see him go. Folks around here weren't too partial to Indians of any degree. The plains ran red with blood from the uprisings back then, and Linc was a hothead, real touchy about his mixed breeding, always in one fight or another. He got mighty dangerous when he took up using a gun. He was good at shooting, had a keen and deadly eye for it. I know, because I taught him. He's earned himself quite a reputation as a fast gun since then."

Victoria stared at Clinton Dandridge, surprised by all she'd just heard about Linc. For the first time, she noticed that the rancher wore a gun and holster slung low on his hip, at fingertip level. Was everyone in this savage Wyoming Territory a gunfighter?

Another question troubled her thoughts as she glanced back at the empty doorway to the sheriff's office. Why would Linc Masterson return to a town and family that didn't welcome him?

Chapter Four

"But why can't I go down to dinner with Uncle Giles and Victoria?" Deborah persisted. "I've been confined in this hotel room all day."

"Stop whining!" Hannah snapped. "You're trying my patience, as usual."

"Please, Hannah, I—"

"Silence!" The servant woman whirled on Deborah, raising her hand threateningly. The younger woman shrank back against the bed, a frightened look on her face.

Victoria jumped to her feet from the chair, dropping the book she'd been reading. "Don't!" she warned, stepping between her sister and the servant woman.

"Then *you* take her punishment for insolence instead!" She struck Victoria hard across the face.

Deborah gasped. Victoria's hand flew to her stinging cheek, but she wouldn't shrink away. Not this time. Standing straight before Hannah with her chin up, she made herself smile. "Take care. Sir Giles won't be pleased if I show bruises."

"Bruised or not, you'll attend this dinner with him and Deborah will remain here with me. Those are your uncle's express orders." Hannah folded her arms across her chest. Her thin, dry lips pursed together.

"Victoria! Are you all right?" Deborah's lovely face was marred with fear and worry as she gingerly touched the reddening side of her sister's face. "Oh, I'm so sorry. I'm a wretch to infuriate Hannah. Then she takes it out on you when you defend me. We must be obedient. I can't bear to see you harmed."

"I only have so much obedience in me, Deborah," Victoria answered, keeping her cold stare directed at the servant woman. "I'm all right. Please don't fret."

"You won't be all right if you defy me again!" Hannah wagged her finger in Victoria's face. "Perhaps a reprimand from your uncle would be more to your liking."

"Oh, no, please, Hannah," Deborah begged, her countenance growing noticeably paler. "We'll do as you say, won't we?" She looked beseechingly at her sister.

"If you wish," Victoria answered half-heartedly, only to relieve Deborah's worrying.

"That's better," Hannah agreed. "You're to wear the gold silk gown, Victoria. Your uncle insists on that." She waved a hand to where the expensive, full-skirted dress lay over a wing-backed chair in the corner. "Get dressed! This savage railroad town is hardly sophisticated London, but Sir Giles wants you to look your best tonight, for the guest who will be joining you."

"Guest? We know so few people here in America. Who is it?" Victoria asked, wishing she could curb her curiosity. Linc Masterson flashed through her mind, causing a second of alert interest to sweep over her. But her uncle hated the gunfighter. He certainly wouldn't invite him to dinner. And she didn't like the brash American either, she told herself. His violent and arrogant nature appalled her.

Hannah's tone sounded smug when she answered.

"*You* know no one of importance in the United States, but your uncle does. He's a very wealthy and important man, remember."

"In England, yes, but not here," Victoria remarked lightly.

Hannah frowned. "You know nothing about his business enterprises. You could have no comprehension of them even if he chose to tell you. You're much too fluff-brained to ever be able to understand such things. That's why he's the guardian of both your fortunes. Your father knew you weren't intelligent enough to manage such wealth."

The cruel insults stung. But Victoria willed herself to control the urge to retaliate against Hannah's nastiness so Deborah wouldn't be further upset. Her little sister looked so thin and frail. She wished she could shield her from all hurtful words and harm.

"Why does Sir Giles want that gown?" she asked to change the subject. "The decolletage is so revealing."

Hannah gave her a snide smile. "Precisely why he instructs you to wear it." She roughly grabbed Victoria by the chin, forcing her face up. "You'll obey him or feel the pain of his wrath. And you don't want that, do you? Remember the last time you displeased him?"

She cringed, for she still bore the marks of his leather belt on her back because she didn't want to take this trip to the United States.

"Yes, I see you do remember. Good. Now, put on the dress!"

"Ah, Victoria, how lovely you look." Sir Giles stood when she approached his table in the hotel dining room. A burly man well over six feet tall, he towered over her thin, five-foot, four-inch frame. His smile was cold beneath the graying brown whiskers of his bushy moustache. As usual, he was impeccably dressed in a dark blue suit, reflecting the height of fashion in England.

He looked out of place in the rustic hotel dining room, with its crowded wooden bar counter lining one wall. Most of the diners present wore much less formal clothing. Victoria's entrance in the full-skirted gold gown had caused a stir among the other customers. Several men had turned to watch her walk across the spacious room.

Sir Giles' hazel eyes openly appraised her as if she were some prize animal he was considering buying. He helped her into a straight-backed chair next to him.

"You please me tonight, Victoria, as well you should. Your beauty will suit my purpose. That dress goes well with your golden hair and green eyes. You'll continue to do my bidding, I know, because you realize that's the best action for you to follow while I'm your guardian."

She hated his smirking expression.

"Yes, I'll obey you, for now." She regretted the words as soon as she said them, but somehow they'd slipped out before she could stop herself.

"What do you mean?" Giles demanded, his smile disappearing.

She tried to sound placating, but being in a public place where he could do nothing to her gave her courage to speak her mind.

"I mean, I must obey you while Deborah and I are legally under your guardianship. But in less than three months' time, I'll reach age twenty-one. Under the terms of our father's will, when I marry or reach that age, whichever comes first, I'll inherit my share of father's estate and become executrix of Deborah's share. Since you haven't allowed me to wed a man of my choice—or even become acquainted with one I might wish to consider marrying—I'll soon meet the age requirement." She swallowed hard and forced herself to look directly at him. "Then, Deborah and I won't need a guardian. I'll look after both of us."

His eyes narrowed. He grabbed her wrist, squeezing it

hard.

"You little bitch! Just remember, you have nothing, not even that lovely dress on your back, without my generosity. And you're nothing without my wealth and influence, only a young woman alone, a pretty face, nothing more. Never forget that reality, Victoria. Here in the United States these facts are especially true. We're foreigners. You have no money, no friends. I do. You have no one except me. Don't antagonize me, niece. I assure you, you'll regret it if you do."

His severe tone and malevolent gaze sent a chill of fear down Victoria's spine. She knew he meant every word he said.

"We aren't going to eat yet," Giles continued, tossing her hand roughly aside. "You see the table is set for three. Our guest should be arriving soon."

Victoria said nothing as she rubbed her sore wrist, feeling too miserable to even ask who would be joining them. She had no appetite for eating.

She glanced around the crowded dining room. White ruffled curtains hung at the wide front window. Red tablecloths were set with plain white china dishes and unadorned flatware. A large painting of a mountain scene hung on the wall behind the bar. Several young women dressed in long black skirts and starched white blouses hurried about taking orders and delivering food to the many customers.

"Ah, here's our guest now." Giles lifted his arm and waved.

Victoria followed the direction in which he gestured. A sickening dread washed over her when she recognized the short man standing in the arched entranceway leading from the hotel lobby—Alden Cummings.

Sir Giles rose to his feet, clasping the other man's outstretched hand when he reached their table. "Alden, my boy. Punctual as usual."

"Good evening, Uncle. Victoria."

He gave her a nod as his eyes drifted over her. She felt gooseflesh sweep over her when his bold look came to rest at the spot where the tops of her breasts showed above the low neckline of her gown. Disgusted, she looked away to hide her feelings.

"Sit down there next to Victoria, Alden. You two need to become reacquainted." Sir Giles turned to her. "Alden has revealed himself to be most astute and committed to furthering my business interests here. He's quite valuable to me."

"Thank you, Sir Giles," Alden remarked, looking pleased. "You honor me with your compliments and your decision regarding Victoria. She is beautiful and quite appealing."

Apprehension filled Victoria at his mention of some decision.

"I'm certain Victoria will see the merit in our plan, Alden, though she has no choice in the matter anyway," Sir Giles continued. "As you know, I'm her legal guardian under my late brother's will and her only living blood relative besides that sickly brat Deborah. I know what's best for her. She needs a firm hand. At times she can be willful."

"I've found every woman needs to be shown who's the master. I know how to make her obedient and submissive."

Victoria nearly gasped aloud as Alden's icy blue eyes darted to her again. His tone held almost the same timbre as her uncle's did whenever he explained why she needed to be punished, usually as he was wielding his leather belt over her back.

"Well, I see no reason to delay informing her of our plans," Sir Giles remarked. "The sooner known, the sooner carried out. Victoria, Alden has generously agreed to take you for his wife in marriage. At last the burdensome responsibility of taking care of you will fall to someone else." He snorted a laugh and slapped his nephew on the shoulder. "I hope you know what you're getting yourself into, my boy."

"Oh, I'm certain marriage to Victoria will be most suitable and pleasing." Alden smiled and leaned forward, stroking his fingertips down her bare forearm. "I'm eager to take on my husbandly duties."

Victoria felt the blood drain from her face. Nothing moved on her body. Her eyes didn't blink. Her chest didn't rise or fall, because her lungs had ceased working. Not one muscle twitched as she sat frozen with shock. Then suddenly, reactions exploded within her. Her stomach felt as if a brick had been dropped into it. Her heart beat frantically. Her mind cried out against the fiendishness of her uncle's plan for continuing to control her and her fortune. Now she realized why he'd dragged her across the ocean to this wild, God-forsaken country. She knew no one here. The United States, its people, their ways were all foreign to her, making her completely dependent on her uncle, just as he'd said. She must obey him.

She would not obey him!

Letting her anger overpower her fear of him, she snatched her arm out of Alden's grasp and jumped to her feet, knocking against the table so hard that both men had to grab hold of it to keep it from toppling over.

"You're insane! I will not marry you, Alden Cummings! I'd rather die first!"

Lifting her skirt, she whirled on her heel and ran from the dining room, only too aware that the other customers had grown silent at her outburst. Passing through the archway, she reached the hotel lobby and dodged around several people to make her way to the open front door. Rushing outside, she ran along the wooden sidewalk, sucking in the cool night air to fill her straining lungs.

She had no idea where she was going. She only knew she had to get away.

Up ahead, several people loitered on the sidewalk in front of a noisy saloon. Victoria started to hurry past them, but when she stepped sideways to avoid two men talking together, she careened into a tall man and gaudily dressed woman coming out of the saloon.

"Whoa there, English," Linc Masterson cautioned, his arms closing around her. "You need steadying."

Victoria's eyes flew to his face. His compelling dark gaze locked with hers, causing her words to stumble over her lips. "M-Mr. Masterson." The glaring light coming from the open doorway streaked across his handsome face and curly black hair.

"Lose your way, Miss Spencer?" A smirk curled up his full mouth. He made no attempt to release her from his firm hold, which held her body close against his hard-muscled length.

Her senses reeled from the close contact, adding to her panic. She pushed against his chest. "Release me, sir! I have my balance."

"You sure?" One arched black brow cocked toward her. "I don't mind helping you again."

His woman companion grabbed Victoria's arm and tried to yank them apart. "Let her go, Linc! I'm your woman tonight!" She pressed so close to him that her ample breasts nearly pushed out of her tight-fitting purple dress. The skirt only reached to her knees, showing long, black-stockinged legs.

"Let go of me!" Victoria ordered angrily, twisting out of Linc's grasp before he could say anything else. Grabbing up her skirt, she dashed away from him down the sidewalk. At the far side of the building, an alley loomed. Yellow light flooded from a side window of the saloon, illuminating the narrow dirt street. She made a sharp turn to the left and plunged headlong down it.

Suddenly, three men on horseback rode out of the shadows from the opposite direction toward her. Before she could turn to elude them, they surrounded her with their horses. Immediately, the biggest of the men dismounted and caught hold of her by the waist.

"Well, looky here, boys," the fat man declared, laughing and showing missing front teeth. "We don't even have to git to the saloon. The pretty gals is jus' arunnin' right into our arms!"

"Unhand me!" Victoria cried, struggling against his hold. He looked dirty and smelled of a long time without a bath. A foul odor from a wad of chewing tobacco reeked into her face as he brought his mouth close, then turned it away to spit a stream of brown juice into the dirt at her feet.

"Hol' still, you little she-cat!" He gripped her wrist with one hand, keeping his arm tightly around her waist. "I shore enough do like this here fancy dress you got on. But I'd like it better if'n it was *off.*" He let go of her wrist and yanked on the silk material at her shoulder, ripping it down her arm, exposing her breast.

Victoria screamed, clutching for the thin fabric to try to cover herself. The other two men quickly dismounted, coming toward her.

"How's about a little kiss, honey?" The big cowboy holding her sneered as he brought his mouth close to her face and pawed at her bare breast with his grimy hand.

"No! Stop!" she pleaded, twisting her head away and trying to push him back. In desperation she raked her fingernails down the side of his face.

"Yow! You hellion!" He shoved her hard toward one of his companions, clutching at his bleeding cheek.

The man grabbed her from behind, pinning her arms helplessly at her sides. He laughed against her ear. "Well now, sweet thing, looks like ol' Clem there can't tame you, but I kin! Let's jus' see what else nice you got under this here frilly dress."

"Yeah, git it off her, Mel!" the third man urged, rubbing his palms together.

With one hand, Mel started to pull the intact sleeve down off her shoulder.

"No!" Victoria cried, flailing out with her fists, but he easily kept her imprisoned. Tears of terror and humiliation blurred her eyes. She gasped for breath, struggling desperately to protect herself.

"Hold it, boys!" a deep voice ordered, reverberating off the building walls on either side of the alley.

The assailants turned toward the main street where the alley began. A man stood in the wide shaft of light cast from the saloon window, long legs slightly apart.

Victoria shot a fearful look to the newcomer's face. Linc Masterson! His handsome features no longer showed the bemusement they had a few moments ago. His square jaw looked firmly set.

"You talkin' to us, mister?" Mel asked gruffly.

"That's right. Let the lady go."

"Ha! She ain't no lady!" Mel shouted back. "You want to have yer turn with her, you got to wait till we're done with our fun."

"You're done now." His thumbs had been hooked into the top of his belt. Now his right hand dropped to his side where his gun hung holstered at fingertip level.

Clem brushed the blood from his scratched cheek and stepped away from the others to the middle of the alley. "Yer stickin' yer nose in where it ain't got no business bein', mister."

"A bad habit of mine. Before you make any more moves, friend, you might want to ask yourself if the gal's worth dying for."

Mel held Victoria pinned against him by the waist. Frantically, she crossed her arms in front of her, trying to hide her nakedness. For several long seconds, no one moved. Tension mounted.

"Take 'im, boys!" Mel shouted, shoving Victoria to the ground.

Linc's gun exploded, flashing fire into the night. Victoria screamed. Mel cried out and pitched forward headfirst into the dirt, his weapon barely out of its holster. Linc dropped to one knee and fanned the hammer of the Colt, downing Mel's fat accomplice just before he could fire. He crumpled into a heap at Victoria's feet. She screamed again, scurrying to get away from his body.

"Don't shoot! I give up! Don't shoot!" the third man yelled, raising his hands high in the air.

People ran out of the saloon, but Linc ignored them as he stood upright again and walked forward, smoking gun still held out at the ready.

"Drop your gunbelt," he ordered the man still standing.

"Yessir, I will, I shorely will!" he quickly replied, keeping one hand raised while he tried to unhook the buckle at his waist.

When it fell at his feet, Linc kicked it out of reach. He did the same with the other men's weapons, while keeping his gun trained on each one in turn. But even when he nudged them with the tip of his black boot, neither moved.

"You all right?" he finally asked Victoria.

Too stricken with fear and horror, she could only blink back her tears and stare up at him.

"Are you all right?" he demanded, his tone sharper. He glanced toward her, but kept his gun pointed at the man with his hands raised.

"Y-yes, I think so," she stammered, fumbling with the torn pieces of her dress to cover herself.

"Hellfire, woman, you got no business being in this part of town, running down alleys! I don't appreciate having to shoot two cowboys because of you!" His look was thunderous.

Suddenly, two men pushed through the crowd.

"Victoria!" Sir Giles rushed to her, followed by Alden Cummings.

"Looks like there's bin some trouble here," Sheriff Boswell stated, approaching from the street.

" 'Evening, N.K.," Linc greeted, holstering his gun.

"Now why ain't I surprised to find you involved in this gunplay, Linc?" The lawman lifted his high-crowned tan hat and adjusted it down on his head again. "Yer makin' a heap of paperwork fer me."

"Put this on immediately, Victoria!" Alden ordered, frowning as he took off his black suitcoat and threw it around her, then pulled her to her feet.

"Is this going to take long, N.K.?" Linc asked, but he kept his eyes on Victoria. "I got two appointments tonight." He thought of the meeting with Drumm and also the nice little tumble in bed he'd planned with the scantily clad Carmen, who was standing with the other onlookers.

"Appointments kin wait. We're all headin' over to my office agin to get to the bottom of just what happened here. Come along, ma'am. You come, too, Sir Spencer. Linc, lead out. You know the way good enough." He took hold of Victoria's elbow with one hand and grabbed the third assailant by the back of the collar with the other. Then he turned to the people on the sidewalk. "Couple of you fellers git these here two unlucky cowpokes over to the undertaker's. Let's go, folks."

Victoria appreciated the sheriff's supporting hand, for she was trembling all over from the terrible experience and wasn't certain her weak legs would hold her. Such horrible violence shocked her to the core. And she greatly feared Sir Giles, for she could tell by his fierce scowl that he was livid with fury. At the moment, she preferred going to the jail office in the company of the sheriff rather than face him and Alden alone.

She saw Linc pull on his black hat, which had been

hanging down his back by a cord around his neck. When she passed him, he expelled his breath in what sounded like exasperated anger. She raised her eyes to his and felt a jolt to her churning insides, suddenly realizing that Linc Masterson had just shot two men to death to save her from harm.

Chapter Five

Close to midnight, Linc cautiously approached the ramshackle remains of Carbon Timber Town. After the hostile welcome Drumm had given him in town and then the strange message from the Mexican boy, he wasn't sure what to expect in coming here.

Tense with apprehension, he halted his horse at the edge of the ghost town and drew his Colt, raising it to catch the bright moonlight shining over his shoulder. After rotating the bullet chamber to check for six full cartridges, he smoothly slid the revolver into the holster at his side and squinted into the darkness.

The weathered white stones of a small cemetery cast ominous shadows across the rutted, grass-choked road leading down the center of what once had been a thriving mining town. Clenching his gun hand into a fist, he slowly released it, feeling his fingers twitch with readiness. He nudged his boot heels into his mount's sides, urging the animal toward what remained of the old church. If Drumm showed up tonight, he'd be there, the place where they'd played as boys, target practicing at the bell in the steeple.

When he put his mind to it, he could remember a few good times spent with his older half-brother. But the intense rivalry and many bloody fights with him during their growing-up years, and the bitter conflicts over Abby, dominated his memories, souring them.

He guided his horse past the black silhouettes of the few sagging buildings still standing. Darkness surrounded the single-story, wood-frame church. Linc dismounted, throwing the reins over the broken hitching rail in front. Glancing up, he saw the outline of the bell still hanging in the steeple. He drew his gun and cautiously mounted the three rickety steps to the porch, staying to the side to avoid being a straight target from the doorway.

Suddenly an owl hooted, halting his steps. His horse snorted, tossing its head. An answering neigh sounded from behind the church.

Linc waited, every muscle in his body alert. His own heartbeat loudly filled the silence. He cocked back the hammer of the Colt, then used his free hand to turn the rusty knob of the front door.

"Drummond?"

"Here," came his brother's voice from the darkness inside.

A match was struck and touched to a candle on the pulpit rail. The soft yellow glow revealed a tall figure standing behind the wooden lecturn.

"You alone?" Linc asked, making no move to lower his weapon.

His brother stepped out into full view, holding his brown suit coat open. "I'm alone. And unarmed. I wasn't sure you'd come."

"Well, I did, so get to the reason. I don't figure this for a social visit." He darted his eyes around the shadowy room before he uncocked his gun and ran it back into the holster.

Drumm snorted and took off his flat-crowned hat, pulling the brim around through his fingers. Linc recognized the nervous gesture.

"Believe me," Drumm continued, looking at the candle instead of his brother, "having you here is the last thing I really want right now. But I got no choice." He raked a hand through his black hair. "I hate admitting this, but I'm in trouble. I can't trust anybody." He finally glanced at Linc. "Except maybe you. Because this involves the ranch. When Callie showed me one of your letters to her, I knew where you were and decided to send for you. We might hate each other's hides, but that never carried over to how we always felt about the Diamond M." He paused again, blowing out a long breath. "God, I'm going to lose the ranch. The bank's about to foreclose."

Linc kept his face set in an emotionless mask. "I'd like to be around to see you lose something. Too bad it has to be the ranch."

Drummond's look darkened and his hands clenched into fists at his sides. "That all you got to say? Damn it, you know what it felt like to have to send you that telegram, asking you to come here? It took weeks of arguing with myself before I finally did it. I don't much like eating my pride!"

"Mighty bitter, isn't it?" Linc let a smug smile of satisfaction curl up his mouth. This meeting was costing Drumm dearly, and that suited him just fine.

"I knew this wouldn't do any good!" Drumm slammed his hat down on his head and started to storm toward the door.

Linc grabbed him roughly by the arm, stopping him short. "Damnation, Drummond, you have everything I ever wanted! The ranch. Abby. I walked away, left it all to you five years ago. You'll get nothing more from me, you bastard!"

Drumm's fierce glare matched Linc's before he wrenched his arm away.

"Then Clint Dandridge'll own Masterson land."

For a long moment, the two brothers scowled at each other eye to eye in tense silence. Finally, Linc looked away and spoke.

"I reckon that's a hell of a lot worse situation than you

having it."

"I was hoping you'd see it that way."

"All right, I'm listening. What happened?"

Drumm turned to pace a small circle in front of the empty altar.

"Eleven months ago, I took out a big mortgage on the ranch to cover setbacks. A hard winter two years before cut the herd. The last couple of years, I been experimenting with some high-priced English Shorthorn stock from Idaho and Oregon, trying to breed meatier beef on the hoof from our tough Texas longhorns. But an epidemic of scours just about wiped out my calf population. I got so caught up with all the working end of the ranch, I let the business end go. You know I never was one for keeping books. Abby took on that responsibility when we got married, and she's done a fine job, but it came down to the hard numbers that more money was going out than was coming in. I got the mortgage to restock the herd, pay the men the back wages I owed them, and build a new, bigger barn. Now I'm behind in the payments. My two Shorthorn bulls have turned up dead in the last three months. The cattle agent looks down his nose at my mix-breed stock and won't get me the on-the-hoof price I need to make ends meet. Dandridge made me a buy-out offer a month ago—only half what the ranch is worth. But he's holding out cash. Abby's pressuring me to take it before we go bankrupt and lose everything. She hates being stuck living out on the ranch. She wants to move back East, where people are civilized, she says, and there are social occasions to go to." He gripped the edge of the high lecturn with both hands. "Damn, I don't know what to do. The thought of leaving the ranch tears my guts out. Back East's no place for me. But Abby's my wife. I can't lose her." His gaze drilled into Linc; his features hardened. "The devil curse me, but I love her—even knowing it was you she always wanted, you she thinks about when we're

. . . together."

Linc stared at his brother, stunned by his words. The old pain connected with Abby sparked from the embers of memory in his mind. His voice was tight when he spoke again.

"She hitched up with you, not me."

Drumm looked up, his eyes narrowing.

"She married me 'cause Pa gave me the ranch. I know that now. She had lofty ideas about me being a big cattle baron someday, rich and powerful. She made me believe it, too. Talked me into taking risks with a new breed. But then the setbacks started and the comparisons to you. 'Linc would've done this not that. Why can't you be more like Linc?' I got sick of hearing your name!" He banged his fist down hard on the pulpit rail, causing the candle to wobble. The flickering light accentuated the wrath on his face.

Linc felt a triumphant smile reach his lips at the thought that Abby had really wanted him. Maybe she'd suffered like he had during these years for throwing away their love for the promise of money and power.

He heard the ache of need in Drumm's voice—the need that bordered on obsession. He'd felt it himself because of Abby, and hated being so vulnerable to another person's whims.

"A woman can cut a God-awful wound into a man and leave him bleeding inside, if you let her," he said, more to himself than to Drumm. "The trick is not to let her." In his mind he thought about how Abby had bulldogged him to his knees, then run him out to barren range when Drumm offered her more. After that he'd drawn in his heart so deep, nobody could reach it. So what if he felt like a piece of granite inside—cold and hard. He'd been able to see Abby today, even get close to her, without feeling anything.

Unbidden, Victoria Spencer's beautiful green-eyed features flashed in his mind's eye, startling him. Why would he think of her now? She'd caused him nothing but trouble since he'd met her—just like Abby. That must be the reason.

"So you're an expert on women now as well as gun handling," Drumm noted sarcastically. "Well, you better know right off that Abby's mine. She married me and she's staying my wife."

"You can have her. I'm not interested. Besides, I'm enjoying what she's doing to you. Just how high do you buck when she yanks your reins?"

Drummond lunged for him, grabbing him by the shirtfront, his face livid with rage. Linc's gun jabbed into his belly at the same instant.

"Back off, Drumm. This Colt's got a hair trigger, especially for you."

Slowly, Drumm slackened his hold and stepped away. "Clint Dandridge would like it just fine if we killed each other. Then nothing would stand in his way for getting the ranch."

"Yeah, reckon that's true enough." Linc holstered his gun. "So why don't we get to the point. Just what do you want from me? Give it to me plain." He watched his brother's throat work as if he were swallowing hard.

Drumm sighed heavily, then spoke.

"Money. To keep the bank wolves off my back. Do you have anything left from that five thousand Pa left you?"

Linc smirked, shaking his head.

"That's long gone. There was this pretty gal in Texas . . . but I got a few friends who owe me favors. I could put my hands on two or three thousand if I had to. What's in it for me?"

"Two or three thousand isn't enough, but it could hold off the bank for a while. We keep this deal strictly business. I'll give you a promissory note, all legal-like. You'll have your money back with plenty of interest, soon as I can sell the herd."

Linc stared steadily at his half-brother.

"I don't want money."

"What then?"

"The mountain acres."

"What? No! That's prime grazing land! I won't have the likes of you—"

Now it was Linc who grabbed Drumm. Wadding his coat front in his fists, he spoke through gritted teeth.

"Be real careful what you say, dear brother. I know how you hate being reminded, but Masterson blood runs through my veins just like it does yours. I got a right to that land. I named my price. Take it or leave it." He shoved Drumm away hard, into the lecturn.

"You bastard!" Drumm swore, lurching sideways to keep his balance. "You know I got no choice. But if I agree to your terms, I want your gun thrown into the deal. Clint Dandridge seems to be looking to own the whole damned Laramie Plain. One way or the other, he's been buying out the ranches all around here, using money from those English fellas. I can't prove he's doing anything illegal, but bad accidents happen to anybody who doesn't choose to sell out to him, like my bulls turning up dead. He wants the Diamond M. I don't figure to give it to him. It could come down to one hell of a fight."

Linc thought for a moment, his mind racing with the thread of a scheme. "Dandridge wants my gun, too. Offered me a job this morning. I could take it and get inside his operation, try to catch a look at his ledgers, see what he's up to."

Drummond rubbed his chin with his hand, then nodded. "That's a real dangerous idea. I like it. Could get us something. Reading all those books like you used to do could pay off if you can figure out his business."

"I'll find out all right. You just keep the bank from foreclosing and get the deed to my mountain land ready.

I'll let you know when I have the money for you. Deal?" Reluctantly he thrust out his hand.

Drumm looked just as hesitant to take it, but he did. "I reckon I have to trust you. Don't expect any thanks though. When this is all over, we go separate ways, just like before."

"Right, only we'll be neighbors." Linc let a snide smile curl his lips. "Won't that be just fine?"

"More like pure hell! Damn Clint Dandridge for forcing me to this!" He frowned angrily as he strode toward the front of the church, throwing one last remark over his shoulder. "If I have to get in touch with you, I'll send Miguel, the Mexican boy."

After the door slammed behind Drummond, Linc stared into the flickering candle for a long time, thinking about the part of his scheme that he hadn't told his brother. Here was his chance.

"I'll be glad to help you fight off Clint Dandridge, Drumm," he murmured into the emptiness of the abandoned church. "Just long enough for me to get my hands on enough cash to buy your note from the bank. Then the Diamond M will be all mine."

That thought pleased him well enough. Victoria Spencer loomed into his mind again. The pretty little English heiress was set to marry that greenhorn Cummings, according to what her uncle told the sheriff after that skirmish in the alley earlier tonight. She was probably worth plenty, and she owed him for saving her life more than once. She wasn't hitched to that skinny high-nose yet.

"And you never will be, Green Eyes, not if I can get to you first . . ."

Chapter Six

Victoria took great care closing the bedroom door behind her so she wouldn't make a sound. After listening for a moment to the silence of the Dandridge ranch house, she lifted the long skirt of her white cotton nightgown and tiptoed to the curving mahogany staircase. She stared hard into the darkness below on the main floor, then gingerly tried each step in turn until she reached the bottom.

Suddenly, a tall grandfather clock bonged next to her at the foot of the stairs, nearly stopping her heart. It struck twice, marking the early morning hour. When she could breathe again, she glanced around, then hurried across the wide foyer to turn the key kept in the lock and yank the solid front door open. The outside night air washed over her, feeling cool on her perspiring face.

With barely a sound she pulled the door closed behind her and ran around the side of the two-story stone house to a grove of cottonwoods surrounding a small pond. Not a leaf stirred. Moonlight glistened mirror-like on the still water.

Lifting her face to its soothing glow, she started to lean against one of the sturdy tree trunks, then winced away from it when pain shot through her. The thin fabric of her nightdress offered little protection to her back where Sir Giles' leather belt had raised bleeding welts, his harsh punishment because she'd run away from Alden and caused the shooting in the alley in town two days ago.

But at least for a few moments now she was free—free of her uncle's cruelty and Hannah's overbearing sternness. Away from Alden's lecherous gazes. Finally, after the torturous hours of being watched constantly, she'd escaped the confines of Clinton Dandridge's house.

How she longed to find a horse and ride away into the night. But where would she go? The barren desert plain beyond the pond and trees seemed to stretch for miles to the high mountain peaks in the distance. The silvery light from the nearly full moon created grotesque, forbidding shapes from the cactus and sagebrush. Even if she dared to venture out in that open wasteland, she wasn't certain of what direction to take to reach Laramie. And she couldn't leave Deborah.

Her hatred festered when she thought of her uncle's brutality toward her younger sister. Deborah had been distraught over the announcement of the marriage plans to Alden. When Victoria was beaten for running away, Deborah felt the strap, too, as a lesson in obedience. Sir Giles' brutality had brought on one of her severe fainting spells. She was only now recovering.

Hot tears stung Victoria's eyes. She felt so trapped and helpless. She shivered in the cool night air, wrapping her arms around her, but she swallowed back the lump in her throat, stubbornly refusing to cry. She would be strong. Somehow she'd have revenge on Sir Giles for all his cruelty toward her and Deborah. Somehow, someday!

"Damned stupid action, wandering outside at night alone, English."

Frightened, Victoria whirled around to come face to face with Linc Masterson.

"I-I had to get out of that hot house," she stammered, glancing to the shadows cast by the trees to see if anyone was with him. They were alone. Her heart suddenly beat faster when she realized that fact and another—that he wore no shirt. "Is there some danger? E-everything is so quiet."

"Being a foreigner, you likely don't know about coyotes and mountain lions. They're known to come down out of the hills at times to prey on the cattle grazing these parts. You'd taste a far sight better than a tough old longhorn steer. Get back to the house."

His commanding tone reminded her of Sir Giles, setting her already frayed nerves further on edge. She raised her chin.

"Don't tell me what to do, Mr. Masterson. If it's so dangerous to be out here, then why are *you* lurking about?"

"I work here for Clint now. I'm just keeping my eye on things. Besides, I don't care much for sleeping in bunkhouses. There's no danger out here for me. But you'd be wise to get back to the house, if you know what's good for you."

He stepped closer to her, feeling his anger rise at the way her eyes held his without flinching. Men had backed down from gunfights with him just because of the threatening look he could give them. Yet here was this slip of a gal standing her ground right in front of him. She just stood there looking pretty and spirited in her high-necked, nightgown, with the moon-drenched desert wilderness framing her. Her long, straight hair looked like silken threads of pale gold, making his fingers twitch to touch it. Damn, but she was beautiful! And here was a chance to put his plan into action—while he had her alone.

Victoria retreated a step back, feeling her pulse beating rapidly at the base of her neck as his dark eyes locked with hers. She wanted to turn and run back to the house, but her legs felt weak at the knees. She frowned, angry at her body's reactions.

"Don't come any closer, Mr. Masterson. I warn you."

She held up her hand to stop him.

He ignored her protest, lessening the space between them with a half stride so only an arm's length separated them.

"Are you afraid of me, Miss Spencer?" he asked, pointedly using her proper name.

She swallowed hard, feeling the deep timbre of his voice touch her spine and send a tremble through her.

"No," she lied.

He quickly encircled her narrow waist with one arm and pulled her against him.

"You should be frightened, Victoria," he whispered huskily against her ear. "I'm half Sioux Indian. I take what I want. Answer to no one. I could have whatever I wanted from you, but I'll have only this now." He brought his mouth down hard on hers.

In that same instant, he realized he'd made a big mistake. The feel of her body so close to him sent a shock wave pounding through him. He didn't expect such a hunger to explode inside him. He suddenly wanted to taste more of her, to feel more of her.

Her eyes flew open wide with stunned surprise. She pushed against his hard-muscled chest, trying in vain to twist away from his possessive hold and demanding lips. When she had so little breath left that her mind began to spin with dizziness, he pulled his head away, still crushing her body close along his length.

"Danger, English," he murmured, his voice low. "There's more danger out here than you can ever imagine." He abruptly released her, just barely in control of himself. Everything was moving too fast. He had to back away or jeopardize his scheme to get her money. He didn't want to spook her, scare her off so she ran like a panicked filly. But it sure as hell wasn't easy to let her go!

Breathing hard, stunned by his actions, Victoria could

only stare at him, pressing the back of her hand against her bruised mouth. She fought back the tears of anger and confusion stinging her eyes. A turmoil of sensations churned through her. Her injured back hurt from his rough hold. She felt overwhelmed by the taste of his lips and the intimate contact with his hard-muscled body. The helplessness she felt against his superior strength frightened her—and ignited her fury!

"How dare you assault me!"

"I dare anything I please. That was only a kiss, a warning of what could happen out here."

"Savage!"

Now his fury flared. He swiftly reached out and grabbed her arms, pushing them behind her so the front of her body pressed fully against him again.

"That I am. Don't ever forget it." He kept her wrists imprisoned with one hand and raised his other to touch her face. "But I can be gentle." His fingertips slid down her throat. "And pleasure you in ways I doubt you've ever known." He brought his face very close to hers. "Feel this, Victoria . . ."

He brought his mouth down to meet hers again, not harshly as before, but whisper-soft, barely touching her lips. Once, twice, three times he pressed lightly against her mouth. Victoria thought she'd die. No breath moved in her lungs. She was frozen in his arms, held captive by more than just his strength. She couldn't think. She could only feel—such new and alarming sensations. When his lips descended to hers once more and stayed against her mouth, asking, seeking, a small cry of agony sounded in her throat. She swayed against him. He released her hands, and they immediately went to his naked chest to push him away. Her mind shouted the command. But her fingers wouldn't obey. They felt the heat of his body, entwined in the soft, fine hair curling from his taut skin.

Linc's mind whirled as he held the kiss. Sweet. Her mouth tasted so honey-sweet. He had to force himself to control the powerful urge to crush her to him again. His body reacted with gunfire quickness again, arousing his senses to a sharp awareness of everything about her. The curves of her body, the warmth of her flesh through the thin fabric of her nightgown. His heart pounded hard. Liquid heat shot through his veins.

Break it off, stop kissing her. Step back, he ordered himself. And he'd do those things as soon as he showed her he could give as well as take if he chose to. When her will surrendered to his . . .

Still holding the kiss, he gently cupped the sides of her face in his hands, then moved them slowly down her throat to her shoulders. When he let them slide over her nightgown along her back, he felt her cringe and knew something was wrong. Her small cry wasn't from desire this time.

She pulled back, putting out her hand to the cottonwood tree next to them to steady herself.

"You must stop, please," she pleaded, lowering her head.

Linc said nothing. He reached out and grasped the fabric of her nightdress where it was unfastened at her throat. With a quick yank he ripped apart the remaining buttons and pulled the gown down over her shoulders. She gasped, fumbling to hold the torn pieces over her half-exposed breasts, but he paid no heed to them. Turning her around into the moonlight, he moved the material lower on her back.

"Who did this to you?" he demanded, seeing the lashes.

"I must return to the house." Unable to meet his gaze, she started to move away, but he stepped in front of her, taking hold of her arms.

"Look at me, Victoria. Who hurt you? Spencer?"

Her large green eyes lifted to his, sparking with anger. "It doesn't matter. Stay away from me!"

Before he could stop her, she twisted out of his hold and ran for the ranch house.

Linc's brow knit into deep lines as he watched the front door close behind her. He knew Spencer had been furious over the alley incident, but to whip her like that . . .

His hand clenched into a fist at his right side, near his gun. Then he opened it and shook off the wrath that churned in him.

"Keep shy of it, cowboy," he told himself. "Mind your own business. She didn't ask for your help."

He intended to keep his involvement with her limited, just enough to get what he needed—the money for the ranch. Only that mattered. The Diamond M was all he wanted. The crucial goal, he reminded himself, was to get her money. He'd remember that ambition and forget about Victoria Spencer's problems. And her body. He'd only planned to kiss her a few times, then leave her hungry for more so she'd be easy to use anytime he wanted her. He could want a woman or put her out of his mind, as he chose. No trouble. After Abby, he'd taught himself the skill, made himself be a piece of granite inside. Victoria Spencer was like any other woman. He'd make whatever use of her he wanted.

He glanced toward the house, wiping the back of his hand across his mouth. Then he bent down and reached out to where a tiny stream of fresh water bubbled up from the rocks near the edge of the pond. Catching some of the cool liquid in his cupped hand, he lifted it to his lips and sucked it in to wash away the taste of Victoria. The sweet, lingering taste . . .

Chapter Seven

Victoria sat across from Sir Giles and Alden in Clinton Dandridge's elegant open carriage, concentrating on the skirt folds of her emerald green silk gown instead of her uncle's glowering stare. Deborah fidgeted on the cushioned seat next to her, obviously excited by the prospect of attending the dinner party at the Masterson ranch. Victoria didn't share her enthusiasm.

She sensed someone's approach and glanced sideways. Breath caught in her throat when she saw Linc walk by the carriage. He was dressed formally for a social call. Gray trousers clung to his muscular legs. His black coat swung open with his stride, revealing a gray vest, white shirt, and black string tie.

His intense brown eyes met hers when he passed, sending a jolt through her. His rugged handsomeness stunned her, making her heart beat faster. He nodded, touching a finger to the brim of his low-crowned black hat, but his passive expression didn't change. Was he thinking of last night at the pond?

Victoria lowered her eyes, fearing Sir Giles would notice the blush of embarrassment she felt rise up her face. Her lips still burned from Linc's stolen kisses. She should be ashamed or affronted, yet a feeling of wonder and surprise remained with her, just as it had the whole sleepless night.

"Where do you think you're going, Masterson?"

Victoria looked up to see Clinton Dandridge's nineteen year old son grab Linc. Zeke Dandridge's six-foot height matched Linc's, but he was lean and round-shouldered, a light-featured opposite of the man next to him.

Linc turned his head to look down at the young man's hand on his arm, then he slowly raised his eyes to Zeke's face.

"You look like a tinhorn dandy in that fancy suit, Zeke. You might want to think real hard about whether you want to wear it to a party or a burying."

"Why you half-breed bastard!" Zeke's face reddened and his hand dropped to his gun at his left side. "I'll teach you to respect your betters!"

Clint Dandridge yanked his son's arm away from the weapon and twisted it behind his back. "You idiot! Tired of living, boy? At his worst, Linc Masterson is twice as fast with a gun as you'll ever be!" He shoved his son away in disgust. "Now get on your horse!"

Scowling, Zeke cast a black look at Linc and then his father, but he said nothing more. Snatching the leather reins from the hitching rail, he mounted his horse and dug his spurs into the animal to urge it up in front of the team of matched bays harnessed to the carriage.

Victoria watched Linc pat his horse's neck, then swing up into the saddle with an easy, supple movement. He didn't appear to be at all disturbed by Zeke's insult or threat. Yet with an aloof casualness, he'd threatened to kill the young man, and she didn't have the slightest doubt that he would have carried out that threat if Zeke Dandridge had drawn his gun.

She shuddered and forced her eyes to look away from Linc. How could he kiss her so tenderly and possessively in the moonlight, shocking her to the core, and then by the light of day nearly kill a man without a blink of hesitation?

* * *

The last golden rays of dusk crept behind distant purple mountain peaks just as the dinner guests arrived at the Diamond M ranch. Abigail Masterson immediately appeared on the front porch to greet them. Drummond Masterson and a boy of about the age of four joined her as a Mexican butler directed a ranch hand to take their horses and see to the carriage.

Alden took hold of Victoria's waist to help her down from the carriage. He didn't release her right away, but instead leaned down to murmur close to her ear.

"Remember to be compliant and silent tonight, my dear. You are here only because I enjoy looking at lovely decorations." His hand stroked her arm. "My fawning over you should make Abigail especially jealous, resulting in a delightful evening. Don't displease me or your uncle in any way, if you know what's good for you."

Alden's smirk sent a wave of revulsion washing through Victoria. She twisted away from him and went to stand next to Deborah, disgusted by his orders and his lecherous hint of some liaison with Abigail Masterson. Never would she become the wife of such a contemptible man! She would escape this nightmare somehow. She and Deborah together.

"Isn't it exciting to be on a real western ranch, Victoria?" Deborah whispered, her blue eyes twinkling with delight. "Mrs. Masterson looks so lovely in that red gown, don't you think?" She giggled behind her fan. "The low decolletage is positively scandalous. Why, if the black lace weren't there along the edge—"

"Yes, she looks very nice," Victoria cut in with annoyance. She felt angry for some reason. Abigail Masterson was more than just passingly beautiful, and Linc seemed to have eyes only for her as he swung down from his horse.

"Welcome to our home, Sir Giles," Abby greeted, smiling as she came forward to take the older man's hands in hers.

She nodded toward all the men in turn. Victoria noticed that her eyes lingered on Linc longer than they had on the others.

"Lincoln, I'm so glad you came," she said, her smile widening. "I've made Drummond promise to be civil to you tonight. You must give me your word you'll be the same with him."

Linc glanced at his half-brother's frowning countenance, then his eyes drifted back to the woman before him. "Drumm doesn't look any too happy about that arrangement, but if that's what you want, Abby, you have my word."

"Good!" Abby finally turned her attention to her female guests. "Victoria, isn't that your name? My, don't you look sweet in that gown. It matches your eyes perfectly, but if you don't mind my saying so, it does wash out your coloring just a bit. But perhaps your health makes you so pale. I understand you are quite sickly."

"N-no, I'm fine," Victoria stammered, surprised by the woman's crassness.

"I'm the one with the poor health, Mrs. Masterson," Deborah spoke up. "I fear I'm quite a burden to my sister." She smiled lovingly toward Victoria.

"How interesting," Abby continued, turning away to give her attention to the dark-featured boy at her side. "This is our son, Patrick." She looked directly at Linc. "Here is a nephew you've never seen," she explained, holding his gaze. Then she stooped down next to the boy. "Shake hands with your Uncle Lincoln, Patrick."

The boy hung back, clinging to his mother's arm.

"Do as Mama tells you, dear," Abby urged. Timidly, he extended one small hand to Linc, who took it.

"Howdy, partner. I'm glad to know you. How old are you?"

Slowly, the boy raised the fingers of his right hand. "Four," he said proudly, grinning.

Victoria saw Linc's eyes dart to Abby, but she looked away.

"That's a good boy," Abby said quickly, patting his thick black curls. "You can get to know your Uncle Linc better later on. Now, please do come in, everyone. Dinner's about to be served."

Alden took hold of Victoria's elbow, but she hung back to stare at Drummond and Linc and little Patrick. The boy was the living image of his father—and his uncle. She wondered about the strange look that had crossed Linc's face when the boy told his age. For a moment, he'd seemed so surprised.

"Lincoln!" A pregnant woman with dark hair streaked with gray appeared in the doorway. She held a hand at her back as if she were in pain and waited for Linc to come to her. Her smile was warm and welcoming when she hugged him.

"It's so good to see you! You're as handsome as ever, you devil."

A smile touched Linc's usually austere expression as he returned her hug as close as he could, considering her bulging middle.

"It's good to see you, Callie. How many young'uns does this one make?"

She drew away, sighing tiredly as she tucked a stray strand of hair back into the coil on top of her head.

"This is my sixth in eight years. Brad and I hope to be stopping after this one."

"That's what you said with the fifth," Abby said derisively.

"Six?" Linc replied, not too pleased with Abby's unkind remark. "That's nearly a tribe, sister-mine."

She laughed and hugged her arm around his waist. "It's so good to have you home. Come, we can talk more inside. The children are anxious to see their wild uncle." She lowered her eyes. "Brad wanted to come, too, but he wasn't feeling well."

"Drunk again," Drumm stated contemptuously.

Callie's head flew up and her eyes flashed. "Don't say such unkind things about my husband, Drummond. You know he tries hard to be a good rancher."

Drumm snorted. "Everything he knows about ranching you could fit into a lady's sewing thimble."

"Drumm, please," Callie beseeched.

"I think Abby said dinner was ready," Linc cut in, sending a glaring look at his brother. "I reckon we should all go inside *now.*"

Linc took his sister's arm and guided her into the house, glad to have the scene outside finished. In the space of five minutes, he'd had two gut-wrenching shocks. He hadn't known anything about Patrick. The boy's look and age raised a mighty big question in his mind. He'd have to talk to Abby alone.

Then seeing Callie again shook him to the boot tips. She was only two years older than he was—thirty by now—but she looked ten years beyond that, haggard and hardworked. This land could do that to a woman—beat her down, wear her out with the chores of birthing and living. He recognized the yellow dress she had on. It had been one of her favorites five years ago, and she was still wearing it, only now it was frayed and worn, showing marks at the seams where it had been let out. Damn Brad Morrow for keeping her pregnant all the time, and damn Drummond for not helping to lighten her burdens.

Chapter Eight

Victoria ate little of the abundant food served at the Masterson table—heaping platters of roast beef, leg of lamb and several kinds of fish, bowls of baked and creamed potatoes and buttered vegetables, along with breads and biscuits served with preserves. Then there were Mexican dishes unfamiliar to her—bean and meat combinations in dough shells and wrappings, accompanied by sauces. Everything looked delicious, but she had no appetite for any of it. The tension around the long maple table was almost tangible. Drummond Masterson never stopped scowling. He showed no openness to Clinton Dandridge's business offerings. Even his lawyer, Taft Denton, who'd arrived from town just in time to join them, couldn't persuade him to consider any proposals. He sat stubbornly at the head of the table with his square jaw that was so like Linc's set in a firm clench.

On the other hand, Abigail Masterson was the epitome of the perfect hostess. She flirted openly, fluttered her long, dark eyelashes, laughed, and kept up a running conversation of amusing little stories and compliments to the men. She asked Sir Giles endless questions about England and London social life.

"How fortunate you'll be, Victoria, to return to London with your handsome husband Alden at your side," Abby noted, sending the Englishman a warm smile. She sighed dramatically. "I can only imagine the fine parties and balls you'll be attending."

"Those dalliances will have to wait," Alden stated. "Victoria and I will be staying in Laramie for some time, while I continue to oversee Sir Giles' business ventures here. I've already looked into buying a small ranch near Dandridge's place, and plan to run a few hundred head of cattle of my own. There's a great deal of profit to be made from beef. I'm certain Victoria will make a wonderful prairie wife." He leaned over and put his arm around her shoulders, but he kept his eyes on Abby Masterson.

Victoria tried to swallow, but her throat constricted. His touch sickened her. She felt glad now that she hadn't eaten much, because she was certain she wouldn't have been able to hold it down if she had. Not only was the thought of staying on a cow ranch in this God-forsaken country with Alden totally revolting, but Alden's barely disguised attention to Drummond Masterson's wife left little doubt of his fidelity—or hers.

"Why, Victoria, you look positively ill, my dear," Abby said sweetly. "Why don't you go and lie down for a while until you feel better." She motioned to the maid standing nearby. "Anita, show the señorita to one of the guest rooms. Drumm, take these gentlemen into the parlor for some of your brandy and awful cigars. I'm sure Sir Giles would like to see your gun collection."

She rose from her chair before anyone could contradict her. The men stood also, and Drummond begrudgingly led the way out of the dining room. Victoria gratefully followed the young Mexican girl to the wide staircase leading upstairs.

Linc was the last to leave the room. Abby caught his eye and tilted her head slightly toward the kitchen door, then she turned and smiled at Callie and Deborah.

"I think I'll go and check on the children to see that they've been fed in the kitchen and are on their way to bed. No, don't bother, Callie," she said, holding up a hand when her sister-in-law started to come with her. "Sit down and chat with Miss Spencer. You can use a rest from taking care of those children all the time. I'll see to them."

Victoria was glad to be alone in the spacious bedroom. She barely noticed the expensive lace curtains at the windows or the mahogany canopy bed located against one wall. Instead, she wrapped her arms around her and walked out the open French doors onto the veranda that ran all around the outside of the second story of the ranch house.

The night was serenely quiet, filled with a peacefulness that evaded her. None of this could be happening. It was all a dream—a bad dream, like the terrible nightmare she kept having about her father's death. Soon she would wake up and be home again in England. Her birthday would come, and there would be no marriage to Alden Cummings, no beatings, no Sir Giles cruelly spying on her every movement.

She put out her hands to the wooden railing in front of her and turned her face to the star-dotted sky. *How can I stop this nightmare,* she wondered, feeling a deep sense of hopelessness creep over her.

"Oh, Linc, at last we're alone together! I pretended to be checking on the children to get out here to you."

Victoria gripped the railing, stunned to hear Abby Masterson's voice coming from directly below her.

"Hold me in your arms, my darling. I've longed to touch you."

Victoria started to turn away, her stomach twisting in a

knot. But then she stopped, unable to move, drawn to listen.

"Yes, you feel the same to me," Abby murmured. "So powerful, all man. In your strong arms I fear nothing. I want you, Linc. These years you've been away have been such torture. Every time Drummond touched me, I longed for him to be you. You can't know what it's like being married to him. He's a cold, cruel man. He's kept me a prisoner here on this horrible ranch. But now you're back. We can go away together, love each other as it was always meant to be. You want me, don't you, darling? Kiss me, Linc. Please . . ."

Victoria closed her eyes, paralyzed by the silence that hung in the air. Against her will, she thought of another kiss—last night's. She hated remembering it. Hated Linc Masterson!

"Back off, Abby!" Linc's voice sounded low and angry, but a little breathless, as well. "I finished playing your little games long ago when you decided to hitch up with Drumm."

"Oh, Linc, I was so young. I made a mistake, a terrible mistake, and I've been paying dearly for it these last five years. Please, don't punish me more. You're the only man I've ever loved, and you love me, too, I know. I can feel it in the way you hold me. I felt the desire in your lips just now and the fast pounding of your heart against my breast. Here, give me your hand. Feel how happily my heart beats at being with you again."

"Hellfire, Abby, I said back off! What do you want from me?"

"Please, you're hurting my wrist, Linc! I told you, I want to go away with you. I want us to be together. We can go east to New York or Boston. I've managed to save a little money, and I have a deal going that could reap a lot more for us. Share it with me, darling. No man's ever made me feel the way you could. Only you opened my heart and drove my body to madness with wanting you."

"What about your son? Can you run out on him as easily as you can Drumm?" Linc's voice was cold, accusing.

Abby laughed softly. "Oh, darling, surely you know. You must have realized the minute you looked at Patrick that he's your son. Even if I could bear to have Drummond touch me any more, he isn't capable of giving me children. There have been no others besides Patrick. He was born eight months after you left Laramie."

"My God, Abby, why didn't you tell me you were pregnant?"

"I didn't know until after you'd already gone. I tried to find you, but you seemed to just disappear into thin air."

"Does Drumm know?"

"No. I made certain I was a most amorous wife when I found out I was pregnant. He thinks Patrick is his son, his precious heir. Heir to what? Sand and lizards and dead sagebrush? I hate this place! The wind, the dirt, the foul smell of cattle! I want to do more with my life than waste away here on this miserable ranch. I want more for Patrick. You must know the feeling, Linc. You've been traveling, seen places better than this. Callie told me about the letters you wrote to her from all those different cities. Take me to those wonderful places, darling. And Patrick, too. We'll raise him together. He's a wonderful little boy, bright, quick to learn. Just like you, Linc."

"My son . . ." Linc sounded pensive, less resistant than before.

"Abby! Where are you?" Drummond Masterson's voice boomed from the house. "We're ready to have dessert."

"We mustn't be caught together," Abby murmured quickly. "Return to the house by the back way. I'll go in here. Think about all I said, darling. I love you with all my heart. Remember how it was with us before, the need, the wild passion that was between us. I'll send a message by Anita to meet you at the old Franklin ranch in a few days for your answer."

Silence ensued. Victoria still gripped the veranda railing, unaware that her knuckles had whitened with the force of her hold. Lies, deception, adultery. Abigail Masterson seemed to feel no reluctance at all about committing any of those indecent acts. Apparently Linc didn't either.

So the two of them did have a past together. She'd read the smoldering looks between them at dinner correctly. Well, they deserved each other! She only wanted to get away from this awful place!

Turning, Victoria ran along the veranda until she found an outside stairway leading to the ground floor. Dashing down the steps, she started toward the corral. Suddenly a figure stepped out of the shadows.

"Hold it!" he ordered sharply. The click of a gun hammer stopped her short.

"Please don't shoot!" In fear, she spun around, raising her hands.

"Damnation, woman! Don't come up fast on a man like that unless you're tired of breathing!" Linc uncocked the gun and slid it back into his holster. Light from a lamp coming through a side window crossed his face, showing his angry expression.

Victoria sucked in breath, her hand to her throat. "I didn't expect to be shot just because I came outside!"

"You have a real penchant for walking into unexpected situations, English." He stepped closer to her, lowering his voice. "I thought we had a little talk about that last night."

She backed up, frowning. "Stay away from me, Linc Masterson! You are a snake of the lowest breed! You have no honor, no sense of decency!"

He grabbed her by both arms. "What in the hell are

you talking about? I haven't done anything to you except save your pretty little hide—more than once! If I took a few kisses for my trouble, I reckon you got off mighty cheap on paying me back for your life."

"I'm not referring to myself, though the liberties you took with me last night were disgusting enough!" She glared at him and tried to twist out of his grasp.

He yanked her closer. "Disgusting, were they?"

For a long moment, they just stood there glaring at each other. Linc felt his anger begin to boil. Damn, but she looked more beautiful than a female ought to in that gown! All feminine flounces and silk, with her pale yellow hair done up high and coiled in locks on one side. The glow from the window lit the delicate contours of her face, highlighting her fragile loveliness, yet her large green eyes sparkled with a fury reflecting a defiant spirit. Too well he remembered the taste and feel of her from last night—and the same of Abby just now. He had to kiss Victoria again, just to see .

He pulled her against his chest and brought his mouth down hard on hers. Wrapping his arm around her narrow waist, he kissed her long and deeply, drank in everything about her that his senses could gather. The softness of her lips, the sweet taste of her mouth. The tension in her body as she tried to pull away from him.

At last he let her go. She stumbled back a step, then slapped him hard across the face.

"Vicious beast!" she spat, breathing hard. "You have a licentious rendezvous with your brother's wife, then turn your filthy lust to me! You're an animal, not a man! I hate you!"

With hot tears stinging her eyes, she whirled around, grabbed up her full skirt, and started to run. She had no idea where she was going, she just had to get away from *him!*

She dashed toward the barn. Just as she started to pass the big double doors in front, they burst open, and a man on horseback charged out of the dark interior right at her. The animal's huge chest hit her a glancing blow, knocking her to the ground.

"Victoria!" Linc ran up, drawing his gun. Dropping to one knee next to her, he raised his arm and fired the Colt. The fleeing man's horse reared and pranced sideways as its rider tumbled off backward, hitting the dirt with a loud thud. He didn't move. The animal neighed loudly and galloped away into the darkness.

Suddenly a loud explosion shattered the air from inside the barn. The shock wave erupting through the open doors blasted into Linc, knocking him over on top of Victoria. Dirt, hay, and splintered timbers rained down on them. Linc covered her as much as possible with his body. After the debris settled, he scrambled to his knees.

"Are you hurt?" He looked her over, brushing dirt from her shoulders.

"No, I think I'm all right."

"Then get to the house where it's safe!" He stood up, pulling her with him. "We've got big trouble."

His eyes were on the barn where billowing black smoke and bright flames shot through the side wall. The frantic cries of horses and cattle trapped in the burning building filled the air. Linc headed for the barn at a run, pausing only long enough to stoop down to the still body of the man he'd shot. Then he was quickly back on his feet, dashing through the open doors.

"Wait! Don't go in there!" Victoria called after him, but he paid no heed.

Drummond Masterson ran up beside her. "What the hell happened?" Everyone from the house followed him, and men swarmed out of the bunkhouse nearby.

"I don't know," Victoria answered in confusion. She

pointed to the body on the ground. "That man rode out of the barn, then there was an explosion. Linc went in there! You must help him!"

"Damn!" Drummond swore. "My prize stock's in that new barn! Charley! Get the buckets going! Drake! Break out shovels and blankets to wet down!" He turned to his guests. "Anybody wanting to lend a hand would be mighty welcome. We have to save the stock!" He pulled his neckerchief up over his nose to protect his face, and ran for the barn.

Chaos marked the scene. Frightened animals plunged from the building. Men shoveled dirt on burning timbers and passed wooden buckets filled with water hand-to-hand down a line from a trough, but their efforts to douse the quickly spreading fire made little impact.

Clint and Zeke Dandridge joined the bucket line, as did lawyer Taft Denton, but Sir Giles and Alden Cummings remained a safe distance away with Abby and the other women.

Victoria longed to help. She had to know if Linc was all right. Not once had she seen him since he'd dashed into the burning barn. She searched the faces of the men outside and each one who went in and out guiding animals to safety, but never saw him.

"He can take care of himself," she murmured under her breath, wringing her hands. She didn't care what happened to him anyway, she told herself. But not even such a scoundrel deserved to be burned to death in a fire!

"What did you say, Victoria?" Deborah asked next to her. "Isn't this terrible? Those poor creatures trapped inside."

"Yes," Victoria agreed, her eyes fixed on the barn door. "Not just animals may be unable to escape. I'm going to help!"

"What? No, sister, you can't!"

Victoria grabbed hold of her skirt and made a dash for the barn, ignoring Deborah's protest. She wouldn't let herself even look at Sir Giles and Alden as she ran past them.

"Victoria!" Sir Giles shouted, but she kept going.

Smoke filled the farthest end of the barn, but the flames now shooting through the roof above the loft lighted the interior so Victoria could see into the pandemonium. Men struggled to control rearing and kicking horses and force wild-eyed steers toward the doors. No one paid any attention to her when she made her way around stalls and harness equipment. The smoke stung her eyes and lungs. Holding her hand over her mouth, she squinted to try to see each man, but didn't recognize any of them as Linc.

A calf bawled loudly from the stall next to her. Hurrying to the animal, she spoke soothingly to it, patting its neck as she reached for its lead rope tied to a ring in the wall. Pulling with all her might, she coaxed the calf toward the doors. Once outside, she gave it a hard slap on the hind quarters to send it running to safety, then turned and ran back into the barn.

Suddenly a huge bull charged toward her dragging a burning timber by its lead rope. She dived into a stall to avoid its stampeding path and hit the solid wood side hard with her shoulder. Wincing with pain, she scrambled to her feet and stumbled on.

Burning timbers crackled overhead as the fire spread along the hay-filled loft. She heard the wild neigh of a terrified horse, and shot a look ahead to see Linc struggling to control a rearing stallion. Man and horse were nearly surrounded by flames and smoke.

"Pull back! Everybody pull back!" Drummond Masterson shouted from behind her. At that instant, a huge burning loft beam gave way over Linc.

"Look out!" Victoria screamed.

Linc's arm flew up and he twisted away to protect himself from the crashing timber, but the smoke, sparks, and fire that engulfed him kept Victoria from seeing what happened to him. The stallion plunged past her toward the clear doorway, snorting and tossing its mammoth head. She jumped aside just in time to avoid being trampled by its pounding hooves.

Clutching her skirt close around her, she side-stepped around two stalls and the end of the burning timber.

"Linc!" she cried, searching frantically for him. The acrid smoke bit into her lungs, choking her. Brushing at tears streaming from her stinging eyes, she spied a slight movement on the floor in one of the few spots where the fire hadn't yet spread. Linc!

The edge of his black coat caught fire just as she reached him. Using the full skirt of her green gown, she fell across his back to smother the flames.

"Get up, Linc!" she shouted, coughing and gasping in what precious air still remained. She rolled him over and grabbed his arm to try to raise him.

Another burning beam cracked and split overhead, showering sparks and hay down on them, but for the moment it held its deadly load.

"Hurry! Get up, damn you, or we'll be killed!" she swore, using her fear and anger for the strength to yank him to his feet.

Linc seemed to come to his senses enough to throw an arm around her shoulders and stagger along with her around the burning beam and stalls to the other end of the barn. When they stumbled out into the clear air, they both fell to the ground, gasping for breath. In the next instant, a bucket of water doused Victoria.

"Sorry, ma'am. Your dress was smokin'," a ranch hand explained, kneeling down next to her.

She nodded, grateful just to lie in the dirt while the

cool splash of water dripped down her face. Linc coughed and rolled over onto his side to look at her.

"And just what in the hell do you think you were doing in there? God, you look like a drowned polecat." He coughed again.

She turned her head to meet his gaze, frowning.

"What do you think I was doing in there? I was saving your life!" She started to get up, but groaned and fell back when a wave of dizziness hit her.

He put his hand on her arm. "Take some more deep breaths and don't try to move yet. You'll live." He sat up and wiped his coat sleeve across his grimy forehead, then glanced over his shoulder at her, adding, "We both will."

It took over three hours to fight the fire and keep it from spreading to the ranch house and other buildings. Finally, only a few blackened timbers smoldered where the new barn had stood.

"Who was he?" Linc asked tiredly, leaning over Drummond, who had stooped down to peer at the dead saboteur.

"Don't recognize him. Anybody else know him?" Drumm glanced at the circle of people around him, but no one spoke up. "How about you, Dandridge?" He frowned toward Clint.

"That almost sounds like an accusation," the big rancher answered coolly.

"Well, somebody hired this cowpoke to set the dynamite." Drumm clenched his fists, looking at the charred remains of his barn. "Losing my building and so much stock will set me back plenty. This fire can only help your cause, Dandridge. The bank's bound to foreclose now."

"You going to take that kind of talk off Masterson, Pa?" Zeke Dandridge stepped up beside his father. "Let me answer him."

He started to move forward, dropping his hand to his gun. Clint stopped him with an arm on his chest.

"Hold up, Zeke. Drummond's just upset. I can understand that. He's got no proof of anything. I'd say this little party is over. Time for us to leave. Luckily, our horses were in the corral. My offer to buy you out still stands, Drumm. Of course, the loss of the barn and so many animals will have to be taken into consideration regarding the price. I'll send a new agreement to Denton tomorrow for you to look at."

Drummond's face was livid with rage as he took a threatening step toward Dandridge. "Why you filthy—"

Abby darted in front of her husband and raised her hand. "No, Drumm, stop. We're all upset by what's happened. My God, a man's been killed. The barn's gone, but some of the animals escaped the fire. Just be glad nothing else happened. I think Clinton is being very generous to still let an offer of any kind stand. We'll discuss all this in the morning, after we've had a chance to rest and think more clearly."

"Sound reasoning," Clint agreed. "Listen to your wife, Drumm. Zeke, see to the carriage and horses."

Victoria didn't look at Linc as she walked beside Alden toward the corral. She felt drained of all energy. She'd had time to think about her impulsive actions when the fire first started, and she greatly questioned her own judgment. Now she realized how easily she might have been killed—and Linc, too.

Unwittingly, she glanced to his face and felt the now-familiar twinge hit her insides. He looked exhausted and dirty from dealing with the blaze. His broad shoulders drooped slightly as he pulled on his singed coat, but even with his face streaked by smoke and grime, he looked handsome, even heroic to her. Sir Giles hadn't allowed her to help any more after she and Linc had first escaped the barn, but Linc had worked side-by-side with his brother and the others for the hours it had taken to conquer the fire.

She felt confused over her feelings for him. She'd helped him escape certain death. If it hadn't been for her, he might have been crushed under that falling beam and burned to death. She was glad she'd been able to help someone. Anyone, she told herself. It didn't matter that it was Linc Masterson she'd been able to save. Or did it?

She groaned inwardly, deciding to focus her attention on her ruined gown instead of a man who put her whole being into a terrible state of turmoil. What a sight she must be. She was dirty, and her hair hung in tangled scraggles around her face. Her shoulder hurt where she'd bashed it against the horse stall.

Feeling dazed and weary, she let Alden pull her along toward the corral. Neither he nor Sir Giles had said anything to her yet about what she'd done, but she knew they would, and she dreaded the confrontation. Why didn't she think before she acted? But then, if she had, Linc might be dead . . .

As they approached the enclosure, Alden yanked her aside into the shadows of the tool shed.

"Your stupidity tonight surprised even me, Victoria!" he seethed viciously at her ear. "I don't know what possessed you to want to help these people—and that bloody killer specifically—but I swear to you, you're going to regret your actions. Do you know what would have happened if you'd died in that fire? Your stupid little sister would get your share of your fortune. Then I'd have to marry *her.* And I can't abide sniveling children!" He pulled her closer, gripping her arms hard. "I prefer fiery women with spirit, like you. Oh, I've seen how you try to hide your hatred, but you haven't fooled me. After we're married,

I'll enjoy taming that rebelliousness of yours, by teaching you the proper submissiveness a woman should have toward a man. We'll be married soon, my dear, very soon. With Uncle Giles' blessing, I'm going into town tomorrow to make arrangements with the good Reverend Henderson. The poor man does have a problem with drink, but he's legally licensed in this territory to perform marriages and won't ask any questions if the payment's right. Clint Dandridge has already agreed to be my best man and witness our joining to the world—for a price, too, of course. So you see, I have quite an investment in you, Victoria—one that I intend to safeguard."

He pushed her ahead of him toward the carriage where the others were already seated. Victoria felt too tired to argue with him. Besides, she knew doing so would gain her nothing. Alden thought of her as an insignificant thing, merely a means to an end he coveted—her family fortune, and she had no hope of help from anyone. Her uncle supported her union with his nephew, likely for a good share of her money once Alden could legally get control of it as her husband. She was in a strange land, with no friends, no money. Sheriff Boswell seemed like an honest man, but he, too, regarded her as an undesirable foreigner, just as the rest of these Americans did. And she must think of Deborah, as well. If she could manage to run away somewhere to escape Alden and her evil uncle, she must take her sister with her. But Deborah's health couldn't endure a hazardous journey.

She slumped back in the velvet cushion of the carriage seat next to Deborah, feeling doomed. She looked at the men in the vehicle with her, but their faces held angry scowls. Her fate and Deborah's were of no consequence to any of them except for what profit they could gain.

Against her will, her eyes sought out Linc, riding on horseback just ahead of the carriage. But if she entertained the slightest hope that he might help her, that hope was quickly doused when, as if in answer to her thought, he spurred his mount to a gallop and rode ahead, disappearing into the darkness.

Chapter Nine

Linc stood outside the window of Clinton Dandridge's study. He was taking a big chance sneaking around in broad daylight, but he had no choice. Dandridge had gone to town to talk to Taft Denton about the new offer to Drummond. The servant women were occupied doing laundry at the back of the house. He'd have no better chance than now to try to get a look at Dandridge's files and ledgers.

He scanned the yard and out-buildings around him. Some of the men were breaking mustangs in the corral, but they were too far off to give much notice to what might be going on near the ranch house.

Taking off his hat, Linc reached under the leather band around the crown and withdrew a diamond-studded stick-pin. The expensive little tie ornament had come in handy more than once when he'd needed money. Now he was going to put it to another use.

Sliding the pointed end up between the top and bottom window frames, he snapped the lock open. After slowly lifting the lower window, he bent in half to get his body and long legs through the opening, then closed the window after him.

The spacious room was hot and stuffy because it was always kept closed and locked when Dandridge wasn't about. Linc glanced around at the filled bookshelves lining three walls of the wood-paneled study. Expensive brocade chairs faced a black marble hearth on the fourth wall. There were any number of places where a safe for keeping cash and records might be hidden, but before he started a random search for it, he decided to try looking through the massive oak desk that took up one corner of the room.

The drawers to the left and right of the swivel armchair were locked. The center drawer wasn't, but it held only blank paper and writing instruments. Time to put the stickpin to use again.

In a moment, the lock on the right side drawers yielded to his proding. The bottom drawer creaked loudly when he pulled it open. Glancing to the door leading to the hallway, he listened hard, wondering if anyone had heard the noise. After a minute of waiting, he turned his attention back to the drawer and found two large leather-bound ledgers inside a cloth portfolio.

Looking through the most recently written entries, he saw only the typical figures connected with running a big cattle spread like Dandridge's Lazy River Fork ranch—stock purchase and sales receipts, feed and equipment costs, wage expenses for the ranch hands. Nothing appeared out of the ordinary, except the entries showing how much Sir Giles Spencer had invested in the ranch. The Englishman must be a very wealthy man to put up so much money—or he'd borrowed up to the neck.

Thinking about that money made Victoria flash into his mind. He wondered again why she'd risked her life to get him out of the barn during the fire last night. He didn't know quite what to expect from her. She puzzled him, but he never put much time or thought into a woman. Not since . . .

Abby. God, but she'd looked beautiful in that red dress. Just the way he remembered her. And she'd been so warm and soft and willing in his arms outside in the dark when she'd told him about Patrick. They had a son together.

That's what Abby had told him. Could he believe her? She'd lied so well before. Used him. He'd sworn he'd never fall into the trap of her beauty and wiles again. But he had a right to know his son, show him the love a father can have for a boy. The kind of love he'd never had from his own father . . . Somehow he had to find out for sure who had fathered Patrick.

He smiled. He knew how to get Abby to reveal that truth—when she was vulnerable, helpless. In bed, she'd always shown her weak side, when he made love to her, drove her to near madness with the pleasure he could give her.

He'd told Drumm he'd keep his distance from her, but that was before he knew about Patrick. The boy changed everything.

Frowning, he wondered why the thought of bedding Abby again for any reason didn't have the same appeal it once had. She was as alluring as ever, and he didn't have any trouble remembering how she could scratch and moan and pretend to resist him—to a point, then completely surrender. Had any man ever experienced that with Victoria Spencer?

Linc's frown deepened, bringing his black brows nearly together. What had made him think of Victoria with a man? He didn't like that idea for some reason. How would she make love? She seemed so meek. Always doing what she was told by that uncle of hers and that tinhorn Cummings. Yet meekness hadn't pulled him out of the barn fire.

He could find out how she was with a man and accomplish his goal of gaining some of her money at the same time. A little more time alone with her and he'd have her in bed easy enough, just like every other woman he'd ever set his sights on for taking care of his need for a female. Then he'd claim to want to save her honor by marrying her, because Cummings wouldn't be interested in having her after that.

But getting her alone presented a problem. He needed time, and that was one thing he was running short of, especially after the fire last night. Drumm was sure to go under now, and the ranch would be up for grabs.

He tried the left side of the desk. Neatly labeled file folders filled the big bottom drawer. He sat down in the upholstered armchair and fingered through the tabs, recognizing some of the names of ranchers he'd known five years ago—men who owned land around the Diamond M and along the fertile river valley. After quickly skimming through letters and legal documents in some of the files, he pensively stared off into space. A pattern formed in his mind. Dandridge *was* out to own the whole damned valley, any way he could get his hands on it, just as Drumm had said.

He reached back into the drawer for the file marked "Diamond M." Spreading it out in front of him on top of the desk, he leafed through the papers inside. Several letters to and from the bank in Laramie revealed that Clint Dandridge had a bid in to take over the loan note on the Diamond M if Drummond defaulted on the payments.

Another letter made Linc's dark brows knit into a deep frown. He read it twice, then folded it carefully and stuffed it inside his tan shirt before replacing the folder with the others in the drawer.

Suddenly a key rattled in the hall door lock. With lightning swiftness, Linc closed the drawer and shot a look around the room. No time to get out the window. Nothing to hide behind—except the desk!

Pulling off his hat, he drew his Colt and ducked down into the cramped leg space under the desk top, quickly yanking in his feet and then the chair as close as possible. Had he left anything on top of the desk? The stickpin? No, he'd stuck it through the cuff of his sleeve for safekeeping.

"Come on in here, Dorn. I'll get you the cash you'll need," Zeke Dandridge's voice sounded from the doorway. "See, I told you nobody was in here, José."

"But, señor," a third man protested, "I know I heard a noise come from here just a few minutes ago. I do not have a key, so I could not check."

"You're hearing things, old man," Zeke said. "Get back to work. And leave the door open. It's hot as hell in here. Come on Dorn."

Bootsteps crossed the room toward the fireplace. There was a rattle of metal keys.

"Damn I don't have the safe key," Zeke cursed. "Check the middle desk drawer there, Dorn."

Steps approached across the inlaid wood floor. Linc clenched his teeth and gripped the Colt tighter.

"No, wait. It's here with these others after all," Zeke said.

Dorn retreated, and Linc slowly expelled the breath he'd been holding. He listened to the sound of a key being fit into a lock and then a lever being pulled.

"This money should pay for some more good men," Zeke continued. "Pa wants them big and mean and handy with six-shooters. He thinks the showdown with Drumm Masterson isn't far off. Masterson's back is against the wall, especially since he lost his barn and a lot of stock last night. It was real nice of good old Linc to plug Gibson for us. Now he can't ever say we hired him to set the dynamite, and Pa won't have to pay him!" Zeke laughed. "If we get real lucky, maybe Linc'll shoot that stubborn bastard brother of his for us. No, I got that wrong. Linc's the dirty Injun bastard! Maybe Drumm'll shoot *him!*"

Both men laughed. Linc clenched his jaw again and fingered the trigger of his gun. If so much wasn't at stake, he'd show Zeke Dandridge just what an Indian bastard could do to him! But not yet. He'd have to wait. Unless Zeke came over here to the desk . . .

"Try to get me at least four men by tomorrow," Zeke continued. "I want to take some boys over to Joe Two Eagles' place. That old man's being mighty stubborn, too. He can't run that spread by himself any more, but he's holding out on selling. He needs a little more persuasion. Injun's got no right owning land anyway. Pa'll be real pleased if I can get the old man to sign off the deed Holden Masterson gave him to those grazing acres."

"Should be easy," Dorn agreed. "Old folks like Joe have accidents all the time, I hear. Get dragged by a horse. Fall down a well. Real tragic."

"You got the idea. Now, nobody in town's to know we're hiring on more men. Keep it quiet. There should be enough money there to buy silence, too."

"Right, Zeke. I understand."

"Good. Get going."

Linc heard Dorn's footsteps leave the room. After the safe door banged shut, Zeke's boots clicked on the wood floor, too.

Linc waited a minute longer after the hall door closed and the key turned in the lock again. Then he cautiously pushed the chair away and stretched his crampled legs to crawl out from under the desk.

So Clint Dandridge was behind the fire at the ranch last night after all. He wasn't surprised, especially after what he'd seen in the files just now.

The mention of Joseph Two Eagles made Linc's frown deepen again. He'd have to waylay Zeke's plans. He owed the old chief that much.

Wiping his hand over his brow to get rid of the sweat dripping into his eyes, he quickly crossed the room to the window and glanced outside. Still nobody around.

Raising the window again, he bent to go through it, then closed it behind him and headed for the bunkhouse.

Chapter Ten

Victoria pretended to be asleep. She sat with her eyes closed in the bedroom window seat, tilting her head over to the side and letting the book she'd been reading rest in her lap. She kept her body perfectly still, trying to forget how hot the room was now at noonday. But the perspiration trickling down between her breasts under her yellow dress made the heat difficult to ignore.

After a while, she heard the bedroom door open and then close softly. No key turned in the lock. She opened her eyes just enough to look around the room through her lashes. As she'd hoped, Hannah Perkins was nowhere in sight.

Jumping up from the window seat, she hurried over to the canopy bed.

"Deborah, wake up!" she whispered, shaking her sister's arm.

Drowsily, Deborah opened her eyes. "What is it, Victoria? Is something wrong?" She sat up.

"I haven't much time to explain," Victoria said, going to the wooden wardrobe cabinet. She threw open the double doors and continued talking while she searched around inside. "I've made a decision, Deborah. You must listen carefully and not argue with me. This is very important. I'm going to try to get away from this ranch." She pulled out a white blouse and maroon riding skirt, and quickly put them on.

"What? No, you mustn't, Victoria!" Deborah cried.

"Sh, please keep your voice down! I have no choice. In a matter of days, or sooner, I'll be forced to marry Alden. If that happens, we'll never escape Sir Giles' control. I must act now. No one will expect me to try to get away during the day."

"But what will you do? Where will you go?" Deborah crossed the room to stand by her sister, a worried look on her face as she watched Victoria rummage in the bottom of the cabinet.

"I have a plan," Victoria continued, her voice muffled by the clothing around her. "It's insane and has little chance of success, but it's all I can think of in this desperate situation. I'm going to need help escaping from this God-forsaken territory."

"I'll do anything you say, Victoria." Deborah put her hand out to touch her arm.

Victoria stood up and smiled at her brave little sister. "I know you would, but this time you must do nothing. You must pretend you have no idea of what I'm doing."

"But you aren't going to leave me here? You're taking me with you?"

Victoria paused to take Deborah's hands in hers and look into her eyes.

"No, dear, I can't. There's only a small chance that I can escape. If there were two of us . . ."

Deborah bowed her head. "I know. I would only be a burden, as always."

"No, don't say that." Victoria raised her chin with her hand. "I love you, Deborah, and I worry about you so much. I couldn't concentrate on getting away if you were along. I promise you with all my heart that I'll return for you as soon as I can."

"But who will help you?"

A single name came to Victoria's mind in answer, and it wasn't a very reassuring one. But she spoke it anyway.

"Linc Masterson, I think."

"Victoria, no!" Deborah looked horrified. "He's a gunfighter. A killer!"

"He's the only person I know here who isn't afraid of Sir Giles, Alden, or even Clinton Dandridge. He has courage. I know that from the way he faced the train robbers and those horrible men in the alley in town. And he's mercenary enough to take a job from Mr. Dandridge, who's working against his own brother. If the price is right, he might help me. I have to try."

Victoria almost felt defeated before she started as she kept searching in the cabinet. To put her fate in the hands of a man like Linc Masterson seemed absurd. What price would he exact from her for his cooperation? She planned to give him only money, but he might have other ideas—especially after . . .

She wouldn't let herself think about the way he'd kissed her last night and the night before. Or how those kisses had made her feel. If he went along with her plan, he must also agree to keep their relationship strictly business.

"But you have no money," Deborah lamented, wringing her hands. "How will you get Mr. Masterson to help you? Oh, Victoria, please don't do this. There must be another way. He's such a violent man."

"But everyone has a price, Deborah. Ah, here it is!"

Victoria had turned back to the wardrobe cabinet. Now she dragged out a small tapestry valise. Yanking it open by the handles, she began pulling out the clothing inside.

"But that bag belongs to Hannah," Deborah said. "What are you doing?"

"Getting back what is rightfully ours to insure our future. Whenever our uncle gave Hannah money to spend on our wardrobe or other necessities, she secretly kept some of it for herself and hid it in this valise. I've seen her hiding it away on more than one occasion. Yes, here it is!"

She held up a red leather wallet. The two halves of the folded-over flat case were held together by a worn black velvet ribbon. Quickly unfastening the ties, she ran her finger over the edges of the currency in both sides.

"Mostly British pounds, but there's some American money here, too. I'll have to count it later. I hope a bank will exchange the pounds." She slid the wallet into the deep side pocket of her maroon skirt.

"You're taking Hannah's money?" Deborah asked, astonished.

"*Our* money, dear sister, pilfered from our guardian and meant to be for our living needs. Consider it a loan. Tell Hannah that, if you must. If my plan works, I'll soon have my inheritance and will be able to pay her back—if I choose. But I don't think she deserves it, not after the cruel way she's treated us."

"Oh, Hannah will be so angry. How will you gain your inheritance? Your birthday is still months away, and you don't seem to want to marry Alden."

Victoria looked directly at her sister. "I would rather die first. The man is a lecherous snake! I can't tell you any more of my plan, Deborah. You must trust me. I only told you this much because I knew you'd worry yourself ill if I just disappeared."

"And you think I won't worry now?" Deborah clutched Victoria's arm. "Take me with you, please!"

Victoria's tone softened. "I can't. Please understand. Alone, I have a chance. You must be brave, Deborah. No doubt Sir Giles' punishment will be severe if he finds out you know anything about my plan."

Deborah raised her chin. "I can bear whatever he administers if it will help you. But are you certain there is no alternative?"

"I'm certain. Now Hannah will be returning soon. Get back to the bed and pretend to be taking your nap."

"I'm so frightened for you, sister."

Victoria hugged her. "I know. Just wish me luck and keep me in your prayers." She hurried to the door and opened it a crack to look out into the hall. Then she glanced back at her sister. "Good-bye, Deborah. I love you."

"I beg your pardon." Victoria tapped the cowboy on the shoulder. He looked up from repairing a harness in the shade at the side of the barn.

"Ma'am?"

"I-I was wondering if you might know where Linc Masterson is. Mr. Dandridge gave orders for him to escort me riding." She hoped the ranch hand only knew her to be a guest of Clinton Dandridge's, with no way of knowing she was supposed to be confined to the house.

"Linc? The boss sent him up to the line shack with some supplies for the boys rounding up stray steers."

"Is this shack very far away."

"Naw, 'bout two miles straight out thataway at the bottom of them foothills." He gestured toward the gently sloping plain running beyond the back of the barn. "He should be back soon enough. I'll tell him yer lookin' fer him."

"Yes, thank you," she replied, trying to hide her disappointment. She walked around the front of the barn to get out of the cowhand's view. Every moment she was away from the house, she risked having her absence discovered by Hannah or Alden or her uncle. She couldn't wait until Linc returned to the ranch.

Suddenly a bewhiskered man banged on a big metal triangle hanging from a post by the main bunkhouse.

"Come and git yer grub!" he hollered. The loud clanging sound brought men hurrying from every direction.

The cowboy she'd spoken to tipped his battered hat as he strode past her to join the others heading for the kitchen behind the three buildings used for the ranch workers' quarters.

Victoria knew she must make her move now or lose her chance. She swiftly entered the barn. No one was about, and to her chagrin, she saw that not one horse occupied any of the stalls lining both sides of the building. They must all be in the big corral by the larger barn closer to the bunkhouses. She couldn't risk trying to take one with all the ranch hands eating their noon meal so close by.

She sighed deeply and bit her lip, feeling panic well up in her. She had no choice. If she wanted to get to Linc Masterson, there was only one way to do it—on foot. Two miles toward the foothills, the cowboy had said. Two miles over the desert plain.

Pushing open the back door of the barn, she felt a blast of hot air hit her. She looked out in the direction the ranch hand had indicated. She must try to reach Linc out there. If she left by this door, no one would see her from the ranch house or the cowboys' kitchen.

She raised her hand to her forehead to shade her eyes as she glanced up toward the sun scorching the sky directly overhead. Taking a deep breath, she stepped out of the barn. This wasn't the time of day to be venturing outside, but she had to do it. She had no choice.

Chapter Eleven

The heat waves radiating from the scorched dry land shimmered in the air. Victoria was glad she'd dressed in riding clothes to back up the story she'd told the cowhand. Her tan leather boots offered some protection against the hot sand and rocky ground underfoot.

Scanning the sharp-cut mountain peaks ahead, Victoria was amazed by the stark beauty of the wilderness plain around her. Time seemed lost here, with little change to show the passing of centuries. How very different was this place compared to her overpopulated London, where rain and fog were a given climatic fact nearly every day. This Wyoming Territory seemed so wide open and untouched by the hand of man. The high, majestic mountains reached jagged peaks to a clear azure sky that seemed visible for miles and miles in any direction. She had never seen so much blue at one time. Not a wisp of a cloud broke the solid expanse of pale color. In London, it was difficult to see very much of the sky at all because of the press of buildings everywhere. Even in the less crowded countryside, the view overhead was often obstructed by forest.

Four birds flew above her in a wide circling pattern. She put a hand to her forehead to shade her eyes to see them better, but the sun shone too brightly for her to be able to make out the details of color and feather structure to try to identify the species. Predators, no doubt, searching for food, using eyesight so keen they could easily spy a mouse or small ground squirrel from such high surveillances. She had little knowledge of American birds, hardly more than to know the regal bald eagle was the national symbol of the country. But she really wasn't concerned with what types of birds they were. She didn't plan to stay in this awful territory long enough to learn such information.

In looking skyward, she glimpsed the blazing ball of the midday sun, felt its withering heat, and realized she dare not linger to take in the view. Adjusting the wide brim of her straw hat farther down over her eyes, she continued walking at a brisk pace toward what she hoped was the line shack. Something that looked like a structure was barely visible among a small oasis of trees in the distance.

The blinding sunlight beat down, mercilessly scalding all it touched. Perspiration poured down Victoria's face and along her torso under her clothes. Breathing the hot air made her tongue and throat feel as if no moisture had ever touched them. The line shack still seemed a long distance away.

Her steps faltered. She grew worried that her impulsive decision to set out on foot had been very unwise. Glancing over her shoulder, she fearfully expected to see horsemen in pursuit from the direction of the ranch house. When she saw none, she breathed a small sigh of relief, telling herself she must press on. She'd gone too far to turn back now.

After another quarter hour of walking, she stopped to rest on a flat-topped rock. She'd never felt so hot and thirsty in all her life. Suddenly, a foot-long, horned brown lizard shot out between her feet, startling her. It disappeared over the edge of a shallow gulch before she could even pull up her legs, but its very presence prompted her to ignore her body's signals of distress and trod on.

The gently rolling ground began to flatten out. A small

pool of water appeared directly ahead. Giving a cry of happiness, Victoria started to run toward it. But her legs tangled in her long skirt, tripping her, and she pitched face-first to the ground. Groaning and rolling over, she sat up, spitting gritty sand out of her mouth and trying to wipe it from her sweaty face and white blouse. The sharp particles bit into the tender skin of her cheek.

Tears of frustration stung at her eyes, but she stubbornly blinked them back and made herself get up again. Water lay just ahead. She could still see the shimmering pool.

But the water remained the same elusive distance away no matter how many more steps she plodded. With growing weariness and discouragement, she realized her eyes were playing tricks on her. The heat waves created a mirage. She wasn't used to such severe heat, to breathing air so hot it burned her lungs. Could she even reach the trees near the shack? How she wished she could have found a horse at the ranch to ride. She felt suddenly frightened that this trek into the desert was becoming dangerous, even life-threatening.

Commanding all her stubborn will, she wiped the sweat out of her eyes with her hand and squinted to see the trees where she hoped to find Linc. She was close enough now to see the small line cabin. It would offer relief from the suffocating heat. She'd reach it if it were the last thing she ever did!

Taking one more glance over her shoulder, she determinedly set one foot in front of the other and stumbled forward.

At last the heat mirages gave way to the closer sight of the ramshackle log shack. Tall weeds and spiny sagebrush grew everywhere, showing a lack of maintenance to the whole place. A half-dozen head of longhorn cattle meandered about, grazing on the hardy wheat grass. Five willow trees bent their branches low over a real pool of water. Someone was in the pool. Only his head showed above the water—Linc Masterson. Victoria felt relief at seeing him. She didn't know if he was swimming or bathing, but she didn't care. At this point, she gave no thought to propriety. She was too hot and miserable to care. She could only think of getting into the water!

She watched the longhorns warily as she backed toward the pool. Then she plunged in, clothes and all, splashing the cool water all over herself. It felt so wonderful, shockingly frigid against her hot skin. Gathering some in her cupped hands, she raised it to her parched lips to drink.

"I wasn't expecting company."

"Oh, Mr. Masterson." Victoria turned toward where he stood waist-deep in the water. She wasn't sure how to tell him her reason for being here.

The water only reached to his narrow waist. Blazing sunlight glistened on his wet naked upper torso, accenting his powerful physique.

Victoria swallowed hard, feeling her heart start to pound faster. He didn't appear to have any clothes on at all! Darting her eyes around, she spied boots, a pair of brown pants, and a dark blue shirt lying on the ground near the edge of the pond. Linc's gunbelt and hat lay next to the clothes.

"I'm only going to ask this question once," Linc stated in a tone that sounded anything but friendly. "What in the hell are you doing out here?"

She shot a look back at him and was horrified to see he'd started wading toward her. She scurried out of the pool.

"Stop! Don't come out!" she cried, holding up her hand. Then a wave of dizziness hit her, making her sway on her feet. She fell backward, landing squarely on her backside on the patchy grass. She winced, but managed to scramble to her feet again. "I said don't come out! You're . . . naked!"

"Well, it's damned hard to take a bath with clothes on, woman!"

He sounded angry, but he halted, hip-deep in the water. She could see just the beginning of the untanned portion of his lower body.

"Please don't come any farther, Mr. Masterson! I can explain everything from here. I need your help."

"You need more than *my* help." He put his hands on his hips. "You must be plum loco in the head to be out on the desert in the sun at this time of day. Where's your horse? Did you get thrown?"

"No," she answered, fidgeting with her fingers. "I—I didn't ride a horse. I walked from the ranch."

"What! From the ranch?" he repeated angrily.

Victoria was afraid he'd march out of the pool despite her protest. She started talking too fast, wishing he'd stop glaring at her.

"My uncle is forcing me to marry Alden Cummings so he can keep control of my inheritance from my father. Alden's in town right now making arrangements for the wedding. I have no intention of marrying him. I must escape from him and my uncle and Dandridge's ranch and this miserable Wyoming Territory!" She sucked in a breath to hurry on. "I know you despise me, and that doesn't matter because I despise you, too. But I didn't know anyone else I could turn to for help. Everyone seems to be afraid of you and your gun. I came here to offer you a business proposition."

"Shut up and don't move, Victoria!"

Linc's sharp tone startled her. She frowned and opened her mouth to protest his harsh command, but the fierce look on his face made her think better of speaking.

Suddenly, she heard an odd sound behind her, something like a snort. She swung around and gasped.

"Don't move!" Linc shouted again.

Victoria obeyed his command this time without even

realizing it. Before her was the meanest-looking beast on four legs she'd ever seen in her life. The huge black steer stood only fifteen feet away. It tossed its big head and snorted, shaking its long, curved horns and pawing the sandy ground with a sharp hoof.

"When I make a ruckus, Victoria, run for that tree to your left," Linc said, keeping his voice low and even.

"But—"

"Just—do—it."

He spoke slowly, but there was no mistaking his severe tone. Victoria nodded weakly, keeping her eyes fixed on the threatening bull. Her legs shook violently under her. Would they carry her anywhere?

In the next instant, she heard Linc give a blood-curdling howl amidst a loud splashing of water. Spinning on her heel, she clutched her heavy wet skirt and dashed as fast as she could toward the closest drooping willow, expecting the terrible horns to stab into her at any moment. Her straw hat flew off as she ran, but she paid no attention to it and hurried on. Grabbing a low branch, she yanked up her skirt and jumped into the crotch of the tree, then scrambled to a higher branch. Trying to balance, she held onto the rough branch with both hands and looked below her.

Her mouth dropped open when she saw Linc lunge naked out of the pool still yelling and flailing his arms. The hulking bull bellowed loudly, swinging in his direction. Linc ran to his clothes and snatched up his blue shirt, waving it wildly.

The bull charged. Victoria cried out in alarm. She'd never seen a creature of such size move so fast. It thundered right at Linc, who jumped aside only a split second before the huge animal bent its head toward him. Jamming its front hooves into the sandy ground, the bull swung around in a cloud of dust and pounded toward Linc again. Linc waved his shirt out to the side, and the longhorn went straight for it.

If only Linc could get to a tree as she'd done! Victoria shot a look to the other four willows near the pond, but none of them offered low forked branches for easy climbing.

"Try to make it over here!" she shouted, just as one of the animal's deadly horns caught the edge of Linc's shirt and yanked it from his fingers.

The bull shook off the shirt, then trampled it beneath its sharp hooves. Linc spun around and made a mad dash toward Victoria's tree, with the enraged longhorn swiftly in pursuit.

"Higher!" he yelled, waving his arm toward the sky. *"Get up higher!"*

Victoria glanced above her and frantically strained to reach for the only other limb that looked sturdy enough to hold her weight. She pulled herself up and over it, with her feet still dangling down, just as Linc jumped up into the tree and scrambled to the branch she'd vacated. The longhorn thundered over her lost hat and skidded to a stop only inches from the willow. Lowering its mighty head, it butted the trunk again and again.

Victoria held on for dear life when the whole tree shook violently from the force of the huge beast's blows. The sharp pointed tips of the bull's horns stabbed up toward Linc. He stood on his branch and grabbed hold of a smaller protruding limb overhead to keep his balance.

When the attack ceased for a moment, Victoria pulled herself over her branch and sat up, hugging the thick trunk next to her tightly. Linc's head was even with her lap.

"What are we going to do?" she cried, frightened. Without thinking, she glanced down to see what the longhorn was up to and caught a full frontal view of Linc—a sight of a man she had seen only in great paintings and sculptures exhibited in museums and art books. She gasped and slapped her hand over her eyes, almost falling out of the tree because she lost her balance. Linc grabbed her legs to keep her from tumbling backward.

"Hang on, English. Your modesty could get you trampled!"

The willow shook violently again as the bull renewed its assault. Victoria gave a cry of alarm and hugged the tree harder. Linc let go of her dangling legs to hang onto her branch.

"What a horrible beast!" she lamented. "Why does it keep doing that?"

"Because a longhorn bull is five percent meat and ninety-five percent downright cussedness! It doesn't need a reason to be flat-out mean and unreasonable."

"Well, why didn't you shoot it then when you had a clear reach for your gun?" she demanded angrily, still keeping her eyes turned away from Linc. "Your shirt didn't deter it much!"

Linc frowned up at her. "Shoot it? That'd be crazy. A steer of any kind is valuable in this territory. These animals survive in the blistering heat and the bitter winter cold we have around these parts because of their orneriness and grit! This bull will pass those traits on to offspring and create a mighty hardy stock."

"It seems to me there'll also be a great deal of *stupidity* in that so-called hardy stock!" She ventured a glance downward once more, carefully directing her gaze along the tree trunk.

As if it understood her insult, the bull snorted again and rammed the trunk even harder than before. Then it shook its great horned head and staggered sideways a little, as if dazed. After a moment, it circled the tree, snorting and pawing the ground.

"How long will it stay down there?" Victoria demanded. She didn't know which upset her more—the enraged longhorn or Linc Masterson naked on a tree branch right beneath her! He didn't seem at all disturbed by the fact that he was undressed in the presence of a lady!

"As long as it's of a mind to, unless we can distract it somehow." He folded his arms across his chest and leaned back against the trunk of the tree.

Victoria flicked a quick glance down toward him, glad to see that his crossed arms blocked the view of his lower torso. He looked positively relaxed!

"How can you be so calm? It's trying to *kill* us! Can't you break off a branch and hit it or something?" She darted a look around for some foliage within reach.

"It'd take a chunk of wood about as thick as the branch you're on to stun a bull that size. I'm not hankering to aggravate that varmint any more than it already is. You go right ahead and try anything you want to though."

"Aren't you going to do *anything?*" She worriedly looked toward the direction of the ranch. "My uncle will be searching for me. He's a violent man. He might be coming right now!"

"I reckon he and the bull would get along just fine. Give me your pantaloons."

"What?" She couldn't believe his words.

"I said, give me your pantaloons. Or your skirt or blouse."

"I will not! You've lost your senses!" She pulled her legs away from him and tucked them up under her as best she could without losing her balance again.

Linc frowned.

"Your virtue's safe, I assure you, Miss Spencer. If you want to get out of this tree and away from here, do as I say. I need something to throw down over this cantankerous critter's head for a distraction. As you've clearly seen, I don't have anything to use."

Victoria blushed to the tips of her ears. She'd seen all right—more than any woman should ever see of a man who wasn't her husband! A man who was too handsome and too virile and too . . . dangerous.

She didn't like this situation at all. Not one bit. But she couldn't see anything else to do but obey Linc.

"Would you please not look up here?" She glared at him.

Linc cocked a dark eyebrow at her, but said nothing as he averted his gaze toward the ground.

Victoria held onto the tree trunk and precariously stood up on her branch. Using one hand, she reached into the waistband of her maroon skirt and untied the drawstring of her white cotton pantaloons. Balancing carefully, she lifted her skirt just enough to pull her pantaloons down and over first one boot and then the other.

"Here," she said, thrusting the lace-edged undergarment down to him.

"Hmm, very nice," Linc observed, holding it up to scrutiny.

"Please! Just do whatever you're going to with my clothing without any comments!"

Linc snickered and turned his attention to the animal beneath him. The longhorn had stopped butting the willow. It stood with its head cocked to one side, eyeing Linc's every movement.

"I'm only going to get one chance at this toss, so pay attention to what I tell you," Linc said, sitting down on his branch. He winced from the roughness of the bark digging into his bare backside. "If I get lucky and land it across those horns, the bull's eyes will be covered. That's when we get out of this tree pronto. We won't have much time. Head for the cabin. I hope you English know how to run. Get ready!"

The bull snorted and tossed its head, pawing the ground. Linc looked down. His feet dangled only two feet above the animal's horns.

"Hold still, you mangy black buzzard!"

He held onto the branch with one hand and leaned

down toward the bull. Quick as he could, he wrapped a leg of Victoria's pantaloons around one horn, then did the same with the other. The bulk of the garment fell down over the longhorn's face.

The bull bellowed, jerking its head about as it took off running in first one direction and then another.

"Go!" Linc shouted, jumping to the ground and turning to reach up for Victoria. "Come on, come on! This isn't a Sunday-go-to-meeting picnic!"

"I'm climbing down as fast as I can!"

Linc kept one eye on the bull as he reached up and pulled Victoria off the bottom branch.

"Oh!" she cried with surprise, falling into his arms. He set her down hard on her feet beside him and grabbed her hand.

"Lift that skirt, woman, and run like the devil's after you!"

He took off loping toward the log cabin, dragging Victoria after him. When they'd crossed half the distance to the shack, the bull flung off the pantaloons and thundered after them.

"It's going to trample us!" Victoria cried.

"Don't talk! *Run!*"

They reached the cabin and dived through the doorway a split second before the angry longhorn reached them. Linc slammed the sturdy plank door shut and jammed his weight against it. The bull banged into it with a mighty force that shook the crude structure to the rafters. But the door held. They were safe.

Victoria bent over, gasping for breath and holding her paining side. The crude cabin had a stone fireplace and two bunks built into one wall. A rough-hewn square table and two straight-backed wooden chairs sat in the middle of the rectangular room. Shelves holding tin dishes, cans of food, and sacks of flour and sugar lined the wall next to the door. The floor was hard-packed dirt.

"Not bad running for a woman," Linc noted, breathing hard, too. He still leaned against the door.

"Would you please cover yourself?" Victoria whirled around, turning sideways to look out the curtainless window. The bull stood just beyond the door—the only door in the one-room cabin. She wrapped her arms around her and tried to think about the dangerous animal outside, but the animal inside—the handsome, powerfully built human male animal—worried her more now.

Linc felt amused as he watched Victoria. In profile, he noticed how her wet white blouse clung to the sensuous curves of her full breasts. One side of the blouse hung out of her sagging maroon skirt. A sleeve was torn at the shoulder. Her light blond hair had come loose from its pins at the top of her head and tumbled around her sweaty, dust-smudged face in long tangled tresses. Even dirty and disheveled, she looked beautiful. The fact surprised him. Many things surprised him about Victoria Spencer. She could have been killed by that loco bull, yet she seemed more concerned about his lack of clothes! He couldn't believe she'd sought him out, wanting his help. She'd walked right into his plan.

He reached for the worn Indian blanket on the bottom bunk bed and slung it around his hips, tucking the end in at his waist. Then he walked to Victoria.

"You can look now. Everything's covered except my chest, and you've seen that before."

She jumped hearing his voice so close. Swinging around, she retreated two steps, hitting the wall. Her eyes flicked up and down his front.

Linc smiled. "You mentioned a proposition, English. Is a high-bred lady like you saying you need the help of a half-breed gunslinger? Do you want me to kill your uncle? Or that tinhorn runt Cummings?"

Victoria's eyes widened in shock. "Kill? No, I don't want anyone killed! I must have been insane to think I could come to any kind of an agreement with someone like you. You think everything can be solved by a shooting!"

He stepped forward and grabbed her by the arms, frowning fiercely. "Get one thing straight, gal. You need me and my gun, or you wouldn't have pranced out here all this way on foot to find me. So don't get too almighty righteous on me. You can't tell me you haven't thought about killing that jackass uncle of yours when he whips you!"

She lowered her eyes from his harsh glare.

"I thought so," he went on, forcing her chin up with his hand so she had to look at him again. "You'd better understand this. If I decide to throw in with you, it'll be on *my* terms and at *my* price. And I don't work cheap. I'll be the boss. I know my business, and I know this territory. You'll do exactly *what* I tell you, *when* I tell you to do it! Is that understood?"

"Yes," she answered coldly, jerking out of his grasp. "Just as long as you understand *my* conditions. I'll pay well to hire you for protection and guide services. I have no choice and no one else to turn to for help. Believe me, I wish I did. I have money. And that's *all* you'll get from me in payment. Don't touch me again, Mr. Masterson. This is strictly business. Have I made myself clear?"

Linc smirked. Damn her for being so uppity and so god-awful pretty! He felt his blood stir in his veins. It quickened through his body, triggering a twinge of excitement within him that he hadn't felt in a very long time. She was sure setting a challenge for him, and he was a man who never walked away from a challenge. But for now, he'd keep to business, the way she wanted. He could get everything he had a hankering for from her in due time. But he wasn't about to tell her that.

"Your money's all I'm interested in," he replied, making himself sound convincing. "You need a guide and a gun.

If that's all you want, that's all you'll get."

Victoria swallowed hard. There was more to her plan, but that ultimate goal seemed ridiculous now that she was face to face with Linc Masterson. How could she have ever conceived it? She was risking all—her fortune and future, and Deborah's, too—if she told him the rest of her scheme. But what else could she do to foil Sir Giles? She had to try it, even though all her instincts told her now she was making a big mistake. On the one side stood her uncle and Alden; on the other, Linc Masterson. Alarming, frightening choices. Which was the lesser of the two evils?

Linc glanced out the window, then back at her. "Looks like the bull's finally lost interest in us and wandered off to graze. We can get out of here. My horse is in the lean-to behind the shack."

Victoria stood up straight, holding her shoulders back. She cleared her throat and forced herself to look him right in the eye.

"There's one more purpose for which I wish to hire you." His intense, dark-earth eyes held hers, causing her mouth to go suddenly dry. She ran her tongue over her parched lips, then went on, trying to sound confident in her words. "I want you to take me to a town where there's a legally licensed Protestant clergyman, and I want you to become my husband just as soon as possible."

Chapter Twelve

Linc just stared at Victoria. Rarely was he ever surprised by anything. He'd disciplined himself to expect the unexpected from any situation, whether it involved man or beast. But he was dealing with a woman here, and her last words set him back on his heels with a jolt. *She* proposed hitching up with *him!* After he'd spent considerable time planning ways to seduce her and even deceive her to get at her money, she offered him exactly what he was after, just like that. He was immediately suspicious.

He eyed her with down-turned brows.

"That walk across the desert must have addled your brain, woman."

She made her stance as straight and determined as possible.

"I'm quite sane, I assure you. I told you this is business. We'll be wed in name only. You must understand that clearly. When I'm legally married, I'll inherit my share of my father's estate. I'm not certain how much that will be, but I know the British pound amount of the cash will convert to more than three hundred thousand of your American dollars. There are several valuable properties involved also, including a large country estate just outside of London which has been in my family for four generations."

Linc's brow cocked.

"Three hundred thousand?"

Victoria nodded, her expression hardening. "My uncle

has had control of my inheritance long enough. I won't allow him to continue his tyrannical rule over my life and Deborah's. I must act quickly before he can force me to marry Alden, who is just a puppet to his whims. If you'll cooperate with me in this scheme, I'll pay you fifty thousand American dollars."

"That's mighty generous." Linc was thinking fast. If he hadn't seen those stripes on her back, he'd have thought she was sure-as-shootin' loco. But she seemed serious, all right. No mistaking that stubborn set of her high-held chin. She looked damned determined to go through with this wild plan. And he'd come out with a mighty sweet reward for his trouble—money he could use to get the Diamond M. Fifty thousand out of three hundred thousand. He shouldn't be greedy, but . . .

He'd have to win her trust. Play her along and bide his time in order to get the fifty thousand at least. Keep the situation just business for now. That would be easy enough. She was just another woman, like any other—except that she had a habit of acting like a wild rodeo bronc horse and doing the complete opposite of what he expected!

He didn't really trust her to go through with all the conditions of this deal. He never trusted anybody. But one way or another he'd make sure she did keep her end of the bar gain. He was riskin a lot here—his chance to best Drummond and his highly guarded bachelorhood!

"Just where's this generous payment for my cooperation going to come from?" he asked, getting back to cold business dealings. "You're not carrying that kind of cash with you now, are you?" His interest perked up even more.

"Of course not. Such a great amount of money would tempt even the most scrupulous person into dishonest actions. I don't trust you *that* much, Mr. Masterson. As a matter of fact, I don't trust you at all. But I have no other alternative. I need a husband, and you're the only choice I have!"

She glanced worriedly out the window toward the direction of the ranch house, and felt her heart nearly stop. Was that a cloud of dust rising on the horizon? She squinted, straining her eyes to scan the parched prairie, but couldn't see anything clearly. Clumsily, she fished in the side pocket of her skirt and drew out Hannah's flat leather wallet. Opening the folded halves, she pulled out the cash. An ochre vellum envelope fell to the floor at the same time. She absently bent to pick it up as she thrust the money toward Linc.

"My father's London barristers have an office in your New York City," she hurriedly explained. "We stopped there before coming west. A Mr. Arthur Tuttle is employed in that firm. He's been apprised of our family affairs ever since my father's sudden death five years ago. He was recently transferred here to the Colonies, I mean, your United States. If I present myself to him with a husband in New York, I'm certain he will honor any request I make for an advance on the cash of my inheritance. Then I'll give you the balance of the payment for your services. Take this money now as a retainer."

Linc took the currency from her and thumbed through it. "Most of this is English money—pounds."

"Any reputable bank will exchange it. I'm certain a city the size of New York would have a number of financial establishments willing to perform the transaction."

Linc folded the bills in half and started to tuck them into his denim pants pocket. Then he realized he wasn't wearing his pants. The Indian blanket was slipping down his hips. He grabbed for the end he'd wedged in around his waist just as it gave way and would have fallen off completely.

Victoria saw the same thing. The cabin was unbearably hot, but her face heated up for an entirely different reason. Though Linc caught the blanket just in time before everything was revealed, she still managed to glimpse that the thin covering of dark hair on his chest didn't stop at his tight-muscled belly, but went much lower. Immediately, her mind yanked a thought out of her memory, forcing her to remember what it had felt like to be pressed hard against that broad, bronzed chest and the rest of Linc's body. She should have been repulsed by the recollection, but the stirring in her middle felt nothing like aversion. She didn't understand the feeling at all, but it seemed to speed swiftly through her body like a wave of excitement.

"W-we should leave as quickly as possible," she stammered, turning toward the door. "Sir Giles could be pursuing me already. I'll get your clothes."

She ran out of the cabin, looking around for the bull as she headed for the pile of Linc's clothing on the ground. The longhorn grazed peacefully in the shade at the east side of the cabin. Quickly scooping up Linc's shirt, gunbelt, and other belongings, she spied her battered hat trampled in the dust by the bull. Juggling Linc's clothes in her hands, she retrieved it from the ground. It was ruined beyond repair, but she didn't want to leave any evidence of her presence here for someone to find.

Linc was stuffing canned goods into an empty flour sack when she entered the cabin again.

"I've decided to take you up on your offer," he said, glancing over his shoulder. "We'll head for Cheyenne. Tomorrow's the Fourth of July. Independence Day for us 'colonials', celebrating the end of your country's tyranny," he added with a touch of sarcasm in his voice.

Victoria lifted an eyebrow toward him, but listened as he continued.

"The Fourth's a big time in Cheyenne. People'll be coming to town from all over for the rodeo and races, plus all the other events planned for the celebration. It'll be easy for us to get lost in the crowd and avoid your uncle. I know a preacher who's a Lutheran. That Protestant enough for you?"

"Yes," she answered quietly, handing him his clothes. Now she had a different feeling in her stomach, a queasiness caused by sudden doubt. She'd actually proposed *marriage* to the half-naked man next to her who had just tossed a tin of biscuits into the bulging sack and yanked the drawstring ties closed at the top. She didn't want to marry him under *any* circumstances. He was a half-Indian gunfighter, whose ways were as foreign and frightening to her as this uncivilized frontier territory! She'd need to watch him carefully. And never be alone with him! Going to the town of Cheyenne during a time of festivities sounded safe enough. But she had the unsettling feeling that she was really only exchanging the certainty of her uncle's wrath and punishment for the alarming *uncertainty* of protection given by one Linc Masterson!

"Are you going to just stand there and watch me put on these clothes or do something more useful like get my horse and tie these supplies on my saddle?" Linc posed the question with hands on hips.

"I'll get the horse," she answered quickly, feeling flustered as she backed toward the door. "Of course I don't wish to watch you get dressed. I've seen enough of you already."

Realizing what she'd just admitted, she gulped and whirled around to scurry outside. Linc followed her a few minutes later, fully clothed, his gunbelt strapped low on his hip.

"Can you ride?" he asked briskly, checking how she'd fastened the food bag to his mount.

"Yes, but I'm used to an English sidesaddle." She looked worriedly toward the mustang, then in the direction of the far-away ranch house.

Linc followed her gaze and frowned. Either a dust storm was brewing or a pack of riders was bearing down hard toward them. He suspected men rather than weather. And they weren't more than a half hour away.

"No fancy riding gear here, English or otherwise," he noted, squatting and linking his hands together. "Get that pretty little behind of yours up into the saddle pronto. We're getting out of here."

Victoria glared at him, but still set her foot in his grip and let him heave her up. She grabbed hold of the pommel just in the nick of time to keep herself from falling off on the other side, before she settled in astride the leather seat.

Linc didn't climb up behind her immediately. Instead, he hurried to a big ball of tumbleweed that had come to rest against the side of the cabin. Bringing it to the mustang he quickly tied it behind the animal, using the tail hair to secure it.

"Why did you do that?" Victoria asked as Linc effortlessly mounted behind her and took up the reins. The mare sidestepped and whinnied, as if bothered by the bush dragging behind it, but Linc pulled in the reins sharply to control the animal.

"I don't figure to give your uncle an easy trail to follow. The weed will wipe out our tracks as we go. Hang onto that horn, English. We're riding hard!"

He pressed his spurred boot heels into the mare's sides and the animal lunged forward, immediately breaking into a full-out gallop. Victoria was thrown back against Linc's chest by the momentum. His strong arms encircling her were all that kept her on the horse.

The close contact with Linc frightened her as much as the wild ride! The heat of his body surged through the thin fabric of her white blouse. She could feel the hard bulges of his powerful chest muscles pressing into her back as he leaned forward to match the rhythm of the sturdy mustang's fast pace. As they thundered away from the line shack toward the pine and spruce covered foothills, Victoria only let herself think about staying mounted and escaping her uncle. She pushed aside all thought of the crazy scheme she'd contrived that would soon make Linc Masterson her husband!

Chapter Thirteen

"We'll be stopping at that place just up ahead." Linc reined in the mustang and pointed past Victoria's ear.

A cabin with a sod roof nestled at the base of the mountainside. A tall Indian tipi covered with buffalo hides stood close by. Its crisscrossing support poles, tied together at the top, jutted up through the middle smoke hole nearly twenty feet into the air. Victoria remembered hearing an American guest of her uncle's talking about this type of native Indian lodge once. She'd been curious to see one then. She couldn't imagine how people could live in such a dwelling, though for nomadic hunters who were constantly on the move following herds of roving animals, it might be a practical portable house.

"We're nowhere near Cheyenne," she protested, pulling her eyes away from the peculiar scene to glance over her shoulder. "We must move on." She was glad for the pause in the earnest ride, but worried about who might be pursuing them.

"We can't make it today," Linc explained with annoyance in his voice. "Cutting through that dry gully a ways back might have thrown those riders off our trail."

Victoria leaned forward to get away from the disturbing close contact with his body. She felt hot, sweaty, and thirsty. Sand gritted between her teeth when she clenched her jaws together. Her tongue felt swollen from lack of water.

She half-turned in the saddle to look at Linc. "Perhaps I

didn't impress upon you the gravity of my situation. We can't stop until we reach Cheyenne."

"Mustangs are a hardy breed, but even a cayuse like this one has a limit to what it can do. If this horse goes down from the heat, we'll be *walking* to Cheyenne! I have business with the owner of that ranch ahead. We'll be staying here tonight."

"*No!* Your personal business wasn't included in our deal." She frowned at him, then turned to sit ramrod straight with her back to him.

He leaned down close to her ear. "I changed the details. You'll do what I say." Before she could protest further, he encircled her with his arms again, took up the reins, and spurred the mustang forward.

The cabin was bigger than the line shack they'd left several hours ago, and better maintained. A wall of piled stones two feet high lined the yard area. No grass surrounded the cabin or the nearby tipi. The sandy soil was clear of all rocks and raked in a neat horizontal pattern. Not a tree showed anywhere. Only a tall wooden windmill soared into the clear blue sky, its wide base narrowing at the top where the wheel of paddles spun in a wobbly rotation, powered by the wind. Precious water pumped into a large metal catch-trough for storage.

A dozen longhorns grazed close by. Several raised their heads at Linc and Victoria's approach, then wandered off, chewing cud. A tall man with long, straight gray hair held back by a colorfully beaded headband filled the frame of the open cabin door.

Linc reined in the mustang at the hitching rail and dismounted, helping Victoria down after him. Then he raised his palm toward the older man.

"Joseph Two Eagles. I offer you the respect of our revered forefathers. I would visit with you, my uncle, along with this woman."

Uncle? Victoria darted a glance between Linc and the man in the doorway, who was obviously an Indian. Well past fifty years old, he wore the everyday work clothes of a cowboy—blue cotton shirt, gray duck pants. But hard-soled moccasins covered his feet instead of boots, and two black-tipped white feathers showed behind his head. There was no mistaking a certain regalness in the set of his shoulders and the proud up-tilt of his head as he stood before them. His feet-apart stance reminded her of the same one Linc had used when he'd stood atop the train boxcar in the stand-off against Harvey Trump and his gang during the attempted robbery. The straight nose and square jaw matched Linc's, too.

Joseph Two Eagles' face was magnificent—tanned dark, weathered and lined by the ravages of time and the sun. Creases flaring out at the edges of his dark brown eyes widened into deeper crevices across his forehead and around the sides of his mouth. No middle paunch strained the fabric of his shirt. His waist was as narrow as Linc's, a man half his age.

"You are welcome, Stalking Wolf, and your woman. Many moons have passed since last we spoke."

He stepped out the door toward them, then teetered precariously on one foot. Victoria feared he was going to fall, and started to lunge forward to catch him. But Linc caught her around the waist and yanked her back to his side, fiercely frowning a warning.

The old Indian didn't seem to notice their movement as he grabbed the hitching rail to regain his balance.

"Take horse to the lean-to." He awkwardly gestured a long-fingered hand toward a large three-sided structure at the west side of the cabin. "Squaw come inside."

He stood close to them now. Victoria could smell the alcohol accompanying his words. In that brief instant, her admiring appraisal of him shattered. Squaw and Linc's woman, he'd called her. She didn't like those names. Her brows dipped together. The old Indian turned around and re-entered the cabin. She glanced toward Linc, ready to protest being ordered about in such a manner.

"Follow him," he said sharply, pulling on their horse's reins to lead it toward the lean-to. "Don't say anything and do exactly what you're told. Squaws are seen, not heard."

He walked away then, leaving Victoria with her protests unspoken. Arguing with him would be useless, she could tell. When he set his jaw like that and narrowed his eyes, he meant business. She'd learned that about him during the short time she'd known him.

She sighed with annoyance, grabbing up her wrinkled skirt to follow Joseph Two Eagles inside. She'd do as she was told for now just to get in out of the blistering sun!

Inside, the cabin was sparsely furnished but neatly kept. Victoria gazed around. Two cupboards, a table and three straight-backed chairs, and a bed by the stone hearth were the extent of the furnishings. But the walls immediately caught her attention, filling her with amazement and trepidation. Indian weapons—wooden bows and fringed buckskin quivers of arrows, lances, and tomahawks hung in an orderly array on three of the log walls. The fourth wall held a beautiful headdress made of dozens of black-tipped white feathers held in place by an intricately beaded wide headband. Five brightly painted war shields surrounded it.

She'd read about such Indian weapons in a paper-covered novel she'd bought in New York several weeks ago. She shuddered to think about how they were used—in terrible battles against white travelers, settlers, and soldiers that "made the trails of the Great Plains run red with blood," the sensational novel had quoted. Seeing the ominous display of weapons before her set her imagination reeling and made her feel uncomfortable alone in the presence of Joseph Two Eagles.

He stared at her, adding to her anxiety, his dark brown eyes seeming to search more than just her face. Unwittingly, she touched her tangled hair, fearing he might be examining its length for that horrible practice of scalping!

"Sit in chair."

She jumped at the sound of his voice, and immediately

plopped down in the chair right next to her. The force of her descent jarred the table, causing a half-filled bottle of whiskey to wobble precariously. In reflex, she grabbed for it, steadying it with two hands as she darted a glance toward the door, measuring the distance with her eyes. Even as weary as she felt, she thought she could outrun the older man if the need arose. The liquor bottle might come in handy, too!

Relief startled her when Linc strode through the door in the next moment, carrying his rifle.

"I came to warn you, my uncle," Linc said without any other preliminaries. "Clinton Dandridge means to have your ranch."

Joseph Two Eagles gave a single sharp nod. His chiseled face remained a stoic mask.

"I will not leave my land. Your father give me good piece of earth for saving his life. It is mine." Two Eagles folded his arms across his chest. His mouth, creased deeply at the edges, set into a grim, determined line.

"Then you must fight," Linc continued soberly. "My pony will ride with yours against the white evil puffed with greed."

"This not your battle, Stalking Wolf. You cannot fight against your own kind. The white man's blood flows in your veins."

"So does yours, Two Eagles, through your sister, my mother."

The old Indian nodded. "You no longer deny your bloodline?"

"No, my uncle. I'm a man of two worlds and no worlds. I've tried to accept this, just as you've had to accept the many changes in your life."

Victoria might have been just a tin plate on the table for all the attention either man paid to her. But she didn't care, for she found herself enthralled by the conversation. Much was passing between the two men before her, though few words were being spoken. She was amazed by the determined strength in Linc's voice. Another quality in it puzzled her, for she hadn't heard him use such a tone before. Respect, almost reverence edged around it. She'd begun to think Linc held a bad regard for everyone and everything. Yet now, with Joseph Two Eagles, she heard warmth, even caring in his voice. She suddenly liked having that glimpse of another side of Linc she hadn't known before. What else was there to learn about this complex man?

"Someone after you," Two Eagles went on. "Two on one mount make short journey."

"Yes, I know. The woman's uncle is looking for her. He's from the Land-Across-the-Great-Ocean, like the woman, and he follows Clint Dandridge's moccasin trail with his own greed and cunning."

Two Eagles scrutinized Victoria, causing her to shift uncomfortably in her chair. "She is scrawny, unfit for birthing. This one not bear you strong warrior sons."

"You're right, my uncle. She's not my squaw. But I have agreed to help her fight against those who seek to do wrong to her."

Two Eagles gave a curt nod. "She could do worse than have you for her warrior."

Victoria started to open her mouth to protest old Joseph's insults and the way he and Linc spoke about her as if she weren't present, but the Indian's next words silenced her.

"Another enemy seek you, Stalking Wolf. In town this morning, I hear Ewing Cooper escape from white man's prison. He seek vengeance for brother's killing."

Linc frowned, cursing under his breath. Now he had a crazy Bible-quoting killer on his trail along with being lassoed into this wild scheme with Victoria! The timing couldn't be worse.

"I knew Cooper and I would have to settle that score someday," he said aloud. "The woman and I are headed for Cheyenne. We seek the shelter of your lodgings for the night."

"You are welcome. Woman bed with you?"

A touch of a smirk touched the corner of Linc's mouth as he shot a glance at Victoria and saw her startled look. For a moment, he was tempted to answer yes just to see her reaction. Her emerald eyes glared at him. He let a smile cross his lips, enjoying her indignation.

"No," he answered, adding "not yet" in his mind.

Two Eagles nodded again and stood up. "Woman stay in cabin. Cook meal. Cornbread, salt pork, potatoes. Supplies there." He pointed toward the wooden cupboard.

Linc rose to his feet, still looking at Victoria. "Can you cook at all?" he asked bluntly.

They were making her feel like some object of scorn and she didn't like it! She straightened her back and lifted her chin.

"In England, there was no need for me to acquire such menial skills. There were servants trained for cooking."

"No good for cook. No good for bed. What good for?" Two Eagles' wizened face looked puzzled.

"I'm wondering that myself," Linc replied, cocking an arched black eyebrow at her. He grinned at the wrathful look she shot at him. "I'll cook later. It'll be healthier for all of us."

"Good. Come, men counsel in tipi. Woman stay here."

In two long strides, Two Eagles reached the open cabin doorway and went through. Linc followed before Victoria could stop him. She got to her feet and angrily paced the room, mumbling.

"The nerve of him. The nerve of both of them!"

She stomped to the open window and saw Linc and Two Eagles enter the tipi. Despite her anger, she wished she could go inside to see what the Indian dwelling was like. At least she could see it up close now. The tanned animal hides covering the support poles were painted with colorful symbols. She had no idea what the skillfully detailed designs depicted, perhaps some important or heroic events in Joseph Two Eagles' life.

The wooden stakes anchoring the skins to the ground had

been removed and the hide covering rolled up a foot for ventilation. The door flap was folded back, but she couldn't see the two men inside.

Tapping her foot impatiently, she wondered what Linc and his uncle were talking about. The business of Clinton Dandridge seeking Two Eagles' property? She knew Dandridge wanted the Masterson ranch, too. Linc had called him greedy and cunning, yet he worked for the man. And on the other hand, he'd told Two Eagles he'd help him fight the wealthy rancher. Just whose side was Linc on? She had no idea. With more than a little trepidation, she realized she knew very little about the man she'd asked to be her husband.

Hot wind gusted through the window opening, hitting her face. The movement of a dead piece of tumbleweed over the raked sand of the yard made her look out toward the sun-baked prairie. Her heart leaped into her throat. Dark figures on horseback framed by a wide cloud of dust spotted the horizon. The searchers!

"Mr. Masterson! *Linc!*" she cried, dashing out of the cabin.

He bent and stepped out of the tipi, nearly colliding with her as she ran up. Two Eagles followed close behind.

"Someone's coming! There!" She pointed toward the approaching riders.

Linc clutched her arm and propelled her with him toward the cabin.

"Get inside and stay out of sight." When they were through the door, he snatched up his Winchester from the table. "Do you know how to use one of these?" he asked sharply.

"No!" She stepped back in horror when he thrust the rifle toward her.

"Well, you'd better learn fast!" He flipped the round cocking lever hard and fast, priming the weapon. Thumbing back the hammer, he grabbed Victoria's hand and thrust the wooden stock into it. In reflex, her other hand came up to catch the long barrel.

"Just raise it and fix this sight on what you want to hit." He tapped a rounded bit of metal at the end of the barrel. "Squeeze this trigger easy-like. Cock the handle just the way I did to set another bullet into the chamber to fire again." He took hold of both of her shoulders and looked directly at her, forcing her eyes to lock with his. "Now, listen to me, Victoria. Stay out of sight. Don't do anything unless you hear gunfire outside. Then shoot from the window and be careful!"

He let her go and swiftly left the cabin, yanking the plank door closed behind him. Victoria stood frozen to the spot for a moment, staring at the back of the door. Then her eyes dropped to the rifle in her hands and she suddenly became aware of its heavy weight and the cold feel of the metal barrel against her palm.

Linc only called her Victoria when he was deadly serious. He'd told her to shoot the gun. Shoot at men. The men coming to find her. She'd never shot at anything. The idea sent a lead weight plunging into her stomach. Fear weakened her knees, making her sway on her feet. She wanted to throw the Winchester down and run away. But she didn't. She couldn't move. She gripped the hard metal and polished wood of the weapon until her fingers whitened from the hard pressure, knowing there was nowhere to run, nowhere to hide. Her heart raced. She felt the paralyzing fear and panic a cornered animal must feel, and like such a dazed and desperate creature, she turned to fight for her very life.

With the rifle clutched firmly in her hands, she rushed to the side of the window and pressed her back against the log wall. Her breath welled up in her throat, but she made herself expel it slowly, quietly, so her ears could listen to every sound, catch every movement.

The horses drew nearer. She could hear the loud thunder of their hooves beating against the sun-parched ground.

No curtains covered the window, but she dared to peek around the edge of the wall. She spotted Linc and Two

Eagles leaning casually against the hitching rail in front of the cabin, looking as if they were just having a friendly little visit. But she saw Linc's hand go down to the leather loop securing his gun in the holster. A quick flick of his thumb freed the hammer. Two Eagles now had a gun and a tomahawk behind his back, both stuck into the waist of his gray duck pants. He must have gotten the weapons from the tipi.

She swallowed to try to wet her dry throat. Her arm muscles strained and her hands shook holding the heavy rifle. But she kept the weapon locked in her grip, finger on the trigger, waiting for the lightning of men accompanying the storming hooves to descend on her hiding place.

Chapter Fourteen

Five riders pounded through the entrance of the stone wall into the neat yard, yanking up their mounts so hard the animals dug in their front hooves and skidded, churning up clouds of thick dust. Zeke Dandridge led the men. He shifted in the saddle and adjusted his dirty, sweat-stained hat on his head, but made no attempt to dismount.

"What're you doing here, Masterson?" he demanded. "Thought you were sent to the line shack with supplies."

"I go where I please, Zeke." Linc's tone sounded casual enough, but it held an edge of chilled warning in it.

Dandridge frowned.

"My pa'll be wanting to know that, seeing how he thinks you're working for him."

"Well, you run along home then and tell Clint anything you like."

Dandridge's scowl deepened.

"Don't tell me what to do, half-breed. We're not finished here yet. We're lookin' for that English Spencer gal. She took off this morning. She was askin' about you just before she lit out. Know anything about her?"

"Nope," was Linc's only reply.

"Well, we aim to search this place for her," Zeke stated. "And while we're at it, we're going to get this jackass-stubborn old redskin to agree to sell this dried-up stretch of lizard run to my pa."

Linc straightened, taking a step away from the hitching

rail and hooking his thumbs into the top of his gunbelt. When he spoke, his voice sounded distinctly threatening.

"You and these buzzard-bait boys'll save yourselves a heap of trouble if you ride out of here right now, before Two Eagles decides you're pressing his hospitality."

Zeke's gaunt features tightened as his gray eyes narrowed and his lips stretched across gritted teeth.

"That's mighty big talk for somebody up against five armed cowboys."

Angry murmurs of agreement sounded from the men around him.

Victoria listened intently out of sight, her back pressed against the rough logs of the cabin wall. A big horsefly's menacing buzz struck near her ear. She shook her head to fend off the annoying darting insect, and strained to hear what would happen next outside. She felt frightened and uncertain of what to do. She knew Linc and Two Eagles stood out in the open, easy targets for the hostile men. Was Linc depending on her to lower the odds with the rifle if it came to a shootout?

The metal of the Winchester's long barrel felt hot where she touched it with her nervous, perspiring hands. Zeke Dandridge and his men suspected she might be here. Could she pull the trigger of the rifle to save herself? To save Linc? And Two Eagles, she added quickly to her anguished thoughts. She took a deep breath, running her tongue over her parched lips. Hard, terrible questions. How she hoped she wouldn't have to find out the answers.

"I reckon these dirty redskins all stick together, don't they, boys?" Zeke slung the insulting words over his shoulder to his men, beginning to lower his left hand to the gun holstered at his hip. "Guess we'll have to teach them both a lesson."

Victoria's insides cringed with dread. She hadn't been in this American West very long, just enough time to know that insults like the ones she was hearing wouldn't go unanswered. She let her finger rest ever so slightly against the curved metal trigger of the rifle, peeking through a crack between the wooden window frame and the log wall to see the drama outside.

In that instant, Linc drew his gun and fired at a man who'd reached for his own weapon. The shot shattered the air. Dandridge's man let out a howl of pain, clutching his stomach as he tumbled backward off his mount. He didn't move after he hit the ground. The horses screamed and pranced, tossing their lathered heads, rearing their powerful bodies.

Linc fired again, hitting Zeke Dandridge, whose gun went off at the same time. He dropped his weapon to grab at his left thigh, struggling to hold his leg and control his contorting horse to stay in the saddle. His face twisted with pain and rage.

Two Eagles lashed out with his tomahawk. The hatchet blade struck the man next to Zeke Dandridge full in the middle of the chest. The force of the death-wielding blow knocked him from his horse. As he hit the ground, his gun went off. Victoria cried out and instinctively ducked when the stray bullet whizzed through the window near her head. The Winchester exploded in her hands, triggered by the reflex movement of her finger. With horror, she saw a burly cowboy by Zeke Dandridge grab for his shoulder. Bright red blood instantly splurted through his fingers, staining his gray homespun shirt. He pitched forward, grabbing for his horse's mane to stay in the saddle.

"Drop it!" Linc ordered fiercely, pointing his Colt threateningly toward the only man left unwounded. The cowboy quickly obeyed, tossing his gun away and thrusting his hands high in the air.

"That's real smart," Linc continued. "Now, get down and throw these dead jackals over their saddles."

The man speedily dismounted and did as he was told.

"There'll be hell to pay for this, Masterson!" Zeke Dandridge ground out through gritted teeth. He held no weapon, but if black looks could kill, Linc would have been dead.

Linc showed no intimidation. He stepped forward to grab the bridle of Dandridge's horse, his menacing glare matching the younger man's eye for eye.

"This land's not for sale at any price. It belongs to Two Eagles by my father's decree. Any man fool enough to try to take it will end up boots down just like your boys there. Tell your pa he and I are even now. He saved my life five years ago by teaching me to use this Colt. Now I'm paying him back by not killing you—this time."

"I'll be back, you dirty half-breed," Zeke retorted viciously, "and I'll have an army of men to fill you and that wrinkled-up old man full of lead!"

"Then you'll be a dead man, Zeke," Linc said icily, with unmistakable assurance.

Zeke stared at Linc a moment longer, pure hatred filling his cold gray eyes. Then, clutching his thigh with bloodstained fingers, he yanked his horse's head around and dug his spurs into the animal's sides. Galloping his mount, he jumped it over the low stone wall and rode toward the direction of the ranch. The other men followed as best they could, pulling the dead men's horses, laden with the bodies, along after them.

Victoria pressed her back against the log wall and let herself slide slowly down to the floor, unable to believe the carnage she'd just witnessed. She stared at the Winchester lying across her lap, stunned that she'd just shot a man with it.

Linc's gun. Linc was all right. A strange relief filled her at that thought, clashing with the revolting chill that settled over her heart. She'd fired the rifle accidentally, but she realized she'd been standing ready to use the weapon to protect herself. Dandridge and his men were dangerous, malicious, cruel. She knew now with shocking clarity that she would have shot the gun purposely to save her life—just as Linc had done to save himself and Two Eagles.

She'd seen men die again—one stomach-shot; the other

killed by a tomahawk splitting open his chest. She felt appalled, sickened, stunned. Yet a tiny primal feeling of triumph and strength began to thread through her. They were dead. She was alive. They had been a threat to her existence. They forfeited their lives. She survived.

Is this what being in this savage, nature-ruled frontier land did to a person, she wondered in confusion. Did it strip away civility, decency, exposing the baser instinctive human traits of personal survival at all costs?

Linc burst through the cabin door, rushing over to her.

"Are you all right, Victoria? Were you hit?" Concern lined his handsome face as he knelt down on one knee and took hold of her shoulders, shifting his eyes over her.

She managed to find her voice, though it was hard to speak with his deep brown eyes now gazing at her intently and causing a rolling sensation in her middle. "N-no, I'm all right."

"Damnation, woman! Then why in hell did you yell and fire that shot?" His look of concern changed swiftly to anger. "I hope to heaven Zeke didn't have the presence of mind to hear you and realize someone else besides me or Two Eagles shot one of his boys, or he'll be back here looking for you as well as us!"

She shrank back a little under his harsh rebuke, then let her own anger surge. "I couldn't help it! A bullet nearly hit me. I didn't mean to pull the trigger. It just happened! But it helped you, didn't it? That man was about to shoot you."

"I could have handled him!"

"Fine. Next time I'll let you kill everyone!"

For a tense moment, their eyes clashed. Then Victoria's shifted suddenly to a spreading red stain on the left sleeve of Linc's dark blue shirt. "You're hurt!"

He parried her hand away when she started to reach for his upper arm. "It's nothing. Just a nick."

"But it's bleeding! Let me look at it."

Two Eagles entered the cabin then, carrying the bloodied tomahawk in his hand. He nodded his agreement.

"Squaw work. Let her tend."

"Sit there," Victoria ordered, pointing to a chair by the table. She thrust the Winchester at Linc and got to her feet to go to the washstand, glad to have something to think about besides the shootout. When she returned to the table with water in the shallow tin wash pan, Two Eagles joined her, handing her a ragged roll of white bandaging and a dangerous-looking hunting knife. He took the rifle from Linc.

"I keep watch from lean-to."

"No," Linc countered. "Get your things and some supplies together. We're leaving here."

The old Indian's face remained as expressionless as before, but he shook his head.

"I will not leave land."

Linc's look darkened.

"You know Dandridge'll send more men. We can't fight them alone."

"But you and Two Eagles won against them," Victoria said, staring at him.

"White man many," the older man answered. "Hatred strong. War of our peoples still goes on here and here." He swept a hand toward his heart then his head.

"That's why we're going. We'll find another way to fight them." Linc started to get up.

"Sit down so I can take care of your arm!" Frowning, Victoria pushed on his shoulder, catching him off balance so he sat back down hard on the chair. She felt angry through and through. Mad at Two Eagles for being so stubborn, and at white men who preyed on a single old man of a different race who only wanted to live quietly on his land. Outraged at everything—men being shot, men controlling her life, the unrelenting heat, sand and sweat under her clothes, the fly that had returned to buzz annoyingly around her head. She swatted at it, then took the long-bladed knife and slashed open Linc's shirtsleeve.

"Easy with that," Linc warned, scowling. "My arm's only

flesh-wounded. I don't need it cut off!"

"Then sit still!"

She was glad she felt so stirred up. It kept her from flinching at the sight of his bloodied, ragged flesh when the arm was exposed. She'd never tried to tend a gunshot wound before, but instinctively knew she had to wash it clean if possible and get the torn skin covered with the bandages to stop the bleeding.

She tried to act coolly efficient and ignore the nauseating churning in her stomach as she rolled back the cut edges of the shirtsleeve.

"Is the bullet still in there?" she asked, praying it wasn't. She didn't want to test her nursing skills that much!

"No. Just grazed by. Slap something on it so we can get out of here!" Linc's impatience and the annoying throb of pain coming from the wound made his dark brows dip so they almost touched at the bridge of his nose.

"Don't yell at me! I'm doing the best I can!" Her frown matched his in intensity as she twisted the water out of the washcloth with more vigor than necessary.

Linc seemed to decide arguing with her would do no good. He turned toward Two Eagles.

"I mean you no disrespect, Uncle, but nothing will be served if you're dead. Then Clint Dandridge'll get just what he wants. We need more warriors to keep him from stealing what is yours. We have friends in Cheyenne who will help. The woman and I are headed there. Come with us. Pick your braves and lead them back here to defend what is yours, the way you did in the glorious days when you rode with the great Chief Red Cloud."

Victoria watched Two Eagles out of the corner of her eye while she worked over Linc's arm. A faraway look came into the older Indian's dark eyes. His shoulders seemed to straighten, his chin raised slightly. He turned his head to look toward the lances and bows mounted on the wall.

Victoria started to ask Linc to hold the end of the bandage so she could start winding it around his arm, but his hand shot up and covered her mouth. He frowned again to silence her, then looked back at Two Eagles. After a long moment, he spoke, his voice quiet but pressing.

"What is your answer, Uncle? Will you stay here and fight alone on the white man's terms, or gather a force and confront your enemy on a field of honor of your choosing? I stand with you no matter which you choose."

Slowly Two Eagles' eyes cleared and he seemed to be back with them in the room.

"You are right, Stalking Wolf. Our might is in many. I will come with you to gather warriors. I will ready the horses. Squaw get supplies." He strode from the cabin.

"I don't like being referred to as a squaw," Victoria said as she wrapped the bandage strip around Linc's wound, using none too gentle a touch.

"Whether you like it or not, that's what you are to him, and a lowly one at best because your skin is white." He resisted the wince that shot through him when she yanked on the bandage to tie the ends together. Instead, he concentrated on that pale skin of hers, now tinged pink by sunburn from her walk through the desert plain. Perspiration wet and curled the wisps of blond hairs at the edges of her dirt-smudged face. Weariness showed in her emerald eyes, but the stubborn set of her chin could still be seen.

He thought about all she'd been through since he'd first met her on the train from Cheyenne. The robbery, the shootout in the alley in Laramie, the confrontation with Zeke Dandridge just now. An unfamiliar sensation stirred inside him. He consciously thought about it for a moment, because the drift of it surprised him. It was a feeling he'd had for no other woman and very few men. Admiration.

"What are you doing here, Victoria Spencer?" he asked suddenly, his voice quiet.

"W-what?" His question and change in manner caught her off guard. A moment ago he'd been yelling at her.

"The United States is very different from England, isn't it?"

She gave a little snort of laughter to hide how his steady gaze unnerved her and set her heart leaping in beat.

"As different as distant planets! I hate it here!" Without looking at him, she gave the bandage ends a final twist to secure them and rolled Linc's stained sleeve down over the wound. Purposely, she busied herself rinsing her fingers in the tin wash pan. He startled her by taking hold of her hands and gently wiping them with the worn piece of toweling she'd laid on the table.

"But you've stayed with the bronc all the way," he stated abruptly, for the realization of what he felt sat uncomfortably in his gut. But he had to say it. "You've got grit, English. Real grit."

He glanced away as he stood up and tossed the towel back on the table.

"The supplies are in the cupboard. You'll find some empty flour sacks there, too. Pack up as much as you can in them. I'm going to help Two Eagles strike the tipi."

In the next instant, he was gone out the door, leaving Victoria standing dumbfounded in the middle of the room.

Chapter Fifteen

Linc, Victoria, and Two Eagles rode hard for the foothills after leaving the ranch. Victoria again sat double on the mustang with Linc. Awkwardly, she tried not to keep too close to him, but the galloping rhythm of the sturdy horse threw her into him. Finally, she just gave in, realizing riding was easier when she leaned back against Linc's powerful chest, allowing his strong arms to surround her and hold her to the mount. But this arrangement didn't help her state of mind.

At dusk, they stopped for the night in a grove of pines set against the side of a hill. Even Victoria, inexperienced though she was on the frontier, could see that the thick-branched trees offered a natural covering. Without wanting to, she was learning about this wild country—and about herself and her own instincts for survival.

"Keep watch here. Give a yell if you see anybody coming," Linc ordered, helping her down from the horse. He handed her the Winchester.

Before she could protest, he strode away with Two Eagles, pulling the horses along with him. She frowned and turned her back, knowing it would do no good to argue with him. She was more than a little surprised that he trusted her to stand guard. Not too long ago, he'd made it plain that he considered her a bothersome foreigner, all the more worthless because she was an easily cowed female. She didn't understand the sudden change in his attitude. She felt more uncomfortable than ever about being with him. She liked it better when he was angry and impatient with her. Then she could react with her own defensive wrath. Now she didn't know how to respond to him. She only knew she could still feel the heat of his hands where he'd held her at the waist to help her dismount. And now that he was no longer with her, she felt strangely alone. He'd walked away from the circle of her being, leaving the space suddenly and noticeably empty of his strong presence.

Shaking her head in bewilderment, she hefted the heavy rifle under one arm and walked to the edge of the pines to peer out at the darkening desert plain.

The fiery heat of the day was quickly doused by the encroaching night as soon as the sun dipped behind the jagged green-black mountain peaks. The vast openness of the place, drenched in an untouched, rugged beauty, created a lasting impression in Victoria's mind. This Wyoming was so very different from her beloved England, yet she was moved to appreciate and even admire the stark wilderness.

A shiver crept over her. She had no coat, not even a shawl to ward off the sudden drop in temperature. She hadn't thought of the need for a wrap when she'd made her daring escape from the Dandridge ranch during the scorching midday.

That impulsive escape. Her desperate plan. Everything jumbled together now in her mind, mixed with charging bulls, frantic rides, an Indian tipi, exploding guns, a bloody tomahawk, and threatening, treacherous men, not the least of whom was Linc Masterson.

A sound she'd never heard before broke into her churning thoughts, making her turn. With surprise, she saw Linc and Two Eagles standing together a little distance away, facing the mountains. Their backs were to her, but in the fading light, she could see they'd removed their shirts and boots. Each man now placed a necklace of some kind around the neck of the other. A low, droning chant reached Victoria's ears again, and she realized the murmurings came from Linc and Two Eagles. They raised their arms to the crimson-streaked twilight sky, then lowered them to begin a rhythmic movement from side to side with their bodies. Slowly, they turned to follow each other in a small circle. Their bare feet moved in perfect time to the mesmerizing chant.

Victoria suddenly felt like an intruder, an outsider witnessing some kind of ritual dance. She knew she should turn away and keep to her guard post, leaving the two men to their private ceremony, but she couldn't. The simplicity of the song and the steps only added to the haunting beauty of what she saw, drawing her to join them with her spirit, if not with her body.

After a while, Linc stepped out of the circle and moved away, leaving Two Eagles to continue alone. Victoria spun around to face the desert again, trying to pretend she hadn't seen anything of what the two men had been doing. She gave a start of surprise when Linc suddenly stepped up beside her, for she hadn't heard his footsteps approach at all.

"You'd better take this tonight." He held out his shirt. "We can't risk a fire. You'll need it to keep warm."

"B-but what will you use?" Her eyes inadvertently darted to his bare chest. She groaned inside, upset by his nearness and the strong sense of sheer maleness emanating from him.

"I'll get by." He reached down, took the rifle out of her hand, and tilted it against a nearby rock. "My time to watch. A bedroll's laid out by the horses. Get some rest. We have a hard ride to Cheyenne tomorrow."

"But I can take my turn at guarding," she insisted.

"Like you did just now?" Scorn touched his voice.

She lowered her eyes.

"I—I'm sorry. I didn't mean to watch you and Two Eagles."

He turned away from her to stare out at the desert.

"You were curious," he said flatly.

"Yes. I mean, no, that wasn't all of it." Sensing his withdrawal from her, she struggled to find the right words to explain. "I don't know Indian ways, the ways of your people. I mean Two Eagles' people. I'm sorry. I'm putting this badly. I've been told you are half white, yet from what I just saw, you know the Indian ways as well as the white man's. To which world do you belong?" The blunt question escaped her lips before she could stop it.

Linc gave a derisive snort, glancing sideways at her.

"That's a question I've been asking myself ever since I was old enough to think on it."

Victoria heard the tightness in his deep voice, and she remembered the words he'd spoken to Two Eagles back at the cabin before Zeke Dandridge and his men had arrived. He'd said he belonged to two worlds and no worlds. She suddenly realized the terrible loneliness such a condition would cause, and her heart went out to him.

"Tell me about your family," she said quietly, almost holding her breath. She found herself wanting to know about him, yet fearing he would close himself off from her completely if she pried. He'd brought his presence back to her, and she wanted him to stay. Her fear of others lessened with his nearness. But a different kind of fear and contradiction took its place—the worry that he'd go, and that he'd stay.

"My family is none of your business, Miss Spencer," Linc answered coldly. "You know enough about me to carry out the deal we made."

Hesitatingly, she put her hand on his uninjured arm.

"Yes, but tell me anyway. Please," she urged softly.

He stared at her without speaking. The gathering darkness shadowed his chiseled face, but she knew the details of it so well now, and could fill in his handsome features even when the diminished light distorted them.

She forced herself to be silent and wait for several long moments, knowing he was making a decision of trust. And at that moment she wanted him to trust her. It was important to her. She didn't know why, didn't want to reason out the why of it. She just wanted it to happen.

Linc felt glad the night was coming on so fast. Maybe it would hide the earnest appeal gathered in Victoria's green eyes. He wished he hadn't seen it at all, or heard the sincerity in her lyrical, accented voice. He liked it better when her temper flared at him, when her eyes flashed with anger. He knew how to handle a gal under those conditions. But this side of the woman threw his aim off target. She never did what he expected. After what she'd been through today, she should have been clinging to him for protection, near in a faint with shock and fear. Most gals would be. But she wasn't. Instead, she wanted to know about his life, the life he kept carefully hidden away because of the pain. He shared himself with no one. After Abby, he'd sworn he never would. So why did he suddenly feel the spark of an urge to open his insides just a little now?

She reached out to take the shirt he'd offered. He watched her slip it on. She didn't fasten the buttons down the front. Instead, she pulled the cloth together over her breasts and held it there by hugging her arms about her. A simple gesture, but it startled Linc. She was holding him without physically touching him. She didn't speak, yet he understood what her movements conveyed.

He cocked an eyebrow in wonder, feeling uncertain. This was new to him, having someone reach out. Few people had ever done that for him in his life, not without wanting to take something from him in return. For a moment, he was wary, untrusting. But the beseeching look in Victoria's beautiful eyes held no deception, no cunning as they reflected the last scarlet rays of sunset. He saw only honest caring.

He yielded. It took a long moment for him to overcome his long-practiced inner defenses, but finally he let his guard down a little to take hold of Victoria's arms and draw her close. She didn't resist.

"Your curiosity is going to get you into a mess of trouble someday, English," he said gently, gazing down at her.

"It already has." Her arms came around him at the waist. She felt the heat of his flesh. She hadn't planned to get this close to him, hadn't wanted to be so near. Her heart pounded wildly in her breast. She was certain he could hear it. Her hands trembled touching him.

"Everything's wrong between us, you know that, don't you?" he murmured.

"Yes, I know. At every other moment except now."

He leaned down to kiss her then. Pressed an experienced, searching mouth over hers, gently at first. But when the sweetness of her lips and the close molding of her body along his length ignited his senses, he demanded more in his embrace. One arm encircled her back, imprisoning her hard against him. The other raised so his hand could entwine in the tangled silken tresses of her hair and force her head to remain still to his sensuous assault on her lips.

Victoria felt as if she'd been struck. Her mind reeled dizzily. She couldn't think straight. A small voice of conscience deep down inside her called a warning, but she pretended not to hear it while she drank in the taste of Linc's mouth, felt the roughness of his chin pressed into hers and the hardness of the muscles of his back as she clung to him. It seemed so right to be in his arms, so exciting, frightening, paralyzing. She couldn't move, yet inside her body danced with wild sensations coursing through every part of her. She shivered, both from the crisp desert night air and from being soundly and possessively kissed by this man, this Linc Masterson. She knew he was filled with violence, savagery, and a wildness so like the land around them. Yet at this moment, all that was cast aside. He pressed her close with a firm hold, but didn't hurt her. He claimed her lips, her very being, yet she sensed that he *asked* her to give to him, and she wasn't afraid. With stunned surprise, she welcomed him, answered him with her own need and longing, the like of which she'd never before known.

Suddenly, an animal howled loudly from the mountain-side, piercing the stillness of the night. Victoria jumped, breaking off the kiss and whirling her head around in the direction of the sound. Another matching cry sounded from farther away, making her give a small cry of alarm.

"Don't be afraid," Linc said, drawing her chin around. "They're only coyotes—prairie wolves, we call them out here. They're just having a little chat, checking on each other. But I reckon you don't hear their kind of talk back in London town."

Victoria smiled weakly and shook her head.

"No. I've never heard anything quite like it. Are they dangerous?"

"In a hungry pack, they can get nasty with something they've pulled down, but they rarely take on a man—or woman." Glad to have the kiss ended, he made himself step back and lean down to pick up his rifle from the rock. Pulling away from Victoria left him feeling strangely unsettled. Disturbed by the effect the kiss had on him, he forced his thoughts to magnify the differences between his life and hers, telling himself he should keep his distance from her. He just wished his body would go along with the idea and not keep on urging him to get close to her again, to experience more.

But the coyote had brought him abruptly back to cold reality. He was surprised that Victoria had drawn him away from it. Dandridge and her uncle could have men bearing down on them right now. But at least the darkness would halt them for a while.

"I'd best get to guard duty," he said quickly, cocking the Winchester to put a bullet in the chamber. "We don't want any Dandridges or their boys riding in on us."

He didn't mention their kiss, and for that, Victoria was grateful. Her insides still churned and her heart was just now starting to return to its normal pace. She needed time to sort through these new feelings he'd awakened in her. She knew she should leave him, go to the bedroll he'd spoken of a few moments ago. But she felt very reluctant to move away. Did the kiss mean anything to Linc? she wondered. He seemed to let it go easily. She'd be foolish to think a mere kiss would do to Linc what it had done to her. He was a gunfighter, a man of the world. He certainly hadn't led a sheltered life the way she had. A man as handsome as he would have many women interested in him. Women like that saloon girl in the awful purple dress that he'd been with in Laramie just before the terrible shootout in the alley.

The thought made Victoria bristle. She suddenly felt determined not to show Linc how much his kiss had unnerved her.

"What were you and Two Eagles doing over there?" she asked, changing the subject.

Linc turned his head sideways to look at her. His face showed no emotion.

"It's a serious matter, not meant for a woman."

"I mean no disrespect," she replied, though she felt annoyed by his condescending words. "Please explain it to me. I'd like to learn about it."

Linc looked to the open plain before he spoke.

"Two Eagles offers prayers of thanks to the Great Spirit and the spirits of his ancestors for deliverance from his enemies. A battle was fought and won, but the war is not over. He wishes guidance in knowing what path to take against the white man's hatred and greed. But there is only one path—this." His voice took on a cold, emotionless edge as he raised the Winchester. "This is the only solution men like Dandridge know and understand."

"You can't kill them all," Victoria said quietly.

"I know that and so does he." Linc glanced toward Two Eagles, who was still engrossed in the dance and chant. "But we'll fight anyway. It's the only choice white men have given Indians."

Victoria stayed silent for several long moments, sensing the unshown fury inside Linc. She felt his frustration and anger, for it matched her own. She, too, was being forced by others to do things she didn't want to do. Sir Giles, Alden. They tried to manipulate her life to suit their own purposes, giving her no say. She'd had enough. Her back was pushed against the wall until she had to fight back with any means she could think of. Yes, she knew why Linc and Two Eagles had to fight against great odds.

"Was your mother of such a warrior spirit as you and Two Eagles?" she asked gently, hoping he would share a little more with her.

Linc's narrowed eyes swung to her. The icy edge still remained in his voice when he answered.

"She didn't paint her face and ride a war pony or use lance or arrow, but she fought her own battles—and lost. She chose the wrong man—my father, Holden Masterson. He cost her her family, her people, every shred of dignity and honor a person can have. She was spit on, cursed, treated like she was less than dirt." Bitterness deepened his voice. "He kept her in his house like she was one of his possessions. Flaunted her before his legal white wife. Barely acknowledged her existence, except to say he'd keep her on the ranch no matter what. And she stayed. She and the son they made. She loved him, she told me once. Love . . ." His handsome features hardened. "It took everything from her. When my father died five years ago, she went into the mountains and never came back. But I knew where to find her. I went to the sacrificial cliff used long ago by our ancestors. Her broken body was at the bottom."

Victoria pressed her lips together, deeply moved by the

tragic story. She swallowed back the small sigh of sympathy that welled up in her throat. Linc stood straight and tall before her, his head held high, but she felt his terrible pain when she thought of the agony a boy would experience growing up under such circumstances.

"Your father forced her to . . . stay with him?" she asked, barely above a whisper.

Linc's mirthless laugh was short, derisive.

"He kept her at the ranch all right, but he didn't force her to do anything against her will. The hell of it was she *wanted* to be with him. She told me all she had to face, everything she sacrificed was worth it just to be with him. I hated him for that hold he had on her. I wanted to kill him when I got old enough. But I knew if I did, she'd die, too, from needing him. It's loco to let somebody get hold of you like that. Damned loco!"

Victoria sat down on a rock and remained silent for several long moments, deep in her own memories. At last she spoke.

"My father had such an obsession for my mother. She died from a fever when my sister Deborah and I were small children, but he never let go of her. He spoke about her as if she were alive and just away for a while. I'd search for him to play or read with me and find him in his study sitting by the fireplace, staring up at her portrait for hours on end. When I was old enough to wonder why my mother never came home, our dear nursemaid explained to me that she was not coming back. Death finally released my father from his sorrow and torment." She looked up at Linc. "I think you're right. Great love brings great anguish and pain, it seems. I don't want to feel any of those things . . . ever."

"Right," Linc agreed with a sharp nod of his head. "Business agreements seem a whole lot smarter for dealing with folks, I'd say."

"Then we still have our . . . arrangement? But what about Two Eagles?"

"I gave you my word, didn't I? I'll stick to it. Two Eagles will come with us to Cheyenne. I'll take care of our deal of getting hitched, then round up some friends of mine to take on the problem of Clint and Zeke Dandridge. I reckon there'll be a run-in with your uncle and Cummings, too, because of you and their business with Dandridge."

Victoria rose to her feet.

"You'll be in terrible danger. I want to help. Sir Giles and Alden are my battle."

"I'm used to going up against the odds. You'd only get in the way. While I get all this worked out, you'll be staying in Cheyenne with Lottie Stockton."

"But—"

Linc's sharp tone cut her off. "Get to the bedroll, like I told you before, Victoria. We'll be riding hard as soon as it gets light. We're doing this *my* way. Don't argue!"

He strode away from her then and was quickly lost in the darkness surrounding the thick pine trees. Victoria strained her eyes to watch him, but she could see only shadows. She frowned at Linc's stubbornness. Did he think he was undefeatable, invincible just because he was so good with that gun of his? A bullet could fell him just as easily as any man.

That sobering thought drained away her annoyance. Linc seemed so strong. And although he'd revealed a small chink in the armor covering his emotions when he'd spoken so passionately about his mother and father, he still had an air about him of always being master of himself and in control in any situation. But she'd heard that deadly bullet whiz so closely by her head back at Two Eagles' cabin. She'd seen men die by those same bullets. Linc could die, too.

That realization troubled her deeply. She pulled his shirt around her more tightly. It smelled of him, stirring the memory of their heated kiss. The homespun shirt had touched his flesh, strained against his powerful muscles. She felt comforted having it around her—and uneasy. She was frightened by the thought that Linc might be killed, and fearful of the stirrings he'd ignited in her.

She couldn't think any more. Worry and weariness clouded her mind. The coyotes howled again, causing her to hurry her step back to the camp where Two Eagles was bedding down the horses.

Chapter Sixteen

The town of Cheyenne had been planned to parallel the Union Pacific Railroad tracks. Laid out on a broad plain where the gradual slope of the prairie met the steepening grades of the Laramie Mountains, it was now thirteen years past its beginning, lawless boomtown days, when it had held the distinction of being the first railroad terminal town in the Wyoming Territory. Bearing the name of a warlike Algonquian Indian tribe and centered around a vast cattle-ranching area, it boasted a population of nearly four thousand people and was the capital of the territory. The hastily erected shacks, stores, saloons, and gambling halls of the early days had been replaced by sturdier buildings made of painted lumber, brick, and stone.

The main avenue bustled with buggies, travelers on horseback, and people on foot hurrying about their business when Linc, Victoria, and Two Eagles arrived in Cheyenne during the late afternoon. They'd ridden long and hard throughout the day, stopping only briefly to eat a hasty meal of smoked fish, stale buttermilk biscuits, and apples. Staying close to the base of the mountains, they hadn't encountered any other travelers along the way except an old bewhiskered fur trapper who waved a hand at Linc's hailing, then trodded on, showing no interest in them.

Victoria had started to relax a little as more and more time passed and no Dandridges or anyone else appeared on the scene, but she knew by the tenseness she felt in Linc's body when she leaned back against him as they rode that he was taut with expectation. Even when they'd stopped to eat, he'd paced the small clearing, always looking to the hills and plains, keeping watch.

"From the look of the number of folks around, the Fourth of July tomorrow is going to be a rip-roaring event again this year," Linc commented from behind her on the mustang as they wove their way down the street. He motioned for Two Eagles to follow as he reined in the horse before a two-story red brick building. The painted sign overhead bore the name The Sassy Lady Saloon and Gambling Emporium. "This is Lottie's place," he continued, dismounting and reaching up to help Victoria down. "We'll be staying here."

Victoria eyed the establishment with apprehension. The outside looked respectable enough and well maintained. The wood trimming the doorframe and the windows to each side had had a new coat of white paint recently. But loud laughter and lively piano music boomed through the open doorway. Two well-dressed matrons kept their noses in the air as they passed by.

Just as Victoria stepped up on the wooden sidewalk, two men burst through the doorway locked in combat. Linc grabbed her around the waist and yanked her out of their path just before they tumbled into the street. He stood next to Victoria, laughing at the cowboys as they rolled around in the dirt, swearing and punching at each other. Other people poured out of the saloon to join the small crowd that quickly gathered to watch the two men fight. Some cheered and shook their fists in the air, rooting for their favorite man. Finally, the heavier of the two men pulled his opponent to his feet by his shirtfront, lifted him over his head, and heaved him into the nearby watering trough. The crowd exploded with cheers and raucous laughter.

"Lincoln!" someone shouted excitedly right next to Victoria.

Before she could turn to see who it was, a woman lunged past her to fall into Linc's arms. Her momentum drove him back a few steps, but he managed to keep his balance. A grin spread over his face.

"Damnation, Carlotta, you'd think you were glad to see me or something!" He set her upright on her feet.

She was as tall as his six-foot height, and looked at him eye to eye as she wrapped her arms around his neck. She wore the reddest dress Victoria had ever seen. Her hair, colored a bright auburn, was piled high on top of her head in perfect coils of curls.

"I am glad, you handsome devil! How long has it been? Six months? Seems like two years!" With that, she yanked his head forward and kissed him hard on the mouth. Linc's arms encircled her narrow waist.

The crowd cheered again, with some men whistling and hooting and slapping each other on the back. Victoria frowned, perturbed by what she considered to be a blatantly indecent display. Or perhaps it was something else that spurred her ire, for as the woman called Carlotta pulled back a little from Linc and half-turned to wrap one arm around behind him, Victoria saw that she was beautiful and more than amply endowed with womanly charms. The low neckline of her dress was edged in black lace and left little to the imagination.

Linc's eyes swept over her appreciatively.

"You're as pretty as ever, Lottie. I don't know how I could've stayed away so long."

"Good Lord, but you do know how to sweet-talk a gal. Come on in, darlin'. Your room's waitin', just like always."

Linc held up a hand to stop her from pulling him with her.

"Hold on, Lottie. I'm not alone." He gestured a hand toward Victoria. "This is Miss Spencer from England. She'll need a room, too. Victoria, this is Miss Carlotta Stockton."

Carlotta cocked an auburn eyebrow in Victoria's direction, eyeing her from head to foot. "Scrawny bit of a thing, isn't she? A might frail lookin'." She glanced back at Linc. Her tone became more serious with her next words. "What's she to you, darlin'?"

Linc's eyes flicked to Victoria before he answered.

"A friend is all. We've been riding hard since dawn. Some folks in Laramie had plans for her she didn't cotton to."

"Well, any friend of yours is a friend of mine," Carlotta stated, but she looked as if she doubted Linc's explanation. While Linc turned his attention to Two Eagles, she carefully scrutinized Victoria again. After a moment she seemed to finish sizing her up. Twitching her turned-up nose, she stuck her chin in the air and looked away with an indifferent air.

Two Eagles stepped forward holding the reins of their mounts.

"I take horses to livery stable, then go see Standing Bear. He'll know of braves who will ride with us."

Linc gave him a curt nod, then turned with one arm around Carlotta's waist. The other he swung around Victoria's middle so he could propel both women along into the saloon. Reluctantly, Victoria allowed him to guide her. Some of the people who had gone out to watch the fight followed them back inside.

The big open main room of the saloon was crowded with people. Tobacco smoke clouded the air, obscuring the crystal chandliers hanging from the wood-beamed ceiling. The piano player had resumed his energetic playing for the many customers at the gaming tables situated around the room.

Several men and more than a few of the scantily clad young women present called greetings to Linc as they passed the long wooden bar. It didn't take Victoria long to figure out what kind of place this was. Even if she hadn't seen the sign outside, she would have been able to tell by the scandalous way the women dressed in practically nothing and boldly hung on the men who were drinking and gambling at the tables.

She frowned, casting a disapproving glance toward Linc, but he wasn't paying any attention to her. Instead, his eyes seemed to be following every movement Carlotta Stockton made. Victoria's annoyance mounted as she watched the tall woman walk behind the bar. Reaching underneath the highly polished mahogany counter, Carlotta brought out two keys, which she held out to Linc.

"I'll have the girls tote up a bath for you, darlin', so you can wash off all that trail dust," she said, letting her long, pale fingers stroke along his arm. "Then I'll be up to share a tasty roast beef supper—and anything else you have in mind. You won't be too tuckered for our usual romp, will you, Lincoln?" She said the provocative words to Linc, but cast a smug glance toward Victoria, who was shocked by her words.

"Have I ever been too tuckered, Lottie?" Linc took the keys from her and traced a line down the side of her slender neck with one of them.

Carlotta smiled.

"Never, darlin'."

"Linc Masterson, you ring-tailed varmint!" came a shout from the poker table. A man of medium height with shoulder-length dark hair scooped a small pile of coins into his hand and got up to saunter over to the bar. He wore a battered brown cowboy hat cocked jauntily to the side of his head, dust-covered faded denim pants, and a baggy gray homespun shirt. When he got close enough, he threw his arms around Linc and squeezed him in a bear hug that nearly lifted him off his feet.

"Easy, Calam. You'll crush the daylights out of me!" Linc exclaimed with a laugh.

The man let go of him and guffawed loudly.

"I'd like to do more'n that to you, you good-lookin' polecat! I told you, if you ever git tired of these fancy skirts like Lottie here and hanker for a *real* woman, you come lookin' for me!"

Victoria's eyes widened at that last statement.

"Now what would Flagg have to say about that, Calam?" Linc grinned, throwing his arm around the newcomer's shoulders.

"Aw, he's out chasin' some bank robbers. I reckon he'd be glad for the rest from me!"

"Now, don't tease, gal," Linc went on. "You know you're true to Mad Bart."

"You could tempt any gal to stray just a little, honey. You're at least going to save me a dance at the big hoedown tomorrow night, ain't you?"

"Don't I every year?"

"Well, good! Let's all have a drink on it. Barkeep, set 'em up here! Whiskey!"

"Comin' up, Calamity," the burly man behind the bar replied, immediately setting four small glasses on the counter.

"Victoria," Linc said then, drawing her by the arm closer to the bar. "I want you to meet a good friend of mine, Martha Jane Canary, the best army scout, bullwacker, and Indian fighter you could ever want to cross trails with. Calam, this is Miss Victoria Spencer of London, England."

"England, huh?" Martha Canary grabbed Victoria's hand and pumped it vigorously. "You're a far piece away from home, missy. Don't pay no mind to Linc's braggin' on me. Everythin' he said is true, o' course, but I ain't as good as him in doin' any of them things. I just do my best an' don't ask no quarter from nobody. Folks call me Calamity Jane—Calam for short, I guess 'cause I manage to get into a fix or two now an' then."

"If it were only now and then, it'd be a relief to all of us," Carlotta stated, sounding haughty as she picked up a glass which the bartender had filled from a long-necked bottle.

Linc reached for a glass and handed it to Victoria, before

getting one for himself.

"This is just what we need to wash down the trail dust. Better sip at it, English. That's a small glass, but what's in it can kick like a mule."

He downed the whole amount in his glass in one gulp. Calamity Jane did the same. Carlotta lifted her glass toward Victoria, then took a healthy swig. Not to be outdone by any of them, Victoria sniffed the dark amber liquid, then took a gulp. She started to choke before it reached the back of her throat.

"There, there now, take it slow-like," Calamity cautioned, slapping her hard on the back. "Bein' able to down a whole snort o' good whiskey takes plenty o' practice, don't it, Linc?"

"That it does, Calam," Linc agreed with a smile. "But I don't think Miss Spencer will ever take a real hankering to it. She's used to finer things."

Victoria glared at him as air again rushed into her lungs. She felt like a complete outsider among them, the brunt of their scorn, and she didn't like it.

"Now that you've had your little reunion with your . . . friends, don't you think we should be about our *business,* Mr. Masterson?"

"I was just about to suggest that. This way," he directed, pointing toward the stairway across the room.

Victoria was only too happy to leave the bar. She was bone weary from the traveling and worrying if Sir Giles, Alden Cummings, or any of the Dandridges were close at hand. She had to admit she liked Calamity Jane for her friendly manner and earthy good humor. But she wanted nothing more than to get away from Linc and Carlotta Stockton.

Her increasing irritation with both of them gave her a sudden vigor. She walked briskly away, side-stepping several customers to get across the wide room. Without being obvious, she noticed the expensive furnishings around the room, the gilt-framed landscape paintings on the wood-paneled walls, and the elegant green velvet draperies hanging at the windows.

Linc followed her up the stairs. She waited at the top, tapping her foot impatiently. A young woman dressed only in a robe and a man with no shirt on came down the hall arm-in-arm. The man leaned down to whisper something in the woman's ear. She laughed and squeezed herself closer to him.

Victoria watched them with disdain. She may have led a rather sheltered life on an English estate, but she'd read many books, some of which even her father wouldn't have approved. She'd had very little experience concerning man-and-woman relationships, but she knew about how some people endulged their baser physical urges. Linc Masterson was such a person. Given his upbringing in this primitive land, what else could be expected? Even she had been weakened by this territory and the violent happenings of the past few days to the point where she'd fallen into the trap of Linc's prowess and handsomeness. She'd kissed him and even made a deal to *marry* him! She hated to remind herself of these truths and especially her scheme, but she had to. She wished she could tell him just what she thought of him and then leave this God-forsaken, heathen territory forever! Leave him to his brazen tart, Carlotta Stockton! But she couldn't. They'd made an agreement, and she had to stick to it. Her future and Deborah's depended on it. The only consolation she had was to tell herself that everything involving Linc Masterson was only temporary. She had to stay with him for protection, had to get married to him to get her inheritance, but only for a little while—as *short* a time as possible. She hoped this town of Cheyenne had at least one good lawyer in it who could secure a divorce for her as soon as it was expedient!

"How could you bring me to such a place as this?" she demanded angrily. "This is no more than a cheap bordello!

And these women are just common—"

"They're gals who're honest and damned hard working!" Linc cut in sharply. His dark brown eyes flashed with fury. "They've never had the soft life and advantages you were born to, Miss High-and-Mighty! Seems to me you shouldn't be throwing judgment stones when you're doing just about anything you have to right now to survive, just like they are!" He grabbed her roughly by the elbow and propelled her a little way down the hall to a door. Jamming the key into the lock, he opened the door with such force that it crashed loudly against the inside wall. "This is your room. Get in it and get cleaned up. As soon as I wash off this dust, I'm going to see a friend of mine here in town, Reverend Fitzgerald, to make the arrangements for getting us hitched."

"Then you still intend to go through with our plan?" she asked, the words tasting as bitter on her tongue as the whiskey had. She hated being ordered around by him, or reminded of what she needed to do now.

"Of course, though the idea doesn't sit too well with me. I gave you my word, didn't I? Are you having second thoughts now?"

"Absolutely not," she lied. "What's your plan for our . . . marriage?"

"Fitzgerald's Lutheran. You're likely Episcopalian. That's the religion most of you English lean to, right?"

Victoria was taken aback in surprise.

"How would someone like you know that?"

"I read a lot. I can write, too. Amazing, isn't it?"

There was no mistaking the malice in his voice. Victoria dropped her eyes, feeling more uneasy and annoyed than ever.

"I didn't mean to imply . . ."

"You'll find this room comfortable," he went on, ignoring her remark to wave a hand inside. "Lottie runs one of the best places in town."

The mention of Carlotta Stockton set Victoria's anger on edge again.

"Yes, she seems very . . . accommodating. Especially to certain guests. I only hope the wall between our rooms is very thick. I've no desire to hear any of your indecent carryings-on during your 'usual romp' with her!" She snatched the key out of his fingers and marched into the room, turning to slam the door so quickly that he had to hop back out of the way to keep from being hit by it.

Linc stared at the closed door with narrowed eyes. Damn, but she could rile him! Those emerald eyes of hers could sure flash fire when she got on her high horse. What the hell difference did it make to her what he did with Lottie? It wouldn't affect their deal at all.

Entering his own room, a wry smile began to creep over his lips. He thought about the stolen kisses they'd shared. Victoria had insisted from the start that their deal remain strictly business. But now he knew that wouldn't have to be. A woman got quick-mad like that for only one reason. She was jealous of Lottie! Pure and simple. Even though she called him a savage and seemed to hate everything he was, he'd gotten to her. He could get the money he needed from her and everything else she had to offer, if he wanted it. His plan to have her had worked, and he hadn't even been aware that he was carrying it out! But he'd have to play her real careful-like. One wrong move now, and she might shy and buck like a high-spirited bronc.

Carlotta waited until Linc had closed the door to his room before she tiptoed past it and knocked on Victoria's door.

"You'll be wanting a bath sent up, too, I suppose?" she asked icily when Victoria opened it.

"Yes, as soon as possible, if you please."

As Victoria started to close the door again, Carlotta pushed it open, forcing her way into the room.

"What do you think you're doing?" Victoria demanded,

frowning.

"I'm letting you know the way things are between Linc and me." She swung around to face Victoria. "Linc is my man, Englishwoman. I've had a claim staked on him for a long time. Keep away from him."

Angered by the intrusion and the threat, Victoria crossed her arms and faced the tall woman squarely, refusing to be intimidated.

"Tell me, does Linc know about this so-called 'claim'?"

"Of course. He always comes back to me because *I* can give him what he needs. I know how to satisfy a man like him."

Victoria couldn't resist. She knew it was wrong to say the next words that sprang to her lips, but she couldn't stop herself. She hated Carlotta's arrogance. She looked her right in the eye.

"If that's true, Miss Stockton, then why is he marrying me?"

"W-what?" Carlotta suddenly paled. Her rouged mouth dropped open.

"That's right. We're going to get 'hitched', as Linc put it, as soon as possible."

"I don't believe you!"

"It's true. Ask Linc yourself."

"You can bet I will!"

She rushed out of the room. In a moment, Victoria heard her pounding loudly on Linc's door.

Chapter Seventeen

Victoria stepped into the steaming, bubble-filled water and gratefully sank down until only her head and neck showed above the high back of the portable metal bathtub. Never had anything felt so wonderful. She let out a deep sigh of happiness and indulged in the feeling of the hot water soaking into every inch of her tired body. Here, surely, was one of life's great pleasures. Nothing felt better when you were dirty, sticky with perspiration, and weary. Whether she were rich or poor in the future, at least she could hope that this small delight would always be available to her.

Right after Carlotta Stockton had stormed out of her room, Victoria had summoned one of the chambermaids herself to roll in the wheeled bathtub. For several minutes, Carlotta Stockton's loud voice could be heard throughout the hotel.

Afternoon sunlight streaked through the window of the room. Victoria raised one arm and watched the drops of water and soap bubbles glisten on it. She glanced around. These were hardly the first-class accommodations she was accustomed to having when she traveled with Sir Giles. Once, this had been a fairly elegant room. The flower-patterned paper covering the walls showed a tasteful design, but now it showed the fading of age. Two bricks held up one side of a four-drawer burled hickory dresser where a leg was missing, causing the chest to tilt at a precarious angle. A narrow maple washstand holding a plain white pitcher and basin stood in one corner next to the double-sized bed.

The breeze rolled hot, dry air through the open window, fluttering the age-yellowed lace curtains. Victoria's glance moved to the big bed. She studied the worn patchwork quilt on it for a moment, frowning when she thought about the kind of illicit activities that had likely taken place there. She hated the thought of sleeping in a bed used by the wanton women and crude men downstairs, but it at least looked clean, and she felt too exhausted to be overly particular.

Carlotta Stockton drifted into her thoughts. Victoria's light brows knit together as she wondered about just what kind of relationship the beautiful woman had with Linc. She'd called it a claim. But somehow Victoria knew that Linc Masterson wasn't the kind of man any woman could claim, at least not for very long. There was a restlessness about him, an underlying tension that showed through even when he stood tall and statue-calm before adversaries such as the three awful assailants in the alley back in Laramie. Something was unfinished in his life, something he still sought with a cold-blooded cunning. Was it just that cattle ranch he wanted to wrest away from his half-brother? Or was there something else he wanted, even needed? Power? Wealth? Revenge?

Well, she'd never find out the answers to those curious questions. They wouldn't be together that long, she was certain. Then Carlotta Stockton or any other woman could have him, with her blessing! She wanted as little as possible to do with the likes of Lincoln Masterson. He annoyed her and haunted her. She wanted to run from him and to him at the same time! It made no sense. No one had ever made her feel that kind of confusion before.

Suddenly, the door to her room crashed open. Victoria gasped in surprise and grabbed for a towel she'd left folded over a three-legged stool close by. But before she could reach it, Linc strode into the room, looking furious.

"Leave here at once!" she cried, ducking down below the rim of the tub.

He ignored her order, slamming the door behind him with a loud bang.

"I just spent the last thirty minutes dousing Lottie's explosion! Damnation, woman! Why in blazes did you tell her we were getting hitched?" He stood before her with his hands on his narrow hips, frowning fiercely.

"Well, it's the truth!" She wanted to stand up to counter his bullying, but she found herself in a very awkward position for doing that. Clearly Linc wasn't bothered by the fact that she was naked in a tub of water where the bubbles were fast disappearing!

"There's the *whole* truth and *some* truth!" Linc ranted on. "You're getting mighty selective in which you're telling, I'd say. And I don't like having a hot-tempered, jealous woman on my hands!"

"Miss Stockton is jealous of *me?*" Innocence dripped from Victoria's lips.

"Ha! You could say that, though I don't know why she would be. There's no competition."

Victoria's brow creased.

"Just what do you mean by that?"

"I mean, you're not half the woman she is. Lottie can ride and shoot and slug whiskey better than any two men I know, not to mention how she is in *bed!*"

"Well, those are certainly all *fine* qualities a woman of good breeding would want to have, especially in this God-forsaken territory where a person can't even take a bath without a rude intrusion!"

"You're one highfalutin' woman, aren't you?" He advanced toward her, his face shrouded in anger. "Hellfire! I risk my neck helping you get shed of your uncle's corral! I shoot it out with Zeke Dandridge and his boys so they won't find—"

"You did that for Two Eagles!" she shot back defiantly,

warily watching him advance across the small room.

"Well, it just happened to save that pretty little hide of yours again, didn't it? And what do I get for my trouble? Insults! And not even a bath! *You* got the tub *and* the hot water! Well, not for long!"

He stopped right next to the tub, glaring down at her while he pulled his shirttail out of the top of his pants.

"What do you think you're doing!" Victoria demanded, watching wide-eyed as he started to unfasten the buttons down the front of his sweat-stained shirt.

"Just what it looks like. I'm going to take a bath!"

"But you can't! *I'm* taking one!"

"Not for long, you aren't!"

With his shirt hanging open in front, Linc stepped around behind Victoria, grabbed her under the arms, and hauled her out of the tub, dumping her in a heap on the worn braided rag rug on the floor.

"There, you make a mighty pretty sight right there for now," he noted, letting his dark eyes flick over her. His smile held a touch of wickedness when his glance came to rest on her arms crossed over her ample breasts. Reaching for the dingy towel on the stool, he tossed it to her, then sat down on the edge of the bed to pull off his boots.

"Why, you . . . you . . . *terrible beast!"* Victoria was beside herself with anger and astonishment. She scurried to cover herself with the inadequate towel, unable to think of any stronger names to call him at the moment. "How dare you handle me in such a manner!"

"I dare anything I damned well please, Victoria. You should know that about me by now. Lord, don't they teach you any good cuss words over there in old London? That's another thing Lottie can do a far sight better than you. You should've listened when she was swearing up a storm at me just now." Still frowning, he yanked on the buckle of his gunbelt to release it. Placing the gun and holster on the three-legged stool, he took off his grimy shirt. His pants followed, landing on the floor next to his shirt and boots.

Victoria stared at him openmouthed. He was stark naked again, the way he'd been at the line shack when the bull attacked her! Embarrassment stunned her into silence as she gaped at the full sight of his magnificent, muscular body directly in front of her. Her face flamed with an intense heat which then spread down all over her. Her stomach somersaulted. She tried to look away from him, but couldn't. Everything about him was purely male, all lean and powerful and rippling with strength and sinew.

Linc climbed over the edge of the tub and sank down into the water, letting out a deep sigh of pleasure the same as Victoria had done. When he leaned forward and submerged his head in the bubbles, she hurried to her feet and ran to the bed, where she snatched up the quilt and quickly wrapped it around herself. Seething with anger, she had to fight hard against an impulse to grab his gun and shoot him with it!

He emerged again and shook his head, sending a spray of water at her. Wiping his hand over his face to clear his eyes, he reached for the bar of soap on a small dish on the floor.

"You should have ordered up Lottie's big-sized tub," he said, lathering the soap in his hands. "Then you wouldn't have to wait your turn. This one's a might small for the two of us. You're welcome to use the water after I'm through though."

"How generous of you! I'd rather be thrown into an erupting volcano!" She sat on the bed and clutched the patchwork cover let around her, glaring at Linc with undisguised malice. If she could only leave the room, but that was out of the question when she had no clothes on. She could just imagine what would happen if she went downstairs into the gambling hall with just a quilt around her! And she couldn't get dressed with Linc right here.

"Oh, I hate you for this!" she ranted at him. "You're an uncivilized, uncouth lout with no sense of propriety!"

"Yes, you seem to bring out the best in me, English," he replied with a cocky grin that deepened the dent in his square-angled chin. He snorted a laugh and raked his lathered hands through his black hair.

Victoria seethed. She felt stunned by the strange feeling that suddenly shot through her, and she couldn't stop looking at him. She despised herself for feeling this primitive attraction. It was wrong and ridiculous. She'd just said she *hated* him! And she meant it! How could she feel that way and still be unable to pull her eyes away from this indecent display of his manliness?

Perturbed, she got to her feet and tried to pace around, but the dragging quilt tripped her. She lost her balance and fell toward the tub, grabbing hold of the side of it just in time to catch herself. Linc's eyes were closed against the soap running down his face. The rinse bucket of water sat right within Victoria's reach. Feeling a wicked impulse, she let the coverlet drop to the floor so her hands could be free. In the next instant, she snatched up the big wooden bucket by its rope handle and dumped it over Linc's head!

"What the—" he yelled just as the water gushed over him and the upended bucket covered his head. The rest of his words became angry gurgles as Victoria shoved down on his shoulders, completely dunking him underwater.

Laughing, she stooped to retrieve the quilt from the floor and triumphantly swung it around her as Linc came up sputtering. He yanked the bucket off his head and flung it across the room so hard it hit the opposite wall with a loud crash.

"Why you sneaky little she-cat!" he spat, rising out of the tub like a cobra flared to strike.

Victoria swung toward him and her eyes shot wide open in shock and fear when she saw him jump out of the tub and rush toward her.

"Linc, no!" she cried, trying to dart away from him. But the quilt tangled in her legs again, and she fell onto the bed.

Pulling the coverlet off her, Linc grabbed her by the arm and hauled her up. In the split second she was standing, he swung his arms under her and lifted her off her feet.

"Let go of me!" she yelled, twisting and beating on his chest with her fists.

Ignoring her, he took only two strides to get back to the tub.

"So you want a bath, do you? Well, allow me to give it to you!"

"No, don't!"

Her protest didn't stop him from getting back into the tub and plopping down, carrying her with him.

"Oh, you terrible, evil barbarian!" she raved. The water splashed out everywhere as she thrashed in his lap.

The tub started to roll back and forth on its small wheels, but Linc paid no heed to it. Instead, he wrapped his arms around Victoria and pulled her back against his chest, immobilizing her with a vice-like hold.

"Now stay still!" he ordered fiercely. "I'm going to give you a damned bath, woman, or I swear I'll drown you trying!"

She was no match for his strength, but her fury made her attempt to escape anyway. She tried to twist from side to side, but he only tightened his hold and pressed her harder against him. What she suddenly felt beneath her as he forced her to stay on his lap made her instantly stop moving. Again, her eyes widened in shock. His body was hot and hard—everywhere!

She went limp in his arms, feeling defeated and frightened. He wouldn't hurt her. She sensed that. Her fear was of herself when she was like this with him. She felt confused, bewildered, overwhelmed.

"Why are you doing this?" she beseeched weakly, wearily laying her head back against his shoulder and closing her eyes.

"Because you need to learn who the boss is here, Victoria." Sternness laced his words.

"Why? Why do you have to be in charge? Men have tried to rule my life for as long as I can remember. I hate it. I hate how it feels . . ." She bit her lower lip to stop it from quivering.

Linc shifted a little so he could look down at her. He lifted his wet hand and stroked his fingers gently down her cheek.

"I know how it feels," he said quietly. "But right now this is the way it has to be, my beautiful English, because you haven't the slightest idea of the terrible danger you've gotten yourself into, taking on your uncle, Clint Dandridge, and me, all at the same time . . ."

Her long, pale lashes slowly parted, allowing the deep green gems that were her eyes to come to rest on his face. She looked uncertain, innocent, so vulnerable.

Linc felt an ache start deep inside him. He wanted her. Yet there was more than just a physical need. A fierce protectiveness swept through him. She didn't belong here, didn't deserve what her kin was doing to her. She should be mistress of some old and grand English estate, where she could live a peaceful, stately existence, the kind she'd been reared for. Wyoming was no place for a woman like her. The harsh land would destroy her, if the tough and ruthless breed of men didn't do it first. He had to help her. The deep sense of Sioux honor that Two Eagles had instilled in him when he was a child demanded it. And he had to do it for another reason as well—he didn't want anything to happen to her. He admired her fight, her spirit, her need to find her own destiny at any cost. In that, she was very much like him.

The ache grew to stronger desire as he continued to hold her against him. He slid his fingers down the side of her slender neck to the small indentation at the base of her throat. The warmth and softness of her flesh aroused him, beckoned him to search for more. But the look of timidity in her large eyes spoke of a chastity he hadn't seen in the gaze of a woman in a long time. He felt the tenseness in her body, knew she was paralyzed, not with fear, but with uncertainty.

Linc felt a great weight of responsibility come to rest on his shoulders. He knew how to handle a woman as well as he knew how to handle his gun or a good horse. Each one was different, but with experience, you learned how to read them. One shot with a gun, and he knew the feel of the weapon, its weight and how it fit his hand, the pull of the barrel as the bullet careened along it.

Breaking a wild horse took patience and know-how, too. Just like now with Victoria. He must go slowly, gentle her the way he would a spirited, fine-blooded filly. First, she had to hear his voice, low, steady, coaxing. Then she must learn his touch, come to trust it and the man behind it as one who wouldn't harm her. He wanted to win her to him without breaking her spirit. He wanted this first time with a man to be good for her. This, too, was something he hadn't bothered about in a long time. The pleasure of the moment had ruled his dealings with women over the last few years.

Victoria waited, wondering with all her might what she should do next, dreading and longing for what Linc might do to her. Her heart pounded rapidly. Hardly any air entered or left her lungs, for she barely breathed. She stared into his dark brown eyes, hoping to read an answer to the confusion churning up her insides.

Finally, he spoke.

"You asked for my help, Victoria," he said softly, picking up a strand of her hair that had fallen forward and lay against the top of one lovely, rounded, up-turned breast. He rubbed the silky strands between his fingers. "Trust me. You're in my territory now. I know the way . . ."

His words held more than one meaning, she knew. Instinctively, she also realized what he was about to do to her. She saw the glint of desire and determination light up his eyes, and recognized his dawning need, as only a woman can.

Her body and mind felt split in two. Nothing in any of her very proper experiences during her twenty years of life had prepared her for a man like Linc or a moment like this one. Her mind urged her to remember her training in modesty and propriety, and resist him. This was wrong. Linc wasn't her proper husband. He wasn't even her bargained-for husband yet! She'd always wanted to save herself for the man who would court her traditionally, wed her honorably, and bed her lovingly. A man with whom she could build a life and family and future. She didn't want to spend these precious, once-only moments with a ruthless gunfighter in a stifling hot room of a frontier brothel in the midst of this Wyoming Territory!

Those were the logical arguments of her rational mind. But her body began to pulse out a very different message to her. Every part stirred to life as Linc's fingertips stroked small circles across her shoulder and along her arm. Then he reached out to run one finger lightly and slowly over the top of her naked breast.

"Please . . . don't . . ." she protested faintly, giving some homage to her conscience. Feeling a tremble sweep through her from head to toe, she pressed her lips tightly together to try to hide her reaction from Linc. Though he held no branding tool, his touch burned into her flesh just as surely as the blacksmith's iron had marked the flanks of her father's horses.

Linc sat mostly behind her, so she didn't know where he would touch her next. The suspense further tormented her. She expected him to lift her from the tub and carry her to the bed across the room. But he didn't. Instead, he began to bathe her.

Ignoring the washcloth, he found the bar of soap and lathered it to a thick foam between his hands. Then he slowly rubbed the bubbles along her right shoulder and down her arm. His movements were completely unhurried and deliberate. When he reached the ends of her fingers, he drew them up to his mouth and pressed them against his lips, kissing them softly. Then he did the same to her other arm and hand.

Victoria turned her head to watch his handsome face. He didn't speak to her, but the warmth in the depths of his eyes and the slight lifting of one corner of his sensuous mouth told her he was as pleasured as she was by this bath. The tenderness in his small gesture of kissing her fingertips conquered her will more than brute strength or forced ravishment ever could have.

Linc rubbed the foam over her stomach. Then his hand moved upward and over her breast. Victoria closed her eyes and put her head back against his shoulder. A small moan escaped her lips. She stayed perfectly still, afraid he would stop and afraid he'd go on and do even more to her.

His wet, slippery fingers barely touched her nipples at first, yet they reacted immediately, becoming taut and pointed when his caress went on. Amazement overwhelmed Victoria. Inside, she came alive with excitement. A liquid heat she had never known before radiated from an unlocked depth, spreading throughout her body with quicksilver speed. All of her senses danced with sudden awakened expectancy. Her breath caught in her throat in a small gasp. She couldn't think of anything except his hands, his body pressed against hers.

Linc pushed her a little away from him and slowly used his hands to wash her back. Then he returned to her breasts again. Over and around them, he moved his experienced fingers, gently fondling each hardened nipple in turn. He found great pleasure in caressing Victoria. Feeling her lovely virgin body come alive beneath his touch ignited his own desire to a heightened pitch. Primitive instinct urged him to take her now, but he used his civilized will to hold it in check, knowing that the longer he waited, the better the pleasure would be for both of them. She wasn't ready yet. Her body didn't move with the energy of growing passion. She didn't murmur her need or cry out for fulfillment. But these things would come if he could only be patient.

But each passing moment made waiting more and more difficult. As he kept washing her and then cupped his hands to gather water to rinse her, Victoria began to move against him. She rubbed her back along his chest and turned her head to kiss his neck again and again. She lifted her wet fingers to run them over the side of his face. He caught them with one hand and kissed them, harder than he had before, more feverishly. He slid his other hand more rapidly over the front of her body, moving from breast to breast, then downward over her stomach to the inside of her thighs.

The lower half of her body began to sway on his lap. The contact aroused him fully, ending his patient seduction. He suddenly rose from the tub, lifting her with him. When they reached the bed, he lowered her gently on it, then lay down next to her.

"Don't be afraid, English," he whispered tenderly, stroking her wet hair as he looked deeply into her eyes. "There may be a little pain, but it won't last. The pleasure will make up for it, I promise."

Before she could speak, he began to kiss her. Her lips, her neck, and downward, over her breasts. His tongue and lips teased her straining mounds for long, lingering minutes. Then he used his hands and fingers to trace a path over the rest of her body, touching and arousing every sensitive part of her. All the while he murmured softly to her, coaxing her to surrender her will, give in to her need and desire.

Excitement exploded through every fiber of her being. His seduction was shocking, intimate, overpowering. She had no will against it, nor did she wish to. Her body responded joyfully, eagerly, intensely. She arched her back, straining to follow every movement of his hands and lips over her. Her mind whirled in a frenzy of images that were only Linc. She wanted only him. Nothing else mattered. Just his fingers, his mouth, his soft urgent words drawing her closer, more deeply to him. Then as she writhed beneath his sensual onslaught, his mouth descended over her breast with demanding hunger. He nipped and kissed first one, then the other, sensing Victoria's quickening passion in her movements and small cries of ecstasy. When she murmured his name and raked her hands through his hair, forcing his head down so his mouth had to remain at her breast, he raised himself over her. Her long, slender legs opened to him, and he throbbed to plunge deeply and forcefully into her. But his determination to do her no harm overcame his intense desire for just the moment of time it took to enter her gently. For as long as he could, he moved slowly within her, building her pleasure and his own. She clung to him, gasping his name, urging him deeper and harder into her. Waves of ecstasy washed over her, driving her mad with needing him. He answered her with his own overwhelming longing. The climax of their joining brought an explosion of rapture so tumultuous between them that their breaths were whisked away and their bodies forged into one by passion's blazing fire.

Victoria never wanted to stir from Linc's side. She didn't want to speak or move, fearing the magical spell that had woven between them would be broken forever. She hung onto him as her body cooled and her heart returned to its normal beating. She kept her eyes closed, basking in the wonderful afterglow of their lovemaking. In her mind she remembered his hands on her, tasted his mouth consuming hers, felt him within her, moving in perfect rhythm with her. Never had she dreamed that being with a man could feel so exciting, so all-consuming. Her body still tingled from the demanding touch of his lips and hands. There had been no pain, just a sense of a slight resistance inside her when he entered her. And, as Linc had promised, the ec stasy that came with climax made everything else seem insignificant.

"Are you all right?" Linc asked, keeping his voice low, soothing. She nodded and snuggled closer to his side. He gently stroked her arm and then her breast to slowly ease her back to reality. He wasn't in a hurry to have that happen himself. Touching her kept his own pleasure and arousal alive a little longer. He could have allowed it to surge to life again very easily. Victoria could do that to him. A look from her, a taste of her lips, and he knew he wouldn't want to hold back from taking her again. The hunger was there, a hunger he hadn't known since . . .

Abby loomed into the muddle of his thoughts. Everything he'd ever wanted—the ranch, vengeance on his half-brother—was tied up with her. His passion for her had been wild, uncontrolled. It had cost him a lot. The same fever had filled him when he'd started caressing Victoria. But somehow she'd taken him beyond just physical fulfillment. His body's desire was spent for now, but his heart still hungered for her, wanted to keep her close, longed to open to her. He'd never felt this way before with a woman, not even with Abby. The feeling spooked him. His granite insides were cracking. Victoria was getting to him—to the deep, protected part of him that he never let anybody see. He always knew when a woman was after him, wanted what he could give her. But Victoria hadn't used any beguiling ways on him. Yet somehow she'd gotten into his blood, made him crazy with wanting her, needing her. He didn't know how she'd done it. He only knew he needed to back off now, put distance between them, before she could get a tighter hold on him. If he let her fill his mind and body, he'd never get what he'd set his sights on a long time ago. With Spencer and Dandridge breathing down their necks, he had to stay on the edge, alert to everything. Damnation! Right now, he didn't even know where his gun was!

Swinging his head around on the pillow, he flicked his

eyes around the room until he spotted his gunbelt on the stool by the tub. With a twinge of disgust, he realized how far he'd gotten from it. And he hadn't locked the door to the room either. Dandridge or anybody else could have walked in on them, and they'd have been near helpless to defend themselves. Especially a few minutes ago . . .

Linc felt anger wash over him. Careless. He'd been damned careless. In this territory, that could cost a man his life. And a woman's, too. That's what Victoria did to him—made him lose his edge of caution. He had to get away from her. And he would . . . after he held her for just a few more minutes.

After a while, he felt her relax. Her breathing became regular. He knew she was asleep. He could leave her now and clear his head of this loco-weed passion. Think straight again.

He eased himself away from her and rolled off the bed. While he buttoned his shirt, he let his gaze drift over her, feeling his fingers wanting to touch her again, to move over her soft, warm, yielding body. She was beautiful, nobody could argue that. Slim and graceful reminding him of the fleet antelope that roamed the plains. There was plenty more desire wrapped up in that pretty body of hers, he knew. At another time, under different circumstances, he would have been glad to . . .

Linc shook his head to try to banish the thought of making love to Victoria again. It was crazy. They were as different as night and day. Their paths just happened to cross for a while, that was all. They'd both get what they wanted, then go their separate ways. He'd get the money from her to buy the note on the ranch, maybe get his son in the bargain. Victoria would get her precious inheritance and sail off to England to live a life of pampered ease on some country estate. She'd marry some stuffed shirt with just as much money as she had, with titles as long as his arm, and raise a passel of little short-britches. That's where she belonged.

Here in Wyoming was where he belonged. End of story.

Then why did the thought of Victoria with another man twist his gut so hard?

Frowning, he pulled on his pants, then yanked on his boots. Taking time to search the side pocket of Victoria's discarded riding skirt, he found what he was after and turned to go. Grabbing up his gunbelt and hat, he left the room, quietly closing the door behind him.

Chapter Eighteen

Victoria awoke with a start in the darkness. An instant of panic shot through her when her sleep-clouded senses couldn't register the surrounding room at first. Then the sound of blaring piano music and raucous laughter coming from somewhere below her brought memory rushing back. Carlotta Stockton's saloon. She'd come here with Linc and they'd . . .

She shivered as the cool night breeze flowing in the open window hit her bare skin. With it came sharp recollection of all that had happened with Linc.

Twisting her head toward his side of the big bed, she knew, even in the darkness, that he wasn't there. She had no sense of his presence. The room felt chilled and empty. Yet she moved her hand to the sheet where Linc had been to make sure. No body heat of his remained. He must have left her some time ago.

The realization made her heart and spirit sink. Where was he? Why did he leave her after . . .

"Dear heaven, what have I done?" she murmured in confusion. She sat up slowly and reached for the patchwork quilt, pulling it about her like a protective shield. Drawing her legs up, she wrapped her arms around them and pressed her forehead into her knees. How had it all happened? It was difficult to piece things together. She still felt tired, so utterly spent.

The bath, the fight, the anger. Then the closeness,

Linc's gentleness, the heat of his body . . .

He made love to her. Passionately.

Victoria raised her head to look out the window. Now she knew what it meant to lie with a man. Linc had made her feel as if her whole being had opened to him. She'd never known such wondrous pleasure and excitement. He'd aroused her, satisfied her completely, yet left her with a great need deep inside. How could that be? Need for what?

With a groan of misery she accepted the answer—need for him, for his kiss, his touch, his man's power surging into her, sending her to the magnificent heights of desire and ecstasy.

What kind of a wanton was she? To make such love with a man who wasn't even her husband. Of course, she'd asked him to become her husband, but that had been only a business proposition. She'd never intended to . . .

She groaned again. Such an act with a man went against all of her breeding, all she'd been brought up to revere and cherish. She was soiled now. Not even Alden would want her for a wife once he learned she was no longer chaste.

She tried to reason her outrageous behavior as an act of rape. Linc had forced her. Hanging her head, she knew that wasn't the truth. Yes, her will had been overcome, but not by brute strength or violence. Instead, he'd used his spellbinding eyes and demanding lips, his searching hands and splendid, virile body to break down the barriers of all she'd been taught about womanly behavior.

A shudder drove through her like a sharp blade. Thinking about him and what he had done to her body brought warring feelings of indescribable pleasure and relentless shame. What if his seed should beget a child within her? Dear Lord, what would happen to her then? To the child? Linc's child . . .

So many questions plagued her. Why had he left her? Her heart dropped to a further depth of despair. He must have found her wanting as an intimate partner. She had no experience, no knowledge of how to pleasure a man. In her innocent shock over what he was awakening in her, she'd just lain there, nearly paralyzed from the fear that he would stop and the hope that he'd go on kissing her, touching her.

She felt so mixed up. How she wished she'd never left England! There men and women had civilized laws and moral codes to live by. A savage like Linc Masterson had no rules but his own. Hadn't he told her more than once that he did as he pleased? He paid homage to no man—or woman, for that matter!

A spark of anger ignited in what small reserve remained of her pride and dignity. He'd used her, then disappeared. Cast her aside once the bloom of virginity was off the flower!

Carlotta Stockton loomed into her mind. He was probably with that brazen doxie right now! Laughing with her while he told her the story of the prudish English maiden who'd been such an easy conquest for him!

Now she knew how men could kill! If she had a gun right now and Linc stepped back into the room, she'd shoot him right between the eyes!

But she didn't have a gun. Instead, to vent her wrath, she punched the feather pillow hard and threw it across the room.

"I hate you, Linc Masterson!" she muttered through gritted teeth. "You took—"

She froze, halted by another shock of thought. He'd taken her body and what else?

In panic, she flew out of the bed, dragging the quilt with her. In her haste to locate the kerosene lamp on the bureau and strike a match to light it, she stubbed her toe on the bricks balancing it. Wincing with pain and hopping on one foot, she tried to hold the match steady enough to touch it to the wick. When the lamp's glow flooded over the room, she turned and limped to the pile of her clothes on the floor. Still feeling the frantic suspicion, she jammed her hand into first one side pocket of her riding skirt and then the other. Empty, both of them.

Tossing aside her skirt and then her dust-covered boots and dirty white blouse, she finally spotted Hannah's wallet lying on the floor at the foot of the bed. Snatching it up, she yanked the two leather pieces open. With horror, she saw her worst fear confirmed. Linc had stolen everything. Only the vellum envelope remained. All the money was gone, even the English pound notes. She had nothing left, not even her honor.

Suddenly, someone pounded on the door.

"You in there, honey?" came a slurred voice from the hallway. "Ole Jake's got him a itch, an' Lottie says yer jus' the gal to scratch it!"

A booming laugh accompanied the crude words. In fright, Victoria barely had time to clutch the quilt around her before the door slammed back against the wall and a huge man pitched into the room. He held a half-empty bottle in one hand, using the other to steady himself against the wooden door frame. More matted brown hair covered his face than the top of his balding head. His paunch of a belly hung well over his gunbelt and strained his dirty, red-checkered shirt at the buttons. His shirtsleeves were rolled up to the elbows, revealing thick, hairy arms smudged with dirt.

"Well now, Lottie done tol' me right. You are jus' awaitin' fer me. Ain't you a purty one." The hulking man grinned, revealing a gold front tooth surrounded by empty spaces where other teeth should have been. He lurched forward.

"NO!" Victoria cried in horror, barely escaping the grasp of his huge paw of a hand when he lunged for her.

He got hold of the edge of the quilt as he fell forward, pulling it from her grasp when he hit the floor and rolled.

"Whoee! This here's gonna be my lucky night!" Rumbling a laugh, he moved toward Victoria again with a swiftness that belied his bulk and drunkenness.

Fully naked, Victoria ran around the end of the bed and jumped onto the mattress, snatching up the rumpled sheet and clutching it in front of her.

"Stop! Don't come near me!" she pleaded, not recognizing her own voice for its hysterical high pitch.

He only laughed again.

"You wanna play, honey? That's all right with old Jake! Makes the catchin' an' gittin' a heap more likeable." Showing a lecherous grin, he half-circled the bed, put the whiskey bottle on the washstand, then positioned himself between Victoria and the door.

Seeing that route of escape cut off, Victoria shot a panicked glance toward the open window. They were on the second floor. She could be killed if she jumped.

Jake lunged at her while her attention was diverted for that split second, but she side-stepped out of his way just in time, running to the washstand. Grabbing the whiskey by the bottle neck, she held it up threateningly.

"Stay back, I'm warning you!" she cried.

His drunkenness made him unsteady on his feet. But he kept keen eyes fixed on her.

"Now, honey, you don't wanna be wastin' good liquor like that. Let's have a drink together. Then old Jake'll give you a little kiss!"

He reached out for her again with both arms. She swiftly ducked under them and darted behind him. Swinging with all her might, she hit him right on top of the head with the bottle just as he started to turn around. The glass shattered loudly, scattering a spray of whiskey and splintered pieces everywhere.

She feared to breathe, shocked that the blow didn't

knock him down. She stood frozen, staring as her attacker swung all the way around, raising a big hand to rub his head.

"I declare you got spirit, gal!" He laughed heartily. "I like that in my women!"

He ran at her again. Victoria cried out in alarm and jumped backward. But she wasn't fast enough. One of his hairy arms caught her at the waist. His momentum whirled her around and brought her down. She hit the floor hard with her shoulder. He fell half on top of her, pawing at the sheet she was still trying to hold.

"Now I got you!" he roared.

"NO!" she screamed, frantically hitting him with her fists and twisting her body. It was like fighting with a mountain. Rank smells of liquor and filthiness overwhelmed her. The struggle made her senses reel, but she managed to kick out hard with one leg.

"Oof!" Jake gasped when her foot sank into his fat belly.

For a moment, his grip slackened and she was able to scramble away from him, leaving the sheet clutched in his hands. Naked once more, she jumped to her feet and dashed back to the washstand, grabbing the heavy china water pitcher. Jake quickly got to his feet and dove for her again. She raised the pitcher with both hands and brought it down with all the force she could muster. It hit him squarely in the forehead. Broken crockery flew everywhere. Jake dropped down to his knees right in front of her, stunned.

She shot for the door and ran right into Linc's arms!

"What the—" he stammered, startled as he caught hold of her.

"Oh, thank God!" Victoria gasped, clinging to him.

"Hellfire!" Linc cursed, frowning fiercely as he took in the scene in a quick glance.

Jake was just struggling to his feet again when Linc strode to him and hauled him to his feet.

"Linc!" he shouted, a look of shocked surprise on his face.

"You picked the wrong gal tonight, Jake!" Holding the big man by the collar and seat of the pants, Linc whirled him around and heaved him straight through the window. Jake's high-pitched yell drowned out the sound of the shattering glass.

Linc hurried to Victoria, yanking her back into the room. He snatched up the sheet from the floor and threw it to her.

"Damnation, cover yourself! Can't I leave you alone for a minute? You hurt?"

Victoria's fear and humiliation swiftly changed to rage. Did he think that horrible man's attack had been *her* doing?

"I'm not hurt, no thanks to you! I hired you to protect me! Instead you ravage me, steal all of my money, and leave me alone and defenseless in this terrible bordello! Your wonderful friend Carlotta Stockton sent him up here! Where were you? Great heavens, you threw him out the window!" She angrily whirled the sheet around her like a toga.

"I got rid of Jake, didn't I? He was lucky I didn't shoot him. I expect you to help some in keeping yourself out of trouble! From what I saw, you had Jake down." He put his hands on his hips. He didn't know who he was madder at—Jake for blundering into the room, himself for leaving her in this place alone, or her for looking so all-fired beautiful! His frown deepened. "*I* ravaged you? As I recollect, you were a very willing partner, lady. Hotter than a branding iron. I didn't hear any protests. And I sure as hell didn't see you fighting me off like you did Jake just now!"

"Well, I wanted to! I should have! Why did you steal my money?"

"I didn't steal anything. I took payment for my

services—*all* my services." As her green eyes widened and her mouth dropped open, he added impatiently, "Don't look so outraged. I used the money for that." He flipped a thumb toward a large package wrapped in brown paper lying on the floor near the door. Walking over, he picked it up and tossed it on the bed. "If you're still interested in our business deal, you may want these for getting hitched in. I made arrangements with that parson friend of mine I told you about. You still want to go through with it?"

"How can I think straight when I'm practically naked and an awful man just attacked me?" She sank down on the bed, frowning and biting her lower lip to hold back the hot tears stinging her eyes. She *wouldn't* cry in front of him!

Linc almost went to her. He heard the anger in her voice and the catch in it, too. A need to protect her, even comfort her, swept through him, but he used his strong will to fight it. Clenching his hands into fists to keep them from reaching out and touching her, he forced himself to remember his goal of getting the ranch and keeping her out of Giles Spencer's hands and Clint Dandridge's path as well. He couldn't let her draw his attention to anything else.

"Well, make up your mind quick-like," he ordered sharply, turning away from her and striding to the door. "Time's running out. Your uncle and Dandridge can't be too far off. I'll be downstairs at the bar with Lottie. Come down when you decide."

The room was suddenly empty. Victoria stared at the closed door hanging crookedly on its broken hinges. After a few minutes, she walked to the window and looked down to the street. A crowd of people was gathered below. She couldn't see a body lying anywhere. What had happened to her assailant?

She turned back to the room and forced herself to put aside the terrible incident with the man called Jake and concentrate on Linc.

How could she possibly marry him and keep their relationship strictly business? Yet he seemed willing to do just that. His voice just now had held the same serious, detached tone as it had when they'd first discussed their reasons for marrying. He seemed unaffected by their lovemaking, as if it were just a passing fancy with no meaning to him—and likely it was!

A scowl touched her face as she thought of him with Lottie Stockton now. When a man looked like Linc did—all virile and chiseled and handsome—women were never far from hand. They were attracted to him just as she had been. He could take his pick, and surely did any time he wanted. She was just one in a long line.

"Damn you, Linc Masterson!" she swore heatedly, pounding her fist into the pillow on the bed. "How could you be so stupid, Victoria? To allow a man like him to . . ."

To do what? She sighed deeply, remembering only too well how he'd rescued her so many times, how the taste of his mouth, his touch, his torrid and tender possession of her, and she of him, had awakened feelings in her that she never dreamed existed.

What a fool she was. And reckless. What if the heated lovemaking with Linc did result in a pregnancy? She meant nothing to him beyond the money he needed. He might marry her as part of that deal, but he'd never stay with her. She didn't want him to!

She felt a sickening ache of regret and fear in the pit of her stomach. Why did the man who had reached her heart have to be a rough-hewn gunfighter, a killer? A man who made no promises and asked none. Death rode with him at every turn in this wild Wyoming Territory. It would be just a matter of time before someone faster tested his skill against the professional gunman, Linc Masterson. She'd read the dime novels about American

Westerners. Recalling the blood-thirsty accounts about them, she frowned and rallied her stubborn resolve. She *wouldn't* allow him into her heart, not now, not later, not ever!

Chapter Nineteen

Victoria walked to the destroyed window of her room and leaned her shoulder against the wall next to it, clutching the wrinkled sheet around her. The night sky looked deeply black, lightly dusted with pinpoints of stars. That strange feeling came over her again as she gazed along the rooftops of Cheyenne's main street, the one she'd had before, when Zeke Dandridge and his men had come to Two Eagles' ranch. Her fortitude had been tested again, and she'd come through. Linc had helped her, of course, but she didn't feel broken by the shocking experiences of nearly being raped and having a man thrown out this second-story window to a possible death below—or by making love with Linc. She felt in control, oddly and calmly in control of herself.

But the thought of the future did cause a small shiver of panic to run up her spine now. She must go through with her plan to marry Linc. It was the only way to keep Sir Giles and Alden Cummings at bay until she could settle the legalities of her inheritance. How she wished there could be another way to avoid the clutches of Alden and her uncle. But the pressure of time forced her hand. She held no love or even respect for her father's greedy and cruel brother. She wanted to ruin his plans for her at all costs.

Guiltily, she thought of her dear sister Deborah, still caught in the harsh web of Sir Giles' authoritarian guardianship. How frightened Deborah must be, not knowing what had happened to her after she'd fled the Dandridge ranch. She wished there were some way she could let her sister know she was all right.

All right . . . hardly a good choice of words, Victoria thought derisively. She was on the run with a gunslinger, being chased by men who meant to do her harm when they caught up with her. She'd passionately made love with that same killer, whom she didn't even like, and a drunken lout had nearly raped her, almost within the same hour!

She glanced toward the pile of her dirty riding clothes on the floor near the bureau. She was clean now from the bath she'd shared with Linc. She hated the idea of putting on the dusty, sweaty skirt and blouse again.

Suddenly, she remembered the package Linc had brought with him. She picked up the wrapped package and untied the string. A lovely, slim-skirted satin dress lay within the paper. It was trimmed with a small ruffle of cream-colored lace at the edge of the puffed half-sleeves and around the scooped neckline.

A sigh of delight escaped Victoria's lips as she lifted the dress into the air. Only once had she seen such a delicate pink color—in the hardy summer roses that grew along the northernmost stone wall on her family's country estate in England.

A wave of homesickness washed over her, saddening her. She'd loved finding those roses with Deborah when her sister had been well enough to join her in a morning ride. Her senses now easily recalled their fragile fragrance and velvety petals, the pleasing sight of the gentle pink against the rugged gray rocks.

Blinking to clear the melancholy reminiscence, Victoria rummaged further through the brown paper and found high-button shoes, white stockings, lace-edged pantaloons and matching chemise, and even a wooden-handled hairbrush. Everything looked like it was her size, which surprised her. Apparently, Linc had a good eye for the female form!

Money lay under the pantaloons, the British pound notes that had been in Hannah's leather case. She'd accused Linc of stealing this money. How wrong she'd been about him. The American money was all gone, but she realized he'd likely spent most of it on the costly clothes for her and their lodgings here at the Sassy Lady. *If* he had to pay for their accommodations! More than likely Carlotta Stockton was only too glad to provide him a free bed!

Frowning, she thumbed through the English bills, then retrieved the wallet from the top of the bureau and tucked the notes into it. Again she saw the folded vellum envelope containing some sort of letter of Hannah's. She put it in the wallet, too, absently thinking she might read it later. Her concern now was Linc, waiting downstairs for her.

She quickly put on the dress. It was beautiful, she had to admit. The satin clung flatteringly to the curves of her figure.

Linc wanted her answer about their business deal. Well, she planned to go through with the bogus marriage as planned. She'd look her best when she walked down that staircase with her head held high, showing as much dignity and breeding as all her years of strict upbringing had taught her!

Applying her determination to the hairbrush, she untangled the long, straight blond tresses with more vigor than necessary. Using the pins she'd had before, she twisted her hair into a knot atop her head and secured it there. Then raising her chin high, she left the room.

Linc saw her come to the top of the stairway. Leaning on one elbow with his back to the bar, he'd been watching the battered door of Victoria's room, only half-listening to Lottie's lively chatter next to him. He wasn't sure what Victoria would do. She'd been through a lot the past couple of days. He didn't like the thought of harm coming to her. The need to protect her reared in him again. But he forced himself to think it was because a man was supposed to take care of women, especially well-bred, fragile ones like Victoria Spencer. He wouldn't let himself imagine it was because he was beginning to feel something deeper and more disturbing about her.

He watched her descend the stairs, wearing her pride as boldly as the expensive pink dress. She had spunk, no denying that. But just how much could she take? Maybe he should just ride into the hills with her for a while, until things cooled down. He thought about that for a quick moment, then put it aside just as fast. Victoria Spencer would no more fit into the wild countryside of the land of his Indian ancestors than he would attending some fancy ball in London.

The color of the dress was right. The little shop hadn't had a wide choice of garments, but when he'd spotted the pink one, he'd easily imagined Victoria in it. He wasn't disappointed now. She was a picture of delicate elegance, descending the staircase as if she was about to walk into a fashionable English society party, instead of coming down to a frontier saloon and gambling hall.

He felt something stir in the pit of his stomach. The rest of the smoky, lamp-lit room seemed to go out of focus. He couldn't take his eyes from her. The satin molded over her sensuous curves, and the swells of her breasts showed just above the lace around the neckline. He wished he didn't know what the lower parts of those pale and lovely breasts looked like, tasted like . . .

He let his eyes lift to her beautiful face. Her cheeks were flushed with sunburn. A slight smile turned up the corners of her mouth. She looked completely out of place in the big open room filled with cowpunchers, railroad laborers, tinhorn gamblers, and hardened women who sold their favors to any man with the price.

"My, but ain't she somethin'?" muttered a wizened old miner without any teeth. He leaned on the bar to Linc's left, gazing fixedly in Victoria's direction.

"If you like uppity, skinny foreigners," Lottie noted icily. She stood to Linc's right, a half-filled whiskey glass in her hand. Glancing at Linc's face, she frowned and drained what was left of the amber liquor.

Victoria walked straight to Linc, keeping her eyes fixed on him.

"I believe we have some business to conduct with a friend of yours," she stated.

"You sure?" One of his black brows cocked in question.

She didn't flinch, even though his penetrating dark brown gaze seemed to drill into her inner being.

"Yes," she said firmly. "We have an agreement." She hooked a hand around his left arm and beamed a chilly smile in Lottie Stockton's direction. "We mustn't keep the good reverend waiting."

Lottie's blue eyes narrowed with the glowering look she cast toward Victoria, but she said nothing. Turning her back, she slammed the whiskey glass down on the bar counter and walked away toward the poker table.

There'll be more hell to pay for this, Linc thought, expelling his breath through his teeth as he watched Lottie storm away. Damnation, he'd have to do some fast talking to get in her bed again. But he knew Lottie well enough. She was burning mad at him now, but he knew where and how to touch her to bring her around to his way of thinking. She wouldn't resist him long. He'd see her yet tonight, take his mind off this pink dress and the stubborn, exasperating woman in it!

"Then let's get this chore done," he said impatiently, turning back to Victoria. He didn't look her in the eye, but, instead, nearly dragged her along with him out of the saloon.

The evening hour grew late, but the main street was crowded with riders and other people beginning an early celebration of the Fourth of July. Shots filled the air as men fired their guns for noisemakers. Spooked horses shied and whinnied. Music and laughter drifted to the street from other saloons.

The festive atmosphere didn't spread to Victoria. As she hurried along trying to keep pace with Linc's long stride, she felt as if she were heading toward a fate worse than death, instead of a wedding. The night air was warm, but it didn't dispel the chill of apprehension that filled her.

Reverend Gustav Buchmann guided a modest congregation of Lutheran followers from a wood-framed church at the north end of Cheyenne. He was a short, gray-haired man, close to sixty years old. He bounded toward them with a lively step when they entered the back of the single-story, whitewashed church.

"Lincoln, my boy, so you did bring the lass!" he greeted enthusiastically, pumping Linc's hand vigorously. Then he turned to Victoria. "She is a right pretty one at that. You must be Miss Spencer. Gustav Buchmann at your service in the good Lord's work, miss. Surely I never thought I'd see the day when my good friend here, Lincoln Masterson, would take a wife, but now that I've seen you my dear, I can see why he's decided to pledge himself to you."

He took her hand in his with a firm grip, flashing a warm smile.

"R-reverend Buchmann," Victoria stammered, suddenly feeling uncomfortable under his sincere, blue-eyed gaze. She could tell the wiry minister was genuinely happy for them, likely thinking their desire to marry was motivated by affection. Apparently Linc hadn't told him the cold details of their business arrangement. It was just as well. She couldn't bring herself to do it either. For some reason, she didn't want to be the cause of disappointment to this man.

"I'm glad you approve, Gus," Linc replied, not meeting his friend's direct look. "Could we get on with the ceremony?"

The clergyman gave a hearty chuckle as he smacked Linc on the shoulder.

"Patience never was one of your strong points, but in this case, I'll spare you the sermon on the subject. I remember a man's blood can run hot. Come to the front, and we'll get on with this marrying business. Margret!" he shouted as he turned and led the way down the aisle between the rows of wooden pews. "Linc's here—Fetch my Holy Bible!"

Linc took Victoria's elbow to follow him. A plump, gray-haired woman close to Reverend Buchmann's age hurried into the sanctuary from a side room just as they reached the front of the church. Her brown eyes crinkled with happiness when she saw Linc. Linc grabbed the older woman around the waist and swung her in the air.

"Margret, you never looked prettier!" he declared with a grin.

"Liar! And saying such a thing in the good Lord's own house! Put me down this instant, Lincoln Masterson!" She seemed to be chastising him, but there was laughter in her voice and a smile on her face.

"Victoria, this is Gus's better part—his wife, Margret," Linc introduced when he'd set the other woman on her feet again.

"Mrs. Buchmann," Victoria returned with a nod.

"Oh dear, call me Margret. Everybody does. My, how lovely you are." The older woman's smile matched her husband's in warmth. "I'll be your witness for your marriage. And I'll wish you both all the happiness that Gus and I have known."

Victoria heard genuine caring in Margret Buchmann's voice. It increased her uneasiness, making her hope the ceremony would be over quickly so they could leave this place and these good people.

The simple wooden altar was adorned with an embroidered white linen cloth, and a two foot brass cross rested on a wooden stand in the middle. No stained glass, carved statuary, or other adornments decorated the small church. Sturdy, plain-hewn pine had been used to furnish it. How

ifferent this house of worship was from the old and elegant
aurches of England. But to Victoria, the small sanctuary
lt welcoming in its simplicity.

"Well now, I have the marriage document right here,"
everend Buchanann said, taking a well-worn leather-cov-
red Bible out of his wife's hand. Opening it to the middle,
e withdrew a printed piece of paper. "As soon as the vows
re said, both of you will sign it, to comply with the laws of
ur Lord's good church and this fine Territory. Come for-
ard now, the two of you, and let's be getting you wed."

"Oh, don't start yet, Gus!" Margret said, turning to
urry to the door by which she'd come in. "I forgot my
owers!"

Only a few minutes elapsed while the older woman left
ne altar, then returned with a bouquet of yellow flowers.
Vhen she reached Victoria, she placed the bouquet in her
rms.

"They're from my very own garden out back," she ex-
lained, beaming a proud smile. "I picked them when Linc
old us the news about you earlier. Took all the thorns off,
o there'd be no danger of pricking yourself. You can't
narry without flowers. I hope you like them, dear."

"They're lovely," Victoria answered, holding them close to
er face to take in their delicate fragrance. Roses again.
The smell renewed the feeling of homesickness in her, just
s seeing the color of the pink dress had done earlier. How
he longed to be back in England, away from all that was
appening here . . .

She couldn't look at Linc. Instead, she listened very hard
o the words Reverend Buchmann spoke, willing him to be
lone quickly. The seriousness of his tone sent a wave of
uilt through her. She let her eyes shift around the altar,
hen lowered them in shame at the sacrilege in which she
vas participating, realizing God knew every thought, every
eeling in her heart. He'd know she'd made love with Linc
out of wedlock, and also that she had no intention of keep-

ing the vows she was speaking. Neither did Linc.

Her stomach churned sickeningly. She hoped a fiery bo of judgment lightning wouldn't strike the church, for th Buchmann's sakes, even though she and Linc deserved it!

"And will there be a ring," Reverend Buchmann asked a the appropriate point in the ceremony.

Victoria was amazed when Linc nodded and reache into the side pocket of his thigh-length black coat. She suc denly realized that he had on new clothes, too. She'd bee so angry with him back at the saloon that she hadn't nc ticed he no longer wore his dirty riding clothes. Now h had on what she'd learned Americans called a "Sunday-gc to-meeting" coat, along with black pants, a white shirt, an neatly tied black string tie. Even his black boots looke shiny and new. Apparently Hannah's money had gone long way!

His handsomeness stunned her. His rugged features hel an expression which in daylight would have conveyed rea sternness. But the dim light from the two kerosene lamp hanging from the ceiling took the sharpness from his face He looked as apprehensive as she did as he fished aroun in his pocket. When he brought out a simple polished gol band, her eyes widened in further surprise. It was only a little too big when he slipped it on her ring finger.

"I d-do," she stammered when it came her turn to tak the marriage vow. She had no ring to give him. It wasn' customary, though it could be done, but in her confusio over all that had happened, she hadn't given it a thought nor had the opportunity to get one. She was overwhelme that Linc had. Again he'd surprised her.

But she knew the ring held no more meaning than th marriage words. She noticed Linc's tone hadn't been a strong and sure as it usually sounded when he'd faced he and recited his vows. His voice cracked once, and he low ered his dark eyes from her face to her hand, which he helc lightly in his bigger one.

"I now pronounce the two of you husband and wife! Congratulations!" Gus Buchmann boomed, smacking the Bible closed. Then he slapped Linc on the shoulder, grinning from ear to ear. "It is the practice to kiss the bride right about now, son."

Linc's eyes swept to Victoria's face. For a moment, she caught a glimpse of something in his look. She had to keep her lips from smiling when she realized it was panic she saw there, a split-second realization of what he'd just done. She had the same feeling exactly! But he quickly masked the look when he leaned down to give her a peck on the cheek.

"Well, I hope you'll do better than that later, Linc, my friend!" The older man laughed heartily.

"Oh, Gus, leave them be," his wife chided, though without sternness. Then she hugged Victoria and Linc in turn. "May our good Lord's blessings be upon the both of you. I declare, I'm so happy I could cry a bucket!" She reached for a white handkerchief tucked into the waistband of her plain gray skirt. Dabbing at her eyes, she waved them toward the side room. "Come along now. Get the legal papers signed, so there'll be no question as to the propriety of the joining of the two of you."

Victoria let Linc lead her by the elbow. Almost in a daze, she signed the printed form under his name. The reverend and his wife signed the document, too.

Linc talked with his friends for a few minutes longer, but she could say nothing. She barely managed to say thank you and good-bye when it came time to leave. She walked numbly beside Linc through the front door and out into the warm evening. The night breeze felt cool against her flushed face and bare arms. She couldn't bring herself to look at Linc—her husband now in the eyes of men and God.

Chapter Twenty

"I could use a drink about as strong as a peddler's snake-bite medicine. How about you?" Linc asked, leading Victoria by the elbow into the Sassy Lady Saloon.

It was the first time he'd spoken to her since they'd left the church as husband and wife. Victoria hadn't felt very talkative herself, so she'd been glad for his reticence.

"N-no, I don't want anything to drink," she stammered, making herself look at him. "Why did we have to come back here? Can't we stay somewhere else?"

"Town's full up because of the Fourth tomorrow. You're lucky to have a room at all."

She frowned, just wanting to get away from him, escape to someplace quiet where she could be alone to think through her feelings about him and this business arrangement they'd gotten into together. How could she find some solitude in a place like this? The loud music, talking, and laughter made it hard for her to even hear Linc speaking right next to her. The thick tobacco smoke hazing the area made her queasy stomach turn over with added nausea. The piano player pounded out a lively tune on the battered upright in the far corner of the room, adding to the din around her. Her head began to pound.

"I'm going upstairs," she suddenly announced. Then she felt a moment of panic, wondering if Linc would be coming to the room with her. He seemed to want to keep their dealings strictly business, just as she did. But there was the very disturbing matter of that afternoon, when they'd fought in the bathtub and ended up in each other's arms . . . Legally, he now had the right as her husband to be in her room, in her bed. She didn't want that. Or did she?

Confusion tore her mind in two. She didn't want to feel anything for Linc. A part of her wanted him to be just a hired man she needed for protection and for help in ruining her uncle's evil schemes. But another side of her—the newly awakened woman—couldn't stop thinking about what it had felt like to lie in his arms, to have him unlock sensations and desires in her that she never knew existed.

She saw Carlotta Stockton rise from a round table where four rough-looking men were playing cards, and turn in their direction. She groaned inwardly, dreading the inevitable confrontation. To avoid it, she started toward the stairway, but Carlotta stepped into her path.

"Well, did you get it done?" she asked in a nasty tone, hands on her hips. Despite her frown of disgust, she looked beautiful in a tight-fitting black silk dress, with her thick auburn hair piled high in ringlets on her head. The low-cut neckline went beyond provocative, leaving little of her ample breasts unseen. Her dark blue eyes smoldered with unconcealed hatred as they fixed on Victoria.

"Yes," Victoria answered pointedly, trying to appear undaunted by the other woman's malevolent look. Turning, she started to push past her. Carlotta grabbed her by the arm.

"You won't keep him, you know," she seethed close to Victoria's ear. "He's mine. Always will be. He'll be in *my* bed tonight, not yours. Just you wait and see."

Victoria cast a scathing glance toward Carlotta. The thought of Linc with the sultry saloon woman caused a heated flush of anger and jealousy to flash through her. She quickly denied the jealousy and convinced herself that her wrath was caused by her concern about their business deal.

She wrenched her arm away, knowing the other woman's mean grip left marks on her skin.

"I'm certain bedding you will please Linc no end, Miss Stockton. He prefers a woman of your sort. You're more than welcome to him. I have no further use for him tonight."

"He'll be mine for more than just tonight, you—"

Linc suddenly stepped between them.

"That's enough, gals," he warned sharply. "No use making a big ruckus over this again. I'm not in the mood for it. Don't you go getting possessive on me, Lottie. I've never been a one-woman man, and you know it. I told you I'd see you later. Let her pass." He swung an arm around Carlotta's narrow waist and pulled her out of Victoria's way.

"I'm not putting a claim on you, Linc, darlin'," Carlotta purred, draping herself over his shoulder. "But I know you need a *real* woman to heat up that quick-fire man-need of yours, not some simpering foreigner like her!"

Victoria didn't wait to hear more. The arrogant confidence lacing the other woman's intimate words made her own feelings reel. Anger and disgust jumbled in her tormented mind. Shifting the bouquet of flowers she'd gotten from Margret Buchmann to the crook of her arm, she gripped the skirt of her dress and stepped past Carlotta, whose taunting laugh drummed in her ears.

She was barely aware of her feet touching the wooden stairs as she hurried up them. Reaching the room she'd had before, she slammed the broken door closed as best she could and leaned back against it. Nothing was working out the way she'd planned. She felt as if a black cloud of doom hung over her head, ready to drench her with complete destruction. Even the beautiful wedding flowers she held in her arms had wilted. Their bright petals sagged on limp stems.

She squeezed her eyes shut to keep back the hot tears threatening to spill out. She hated Linc Masterson, hated all these crude, outspoken Americans, hated this wretched, uncivilized Territory! And most of all she despised herself for even beginning to feel anything for a rough and wild gunfighter, a man who killed for a living! Dear heaven, what had she done in marrying him?

"Come on, darlin'," Lottie coaxed, taking hold of Linc's arm. "Let's go upstairs now. I've been hungering for you all evening." She pressed her sensuous body along his side and nuzzled his neck with her lips.

Linc cocked his head toward her, absently aware of her seduction. He'd seen Victoria's emerald eyes flash with fury at Lottie. But she'd controlled herself and departed the room with complete poise and dignity. He'd watched her hasten up the stairs and out of sight, thinking to himself he was mighty glad to be rid of her. But he couldn't help admiring the way she handled herself. She was a proud one, all right, and a beauty. Stubborn, too. She intrigued him more than he cared to admit. Made it hard for him to keep his mind on the first rule a good gunfighter always followed: stay detached, never get personally involved. He'd been curious about her was all. Never had an English gal before. So he'd quenched his curiosity. He didn't need to bed her again. He could keep his crazy business deal with Miss Victoria Spencer.

Startled, Linc was struck by the realization that she was now Mrs. Lincoln Masterson, his wife!

Quickly turning his back to the stairs, he pounded a fist on the bar. "I need a drink, Tiny!" he shouted to the burly bartender. "Make it a stiff one! Better yet, give me a bottle!"

"Shore 'nuff, Linc." The man slid a full bottle of whiskey in front of him.

"We'll take it upstairs with us, darlin'." Lottie grabbed the neck of the bottle just as Linc reached for it. Holding his arm, she pulled him away from the bar, calling over her shoulder, "We don't want to be bothered by anybody, Tiny. You understand?"

"I hear you, Lottie," the big man agreed, laughing as he wiped the inside of a whiskey glass with a towel.

Lottie struck a match to the hurricane lamp, but kept the wick low so the room remained shadowed. Then she hurried around, picking up clothes that were strewn about and tossing them into a tall mahogany wardrobe closet. The big double bed across the room was rumpled and unmade.

Linc didn't wait for Lottie to bring two glasses from a silver tray on top of the three-drawer dresser. Yanking the cork out of the whiskey bottle, he tipped his head back and took a long swig of the amber liquor. When Lottie came to him, he put his arm around her waist again and roughly pulled her against him.

"You're right, Lottie. You're just what I need tonight."

He brought his mouth down hard on hers. Lottie didn't resist. She groaned eagerly and threw her arms around his neck, pressing her body fully along his length. She was breathless when he finally broke off the kiss and pushed her a little away.

"Get out of that damned dress!" he ordered fiercely, raising the bottle again.

Lottie laughed, unfastening the buttons down the front of the long black dress.

"I love it when you get that vulture look in your eyes, darlin'. Can't wait to have me, can you? You know I'm woman enough for you."

Linc watched her with narrowed eyes while she undressed and let down her auburn hair. The red-tinged curls tumbled around her shoulders, framing her face and neck like a twilight sky surrounds the setting ball of sunfire. He took another long drink, then put the bottle on the bedstand and took off his coat.

"Here, let me do that." Naked now, Lottie quickly came to him and started unbuttoning his shirt.

Linc let his eyes devour the pale skin of her shoulders and her ample breasts. Then his hands followed the same path. Lottie gasped and fumbled with the buckle of his gunbelt. When the holster dropped to the floor, she ran her fingers greedily over the rippling muscles of his arms and through the coarse dark hair on his chest.

"God Almighty, you're a fine piece of man, Linc Masterson," she murmured huskily, leaning forward to kiss the middle of his chest.

A small sound of delighted laughter sounded in her throat when Linc grabbed her by the hair and lowered his head to devour her mouth again. She answered him with equal fervor, pressing her lips against his and forcing his mouth open with her searching tongue while she rubbed her hands over his back and down to his waist.

Linc felt the whiskey curling in his belly, heating his insides. His senses were still clear, rousing to life under Lottie's expert handling. He kissed her possessively, letting go of his control so his mouth and hands could take in every part of her. She would be his, willingly, hotly, completely. The tiny cry in her throat and the way she clung to him left no doubt of that.

He whisked her up in his arms and moved to the bed. Nearly throwing her down on it, he quickly covered her body with his and found her mouth again. He closed his eyes to lose himself in the taste of her, in her woman's scent, and the feel of her hot, soft flesh against his. He entwined one hand in her hair and moved the other roughly over her breast. This woman was familiar to him. And she moved her body knowingly against him, knowing just how to arouse his desire the most. His need of her should be rising. His blood should be pulsing like volcanic lava through his veins, igniting every part of him. Why wasn't it? Something felt wrong . . .

The writhing woman beneath him coaxed and taunted him with gasps and small moans. She arched her hips and moved so he could have taken her easily. But he hesitated, not knowing why. When she spoke, the sound of her voice startled him.

"I can't stand this, Linc darlin'. Get your pants and boots off. Don't tease me. I need you to take me *now!*"

The voice was wrong. There was no lilting foreign accent in it. With confusion, he realized that the thick, curly hair in his hand wasn't right, either. It should feel fine and straight, slipping through his fingers like strands of spun silk.

He opened his eyes. The light in the room was dim and cast flickering shadows over the walls and across the bed, but Linc could see the woman clearly enough. No gem-green eyes stared back at him now, wide with wonder and desire. These were a smoldering dark blue, like a deep consuming pool. He ran his tongue over his lower lip, realizing the taste of her was all wrong, too. Carlotta. Not Victoria . . .

"Damnation!" he swore, rolling off of her to the edge of the bed.

"Linc! What is it? What's wrong?" Lottie sat up, looking as bewildered as he felt.

"I reckon this won't work tonight, Lottie. I got too much eating at me."

He didn't wait to say more, knowing he couldn't explain his loco behavior to her any more than he could to himself. Moving quickly, he gathered up his shirt, black coat, and gunbelt from the floor and left the room.

"Linc!" Lottie called after him, but he didn't hesitate one step.

Using the back stairway, he left the saloon and all the

raucous noise and gaiety behind, hurrying out into the night. He pulled on his shirt as he headed for the south end of town. Few people were on the street now.

Buckling on his gunbelt, he walked fast, moving past darkened stores and houses. In no time, he reached the end of the long main street. Ahead sprawled the open desert outskirting Cheyenne. Moon-touched and empty, it offered the precious solitude he sought. He kept walking, leaving the town behind.

The desert air felt cooler away from the buildings. It hit his perspiring chest where his unbuttoned shirt hung open. He stopped and raised his face to the gentle breeze. The desert usually calmed him, pulled him back to the roots of his Indian ancestry, which held the revered belief in oneness with all of the Great Spirit's creations. But now he knew no peace of spirit. One single thought kept churning in his mind: Victoria.

Chapter Twenty-one

Victoria paced the hot, stuffy room. She felt restless, closed in, apprehensive. She hated being here. Carlotta Stockton owned this place. A horrible bear of a man had nearly raped her and then been thrown out the window. He hadn't died. Linc told her Jake Horn ended up with only a broken leg from the fall and a firm resolve to give up women.

She looked at the bed. There Linc had made love to her so passionately and thoroughly that she knew she would never be the same again.

Shaking her head in bewilderment, she walked to the window and carefully raised the broken frame. The last time she'd looked out over the rooftops of the town like this she'd been simply Victoria Anne Spencer. Now her legal name included a new ending—Masterson.

She glanced down at the plain gold ring on her finger, wondering again how Linc happened to have it for the ceremony. Their marriage . . .

Groaning, she jumped up and paced the room, furious with herself because she couldn't get Linc out of her mind. Everything about him, every moment they'd spent together since meeting on the train to Laramie raced through her head in vivid, startling flashes. His dark brooding brown eyes, the deep timbre of his voice, his naked torso, his gentle and fiery possession of her when he made love to her . . .

But she also remembered his gun, for it was always present, always a part of him, along with the death that resulted from it.

She wondered if Carlotta Stockton felt the same dread about Linc's gun, his dangerous line of work. Likely not. When Carlotta had fawned over him and all but proclaimed her intentions to the whole crowded room downstairs, she hadn't seemed concerned about anything except getting him to her room upstairs!

Victoria felt so hot. And inexplicably angry. Removing her dress, she laid it across the top of the tilted chest of drawers to keep it from wrinkling. Her wedding dress . . .

She didn't want to look at it. Not trusting the security of her surroundings, she yanked the rumpled sheet off the bed and wrapped it around to cover herself, tucking in the edge at the top. Hanging loosely about her, it felt a little cooler than the tight-fitting dress had been.

Exhaustion crept over her, stealing into every pore of her being. She longed to sleep, to find release for at least a few hours from all that had happened during the day, all that plagued her mind.

Lying down on the bed, she closed her eyes and forced herself to think about England. That's how she'd calm her troubled thoughts, thinking back to her family's elegant and serene country estate. She'd been so happy there in her childhood, running over the green meadows, wading in the small swift stream that churned over the smooth stones bordering one side of the property. Dressing up in pretty outfits for the many guests her father always entertained. Memories. Such pleasant memories . . .

Linc hesitated with his hand on the knob of the saloon back door. He didn't want to go inside. The blaring piano music and laughter still boomed through the open windows. By going in, he ran the chance of running into Carlotta again, and he didn't want to do that. He'd had enough of her for the time being, though he didn't know why. Lottie hadn't changed. She was still a fine piece of spirited woman. And she wanted him, just like she always did. She'd been eager to bed down with him, no questions asked, no promises required. Just a night of hot pleasure together. So why wasn't he upstairs with her now?

He couldn't answer that troubling question. Even after he'd walked the desert for more than an hour to try to let the crisp night air clear his thinking, he didn't have an explanation.

He was going to spend the rest of the night in the loft of the livery stable with Two Eagles, but he wanted to check on Victoria first, just to make sure she was all right. It was his job, after all. One of the drunken tinhorns at the gambling tables could find his way upstairs the way Jake Horn had earlier. Or Lottie might go looking for revenge over the way he'd walked out on her.

He turned the knob of the back door and entered the saloon, climbing the dimly lit stairs to the second floor. No one was in the narrow corridor. Outside Victoria's room, he paused, putting his ear to the slightly tilted door. No one seemed to be stirring inside, but it was hard to tell for sure because of the noise coming from downstairs. After listening a minute longer, he started to turn away.

A piercing scream suddenly shattered the emptiness of the hallway. Linc's right hand instinctively dropped to his gun as he whirled around. A second scream quickly following the other sent him smashing through Victoria's door.

She was sitting up in the bed, sobbing hysterically. Crouching, he gripped the Colt and darted his eyes around the room. Seeing no one else there, he swiftly holstered his gun and crossed the room in two strides to gather Victoria in his arms.

"Here now, English, what is it?" he murmured against her soft hair. "Are you hurt? Was some cowpoke here again?"

Victoria clung to him, shaking hard and crying uncontrollably. She gripped the edges of his open shirt in her hands and buried her face against his bare chest. Her hot tears seared him where they touched his flesh.

For some time he just held her, sensing her helplessness, her fear. He wanted to hold her, let her know she was safe with him, that he'd do anything to help her, keep her from harm. That feeling stunned him. He'd never had it before. He never thought of anybody but himself, first and foremost. He'd set that rule in his mind long ago. But now an intense feeling of protectiveness toward her swept over him. He hated whatever it was that had frightened her so much. It instantly became his enemy.

Only the thin sheet covered her, and it had slipped down when he'd pulled her to him, so her lovely full breasts were half revealed as they pressed against his bare belly. His body reacted instantly to her nearness and to the softness and heat of her naked flesh. He longed to touch her more, move his hands over her beautiful body to prove to her that he was as close as possible, as near as she needed him to be.

She was very vulnerable at this moment. His need to care for her warred with the sudden fire of desire that ignited within his body. Her silken blond hair tumbled in disarray about her face. He stroked his hand over it to soothe her and also to feel the fine tresses slip through his fingers. He longed to press his lips against her forehead and then move down to her soft, yielding mouth.

Damnation! He cursed himself. How could he think of such things at a time like this, when she was so like a child needing gentle, fatherly comfort? He really was a selfish bastard, thinking of his own heated need for her now.

He tried to focus his mind on something else while he held her. He should have gotten her out of this room. Maybe what had happened with Jake Horn was the cause of her hysterics. But because of the Fourth celebration tomorrow, he knew all the boarding houses were as filled up as a stockyard corral at shipping time. There wasn't another room in the whole damned town where he could have taken her!

"I—I'm so glad you're here," Victoria finally managed to whisper, pulling a little away from him. "I was so frightened. A terrible nightmare. I have it often. About my father's death. It always seems so real."

Her liquid green eyes stared at him intently. Brimming tears still wet her long dark lashes. Her voice sounded breathless, touched by fear when she spoke again. "I'm glad to be awake. I don't know why his death haunts me so. It's as if something still needs to be done, something remains unresolved. Yet he's been dead for over five years."

She looked away and self-consciously pulled her hand away from his chest to reach for the linen sheet and pull it up to cover herself.

"You all right now?" Linc asked gently, almost raising his hand to her shoulder. But he stopped, knowing he had better not touch her again. He didn't trust his control.

She nodded. "Thank you for coming in," she whispered then paused, lifting puzzled eyes to his again. "How did you happen to be so close by?" One brow dipped downward in the beginning of a frown and her tone became sharper. "Did you have to leave Miss Stockton?"

Linc's own testiness flared at the mention of Lottie, mainly because of what had happened between them—or, more to the point, what *hadn't* happened! He didn't like being suddenly reminded that thoughts of Victoria had interferred with a wild tumble in bed with Lottie Stockton, of all women!

He got to his feet, needing distance from her. She was stronger now, herself again, no longer clinging to him.

"Hellfire, woman, what difference does it make why I was close by? I just was. I heard you scream and busted in, thinking you were in trouble. I took on the job of protecting you, remember? I've had a lot of cause to regret that decision, but I'll finish the job. That's all there is to it."

He strode across the room and made himself focus on the broken door lying on the floor. Picking it up, he examined the hinges.

"No fixing this tonight." He propped it against the opening. "Push the bed up against it after I go out. That'll hold it in place till morning. I'll be back then."

"Are you going to her?"

The question surprised him. He wasn't quite sure what he heard in her voice this time—anger, yes, but also a slight touch of that vulnerability again.

He kept his back to her.

"That's none of your business, Victoria."

"You are going to her."

The simple statement poked the ashes of his anger to heated life. He swung around to face her.

"No, I'm bedding down at the livery. Lottie and I didn't—"

He couldn't finish the sentence. The shadowy sight of Victoria sitting in the middle of the big bed with her hair cascading around her and the thin sheet barely covering her sensuous body hit him with full force. He'd never seen a more arousing sight in his whole life.

"I thought she was the woman you wanted."

More simple statements, asked by her lyrical voice and compelling deep green eyes. He felt his own eyes unwaveringly lock with hers. He crossed the room, stopping next to the bed, angry that she could make him feel so edgy.

"Of course, I wanted Lottie. Why wouldn't a man want her? She's one of the most hot-blooded women I've ever come across! She knows what she wants and she goes after it."

"She isn't the only woman like that!" Victoria shot back. "*I* know what I want, and it *isn't you!* You stand for everything I hate in this uncivilized place, everything I hate in a man!"

She whirled away from him to face the wall, but he grabbed her and knelt down on the bed, pulling her around by both arms so she had to face him again.

"Is that so. Well, you weren't singing that tune right here in this bed with me this afternoon! Seemed like you knew what you wanted from me bad enough then!"

She tried to twist away from him.

"That's a lie! I didn't want you to—to—"

"What's wrong, Victoria? Can't you say it? You didn't want me to make love to you, is that what you're trying to say?" He yanked her against his chest, putting his face close to hers. "You're a liar . . ."

His mouth descended on hers with the force of a hot wind plummeting down a sheer-rock canyon. When she was gasping for breath, he pulled back and, taking both of her wrists in one hand, used his other to catch hold of the sheet and yank it away from her. It was still wound around her legs, but he let the material remain for it kept her from struggling, the same as a rope. He pushed her back on the bed and straddled her with his knees, pinning her hands against the mattress on either side of her head. She twisted and tried to turn, but he held her fast.

"I think I need to teach you to enjoy what can be between us, English, so you can never deny it again!" A cool smile turned up the corners of his mouth.

Before she could protest, he kissed her again. More gently this time, he pressed his lips over and around her delicate mouth, drinking in the taste of her. If he was going to play teacher, he was determined to enjoy himself!

The softness of the skin of her face startled him as it had before. He ran his cheek along hers, knowing the beginnings of his whiskers on his jaw would feel rough to her but not painful. He buried his face in her smooth, straight hair, relishing the feel of it against his skin.

His body reacted sharply as each sense took in something more about her. He felt his fingers tingle to touch her naked flesh, knew in only moments he would be ready to penetrate deep inside her. He could take her easily. He was much stronger than she was. But he held back, used long-practiced discipline to wait to have her, wanting her desire and pleasure to be as great as his. He wanted her to feel the deep, driving need he felt. He closed his eyes and gasped for breath, willing himself to slow down, pause, hold.

Victoria knew she was no physical match for Linc. He could rape her or hurt her in any other way he wished. There would be little she could do about it now or even after. They were legally married. A husband had his rights regarding the marriage bed.

She set her mind. Using every ounce of self-control, she decided she wouldn't enhance his cruel pleasure in any way. She'd lie like a stone on this bed, no matter what he did to her. She'd see how much he enjoyed forcing himself on someone who was unresponsive and as wilted as the flowers on the dresser.

Squeezing her eyes tightly shut and pressing her lips together hard, she tried to resist the onslaught of his mouth and hands on her by lying perfectly still and showing no sign of the volcanic heat that began to course through her body. When his lips gently moved over one breast to kiss the tightened, aroused nipple, she made herself gulp hard to suppress the moan of agony that started to sound deep in her throat. He was torturing her, determinedly, methodically, exquisitely. She should hate him, hate what he was doing to her. She tried hard to loathe him. Any decent woman would, she raged in her mind, directing her thoughts away from him. But his hands kept caressing her, touching her everywhere, as if they didn't even notice her pathetic resistance, and she couldn't keep thinking of malice and opposition.

Never had a woman lain so passively in Linc's arms. She was as limp as a thrown lasso that missed its mark. Again he was surprised, taken aback by Victoria. She never did what he expected. That trait in her made him mad as hell because it kept him unsure, off-balance, and he didn't like the feeling. But at the same time, not knowing what she would do next intrigued him, drew him back to her again and again. Even now, when her resistance to his seduction of her sensuous body seemed strong and should have put him off, he felt the fire of desire blaze even hotter in his veins. He would make her feel the heat, ignite her passion if it was the last thing he ever did! He added huskily murmured words to his caresses.

"You're so beautiful, English, and you have a mighty strong will. But mine's stronger. I want you and you want me. That's the way of it between us. Accept it, and give in to the pleasure we can have. In the eyes of God and men, we're joined as husband and wife. But even if we weren't, we're joined here." He touched his hand to his heart and then to hers. "And you know it. I see now it's been that way since we first laid eyes on each other. Destiny's dealt us this hand, and we're going to play it out. I don't need this ring on your finger to make you mine,

Victoria. Now kiss me, damn it, and let me make love to you!"

His mouth found hers, and she moaned in anguished defeat and surrender as the warmth and taste of his lips and the tender, possessive movement of his hands on her body overwhelmed her senses. With her eyes closed, she couldn't see where he was going to move his expert fingers next. So the intimate places he chose startled and aroused her even more. An aching need began to grow deep within her. His closeness scalded her flesh, set it afire along her whole length.

Slowly, he drew the sheet from between them. Pausing just long enough to strip off his clothes, he quickly returned to lie down beside her. Victoria's eyes widened in surprise when she saw his man's need for her and then felt it pressing into her thigh as he entwined his legs with hers.

His mouth found hers again and she was lost in his impassioned embrace. One of his hands clutched her hair, holding her head while he consumed her lips. The fingers of his other hand moved slowly along her bare shoulder and down to her breast. With the lightest touch, they caressed the mounds of her flesh, circling and taunting the nipple to straining tightness. His mouth followed the same searing path, flicking and darting over first one swollen nipple and then the other. His hands stroked her flat stomach and slid over her hips down to her thighs. He parted her legs and slowly stroked his fingers along the sensitive insides.

She writhed beneath him, releasing all control of her will, eager to have him touch her, to drive her wild with need and passion. No longer wanting to hide her body's reactions to him, she let her senses fill with him. All else was lost from her consciousness. She began to move her hands over his hard-muscled flesh, reveling in the heat of his skin and the gasps that came from him. She sought to touch him as intimately as he touched her, to memorize every inch, every part of him. Lacking experience, she let instinct guide her. Her own breath caught in her throat. She held it there, afraid to breathe and risk ending the magical, exciting feelings pounding through her. She longed to be as close to him as possible, to feel his intense passion and his great tenderness. She felt amazed that he could show both extremes and arouse them in her.

Linc lay quiet beneath her, willing himself to hold back his desire so this wondrous exploration Victoria was working on him could go on. The tremendous pleasure she was causing in him sent waves of awe pulsing through him. He'd never felt this way. He wanted her more than any woman he'd ever known, wanted to hold her, sink his throbbing manhood deeply within her, hear her cries and gasps of ecstasy, bring her to the same frantic, pulsing, magnificent climax he would know. He couldn't wait any longer. His body demanded release, and he knew instinctively that Victoria was nearing the same pinnacle of rapture.

Rolling with her, he put her beneath him. Murmuring his love for all of her body, he parted her legs and moved between them.

Victoria arched her back to welcome him into her. She trembled violently from the heat of passion and the heightened anticipation, crying out when he thrust himself deeply within her again and again and caused waves of ecstasy to throb through the heated core of her being. Clinging to him, she moved in perfect rhythm with his splendid body.

At last spent, Linc held Victoria close, breathing deeply and letting his body and whirling mind slowly wind down to a normal pace again. He knew it would take her longer to descend from the rapture they'd reached together. He said nothing while he moved his hand gently over her face and then to the soft swollen curves of her breasts, caressing them. She smiled with pleasure and pressed against his length, murmuring his name and telling him of her great and wonderful contentment.

Chapter Twenty-two

Victoria lay perfectly still, watching Linc while he slept. The first faint crimson streaks of dawn sent fingers of coral-pink color through the window to touch the shadowy walls of the quiet room. She longed to snuggle close against Linc's side, become as intimately near to him as she had been again and again during the night, but she didn't want to wake him just yet. Relaxed in sleep, the tense, almost hard lines around his mouth were softened. His striking handsomeness made her breath catch in her throat. Churning desire welled up within her, along with some other intense emotion she was afraid to define. These feelings were very new to her, exciting, overwhelming, filling her with apprehension.

What would the hurrying dawn bring, she wondered. When Linc awoke, what would he be feeling? She knew there could be only one explanation for the deep-down need and longing she felt for him. She had fallen in love with Linc, quickly, completely, foolishly.

The thought tore her heart in two. She and Linc were so different, their worlds separate except for those few magnificent hours of last night when they were the only two people together in a world that seemed so distant and inconsequential. If only they could keep the outside world at bay. But the increasing light of sunrise dispelled that hope as it stealthily revealed the room around her. Too easily now, she saw where she was, remembered all of what she wished she could forget—Sir Giles, Alden Cummings, her hasty marriage to Linc. Even the thought of her sister brought no comfort, only more dismay, for she knew Deborah must be frantic with worry about her.

Sighing deeply, Victoria closed her eyes and tried to put aside her smoldering passion so she could think clearly, but she couldn't while she lay so close to Linc. The heat of his virile body spread easily to her. Her flesh still tingled from his torrid caresses during the night. Against her rational will, she longed for him to touch her, kiss her more. She ran her tongue over her lips, trying to recapture the taste of him.

A ripple of need and pleasure started to weave through her. Opening her eyes, she just wanted to look at Linc while he lay sleeping, unaware, unguarded. She studied the creases at the outer edges of his eyes, the sharp arch of his black brows, ran her eyes over each lock of curly black hair tousled over his forehead. The beginning of the day's growth of beard darkened his chiseled square jaw, spreading over his cheeks and just above his upper lip. It only added to his rugged good looks.

She would wake him soon, see his compelling deep brown eyes lift to meet hers. Those eyes could see into her very soul, strip away her reason and virtue, leave her longing desperately for him and what he could make her feel,

Tiny beads of perspiration dotted his forehead. Already the room felt stuffy, close. The new day held the promise of sweltering heat.

Lying on her side, she gently touched Linc's face. His eyes shot open as he jerked awake.

"I'm sorry. I didn't mean to startle you," she said softly, pulling her hand away. Linc caught it in midair. A smile spread slowly over his lips.

"You can wake me like that any time you want, English. Or this way would be fine, too." He half-turned and reached out, pulling her to him to kiss her tenderly.

Victoria closed her eyes and melted into his embrace. She couldn't keep a small moan of pleasure from sounding deep in her throat. The taste of his lips on hers was like a honey nectar. His fingers branded her flesh where they touched her. She moved closer to him, so their naked bodies pressed together down their entire lengths. Her breasts responded instantly to the contact with his muscular chest, the nipples hardening at once when pushed against the dark hair. Desire surged through every pore of her being. She wrapped her arms around his neck and devoured his mouth with hers.

His hand slid down her arm to her breast, where he used his thumb to circle over and around the turgid peak. He tangled his legs in hers and used his expert fingers to explore her flat stomach and the roundness of her hips. And all the while he kissed her, again and again. Asking at first, then demanding as much as she when her mouth pressed hard against his.

She remembered all he'd done to her during the night and all she'd been moved to do to him to bring him pleasure, and she repeated everything now. Slowly, deliberately, she placed small kisses about his mouth, over his beginning rough beard, and on the deep indentation in his chin. She seared a path of nipping kisses along his earlobe and then down the side of his neck and along his shoulder. Hearing his quick intakes of breath, she inched lower to kiss his chest and nipples, at the same time parting her legs so he could move between them and enter her.

With his first powerful upward thrust, she gasped and rose up, bearing down with her hips to receive him deeper inside her. As he moved up and down within her, little cries of ecstasy escaped her parted lips. He overwhelmed her in every way. Her mind, her body, her senses knew only him, desired only him, surrendered totally to him.

With the fury of passion mounting to eruptive force inside him, Linc pushed her over onto her back and lifted himself over her. Panting for breath, he plunged into her again, drawing her with him to the heights of rapturous climax. At the moment when the throbbing pleasure burst between them, he opened his eyes and stared deeply, penetratingly into hers, wanting only to burn the image of her emerald eyes and her flawlessly beautiful face into his mind and heart for all time.

He held her close for a long while after, tenderly kissing her hair, her forehead, her mouth. Her hand rested against his chest. He raised her fingers and kissed them one by one.

Finally he asked, "Did you have a medicine woman put a spirit spell over me, English? I can't seem to have enough of you."

"I was wondering if you'd done the same thing to me," she answered with a smile. The mood between them was relaxed, drowsy. With her hand still in his, she saw the gold band on her finger and couldn't resist curiously asking him about it. "How did you happen to have this handy last night at the church?" She wiggled her ring finger so he'd know what she meant.

"I thought you might like it," he replied off-handedly.

He seemed a little embarrassed by the gesture. She wondered if he now regretted giving it to her.

"Don't worry," Linc continued quickly, "your money didn't buy it. A storekeeper friend of mine here in town deals in precious metals and some jewelry. I had him make it yesterday afternoon from a gold stickpin of mine. I've used it to borrow on when I've needed money quickly to get out of scrapes."

Victoria was surprised by his answer.

"But now you won't have it to use."

He smiled at her concern. "I'll find another way to get out of trouble. Do you like the ring? I had to guess at the size."

She let her eyes flick to it.

"It's lovely. I—I wasn't expecting it." She looked up at him. "I wasn't expecting many of the things I'm discovering about you."

She feared to tell him what she was feeling, but knew she must, for she hoped to find out what was in his mind and heart as well.

"We're in a real fix here, aren't we?" Linc remarked before she could say more.

"A fix?" She dipped one of her brows uncertainly.

"I mean, I didn't figure on feeling this way about you, Victoria." The sudden seriousness in his voice matched the expression on his handsome face.

"What way is that?" She barely whispered the words, holding her breath waiting for him to answer.

He sighed deeply.

"I'll tell you, this is as hard to admit as being dragged around a corral by a half-wild bronc. I didn't want anything to happen between us, never planned on it. You're the most exasperating, unpredicable, infuriating gal I've ever come across. You turn my insides upside down, fill up my head with crazy fool thoughts." He blew out his breath, clearly having a hard time with the words.

"Are you trying to say you're in love with me?" Victoria ventured timidly, hoping against hope this was true.

"I reckon that's what you'd have to call it. I can't think

of any other reason for this damned loco feeling." He knew she was part of him now, a deep completing part. She fit with him inside almost the way his hand molded around the smooth pearl handle of his Colt on the outside. If he lost her, something in him would die—the feeling side of him that he'd kept guarded for so long. He'd tried to hide it, tried to deny it. But Victoria had reached that vulnerable place and drawn it out. No other woman had ever touched him like that, not even Abby. He didn't like this opening of himself. His mind wanted to resist it, keep it down where he could use his strong self-control to check it. But his heart and his body would have none of that tethering. Those two parts of him reached out to her now and took her in. He'd protect her from harm at all costs, even his own life. He had to be with her to take care of her . . . to love her. But being with him put her in danger, from his past, from his gun. He felt the conflict welling up in his chest and hated it.

Victoria feared she heard regret in his voice.

"I'm feeling all mixed up inside, too, Linc. I want you and need you beyond all reason. I thought I had everything carefully planned out about you. Our relationship would be strictly business. But somehow, somewhere along the way, all that changed. I'm in love with you. I want to be with you, near you every moment. It's all so crazy and wrong."

He touched the side of her cheek, seeing the starting tears in her glistening green eyes.

"No, not wrong, Victoria. Never wrong. There's a lot I can't explain about what's happened between us. Sometimes there's no reason you can see right away for things taking place. Maybe we can figure it out, the longer you stay here."

"Stay?" His words struck her like a blow. She hadn't thought of remaining in this Wyoming Territory. The whole purpose of her scheme to marry him had been to get free of Sir Giles' tyrannical control of her life so she and Deborah could go back to England and resume the life they'd always known. "I—I didn't think about us beyond the marriage and having proof that I had a husband." She couldn't look at him. "I must return to my home in England. I don't belong here. But I love you. I want to be with you. Will you come with me?"

Linc was silent for several long moments. He felt his gut tighten around a lead weight that seemed to be in it. The quiet hung between them like a fragile thread.

"I couldn't live in your England, Victoria," he answered finally, his voice low but firm. "I'd feel like a trapped animal in fancy London-town with paved streets and tight-together buildings. I've seen pictures of that place." He sighed deeply again, knowing this serious consequence could part them. Their love was so new, like when a filly was just halter-broke and needed a gentle, guiding hand. Somehow he had to make Victoria understand what he was, what he felt about the land.

"I need this wide open space. Sometimes I think there's a kind of wild thing inside me. Maybe it's my Indian blood. I know this land doesn't seem like much compared to England. Sand, rocks, endless horizon. Nothing much grows here except scrub grass. But cattle thrive on it. Herds increase. There's something good and strong in this country, something worth fighting for, working for. This Territory's like a rough gem diamond right now. But someday . . .

"I'm part of it all, Victoria. I need to be able to look out over the prairie for as far as my eye can see and know I'm seeing my land. That's all I've ever wanted—a ranch. The Diamond M ranch. But I'm in love with you now. I'd like you by my side when I get what I want. Stay with me."

His voice was hardly above a whisper when he said the words. Victoria knew speaking his heart like this was difficult for him. Like the Indians she'd read about, he had a stoicism about him that veiled emotions. Her own heart ached for him, for their love.

"I want to be with you, Linc, but . . ." Her voice broke with the uncertainty pulling her in two directions.

"I know . . ." Linc hugged her close, knowing her conflict matched his own. "We have to do some more mighty serious talking about us real soon. But right now, we can't stay here like this, pretending the world is in another territory. I still have a job to do protecting you. I need to find out if your uncle and Dandridge have tracked us here to town."

He kissed her gently and sat up to get out of bed. She wanted to hold him back, stay close in his arms where she felt so safe and happy, but she knew he was right. Their passion, this new, disturbing, wonderful love must wait a little longer. Evil lurked in the form of men driven by greed and the lust for power.

She sat up, holding the rumpled sheet around her as she silently watched him dress in the clothes he'd worn for their marriage. When he buckled on the leather holster holding his Colt and bent to fasten the leather tie around his leg, she felt a wellspring of fear begin to bubble up inside her. He would be risking his life going up against Sir Giles, Alden, and Clint Dandridge. They were so many; he was but one. Yet as she watched him, trying to memorize his handsome features and all of his movements, she saw that he showed no fear, no worry. His mouth that had kissed her so softly only moments ago was set in a stern line now. His dark, sharply arched brows were slightly downturned in the beginning of a frown, but otherwise, he gave no outward appearance that he might be on guard or apprehensive.

He glanced at her in the bed as he crossed the room to the propped door.

"Stay here," he told her. "Push the bed against the door after I leave. I'll try not to take too long finding out what I need to know."

"Please be careful," she beseeched, worrying more about him than herself.

A kink of a smile touched the edge of his mouth.

"I always am, English. Don't worry."

His hand was on the doorknob when she called his name again. He swung his head toward her.

"I—I just wanted you to know I love you," she stammered, unused to saying such words. But she meant them with all her heart.

He smiled, looking pleased as he nodded and then left the room.

Victoria took her time dressing. First, she washed as thoroughly as possible using the water in the china pitcher to fill the matched bowl. She longed to sink down into a steaming tub for a complete bath, but had no desire to go down to the gambling parlor to ask about having one sent up. Doing so would risk a run-in with Carlotta Stockton, and she didn't want that to happen. She knew the woman was an enemy, and she had enough enemies to face for the time being.

As she washed, she tried to keep her thoughts set on the seriousness of the situation with Sir Giles and the danger Linc might be in, but her happiness in knowing that Linc loved her kept creeping into her thoughts, and she couldn't stop herself from humming a merry little tune her father had taught her as a child. It had no words, but she remembered he would whistle the sprightly melody when they took carefree walks around he meadows at the country estate.

Thoughts of her father cast a shadow of sadness over er. She stopped wringing the water from the washcloth o stare off into space. The terrible nightmare had rought Linc to her last night, and for that she was rateful, because it was then they had learned of their ove for each other. Why did she keep having that awful ream? Her father had died years ago, yet his death still aunted her for some reason. Hannah had always corned her concern and worry about the nightmare, dis-nissing it as foolishness and of no consequence. Probably he servant woman was right.

Remembering Hannah made her glance at the leather vallet lying atop the tilted chest of drawers. Only a little noney remained in it, the English pound notes. Her eye aught the corner of something barely visible at the edge f the small case. She put the wet cloth over the side of he bowl and walked to the dresser to pick up the wallet. pening the folded two halves, she saw the expensive vel-um envelope. She hadn't paid much attention to it when t had fallen out before. Now she looked at it more losely.

No name addressed the envelope. Pulling at the sealed lap, she carefully tore it open. Inside was a single sheet f matching vellum, folded in half.

As she read the neatly written words on the paper, her yes widened in shock and horror. So many things sud-lenly fell into place, pieces of an obtuse puzzle that had roubled her all these five years since her father's death. The letter read:

"To the Finder of This Script,

"I always keep this letter with me, for I fear for my life. If this be found, then I have met my death at the hand of an evil murderer. I wish to reveal the identity of the wicked man and the horrible deed he committed. I speak hereof of Sir Giles Spencer of London, my employer for many years. He has allowed me to remain a servant in his household for so long because I witnessed the murder of Mr. Edward Spencer—brother to Sir Giles—and have used the threat of this letter's falling into the hands of the authorities as the means for keeping my employment. Miss Victoria Spencer, Edward Spencer's daughter, also saw the murder by stabbing of her father, though she was taken with a fever at the time and unsure of what she witnessed.

"It is my last wish that justice be done against Sir Giles for the murder he committed in order to gain the property and other holdings owned by Edward Spencer. May God have mercy on my soul for keeping this terrible secret for so long."

Hand to her throat, Victoria read the letter again hardly able to believe the words she saw before her. I was signed Hannah Perkins and dated only two day after her father's death. If this paper could be believed her father had been murdered by his own brother an not by highway thieves, as Sir Giles had reported to th authorities.

Victoria's legs suddenly felt as if they wouldn't hol her. She sank down on the edge of the bed, clutching th paper in her hand. Murder. No wonder the nightmar tormented her. Her father's soul must have been reaching out to her to serve vengeance for the vicious wrong tha had been done to him. She must act.

Hannah was still alive. She might not know yet tha her money wallet had been stolen and the letter revealed.

Victoria glanced down at the paper again. She mus get this to a lawman as quickly as possible. If Hannah could be brought as a witness against Sir Giles, then justice could be served, and her wicked uncle would never be able to harm her or Deborah or anyone else again. She had to tell Linc about this. He'd know how to help her.

Chapter Twenty-three

Victoria paced the room, anxious for Linc to return so she could tell him about Hannah's letter. She'd put on the pink satin dress again, tempted to go out and try to find him, but she changed her mind when she realized she knew very little of Cheyenne. She wouldn't know where to start looking for him. Besides, he'd told her to wait here.

Crossing her arms in front of her, she impatiently drummed her fingers on her arms and walked to the broken window. The street two stories below bustled with people now. Men and women scurried along the wooden sidewalks. Some already carried purchases wrapped in brown paper and baskets of store-bought goods. Children scampered in and out among the pedestrians, playing chase and climbing on hitching rails.

Three men attempted to hang a banner across the width of the street. A rope had been strung between two buildings that faced each other. Two of the men held a tall ladder, while the third man balanced at the top, trying to tie the banner to the rope. They were hampered by horseback riders and people driving by in wagons. From what Victoria could see of the part of the banner already attached, the words announced the Fourth of July celebration.

She caught her breath when she saw the ladder suddenly start to sway precariously. The man at the top frantically waved his arms, attempting to keep his balance. Finally, he reached down, grabbed the top of the ladder, and held on. She smiled when he stopped swaying and began to shake his fist down at his two helpers. She couldn't hear what he was shouting to them, but she could imagine his anger.

Footsteps in the hall made her turn toward the battered door. She felt a surge of relief and excitement when Linc called to her from the corridor. With an effort, she pushed the bed away from the door so he could enter.

"Linc, thank heaven you've returned!" She held up the paper. "Giles Spencer is a murderer. He killed my father. My servant, Hannah Perkins, wrote this letter saying she witnessed it. I didn't know it was in the wallet of money I stole from her to pay you. We must tell the sheriff about Giles' vile crime." She held the vellum sheet against her chest, feeling her resolve harden and grow inside her. She set her heart in icy determination to be the victor in the next confrontation with her evil uncle.

Linc took the paper from her and glanced over it.

"That will convict him and free Deborah and me from his terrible influence," Victoria continued coldly. "I want Sir Giles caught and arrested. Hanging would be too good for him. He should be imprisoned for the rest of his contemptible life so he can have a longer time to suffer for what he did to my father!"

"Hold down your hatred, Victoria," Linc cautioned, putting a hand on her arm. "Keep your head. The sheriff here in Cheyenne can't be trusted. Corbett's known for bending the law to the side that pays him the most. If your uncle got to him, this evidence would likely disappear real quick, making it only your word against his, unless the Perkins woman would testify."

"She wouldn't," Victoria answered angrily. "She's been part of it all along. But who can we trust?"

"Boswell in Laramie. He's a good man. I didn't catch any word about your uncle or Clint Dandridge when I was out just now, but I've got a strong suspicion they're here in town. I'll leave word with Sheriff Corbett that I was looking for them. Corbett'll see the possible money in that news and hightail it to your uncle and Clint. That should bring them to Laramie after us quick enough. Boswell and I'll be waiting."

Victoria nodded, glad to follow Linc's level judgment.

"We have to return there for Deborah, too. I can't leave her to Sir Giles' merciless hands any longer. I only pray she's still all right. Oh, Linc, you must help me protect her from him!"

"Don't worry. We'll see justice done."

Victoria knew he spoke the truth. She trusted him to help her as he had so many times already. They'd confront Sir Giles together. The two of them as one, strong and certain, with the law on their side as well. She felt she could face anyone or anything with Linc standing beside her.

Darkness descended over the desert plain in flaming streaks of scarlet. Linc guided his lathered horse off the trail he'd been following that skirted the edge of the foothills. An out-jutting of jagged rocks offered a natural protection from the openness of the flatland beyond.

"This should be a safe place to stop for the night," he said, dismounting and coming around to help Victoria down from her horse. "These animals need a rest." He didn't add that she needed the same thing.

"But we can't stop, Linc. We must get to Laramie!"

He reached out and grabbed her horse's bridle. "If we don't rest and feed these animals, we'll be walking the rest of the way! We're stopping here."

For a moment, her green eyes clashed with his darker ones. He had to admire her spunk, but he was hot and tired himself, and glad for the cool night air quickly moving in around them. Finally she looked away and dismounted without letting him help her.

"Here, drink your fill of this water." He handed her the canteen and his hat. "Then pour some of it in my hat and let the horses drink from it. After I unsaddle them, I'll rustle us up some beef jerky to eat. You set the bedrolls out."

Fatigue made Victoria's anger flare at Linc's high-handed manner. But she thought better of arguing with him, for she'd learned that in matters of survival in this frontier, he was the expert. And her limbs didn't seem to want to move any more. Her arms felt weighted with lead as she held up Linc's hat to each horse in turn. Her body ached with weariness from the long hours in the saddle. Linc was right. They had to rest.

She let her eyes drift to him as he easily hoisted the heavy saddle to a flat place on the ground. So tall and handsome, he seemed to have unending strength and vitality. But she knew he must be tired, too.

She saw him pause to glance toward the horizon again. He'd done this often during their ride. She should feel frightened that Sir Giles, Alden Cummings, and Clint Dandridge were probably riding the same trail they had, but she felt safe with Linc.

The beginnings of his dark beard shadowed the lower part of his rugged features. The white creases at the edges of his eyes and mouth were deepened by fatigue and streaked with dust and sweat. His dirty white shirt was unbuttoned nearly to his waist, revealing a wide expanse of dark hair on his muscular chest.

Victoria felt the now familiar stirring in her middle, the surge of excitement caused from being near him. This man had indeed caught her by surprise. Overwhelmed her. Changed her, changed her life. She knew she'd never be the same again, knew she never wanted to be that empty, unfulfilled woman.

She stepped up close to him. When he turned to reach for the other saddle, he abruptly came face to face with her. She slipped her arms around his waist and drew him against her in a tight hug.

"What would I do without you?" she murmured, looking up into his dark brown eyes. "I don't even want to remember what my life was like before we met."

"Victoria, you know we're both loco to—"

She put a finger to his lips to stop his words.

"I'm uncertain enough about this love I feel for you. I know it makes no sense. We're as different as night and day. But I feel love for you in my heart and to the depths of my being. I don't want to think past those feelings now."

"My English . . ." Linc murmured, shaking his head as he closed his arms around her. He kissed her long and deeply, relishing the taste and feel of her mouth on his. His weariness was suddenly put aside as desire awakened in him. Her soft, yielding body molded against his, touching to life sparks of need he couldn't hold back. Mixed with his growing excitement was a deep contentment from being with Victoria like this, alone in the vast, wide-open land he knew so well, with a million stars overhead and the deep, endless night going on as far as the eye could see. But his eyes saw only his wife as he gazed steadily at her lovely face. His wife . . . the words slid easily through his mind. He liked the thought, the meaning of them.

He smiled and stroked his hands up the sides of her slender neck to cup her face with his palms. Slowly, he lowered his head to kiss her again, this time letting his mounting fever show in the way his lips clung to hers. His fingers trailed back down her neck and over her shoulders, then to the buttons of her blouse. When the material parted, he drew Victoria down to the saddle blankets she'd spread on the ground before.

He didn't hurry to undress her. He forced himself to go slowly so he could savor the sight of each part of her lovely body as it was revealed to him. Letting his hands caress over her, he then followed the same path with his mouth. He lingered long on first one ample breast and then the other, feeling the heated need in him send liquid fire through his veins when her nipple tightened and she arched her back to press it deeper into his mouth.

Victoria gasped and raked her fingers through his dark hair. That he could make her feel such desire and sheer ecstacy amazed her and made her a willing and eager part of this lovemaking. Her body shuddered, aroused with all the energy of her woman's passion. Her heart pounded hard, sending a pulsing hunger to every fiber of her body. Her breath caught and held in her throat when Linc's lips devoured her straining breasts and his hands stroked over her flat stomach and then moved down to part her legs. Impatiently, she fumbled with his shirt to remove it so she could feel the hot flesh of his powerful chest and back beneath her own fingertips. She loved his body, loved all of him, and cherished this breathtaking, all-consuming intimacy with him. The rising force passing between them seared her to her very soul, creating a compelling bond that went far beyond just the physical joining of their two bodies.

She kissed him again and again, his lips, his face, his chest, his muscle-rippled belly, freely offering everything she had to give and opening her body, her entire being to all he gave her in return. She realized no thoughts about the place they were in, heard none of the night sounds that were still so foreign to her. There was only Linc beneath the sparkling stars of the cool, blanketing night. Only Linc to send her soaring to the height of complete bliss and explosive passion.

Clinging to each other, they rose together, she opening, he coming to her, into her. At last, the exquisite shudderings of rapturous climax passed between them, forging them into one.

Later, Victoria lay on the saddle blanket, snuggled happily and contentedly against Linc's side. She quickly fell into a deep sleep. Taking care not to wake her, Linc pulled the bedroll blanket up over her shoulders to ward off the chill desert air. The moon hadn't risen yet, so the night remained dark and close around them. He preferred the lack of light. The darkness hid them well here. Some of the tension began to wane from his body.

He glanced down at Victoria sleeping in his arms. He didn't need moonlight to see her clearly. He knew every eyelash and brow, every contour of her lovely face. He remembered the softness and curves of her flesh under his touch, the sweet taste of her lips, the silken tresses of her pale yellow hair. Every part of her was carved into his mind, branded on his soul. No harm could come to her. While he had life and breath in his body, he'd keep her safe in his protection. God, how he loved her . . .

A coyote howled in the distance. Linc looked toward the baleful sound. An answering yip sounded from an adjacent hill. Normal night sounds for the desert. He was used to them. He eased himself back against his saddle and let some of his tight alertness settle down. He felt tired, but he knew his senses wouldn't fail him. His sixth sense—for survival—wouldn't sleep.

He took one last look around their small camp, then drew his Colt out of his holster and checked the bullet chamber. Holding the gun down at his side away from Victoria, he rested his head back on the saddle and closed his eyes, allowing himself to drift into a light sleep.

Chapter Twenty-four

"England ain't hardly in my jurisdiction," Sheriff Boswell stated, scratching his head as he leaned back in his desk chair and stared hard at Hannah Perkins' letter in his hand.

"But a terrible crime has been committed!" Victoria cried, putting both hands on the battered oak desk and leaning toward the lanky lawman. "You have proof of it right there. Giles Spencer murdered my father and Hannah Perkins witnessed it! She's kept her position in my uncle's household by threatening to expose his vile deed, I'm certain of it! That, too, is a crime. Surely your American laws recognize these wrongs as much as British jurisprudence!"

"Easy, Victoria." Linc stepped away from the jail office window where he'd been watching the street outside. Putting a hand on her shoulder, he drew her back from her forceful position. "What the sheriff means is that things are a bit more complicated since the murder didn't happen in the Wyoming Territory. Isn't that right, N. K.?"

"Right, ma'am." He twisted the end of his bushy moustache. "The usual procedure is when a criminal's arrested for breakin' the law, he's got to be took back to where the crime was committed for trial. That'd be England in this here case, I guess. I ain't never run into this situation b'fore. I'll have to send a telegram to the circuit judge an' see what he says to do."

"But while you're doing that, Giles Spencer could escape!" Victoria's impatience with the sheriff's slow legal thinking made her pace a small circle in front of the desk, tapping her fingers on her crossed arms. The sweltering heat of the cramped room didn't help her agitated state of mind. She rubbed her hand over the side of her perspiring neck, then pulled back and forth on the front of her grimy white blouse, fluttering the fabric to try to create some air to cool herself. She'd changed her pink satin dress for her blouse and riding skirt before she'd left Cheyenne with Linc.

"Well, I suppose you could sign a complaint," Boswell continued, "an' I could get the circuit judge to swear out a warrant to arrest Spencer on suspicion of murder. Then I can hold him in jail till the judge gets here for a hearin'. Take about three days to get done."

Victoria shook her head angrily.

"That's too long. My uncle—"

Suddenly the door to the jail office burst open. Linc instantly tensed and drew down on the cowboy who burst in.

"Don't shoot, Mr. Masterson!" the tall man cried, halting dead in his tracks and throwing up his hands.

"Damnation, Duggins, what are you doing charging in here like a stampeding bull?" Linc frowned as he recognized the young ranch hand from the Diamond M. Uncocking the Colt, he slid it back into his holster.

Looking visibly relieved, the young man turned to Boswell.

"You got to come out to the ranch, Sheriff! Mr. Masterson's been hurt real bad!"

Linc's frown deepened as he grabbed him by the arm and spun him around to face him.

"What do you mean? What happened to Drumm?"

"A couple of the hands brung him back home just a

little while ago. He was up in the west forty pasture checkin' for some stray heifers. Looks like he got caught in a stampede the way he's busted up. I got the doc on his way out already. The foreman sent me to get you, too, Sheriff. Said Mr. Masterson mumbled somethin' about bein' bushwhacked. I got to find Mrs. Masterson. She's somewhere here in town shoppin'." He turned and dashed from the office before anyone could say anything more.

Linc and Boswell exchanged glances.

"Let's go," the sheriff said, grabbing his hat from a peg on the wall.

"Victoria, you stay—"

"I'm coming with you!" She stepped quickly past Linc to follow the sheriff out the door.

Victoria winced and drew back when she entered the ranch house parlor with Linc and saw Drummond Masterson lying on the tapestry sofa. Two cowboys stood nearby, hats in their hands, glum looks on their sun-weathered faces. An older man with graying hair worked over Drumm with bandages, blocking some of her view, but still she could see enough of his battered and bloody body beneath the torn plaid shirt and leather chaps to make her put her hand to her lips to fight back the nausea churning in her stomach and beginning to rise in her throat.

She made her eyes move around the wood paneled room. Four elegant tapestry covered chairs edged in smooth dark wood that matched the sofa sat in a half circle around a marble fireplace. A bookcase lined with leather bound volumes stood against the opposite wall. Above a massive cherry desk hung a portrait of a man who could only have been Drummond and Linc's father.

The brass engraved plate on the sturdy wood frame stated the name of Holden Masterson. The black hair was the same as the sons', and the deep cleft in the chin. The square-chiseled jaw seemed to have a harder line to it than she'd ever seen in Linc's features. But the dark brown eyes held the same glint of strong, unyielding pride.

She followed Linc with her glance as he went to stand by his half-brother, followed by Sheriff Boswell.

"How is he, Doc?"

The gray-haired man looked up from using a wad of cloth to soak up the blood oozing from a deep cut on Drummond's forehead. His grim expression didn't lessen when he shook his head.

"Linc . . ." The hoarse whisper came from Drumm's dirt-smudged lips. He opened his eyes. The doctor shook his head again and stepped away.

Linc knelt down on one knee beside the sofa, shaken by his brother's condition. He'd seen men gut-shot who had bled less. It was hard to believe the cut and mangled man before him covered with dirt and blood could be the half-brother he'd hated all his life.

"What happened, Drumm?"

"Z-Zeke Dandridge . . . and his boys . . ." He stopped, gasping for breath. Grimacing with pain, he hugged his arm over his crushed midsection and labored to go on. "Stampeded the herd . . . the gulch . . ." He lifted his left arm and grabbed hold of Linc by the shirtfront, pulling him closer. "You know . . . Clint wants . . . ranch." A breath-taking coughing spell halted his words for a moment, but he still held onto Linc.

"Take it easy, Drumm. Save your strength," Linc cautioned, easing his brother back against the cushions.

"Got to talk . . . while I can." Drumm brushed at the blood streaking down into his eye from the cut. "Clint can't . . . get ranch. Swear . . . he won't. Swear!" Another coughing jag cut off his raspy voice. Clearly what strength he had left was waning.

"I hear you," Linc answered coldly, fighting back the wrath and loathing he felt, not for his brother, but for the heartless men who would do this to another man. "You got my word, Drumm. No Dandridge will ever put his name on this range."

Linc's solemnly spoken vow seemed to calm Drumm a little. He inhaled a deep breath and nodded slightly. A smile touched the corners of his mouth.

"Mastersons . . . only, Linc." For a long moment Drumm's hazel eyes focused clearly and steadily on his brother. "You . . . Patrick. Papers in . . . pa's old desk. Give money to Abby . . . for East."

He winced and stiffened, his strength cut by pain. His face, so like Linc's in the ruggedly handsome features, paled to ashen. He reached out a shaking hand. Linc took it in a firm grip. One last time Drumm's eyes locked with Linc's and held. Then his chest stopped moving as the breath of life passed from him.

Linc stood silently at his brother's side. Victoria watched his handsome face, saw emotions there she'd never seen before. Not anger or hatred or even grief now. She saw regret. And sadness. Her heart ached for him and for Drummond Masterson, cut down so brutally in the prime of his life. She stepped to Linc and put her hand on his arm. Absently he glanced toward her, then back to his brother's body. Letting go of his brother's limp hand, he reached up and touched the open eyelids to close them.

"Drummond!" Abby screamed, running into the room. She rushed past Victoria and Linc and fell to her knees next to the sofa. "My God, Drumm! Drumm!" She clutched his bloody fingers to her cheek.

Linc put a hand on her shoulder.

"He's dead, Abby."

"No! No! He can't be dead!" She raised up and threw herself across Drumm's still chest, sobbing hysterically. The doctor stepped up to her and put an arm across her shoulders.

"Mama! Papa!" Patrick cried, trying to hurry to his mother. But Sheriff Boswell knelt down in the boy's path and caught him around the waist when he tried to run by.

"Whoa, son," he said gently. "Best stay here for a minute an' let your ma and pa be."

Linc looked at Abby. Victoria saw something flicker across his face that she couldn't read. Her heart turned over with fear, fear of what had once been between Linc and his brother's wife, and what might be again.

Linc didn't look at her as he moved to Boswell and reached down to pick up the crying boy.

"Don't be afraid, Patrick. Let's go outside for a little while. Then you can see your ma, I promise."

Little Patrick buried his small round face in Linc's shoulder, sobbing as he hugged his arms around his neck.

Victoria followed them out of the house. He stopped on the front porch and stood staring at the flat, windswept grassland stretching before him as far as the eye could see. Running a soothing hand over Patrick's black curly hair, he hugged the boy close to him.

"Don't worry, son," he murmured, patting his back. Then he leaned down to set Patrick on his feet. Squatting before the boy, he put his hands on the small shoulders and spoke slowly and quietly. "You saw your pa hurt real bad in there. He's dead, Patrick. He won't hurt any more. You're ma's going to need you to be real strong for her, be a man. You and I'll take care of everything.

You watch over your ma while I make sure the bad men who hurt your pa pay for it. Whenever you need me, I'll be here. Do you understand that, son?"

Patrick's bright brown eyes were wide as they stared back at Linc. After a moment, he wiped the back of his hand across his runny nose and nodded.

"You can be strong for your ma?"

The black curls bobbed as he nodded again.

"Good boy. Your pa would be proud of you."

Victoria watched from behind them, her heart going out to the frightened little boy. Too well she remembered the conversation concerning Patrick she'd overheard between Linc and Abby Masterson the night of the dinner party. Abby had said Patrick was Linc's son. It could be true. Now that Linc and the boy stood so close together, she could see the distinct resemblance between them.

Her heart felt deadened by the weight of despair filling it. Her mind reeled with the echo of Linc's words. He'd be here to help Abby, to help Patrick, who might very well be his blood son. Where would that leave her? She loved Linc so desperately, so completely that she knew she couldn't bear it if he turned to another woman. Yet Abby held a claim to his heart from long ago. She might have given him a son . . . with Drummond dead, there was no one to stand in the way of Linc and Abby being together again.

No one except me, your wife, she whispered inwardly, feeling agony tumble over her. Abby would get the ranch, and through her, Linc could become master of the Diamond M. And that was his dream, his need, his obsession.

But somehow I'll gain this ranch for you, she vowed, wishing with all her might she could speak the words out loud to him. But his attention was on Patrick, and she didn't know how she would fulfill her vow. Her inheritance was far away in England, entangled with the complications of her father's terrible murder. Abby was here, now, close at hand. In her bereft state of mind, she'd surely turn to Linc, for his strength . . . or his love.

Then another tormenting thought added to the sinking of her spirit. Perhaps neither she nor Abby would have Linc to love. He'd just vowed revenge on Drummond's ambushers, promised to make them all pay for their vile actions. He could die carrying out that vengeance. He could die . . .

An anguished plea sprang to her lips, but before she could speak it, she saw Linc stand up and look out to the east, past the corral. A cloud of dust appeared on the horizon, signaling riders were coming, pounding their mounts hard and fast.

Victoria's hand flew to her throat. Fear shot through her, making her heart race frantically. Without even seeing their faces, she knew the identity of those thundering riders. Sir Giles, Alden Cummings, Clint Dandridge. The chase ended here and now.

Chapter Twenty-five

Linc slipped the leather holster loop off the hammer of his Colt.

"Go into the house, Victoria," he said, his tone broaching no argument. "Take Patrick with you." He didn't look at her. Pulling his hat brim low over his eyes, he stepped down off the porch into the sunlight.

The last thing she wanted to do was leave Linc to face the coming men alone. But she did as he told her, for Patrick's safety. Taking the boy's hand, she hurried into the ranch house, heading straight for the parlor.

"Sheriff Boswell, you men!" she called to the lawman and ranch hands when she reached the open doorway. "Linc needs help outside! I think my uncle's coming. You must arrest him!"

Abby stood away from the sofa now, weeping against the doctor's shoulder. Patrick ran to her and hugged her around the legs. Someone had covered Drummond's broken body with a blanket. His dirty and bloody right hand—the one Linc had clutched at the last—hung down below the edge, touching the inlaid wood floor.

"You just been deputized, boys. Let's go!" Boswell ordered, leading the way out.

For a moment, Victoria hesitated. Linc had told her to stay inside. Perhaps she should go to Abby to comfort her. But she couldn't. She had to know what was happening out in the yard. Whirling around, she followed the men through the dining room to the front door.

The scorching July sun beat down like fierce spears, stabbing the parched ground with blistering heat. Sheriff Boswell stood beside Linc near the front steps. Victoria saw him slip the guard loops from the hammers of his two holstered guns as Linc had done. The two armed ranch hands stayed just behind them in the shade of the porch roof.

Linc stood in an easy stance, legs apart, his thumbs hooked into the top of his gunbelt. Victoria could see his face in profile. He squinted against the bright sunlight and wind. His square jaw showed a hard chiseled line. Rugged, handsome, fierce, savage, courageous. All these words tumbled through her as she watched him. Her heart filled with love and then great fear for his life. This was insane. Within moments there could be brutal death all around her, just as there was with Drummond inside. Drummond who had looked so much like Linc . . .

She hated this ever-present violence, the impending doom. It was everywhere in this land, in the people who were part of the land. How well she knew that fact now . . . and accepted it. Not long ago she'd recoiled from it. Now she was drawn to this scene, still despising the violence, the lurking threat, but knowing there was no other choice except to stand and face it with your whole being. This was life—raw, exciting, primal. A test of strength and will and bravery.

She stood in the doorway, wishing she had the skills to help the men before her survive. The skills could be learned, she knew, and she would learn them. Linc would teach her in time. Together . . . if they had the chance.

Fear pitched in her middle again, but she willed herself not to shrink back.

The hot breeze laced with gritty sand stung her eyes, making them water. She blinked hard to clear them so she could see the horsemen ride up and rein in their mounts. As she feared, the eight riders included Sir Giles, Alden Cummings, Clint Dandridge, and five gunmen.

"Good that you're here, Sheriff," Sir Giles stated when his winded horse stopped prancing. His hazel eyes narrowed into a furious expression as he pointed at Linc. "I want this man arrested for kidnapping my niece!"

Victoria swiftly stepped forward, walking off the edge of the porch to stand between Linc and the sheriff. Her hatred for her uncle gave her the courage to hold her head high and speak.

"He didn't kidnap me. He's my husband. I'm with him of my own free will."

She heard a gasp from behind her. Turning her head, she saw Abby Masterson standing in the doorway, pressing the back of her hand against her mouth. Her face was pale as she stared past Victoria to Linc. But it was Alden Cummings who spoke first.

"*What?* A woman of your breeding married to Indian trash like him! What are we waiting for, uncle? We outnumber them!" He started to reach for a gun at his waist.

Victoria was aware that Linc tensed next to her, but the motion of his hand was so swift that she didn't comprehend what was happening. A shot exploded. The bullet caught Alden in the right shoulder. He yelped and tumbled backward off his horse. The other horses whinnied and shied at the gun blast, so for a moment their riders were occupied with controlling them.

"Hold them steady there, boys," Linc warned with calculated calm, still pointing the smoldering Colt at Cummings writhing on the ground clutching his bleeding shoulder. "And don't reach for any of your hardware. This Colt's got a hair trigger."

"You heard the man," Sheriff Boswell added, drawing one of his guns. The deputized men behind him did the same, cocking back the hammers on their weapons.

Linc glanced down at Cummings.

"Take care with your worthless opinions, Englishman. The next bullet'll be right between your eyes. Wouldn't cause much of a loss by my reckoning, except for the lead. What Victoria told you is true. We were married in Cheyenne. That puts an end to the plans you and Spencer were cooking up for her inheritance, doesn't it?"

"Why you fortune-hunting, half-breed bastard . . ." Giles Spencer's scowl turned malevolent. Sizzling tension mounted, as tangible in the air as the blistering heat.

"*You* are the fortune-grasping swine, uncle!" Victoria shouted angrily. "Your vicious schemes to gain all of the Spencer family holdings have been exposed. I know you murdered my father. The sheriff has proof I gave him in a letter written by Hannah in which she accused you!"

"Letter . . . Hannah." Sir Giles looked shaken for a moment, then swiftly recovered, masking his face to look at her fiercely again. "My dear, I'm afraid this hot sun has damaged your faculties. You must be demented. If there could be such a letter, it is surely a slanderous forgery."

Victoria's fury exploded. He sounded so self-assured and condescending. He was a murderer, yet he called her insane!

"Your lies will no longer be believed, Giles Spencer! I will see justice done, if I must administer it myself!" She made a grab for Sheriff Boswell's unused gun in the holster nearest her, but Linc's left hand shot out, gripping her wrist hard to stop her.

"That's enough, Victoria! This isn't the answer."

She glared at him, wrenching her wrist free of his rough grasp.

"It's how you solve everything!" she shot back.

"When there's no other way. Let N. K. handle this. He's the law."

His narrowed dark eyes locked with hers in silent combat, but yielded no ground. Her wrath railed at his interference. She wanted to *kill* Giles Spencer!

"I'll take care of it, ma'am," Boswell assured her, drawing the gun she'd reached for. "A crime's been reported to me an' evidence given. Enough so's I figure on takin you in, Spencer, an' holdin' you in my jail till the circuit judge decides what's goin' on in this case. You got any argument with that, Clint?"

The other riders had raised their hands when the guns came out against them, but Dandridge's hand started to move toward the weapon at his hip.

"Just give me a reason, Clint." Linc cocked his Colt

and pointed it directly at Dandridge's chest. Dandridge slowly raised his hands, giving Linc a malicious look.

"Now that's right smart, Clint," Boswell noted. "Get their guns, boys," he said to the ranch hands. "An' keep the drop on all of 'em. I'll just be puttin' these manacles on Spencer." Without lowering his own weapon, he reached into an inside pocket of his vest and drew out a pair of tarnished metal handcuffs. While he clicked them into place over Sir Giles' wrists he glanced up at Dandridge. "No need for the rest of you to be stayin'. Head on out before I find a reason to arrest all of you."

Dandridge's fierce scowl deepened, but he said nothing more as he yanked roughly on the reins to pull his horse around.

"Come on, boys," he ordered gruffly, digging his spurs into his mount.

"I'm going after Zeke," Linc stated, watching Alden Cummings struggle to mount his horse and follow the others.

"Thought you would," Boswell replied. "But you best hold up some. I know you're mighty good with that gun, but you can't take on all of Clint's boys by yourself. You know Clint won't give up Zeke easy. Let me take care of the Englishman here first, then we'll round up some more boys for deputies an' go after Zeke together. It'll be dark soon. Don't cotton to ridin' out to the Lazy River Fork ranch at night. Give Clint an' Zeke an' their boys too much advantage. Reckon we'll wait till tomorrow. Let's do it legal, Linc."

"All right, N. K.," Linc agreed, sounding reluctant. "We'll get Drumm buried in the morning, then some of the ranch hands and I'll meet you in town about noon."

"Too bad about Drumm," Boswell noted with little

emotion in his voice. He lifted his hat and rubbed the sleeve of his blue shirt across his sweating brow. "Good man."

"I reckon you could say that," Linc replied, his face expressionless.

Chapter Twenty-six

"You wanted to see me?" Linc asked, coming into the parlor.

The room was empty now, except for Abby sitting at the desk. Crimson twilight shadows filtered through the western window, giving an eerie glow to the book shelves and Holden Masterson's portrait. Drumm's body had been taken out, and the bloodstained sofa.

"Are you and your *bride* staying here tonight?" Abby's voice held a bitter edge. She didn't look at Linc.

"I reckon that depends on you."

Abby pounded a fist on the desk and jumped to her feet, looking furious.

"Damn you, Linc! How could you do it? How could you marry that—that *bitch?*"

Linc's brow dipped in a frown. His own anger had been boiling very near the surface for hours, and he wasn't sure why. He felt agitated, edgy—bound up inside with feelings he didn't like because he didn't understand them. He should be glad Drumm was dead. Drumm had been his enemy. But he wasn't happy about it. And that mixed him up mightily. He held his temper in check, knowing Abby was in a distraught state of mind right now.

"I married Victoria because I wanted to, Abby. It was a way to get my hands on some big money."

"Then you don't love her?" Abby's voice raised in

hopefulness. She didn't wait for him to answer, but instead rushed forward to throw her arms around him. "No, of course, you don't! You love *me.* You've always loved me. And I love you. I always knew you'd come back for me someday. Thinking of being with you was the only way I could endure living with Drumm. I'd close my eyes and think of you whenever he touched me."

Linc roughly pulled her arms from around his neck and let his anger surge out.

"Don't talk like that, Abby! My God, Drumm isn't even in the grave yet!"

"Well, he will be tomorrow, or what's left of him. And I don't care! I never loved him. You know I only married him because he had money and the prestige of owning this ranch and you didn't. But at the end, he didn't even have money. He could never give me what I wanted. I need beautiful clothes and civilized people around me. I want to live in a real city where there are theaters and society affairs and places to dance and go to parties. Look! Look at these lines near my eyes. That's what living in this God-awful desert is doing to me. I'm still young! I want to do exciting things, see places. I don't want to shrivel up and die on this miserable ranch!" Frantically, she moved forward again and put her arms around Linc's waist, hugging him tightly. "The ranch is mine now, my darling. I'm going to sell out to Clint Dandridge. I'll have enough money to last a long time. Come east with me. We'll have a wonderful life. We'll raise Patrick together. Our son. I don't care that you married that woman. You can get a divorce somehow. It doesn't matter. I know you've always loved me and that's what counts."

Linc felt his anger drain away and become pity, making him wonder how he ever could have loved this woman. He saw her now for what she was—vain, selfish, even cruel. He remembered the letter he'd found in Clint's desk. Drumm must have lived in hell being married to her. Perhaps it was good now that he was free . . .

Victoria flashed into his mind. She'd gone to the servants' quarters with the maid, Anita, to help with preparing Drumm's body for burying. The contrast between Abby and Victoria left him shaken. Both women were beautiful, desirable. But it was the way they were inside that made them so different. Abby was conniving and spoiled, a whining, desperate child in a woman's alluring body. Victoria's strength and spirit and unselfish love could fill him inside as no other woman ever had.

Once more he pushed Abby away.

"It's no good, Abby. I'm in love with Victoria. It was over for us a long time ago. Besides, I couldn't trust you now. I know about your treachery with Clint Dandridge against Drumm, how you fixed the record books."

She stared at him steadily. Her face changed from showing child-like hope and expectation to pure hatred. Straightening her shoulders, she lifted her chin and spoke coldly.

"You can't prove anything! You're a fool, Lincoln Masterson. Half-breed scum and a ridiculous fool. I know how much you've always wanted this ranch. Well, you won't have this land or me or your son!" She pointed to a paper lying on the desk. "That's Drumm's will. He left everything to *me.* And I'm selling out to Clint Dandridge! Stay here at the ranch tonight if you want to. Watch me sign it all away tomorrow! Have your little English whore! But you'll never have the Diamond M, I swear that on Drummond's grave!"

She rushed past Linc out of the room. He was glad to have her gone. He needed to think. He let his eyes roam slowly over the parlor. Maybe this would be the last time he'd ever come here.

The thought left a hollow ache in his gut. He hadn't known much happiness in this house or even this room, but he felt a kinship with all of it, a belonging. It was loco. He belonged here less than anyone—the half-breed bastard son who always rebelled against the strong-willed father.

The shadows in the room lengthened as dusk gave way to night. Linc glanced up at his father's portrait. No smile or warmth or compromise showed on the still face frozen in time on the painted canvas. A stern, even severe man. But fair. He'd insisted on giving his half-Indian son a place in his household, and the squaw mother, too. It had cost all of them so much hardship.

Linc remembered his stepmother Eunice—Drumm's mother, his father's white wife. And the hatred. This house overflowed with it all the while he was growing up. But he realized something now that he never had before. All the while his father had been strict, demanding, even harsh in his dealings with him, he'd really been sculpting him. Like the relentless wind and rain shaped the formidable mountains, he'd whittled away the soft parts of the boy, the weaknesses, the vulnerabilities, and left so much of the tough, gritty, self-preserving man he'd become. He realized now that he was able to survive in this wide-open, untamed territory because of his father's hard hand, what he'd taught him, instilled in him with words and actions.

He blew out his breath in a heavy sigh, staring at the portrait again. He still hated his father. That vein ran deep, had been made rock-strong by years of anger nd conflict. But now he understood some about why is father had been so demanding, even ruthless to-vard him.

He glanced at the paper on the desk, then walked ver to it. Being of sound mind . . . last will and tes-ament . . . He read the words solemnly. Drumm gave verything to Abby, just as she'd said. Tomorrow Clint Dandridge would own the Diamond M.

Linc looked up at the painting once more.

"What would you think of that, pa? A Dandridge wning Masterson land. Enough to make you turn ver in your grave, I'd bet on that." The idea didn't sit vell with him either.

Abby would take Patrick away. Was the boy his son? Iow would he ever know for sure?

The bright-eyed, curly-haired youngster melted into is mind's eye and he caught himself smiling. He'd ever been much taken with children before, but he elt something for Patrick, a bond of some kind. Was it ecause of a blood kinship, or was he just seeing the oy's pain now and remembering his own as a child?

The smile faded and the anger returned. Patrick was ust a pawn to Abby, something else to use to get what he wanted.

Victoria heard the pounding, but she hesitated to go nto the blacksmith's shed. It was late. The night was leeply dark and cool. She pulled Anita's crocheted lack shawl up higher on her shoulders, determined to ind Linc. She felt sure it was he working with the ammer.

Being careful to stay back in the shadows, she raised ip on tiptoes to look into the open window. The glow rom a kerosene lamp cast flickering shadows over the

rough-hewn log walls of the three-sided enclosure. Sh
saw Linc bending over a long box laid across two saw
horses. With even, rhythmic strokes, he swung a ham
mer against the raw wood, pounding nails in a straigh
row down the edge of the nearly finished coffin. He
glance slid down to the gun at his hip. He was neve
without it, it seemed. It was as much a part of him a
his hand. She had trouble understanding his need fo
it. But then she remembered the confrontation with Si
Giles and the others earlier in the afternoon, and th
sudden realization struck her that she herself hac
nearly used a gun today. If Linc hadn't stopped her
she would've used Sheriff Boswell's gun to shoot Si
Giles!

The anger and hatred she felt toward her uncl
flared through her in a lightning burst. He was evi
and cruel, with no goodness in him—a murderer con
sumed with greed and a lust for power. He was in jai
now, but she felt no assurance that he'd ever come tc
justice. She wanted to believe in laws and civility
among people, but she knew right didn't always tri
umph. Sometimes evil must be met on its own terms
and in this time and place, a gun evened those terms

The hammering stopped. She saw Linc reach for an
other board. He wore no shirt. His upper torso glis
tened with sweat in the lamplight. The thick cords o
muscle in his right arm and across his chest ripplec
with each swing of the tool. His wavy black hair hung
down over his forehead like a thick dark mass clouding
his eyes. But she knew what they looked like—his deep
earth-brown eyes that could penetrate to the depths o
her soul when they flashed over her.

Victoria bit her lower lip, captivated by the sight o
him, by the magnificent man he was. Her body
swelled with desire, and she felt an aching need to be

eld in his arms and to hold him. Her heart wept for he hatred and anger and hurt she knew he held inside im. She wished she could get rid of her own confused eelings of love and sadness and futility. So many obtacles stood between them, divided their love.

She must talk to him. She couldn't wait any longer.

He looked up when she entered the shed, then went n with the pounding.

"You're working late," she said lamely, unsure of how o begin to say what was in her heart.

"This needs to be done."

He picked up another pine board from the evenly ut pile on the dirt floor and carefully fit it into place ext to the one he'd just finished hammering. She ouldn't say anything while he hammered away again. The sound seemed deafening in her ears, created a arrier between them. She stood off to the side out of is way, hugging the shawl around her, wishing he'd top and look at her, talk to her, but knowing, too, hat he needed to do this, needed to be the one to nake his brother's coffin.

After several minutes, he put down the hammer and eached for a red rag hanging from a nail on the log vall next to him. Wiping the cloth over his sweaty orehead and neck, he finally spoke.

"What do you need, Victoria?" he asked abruptly, oncentrating on rubbing the rag between his hands. It's late. You should be asleep."

His gruff manner hurt her to the quick. She had to hange this between them. But how? She felt so unchooled in this thing called love, this needing someone o desperately she could hardly think straight or act raionally. Her pride, her reason sparked, ready to flare o life and divide them further, but she willed down hose parts of her, deciding she must speak with her heart instead. The words were barely a whisper from her lips.

"I—I need you, Linc . . ."

He slowly raised his eyes to look at her. One of his sharply arched black brows dipped down as if to start a frown, but it didn't spread to the rest of his features. Instead, he blew out his breath and glanced away from her.

"I know," he murmured. "We've got one hell of a mess here, English."

She walked to him and put a hand on his arm, feeling his flesh hot beneath her touch. The words she had to speak caught in her throat, nearly choking her, but she forced herself to say them.

"Are you still in love with Abby? All you've ever wanted is right at hand now. The ranch, Abby, everything. Only I stand in the way."

He turned on her fiercely, grabbing her by the arms. "Don't be such a damned martyr! You don't know anything that's going on here!"

"Then *tell* me!" she demanded, feeling her own anger and frustration burst forth. "I don't know what's happening! Murder, death, deception are all around me. And in the midst of it, I want to love you, but I don't know how, and if I knew how to love you, I don't know if you'd let me!" Her voice broke as a sob filled her throat, cutting off her breath. She pressed her palms against his chest and gasped in air.

Linc pulled her to him, wrapping his arms around her.

"God, Victoria, we have to sort this out." He stroked her hair, relishing the long silken tresses. Then he used two fingers to tip her chin up so she had to look at him. Tears made her eyes liquid glistening emeralds. He felt his heart turn over with longing. The words came hard for him, but he made himself say how he felt. "I'm not in love with Abby. I'm in love with you. I'm your husband and I'll gladly keep on being your husband if you'll have me, but that'll mean staying here in Wyoming. Guns are a way of life on the frontier. I'll be using mine. There are some wrongs to be made right—you have to understand that."

She closed her eyes and leaned forward to rest her forehead against his chin. She knew she had to make a decision now that would affect the course of the rest of her life. It was an easy one to make. Linc loved her. He wanted to be her husband.

She brought her arms up to encircle his neck, touching his black hair with her fingers and drawing his head down closer.

"So be it, my husband. If this is where you must be, then I'll stay here with you." She kissed him. Long and deeply, she pressed her lips to his, nourished by the salty-sweet taste of his yielding mouth. She felt dizzy with the sensations that spun through her from just kissing him, pressing close to him. His power and heat surged into every pour of her being.

For several moments, Linc let her kiss him. He moved his hands slowly up and down her back, feeling his insides begin to churn from touching her. But he willed down his body's need, commanded it to wait until later. Now he just wanted to feel her in his arms, know her warmth and her giving love. He needed that so badly, needed her to fill up all the emptiness inside him.

"Victoria . . ." he murmured, bringing his mouth down hard on hers, giving back all she gave to him.

For long, suspended minutes of time, they kissed and clung to each other. Finally, Linc pulled a little away.

"You should go inside now. I have to stay to finish

the coffin."

Victoria nodded but didn't move out of his arms.

"What will happen now with the ranch?" she asked

His eyes took on a cold glint, his sensuous mouth a grim line.

"Drumm and I had a deal for some prime acres, if I could get him the money he needed to keep his creditors off his back. But I didn't have a chance to pay off my end of it. Drumm didn't want anybody to know about the agreement. He didn't put anything in his will about it. He left everything to Abby. She's going to sell out to Dandridge."

"Oh, Linc . . ." She knew the pain that would cause him. "But now with my uncle in jail, I'll be able to get my inheritance without any contention. We can offer her more, a higher price. You can buy the ranch."

"It could take months to get your money straightened out now. Abby's selling tomorrow, right after the reading of the will, I'd say. She wants money, but more than that, she doesn't want me to have the Diamond M."

"But there has to be a way, Linc. We can't give up!"

A slight smile touched the edges of his mouth.

"You've got spirit, woman. I'll give you that. The deed isn't signed over to Clint yet. A lot can happen tomorrow. I've got plenty of fight in me yet. When I go with Boswell to Clint's place—"

"Linc! Deborah's there, at Clint Dandridge's ranch!" The sudden thought of her sister sent panic through her. "If there's a showdown, she might be hurt!"

"Damnation! With Drumm dying, I forgot about her." He frowned, thinking hard. "And the Perkins woman is likely still there, too. She's your only witness against Spencer for the murder. No telling what he'll manage to do to keep her quiet, even if he's in jail.

His money makes him a powerful man no matter where he is."

"What are we going to do?" Fear and dread welled up inside Victoria, waiting for Linc to answer.

"We're going to get your sister and Hannah Perkins off the Lazy River Fork ranch—*tonight!*"

Chapter Twenty-seven

"Damnation, Victoria, you can't go with me! It's too dangerous!" Linc yanked hard on the saddle cinch, tightening it.

"But Deborah won't come with you!" Victoria argued. "She'll be frightened of you just as I—" Her voice dropped off and she looked away.

Linc stopped adjusting his mount's halter.

"You afraid of me? I didn't think you were afraid of anything."

"I was at first," she answered uncomfortably, smoothing a rumpled place on the saddle blanket. "You scowl at everyone all the time. You can get this cold, deadly look in your eyes, giving the impression of someone who's rock-hard and doesn't feel anything."

Linc stepped around the horse and touched Victoria's arm to turn her to face him.

"And what do you think now?" he asked gently.

She looked up, her eyes sparkling from the fluttering wick of the kerosene lamp sitting on a barrel in the corner of the barn.

"I think you would like everyone to believe you're cold and ruthless, invincible. You're strong in many ways. But I've seen the warmth, the compassion you try to hide. It showed in your eyes, your voice when we were with Two Eagles, and I saw it again this afternoon when you spoke to Patrick." She raised her hand to touch the side of his face, feeling the rough beginnings of his coarse dark beard. "And when we make love, you give me so much, such joy and pleasure and hope."

The piercing depth of his near-black eyes melted her insides, making her legs weak. The blood pulsed hard through her veins, sharpening her senses and letting her take in all of him, his heat, his strength, his life energy. She moved closer, slipping her arms around his waist. He'd put on his blue cotton shirt again, but it hung open down the front. She closed her eyes and pressed her lips into the soft hair on his bare chest, murmuring her need, her longing.

"I love you, Lincoln Masterson—with all my heart and soul. I know it doesn't make sense and I know we'll have mountains to overcome—"

His lips stopped her words. His warm, demanding, possessing mouth consumed hers and his arms crushed her against his length. It was a time to cease words and reason, and just feel . . .

Long minutes later, they parted a little, short of breath. Linc took her face in his hands and smiled.

"Victoria . . ." For a moment, he couldn't find any other words to say to her. The look in her eyes told him they had no need for words. She knew his heart and he knew hers. Finally, he let his hands slide down her arms and away from her. "I love you. I want you. But I think I better round up your sister and that witness. I'll be back as soon as I can."

He stepped away and grabbed his hat from where he'd hooked it on the saddle horn. Putting it on, he started to button his shirt. Victoria swallowed hard, following his movements with her eyes. He was closing her out again, putting more than just a few steps distance in the barn between them. Her glance dropped to the ever-present Colt in the holster slung low on his narrow hips. She took a deep breath, summoning her courage.

"I'm coming with you, Linc. Deborah will cooperate if I'm along. I'll follow you after you leave if I have to."

A fierce glint flashed over his gaze.

"Victoria—"

"We're wasting time arguing! You'll have to tie me to a post to stop me!" She crossed her arms in front of her and stood her ground before him, letting her stubbornness cut free.

"I could do that easy enough."

"I know. But we're foolish to fight each other when there are enemies to face!" She strode purposefully to the next horse stall and struggled to lift the heavy saddle off the side wall.

"Here, give me that!" Linc demanded angrily, grabbing the saddle from her. For a tense moment he just stood there holding it, glaring at Victoria. Then he blew out his breath with exasperation and tossed the blanket and saddle over the back of the roan in the stall. "Tie that black shawl close around you so your white blouse doesn't show!"

"Shouldn't we have brought some men with us?" Victoria whispered, lying on her stomach on the ground next to Linc. They'd left the horses a distance away and crept up to a small sand dune, taking care to stay low and out of view of the ranch house ahead. A narrow crescent of moon had risen over the jagged mountain peaks, but it gave little glow to the black night.

"More men would just draw attention," Linc answered, keeping his voice low. He laid the coil of rope he'd brought on the sand beside him and cocked his Winchester, squinting to see through the darkness. "This is the Indian way. A quick raid in and out before the enemy knows what hit him. Damnation! It's just like I thought. Dandridge has an armed camp down there. Guards all over the place."

He pointed to the front porch of the house, the corral, the corner of the barn. Victoria could just make out the shapes of two men standing at each of those places.

"How can we go up against so many?" she asked worriedly.

"We're not going to take them on. If we do this right, they won't even know we've been here till we're gone. Where do you reckon your sister and the Perkins woman are in the house?"

Victoria stared hard at the imposing double-story building, then pointed.

"There, that upper window to the left of the chimney. The room I shared with Deborah was near that corner of the house. Hannah's room was right next to ours."

"Nice of Clint to build that veranda all the way around the house on both levels, no doubt so he can look out over all his land any time he wants. Well, it's going to work for us now." He reached for a gun he had stuck in his belt near the buckle. "Do you think you could shoot this if you had to?"

She nodded, taking it by the cool, smooth wood and metal stock when he handed it to her. It felt awkward, heavy, unfamiliar in her palm.

"If I tell you to shoot, just pull back on the hammer, then pull the trigger," Linc continued. "Keep firing, all six bullets. Shoot at the sky if you have to, but make as much noise as you can. Understand?" She nodded again. He reached out and took her chin in his hand. "Do exactly what I tell you, Victoria. Our lives depend on it."

"I will," she promised.

Keeping low, they moved in quick bursts across the open ground whenever the circulating guards turned their backs to them. At each step, Victoria expected to hear a shout of alarm or a gunshot. Her heart pounded rapidly in her chest. She felt frightened, but some energy pulsed hard through her, giving her legs strength and speed to follow Linc's fast strides. When they reached the back corner of the main barn, Linc stopped, pressing against the whitewashed boards.

"We'll have to go this way," he whispered. "Can't risk the corral side. The horses might spook and rouse the guards. Stay close."

Just as Linc stepped out from behind a stack of straw bales, a man sauntered around the front corner of the barn, carrying a rifle. Linc froze to a halt so quickly, Victoria crashed into him. Hitting his rock-hard body was like colliding with a tree. She had to clamp her mouth shut tight to keep from muttering an exclamation. She dared not breathe, petrified that the guard had seen their movements even in the thick darkness. Certainly he could hear the thunderous pounding of her frantic heart!

For a moment, he stopped and stood still, seeming to listen, but then he leaned his rifle against the barn, showing no signs of alarm. Suddenly a match sparked to life in his fingers, then lighted his bewhiskered face when he touched it to the end of a cheroot. He shifted his weight and turned his back to them, leaning his right shoulder against the barn wall.

Still Linc remained motionless. Victoria felt the tension in his rigid body, the taut readiness of muscle and sinew. The ominous danger of immediate detection permeated the cool, silent night air.

Cautiously, Linc eased away from her, taking almost imperceptible steps toward the unsuspecting guard. Victoria backed up, then ducked behind the straw bales again, peeking around the end of the pile. She hated watching Linc skulk closer to the guard, knowing the life-threatening danger, the terrible risk. But she felt mesmerized by the shadowy scene, drawn to squint in the darkness to see what would happen next. She couldn't suppress a gasp when a stone crunched under Linc's boot. The guard instantly grabbed his rifle and spun around, but his reaction paled compared to Linc's lightning-quick movements. He swiftly raised his gun and brought it down like a battering ram against the side of the guard's head. The man didn't mutter a single sound as he crumpled to the ground in a heap.

Victoria ran forward to watch around the corner while Linc dragged the guard out of sight well behind the barn. Nothing else stirred. She saw five other cowboys standing guard at strategic places around the front of the ranch house, rifles in hand, but they made no move to leave their posts and come toward the barn.

"Victoria!" Linc called in a low whisper.

She hurried back to him.

"Help me spread out some of this straw." He bent to grab a knife out of the top of his left boot, then used it to slash at the twine securing a bale.

"What are you going to do?" she asked, her own voice muffled.

"Create a diversion. Draw those men away from the house."

Linc crept to the place where he'd knocked out the

gunman, and bent to pick up the smoldering cheroot from the ground. Taking care to keep his back to the ranch house, he clenched the cigar between his teeth and drew on it hard to set it glowing again. Then he returned to where Victoria was spreading the dry straw and knelt down on one knee to touch the red end of the cheroot to a handful of the prickly stalks. They crackled and caught fire, fueled by the rising night breeze. Tossing the burning straw and the cigar on the scattered pile, he grabbed Victoria's hand and pulled her to cover behind an empty freight wagon. At the same time, a shout sounded from the front of the ranch house.

Victoria peeked through the spokes of a wagon wheel and saw men running toward the barn from three directions. With a shudder, she realized many more men had been out in guard positions, men she hadn't seen. Somehow Linc had sensed their presence and eluded them.

Ranch hands clamored out of the two bunkhouses. Lamplight glaring through the doorways revealed their clumsy efforts to pull on their clothes as they ran to fight the fast-spreading flames. Shouts of "Fire!" and the pounding of boots on the hard ground shattered the quiet.

"Come on!" Linc urged in a rough whisper, pulling on her hand again.

Their quick dash across the yard went unnoticed by the gunmen and cowboys forming a bucket line by the well. Thick smoke billowed around the barn, which had caught fire. The neighs and bellows of frightened animals added to the noisy chaos. Linc stopped at the edge of the house to look back.

"That's for the Diamond M barn, Clint," he murmured. The bright flames flickered in his dark eyes, revealing their relentless coldness.

A score was being settled, Victoria knew, remembering the terrible night of the dinner party hosted by Drummond and his wife. She could only wonder and dread what Linc would do to settle the debt he calculated against Zeke Dandridge over Drummond's murder.

"I'll go up first, in case anyone's still on guard on the veranda." Linc drew his Colt as he spoke.

Clutching the gun he'd given her, Victoria followed several steps behind him, determined to go on to reach her sister, even though her fear made her legs seem less than reliable beneath her.

Keeping their backs pressed along the outside walls of the house, they made their way to the west side. No guards challenged them. One of the double French doors to Deborah's darkened room stood slightly ajar. Linc was just about to push it open more when a loud pounding on the hall door in the bedroom made him swiftly draw back against the wall again next to Victoria.

"W-who is it," Deborah called out, sounding frightened. Victoria took a step toward the French doors, but Linc's arm shot out to stop her.

"Clint Dandridge. Open the door, Deborah."

Lamplight flooded through the windowpanes, then diminished some as Deborah carried the kerosene lamp away with her to the hall door.

"What's the matter, Mr. Dandridge? I heard a commotion outside."

Victoria knew the flutter in her sister's voice stemmed from fear. She had to fight back the urgent impulse to plunge into the room and throw herself between Deborah and Clint Dandridge to protect her little sister as she'd always done. She was glad Linc's wide girth of shoulders prevented such a rash action. She feared putting Deborah in more danger. Her heart missed a beat when she stood on tiptoe to peer over Linc's shoulder into the bedroom.

"There's a fire at the barn," Clint Dandridge explained, filling the doorway with his straight-postured frame. "You're to stay here in this room, understand? My man Craine will be right here in the hallway to make sure you don't try anything." He started to turn away, but Deborah put her hand on his arm to stop him.

"Is there danger the fire might spread here to the house?" she asked.

"None," Clint answered gruffly. "But there's something suspicious about all this. I'll be busy fighting the fire and trying to save the animals. I don't want to give any thought to you, so mind my orders to stay here. And lock that veranda door."

"But where is Hannah? Could she come in to stay with me?" Deborah's pleading voice rose in pitch.

"Your uncle has plans for Miss Perkins. Craine will be all the nursemaid you'll need. Now do as I say and I'll keep him *outside* your room instead of inside with you. He can be a rough sort."

"Y-yes, Mr. Dandridge," Deborah submitted as he slammed the door in her face and locked it.

Victoria couldn't wait any longer. She darted around Linc and yanked on the partially opened French door. At the sound behind her, Deborah gasped and whirled around, hand pressed to the high neck of her nightgown. Her blue eyes widened with fear and disbelief.

Victoria quickly pressed a finger to her lips to signal Deborah to silence as she hurried past her to listen at the hall door. Deborah gasped again and the glass lamp shook in her hand when she saw Linc step into the room from the veranda.

"Don't be afraid, Deborah," Victoria soothed quietly, coming to her sister and gathering her in her arms in a tight hug. "Linc's here to help us. Are you all right?"

"Yes, but what happened to you? I thought you were dead. You've been gone so long. Uncle Giles and Alden and Mr. Dandridge questioned me again and again about your plans. They went away to find you." The hushed words spilled from Deborah's lips as she looked lovingly at her sister and then warily at Linc.

"I'll explain everything once we're away from here. We must hurry. Where's Hannah?"

Deborah shrugged, her eyes wide and glistening in the lamplight. "Mr. Dandridge came for her today and made her go with him somewhere. He locked me in here. Oh, Victoria, Uncle Giles has been arrested for father's murder!"

"I know, Deborah. Please come now. There isn't time to talk!" Victoria kept her voice low, but filled it with firmness. "We must leave now while the fire holds everyone's attention."

"*You* started the fire at the barn. And you have a gun!" For the first time, Deborah noticed the weapon in her sister's hand.

"Yes. Now come, follow us."

"Follow you where?" Deborah hung back. "I must get dressed. I can't go outside in my nightgown!"

"Yes, you can." Linc stepped forward and grabbed Deborah by the arm to propel her toward the veranda door.

Suddenly the hall door crashed open and Dandridge's man, Craine, barreled into the room. A heavy man, wide-chested and thick-limbed, he moved cumbersomely, but with massive power. When his close-set eyes shot to Linc, he targeted that bulk into a full-frontal attack. Catching Linc around the waist, he carried him down hard to the floor.

Linc felt the breath explode out of his lungs when the big man's weight crushed over him. For a moment, his senses reeled as he gasped for more air. Craine lost no time in straddling him and grabbing him by the shirt-front. Pulling Linc up some, he swung out with his right paw of a fist and smashed it across Linc's jaw, stunning him even more.

Victoria's initial shock at seeing the man burst into the room left her paralyzed, until she saw Linc's dangerous position. Feeling a force of energy burst through her, she searched frantically for a way to help him. She feared she might hit Linc by mistake if she tried to shoot the gun, or a shot might bring others to the room. Instead, she grabbed hold of the barrel of her gun and leaped at Craine. Swinging it like a club, she landed a glancing hit on the side of his head. Caught off guard by her assault, the hulking cowboy raised his arm to ward her off, lost his balance, and toppled backward.

The few seconds of Victoria's attack gave Linc a chance to regain his senses. He twisted out from under Craine and tried to scramble to his feet, but Craine pounced on him again, clutching him in a bear hug and tumbling to the floor. Locked in combat, the two men rolled across the oval braided rug, grunting and breathing hard from the exertion of battling each other. Craine rose up and brutally struck out, burying his fist in Linc's midsection. Linc rolled away, clutching an arm across his aching belly, but he forced himself to ignore the pain and turn on his adversary. Kicking out with his boot, he caught Craine on the side of the jaw. The cowboy fell backward again, but was quickly on his feet. Plunging head-first into Linc, he carried him crashing through the French doors out to the veranda. Linc's Colt fell out of his holster from the force of the blow.

Craine's weathered face twisted in an ugly grimace. Teeth clenched, he used his bulk to pin Linc against the wooden railing, then went for his throat with powerful hands that were like steel bands strangling the life out of Linc. The railing creaked, as if ready to break under the heavy weight crushing against it. Farther and farther Linc bent back over the railing, straining to hold off Craine's death grip. His senses began to blur from loss of air to his windpipe. The blackness of unconsciousness tested the edges of his mind.

His strong instinct to survive erupted with a final upheaving burst through him. Clamping his two hands together into a tight fist, he used the last of his fading consciousness to summon his strength and thrust upward with all his might. His blow whipped up between Craine's forearms, breaking the man's hold. Freed of the death grip, Linc desperately sucked in air, opened his fist, and used the sides of his hands to slam two chopping hits on either side of Craine's neck. The man stood stunned for a second, giving Linc the instant he needed to smash a right cross into the big man's jaw. Craine reeled backward, tumbling through the broken French doors to come to a sprawling heap at Victoria's feet. She gasped in horror and jumped back a step when he groaned and started to roll over to get back up. Without thinking, she snatched the glass-globed lamp out of Deborah's shaking hands and smashed it down on Craine's head. He collapsed on his belly, face down, and lay still.

"Come on!" she demanded, grabbing her sister by the arm and dragging her out onto the veranda.

"This way! Stay close to the wall!" Linc called, bending to retrieve his gun. He shook his head to try to clear the lingering dizziness. Keeping the Colt in his hand, he led the way along the wide porch past the other darkened bedroom doors to the back stairway.

The darkness hindered their passage. At the bottom of the stairs, Deborah tripped on the hem of her long nightgown and fell, giving a small cry of pain as she hit the ground.

"Oh, my ankle!" she moaned, clutching at it.

"Deborah!" Victoria hurried to kneel next to her.

"Damnation, girl, you're not making this easy!" Linc swore, jamming his gun into his holster. Grabbing Deborah by the hand, he hauled her up and heaved her over his left shoulder.

"What are you doing?" Deborah cried.

"Be quiet and hang onto my gunbelt!" Linc ordered fiercely, trying to keep his voice low. He winced when her shifting extra weight aggravated the pain in his bruised ribs. Then he turned and headed across the backyard, with Victoria hurrying after him.

Linc veered to the right to go behind the empty bunkhouses and avoid the chaos at the nearby barn. Just as he started to run across the open yard between the main house and the ranch hands' quarters, he heard shouts and gunshots coming from around the barn. Suddenly, wild neighing and bellowing moos punctuated the air, followed by thundering hooves as the barn animals were driven from the burning building and ran at full gallop right toward Linc, Deborah, and Victoria.

"Run!" Linc commanded over his shoulder to Victoria. He pushed his legs to a burst of speed that enabled him

to carry Deborah to safety behind the closest bunk-house. But when he swung around to look for Victoria, he saw her long skirt hampering her from crossing the open area as fast as he had. One of Clint Dandridge's purebred bay stallions was bearing down on her at full speed.

"Damnation!" he cursed, dipping his shoulder so Deborah tumbled off to the ground. Then he dashed away from the protective end of the building and jumped between Victoria and the charging horse. *"Ha! Ha!"* he shouted, throwing his arms up in front of the panic-stricken animal. The big bay dug its front hooves into the dirt and reared, screaming a frightened neigh. One of its thrashing hooves hit Linc's right shoulder. The powerful blow drove him to his knees. He barely rolled clear before the death-wielding hooves crashed to the ground. Tossing its head, the bay snorted and pranced sideways, then galloped away into the night following the other stampeding animals.

"Linc!" Victoria cried, running to him. Her heart beat wildly from the fear of being trampled by the panicked horse and seeing Linc struck down by it. Her legs wobbled weakly beneath her, but she willed them to carry her to him.

"I'm all right," he told her, staggering to his feet.

"Oh, Linc, you're hurt!" The barn flames streaking into the black sky cast enough light to reveal blood oozing through his torn blue shirt at the shoulder—the shoulder of his gun hand.

"No time to fuss about it. Let's go!" he ordered.

Hurrying to where Deborah lay on the ground, he reached his left hand down to her, then pulled her up and over his uninjured shoulder. Without another word, the three of them stole away from the Lazy River Fork ranch into the desert night.

"Boss! Boss!" shouted a young ranch hand, running up to Clint Dandridge, who stood grimly near the well watching the fire consume his barn. The young man thrust a black cowboy hat into his hands and hurried to explain. "That there English gal, Miss Deborah, is gone! Plumb disappeared. An' Craine's got hisself a cracked head that's gonna lay him up fer a long spell! I found this here hat layin' by him. Who do you reckon it belongs to?"

Clint Dandridge's furious expression hardened into granite fierceness. His cold gray eyes flicked to his destroyed barn, then up to the veranda of his house. His fingers moved over the crown of the hat, just under the narrow ribbon band. He found no gold stickpin, but his fingers traced over the two small holes in the felt where the pin had once been. Keeping it there had been a trick he himself had taught the owner of the hat—that trick, and much more.

"There's only one bastard with grit enough to do something like this," Dandridge said aloud, not really speaking to his hired hand. "Masterson. Linc Masterson."

Chapter Twenty-eight

"You did *what?*" Deborah exclaimed in the small servant's room. The flickering lamplight gave an eerie paleness to her pretty face, clearly revealing the disbelief in her expression.

"Shh," Victoria cautioned, opening the hall door and peeking down the corridor. They'd returned to the Diamond M after making their treacherous escape from Clint Dandridge's ranch. "No one's to know you're here, especially not Abby Masterson."

Deborah lowered her voice, but still seemed stunned. "You married Lincoln Masterson? Victoria, are you mad? He's a . . . a gunfighter—an American—an *Indian!*" With each label her voice rose in pitch. "Why in the name of heaven did you marry *him?* He's a terrible man, uncivilized, just like this awful country!"

"No, he isn't like that, Deborah," Victoria answered, annoyed by her sister's name-calling and derogatory tone. Yet she knew that a very short time ago, she'd held the same negative ideas about Linc—and Wyoming. "You don't know him. It's hard to explain the way he makes me feel, the way I've come to feel about him. I don't completely understand it myself. At first it was necessary for me to marry him to have a husband so I could gain my inheritance. Then you and I could get away from Sir Giles."

"So that was the scheme you wouldn't tell me about," Deborah interrupted. "But now that Uncle Giles is in jail, charged with father's murder, that will all change. If he's convicted, all of father's holdings will pass to you anyway. You won't need a false husband. I know it might be difficult, but you could get an annulment or a divorce or something from Mr. Masterson. How could you come to feel so much for him so quickly? Surely, it was only the extenuating circumstances—"

"I don't want an annulment or a divorce, Deborah. I want to stay married to Linc." Victoria made the statement firmly, without wavering.

"But if the marriage hasn't been consum—" Deborah lowered her eyes in embarrassment. "It isn't proper for me to discuss such topics, I know."

"Linc is my husband in every sense of the word. I love him very much." Victoria felt no shame, no hesitation. Her heart swelled with the intense feelings she held for him.

Deborah sat down hard on the edge of the narrow bed.

"Love him . . ." she echoed the words in a whisper of despair. "How, in so little time . . . ? I don't understand."

Victoria sympathized with her sister's bewilderment, worrying about the effect on her weak heart.

"It just happened, little one. I don't know why. I certainly didn't *plan* to fall in love with him, but I have. And he's in love with me. I have no experience in these matters of the heart. I only know I need him. I want to be with him so much."

She looked at the door again, feeling anxious to leave and go to Linc. Deborah seemed very shaken by the experience of the rescue and the news about the marriage, but she wasn't incapacitated. Linc needed her more now. He was hurt. When they'd returned, he'd insisted that she see to getting Deborah safely hidden in a room in the big ranch house while he tended the horses. Reluctantly, she'd obeyed him, leaving the barn feeling torn by her longstanding dedication to Deborah and her new-found devotion to him. She knew he was in pain from the fight with Craine and the trampling by the stallion. How she wished the hurt he felt were her own, that she could take it from him, bear it herself.

"I can't believe all that's happened," Deborah mumbled, sounding miserable. "So much has changed." She raised her large blue eyes to Victoria's face, a look of worry creasing her forehead. "What will become of us, of me? Who will take care of me? Will you be staying in America with him, here in Wyoming Territory? You probably won't want to be burdened by me now that you have *him!*" She crossed her arms in front of her and turned her back to Victoria.

"Don't be foolish, Deborah. You'll stay here with us. I'll still take care of you just as I always have." Victoria put her hand on her sister's shoulder, but Deborah shrugged it off.

"And what will *he* say about that? I don't want to stay in this place, Victoria. I hate it here! I want to go back to London, to our home where mama and papa are buried. We don't belong here. Everything we know is in England."

There was no mistaking the bitterness in Deborah's voice, and the pleading.

"I know how you feel, Deborah. Linc and I have talked about this a little. Perhaps I can make him understand in time."

Deborah whirled around and jumped to her feet.

"I don't want him to understand! I don't want him in our lives! You and I have always been together. It's been the two of us against everyone—Hannah, Uncle Giles. Now you want to throw me aside just because of him!"

Deborah's delicate brows dipped in an angry frown. Victoria was surprised by her vehement outburst. This was a side of her younger sister she'd never seen before.

"I won't throw you aside, Deborah. I'd never do that. You're tired and upset now. We'll talk again in the morning. Trust me. Everything will be fine."

"Trust you? How can I trust you any more, or anyone else? Oh, I wish my heart would fail now. I want to die!" She buried her face in her hands and began to sob. Victoria hurried to gather her into a hug and stroke her light brown hair.

"Please don't say such a terrible thing. I couldn't bear it if anything happened to you. We'll be together somehow. I promise."

Victoria wished she felt as sure as her words had sounded. But in truth she didn't know what the future would bring or where her future would take place—Deborah's either. A heavy weight of responsibility settled over her heart as she gently touched the side of her sister's face.

"Don't worry, little one," she beseeched. "Somehow everything will work out. Please trust me the way you always have. Sleep now. I'll send Anita in to help you prepare for bed. She's so sweet to give up her room."

"But where will you be?" Fear touched Deborah's voice as she suddenly clung to Victoria's hand. "Please don't leave me! I was so frightened when we were escaping. I'm still afraid. Please stay with me!"

Her big blue eyes reflected such a childlike and pleading expression that Victoria felt overcome with guilt. Her conscience and deep sense of duty to her sickly sister took the upper rein for the time being.

"Yes, I'll stay with you, Deborah."

Victoria found Linc still in the barn when she hurried there over an hour later, after Deborah had cried herself to sleep. The horses they'd ridden in the rescue were unsaddled and wiped dry of the sweat they'd lathered up in the frantic ride away from the Lazy River Fork ranch. They stood quietly in their stalls, munching oats from full feed bins.

Linc had removed his torn shirt and was attempting to wash the deep gash in his right shoulder, using a rag of cloth and a bucket of water.

"Here, please let me do that," Victoria offered, stepping into the small circle of light around him, cast by a kerosene lantern hung from a nail on a support post.

Linc was too weary and lightheaded from loss of blood to argue. Grateful that she'd come, he handed her the piece of clean white cotton cloth he'd been about to use. She dipped it into the bucket, then squeezed out the excess water.

"Does this sort of thing happen to you often?" she asked. "Getting hurt, I mean. I'd better change the bandage on the wound you got in your other arm at Two Eagles', too."

"It happens now and then. Hazard of the trade."

She sighed.

"It's such a dangerous line of work. The cut's still bleeding badly. I think it should be stitched." She tried to concentrate on his injury instead of his naked chest as she carefully placed the wet cloth over the torn skin of the bloody wound. He winced when she touched him, but made no sound. Her heart increased its beat and her hands trembled slightly moving over his darkly bruised shoulder. The thought of sewing his flesh made a lump of dread drop heavily into the pit of her stomach.

"Reckon I can roust out old Pete at the bunkhouse to do it," he said.

"I can put in the stitches," she volunteered, sounding more confident than she felt. The lump spread, weakening her knees.

"You ever done anything like this before?" His deep brown eyes lifted to meet hers.

"No, but I've stitched many embroidery samplers in my life."

"Embroidery." He shook his head. "I don't want the scar to look like some woman's sampler."

"I'll try to remember that and sew jaggedly!" she retorted, pricked by his condescending tone. She dipped the bloody cloth in the bucket again and wrung it out. "Here, hold this over the cut while I go to the house to ask Anita for a needle and thread." She pressed his left hand against the cloth on his shoulder. When she started to turn toward the door to leave, Linc spoke, stopping her.

"Sometimes I forget how different you and I are. I grew up herding cattle, using a gun and branding iron. You grew up doing embroidery, having the best of everything. I can't give you that, Victoria, at least not yet."

She looked back at him, smiling.

"I've learned to use a gun a little and I can learn to brand a cow if I have to. You can learn to sew if need be. I'm not asking for the best of everything, Linc. I'm only asking to be with you."

Her eyes held his for a long moment before she turned and left the barn.

Sewing his gouged flesh proved to be even harder than she imagined. The dim light from the lantern and the blood still seeping from the cut hampered every stitch along the deep five-inch gash. Linc winced and his body remained tight with tension throughout the ordeal. Sweat beaded his forehead and dripped down his face as he clenched his fist and endured the sewing.

"This hurts terribly, doesn't it?" she asked sympathetically. Despite what she'd said about sewing jaggedly, she tried to go quickly and make each stitch even and secure, but the tattered edges of the mutilated skin were hard to grasp and pinch together so she could push the needle through. Blood seemed to be everywhere she had to touch. Nausea rolled over her stomach and threatened to inch up her throat, but she forced it down and made herself work steadily.

"Yes, damn it! It hurts like hell! Just get it done, will you!"

"I'm trying! Don't talk. Stay still. Any movement hampers me!"

At last she sighed with relief and knotted the end of the thread, snipping the double strands with the pair of small sewing scissors Anita had given her. Then she bandaged the injury with other supplies she'd gotten in the house, winding a narrow strip of cloth over and under Linc's shoulder and arm to secure a wad of gauze in place over the stitches.

"Not a bad job for the first time," Linc commented, trying to sound casual speaking through gritted teeth. "You seem to have many talents. The way you went at Craine brandishing that gun helped me get the better of him."

Victoria couldn't meet his eyes. She suddenly felt shy about his compliments.

"I—I didn't want him to hurt you. But your ribs are injured, too, aren't they?"

"I don't think any are broken, but you could wrap some of that stripping around them anyway."

She nodded and handed him the end of the roll to hold. Winding the cloth strip around his naked, muscular torso was almost too much for her. She knew he must be exhausted from all that he'd been through in the last twenty-four hours, the last few days as well. Yet his strength, the controlled power of his hard-muscled chest and arms still radiated to her fingers when she touched him, exciting her and making her long to hold him, soothe his pain and tiredness away.

"Thank you for rescuing Deborah and saving me from that stampeding stallion," she said quietly, keeping her eyes on the task of bandaging his midsection. "I'm sorry you were hurt because of me."

"You seem to need a lot of looking after, ma'am," he teased, lifting her chin with his fingertips so their eyes met. His dark brown ones twinkled in the lantern light with a touch of mischief and his sensuous mouth curled up on one side in the beginning of a smile. "Best get yourself a good man for the job of keeping you out of trouble."

She leaned forward and kissed him lightly, then ran a finger down his rough cheek.

"I have found a good man, Linc . . ."

He wrapped his left arm around her narrow waist and drew her to him, meeting her lips again. It was a kiss of love, not heated desire, and it filled Victoria with complete happiness. She wouldn't have exchanged being here with him at this moment for anything in the world.

At last they drew apart, and she continued the bandaging.

"You'll have to make it tighter than that, English, or it won't do a damned bit of good," Linc told her.

She clenched her jaws and pulled, knowing by the grimace on his handsome face that she was hurting him. But his bruised ribs needed the protection of the bandaging. Finally, she tied the ends of the strip in a knot, then wiped the back of her hand over her perspiring brow. Linc caught hold of her fingers when she lowered her hand.

"You do have grit, woman. You get things done, even if it's hard on you." He turned her hand palm up to see his blood still there between her fingers. Then he locked his earthen eyes with her emerald ones. The lantern light danced over her dirt-streaked face. He felt something twist in his gut, something that made him think she never looked more beautiful. "I don't want to be in the house tonight. Stay with me, Victoria, here in the barn . . ."

She nodded, her heart filling with overwhelming feelings of love and gratitude that he was alive and wanted her with him. Extinguishing the lantern, she lay down beside Linc on a blanket thrown over a deep pile of straw in an empty stall. Again, she was torn by her need to go back to the house to be with Deborah in case she awoke in the night, and her great desire to be with Linc right now. But she didn't have the energy to think any more. Cradled in Linc's arm against his uninjured left side, she closed her eyes, so weary, but needing to be near him like this for the rest of the night.

Chapter Twenty-nine

"I feel so weak . . ." Deborah's voice was barely a hushed whisper as she put the back of her thin hand to her forehead and sighed deeply.

Anita's single-width bed in the small servant's room looked large compared to Deborah's frail form lying in the middle of it. She appeared to be so fragile and helpless, breathing laboriously, beaten down again by the heart that worked imperfectly inside her. Victoria rose from the wing-backed chair and hurried to Deborah's side, consumed with guilt that she'd left her sister all night to be with Linc. But he'd needed her, too. And she'd needed to be close to him, to feel his strength, his vital life force.

"You just need to rest, Deborah. Last night was harrowing, I know," Victoria sympathized.

Torn by her loyalties and very worried about her sister's extremely pale countenance, she dipped a clean white cloth in a shallow bowl of water, squeezed out the excess wetness, and carefully placed the cool compress across Deborah's warm brow. Smoothing back the younger girl's tangled light brown hair, she longed for her sister to regain enough strength to sit up against the pillows so she could have her hair brushed. By the hour Victoria would run their mother's silver-handled brush through Deborah's hair. It seemed to comfort her.

Looking again at the bluish tinge edging Deborah's lips, Victoria decided she must fetch a doctor. One had attended Drummond Masterson on his deathbed. Linc had called him Doc Westcott. But she wondered at his competency. What kind of a man would study medicine and then practice in a rough and tumble place like the town of Laramie, Wyoming Territory? She knew that wasn't a fair judgment, but she longed to be able to call on kindly old Dr. Babcock back in England. The saintly physician had tended Deborah and herself since their births, always giving calm advice and heartfelt caring whenever they needed it. When Deborah had developed the weakening in her heart at the age of four, he'd kept a constant vigil at her bedside for the five days it had taken to weather that first of many attacks. There was little he could do to aid her condition beyond giving her sleeping powders to help her rest, but Deborah always seemed to perk up when she knew he was coming to help her.

She'd ask Linc to send Dr. Westcott to the ranch when he went into town to join Sheriff Boswell's posse. But that would have to wait until the funeral was over.

How she wished she could be with Linc now. He'd taken on the full responsibility for seeing his brother buried, since Abigail appeared to be too distraught to make the arrangements.

Victoria could hear the hymn singing coming up from the parlor where the service was taking place. She walked around the end of the bed to look out the window, amazed by how many people had come at such short notice. Horses, carriages, and wagons lined the open yard in front of the ranch house. Because of the hot weather and the very limited talents of the town's undertaker, Drummond Masterson's body couldn't b kept from burial for too long.

Already the early morning sun promised a scorchin day. Not a single breeze filtered in through the ope window.

Linc had wanted her to attend the service with him but she knew Abigail Masterson's hostile feelings abou their marriage. She didn't want to give her any reaso to cause a scene. And Deborah had begged her not t leave her again.

The singing ended and people began filing out of th house. Victoria saw Linc at the beginning of the proces sion as one of the pallbearers of the coffin he'd fash ioned with his own hands. She noticed he used his lef hand to bear the weight, and worried again about hi injured right arm. This morning when she'd change the bandage, she'd seen that the bruised flesh aroun the stitches had spread to the size of a dinner plate ove his arm and shoulder, making her wonder if the stal lion's powerful blow had done more damage than jus cutting deeply into Linc's skin. If any muscles or ten dons had been slashed . . . but she hadn't mentione her concern to Linc. He'd seemed preoccupied with th dismal tasks the day was going to hold.

Three other men carried the rough-hewn coffin wit Linc. Abigail followed, dressed in black, leaning agains the arm of the minister who was presiding over th service. Her shoulders shook. Little Patrick walked be side her, looking bewildered. He tried to take his moth er's hand, but she paid no attention to him. Finall Anita, the Mexican maid, took Patrick's hand and le him along, holding an arm around his small shoulders

Victoria wondered just how sincere Abigail's grief wa for her dead husband, for she remembered too wel what she'd overheard the other woman say to Linc during their little rendezvous the night of the dinner party. Her heart went out to the sweet little boy. Not quite five years old, he'd barely had a chance to know his father. He'd remember little of Drummond. But was Patrick really Drummond's son? Abby had claimed he was Linc's. How would Linc ever learn the truth?

Victoria watched the group of neighbors and friends walk slowly behind the widow toward the family burial plot. A three foot wall made of piled rocks surrounded the final resting ground of the Mastersons. Victoria squinted, seeing two stone head markers already in place beside Drummond's freshly dug grave. They must belong to Linc's father and stepmother, she thought.

There were no trees to shade the graves or the mourners. Only the empty wide desert plain surrounded them, ending in the far distance at the base of the jagged-peaked, tree-covered Laramie Mountains. Though the late morning was hot, all the men present wore their Sunday-best clothes, including dark coats. Victoria wondered where Linc had gotten the black one he now had on. After helping the other pallbearers place the coffin in the grave, he stood tall and straight, holding a brown cowboy hat in his hands. Absently, she remembered he usually wore a black one. She couldn't see his handsome face, but she knew he'd be wearing the mask of stoicism she'd often seen, the expression that hid his true feelings. Those she could always see in the depths of his piercing, dark-hued eyes. Despite his great hatred for his half-brother, he grieved now for him. She'd seen the pain in his eyes, but felt certain he was trying to fight the feeling of loss by focusing on capturing Drummond's killer and keeping the ranch in Masterson hands. The cold determination she'd heard in

his voice and glimpsed in his penetrating glance tol
her Zeke Dandridge was already a defeated man. Th
thought of how that destruction would take place sent
chill running through her, despite the growing heat o
the room.

She longed to be standing beside Linc to share hi
grief. Abigail Masterson would surely claim that privi
lege. The thought caused a jealous twinge to boil u
inside her. She drummed her fingers on the cross sas
of the window frame. But the tense feeling subsided t
be replaced by amazement when she saw that Abb
remained standing next to the preacher across the grav
from Linc. She appeared to be looking directly at Linc
yet she made no move to get closer to him. Could it b
that she no longer harbored any desire for him?

"Victoria," Deborah called weakly, "is the funeral ove
for poor Mr. Masterson?"

"Everyone is gathered at the gravesite for the fina
words," Victoria answered, turning away from the win
dow. "How are you feeling, Deborah?"

"Very tired. I think I shall take your advice and tr
to rest some more. Tell me a story from the Bible t
help me go to sleep. You have such a good memory. I'
like to hear the story of Naomi and Ruth again."

"Of course, dear," Victoria agreed, sitting down reluc
tantly in the brocade chair once more to reach into he
memory for the story, one of Deborah's favorites. Bu
she wished her sister hadn't chosen that Bible text jus
now. The story about a woman's devotion and loyalty t
another woman who needed her help wouldn't calm he
own tumultuous, divided thoughts at the moment.

A short time later, Deborah's eyes closed and he
head lolled over to the side. With sudden panic, Victo
ria sprang out of the chair to the side of the bed

Holding the backs of her fingers close to her sister's nose, she expelled a held-in breath in relief when she felt the movement of air against her skin. Deborah was only sleeping.

Victoria walked to the window again. Everyone was returning to the ranch house. No, she saw that Linc and his half-sister, Callie, still remained at the small cemetery, along with Duggins, the young ranch hand. Linc's head was bowed as he stood beside the grave while Duggins shoveled the desert sand over Drummond's coffin. Linc shook his hand when he finished the somber task. Then Duggins headed back toward the house.

Linc stood beside the grave with Callie. Victoria ached to go to him, to try to ease his grief.

She glanced once more at Deborah, then quietly left the bedroom. Using the back stairway, she went outside, walking with brisk, determined steps through the yard to the small cemetery.

Callie had stepped back a few feet from Linc. She turned when she heard Victoria approach. Holding up a hand, she motioned for Victoria to stop, then walked back to join her.

"Wait, please, Victoria," she whispered when they were side by side. They were far enough away that her voice didn't carry to Linc. "Give him this time alone," she continued, wiping her red-rimmed eyes with a white lace handkerchief.

Linc had told Victoria that Callamae came between Drummond and himself in age. She and Drummond had had the same mother. Callie had Drummond's coloring, not quite as dark as Linc's.

She could only be a year or two older than Linc, yet she looked worn down, ten years older than her thirty

years. Deep creases lined her tanned face, and her lon
raven hair showed distinct streaks of gray. Her rounde
figure was heavy with child—her sixth baby in eigh
years, she'd said at the dinner party. She had none o
the strong, sharp features that were so distinct in th
Masterson men. Her narrow-set brown eyes held
weary gaze, and her small mouth turned down at th
edges with grim resignation. Victoria suspected this ter
ritory could be hard on a woman who didn't have
wealthy husband and servants to ease the burden o
everyday chores.

Her heart went out to the grieving woman now. Cal
lie's pain at losing her brother showed clearly in he
face and in her trembling hand as she dabbed again a
the tears brimming in her eyes. But she kept her shoul
ders back and held her head up proudly.

"Linc needs to make his peace with papa as well a
Drummond," she explained quietly. At Victoria's ques
tioning look, she went on, glancing toward Linc's broa
back. "He doesn't want to feel this loss, you know. He'
like to keep hating Drummond, just as he did all hi
life. He always thought Drumm was Papa's favorite, be
cause he was white and older. How Linc would try t
best him—riding, lassoing, branding, fighting, shooting
everything. Papa was hard on Linc, I think because h
knew a half-breed boy would have to be toughened t
survive as a man. I see that now, and I think Lin
does, too. But I remember so many times when pap
used his leather belt on him, testing his obedience, hi
spirit. Linc would never break. I used to scream fo
him to cry or beg papa to stop hurting him, but h
never would. He'd get this hard, distant look in hi
eyes, like he was shutting everything out. Finally, pap
would get tired and stop the punishment.

"Linc is so like papa now. Strong, iron-willed, bucking under to no man or blow of fate. I was always afraid his heart had turned to stone, keeping him from feeling anything, until I saw the look in his eyes when he laid Drummond in the coffin this morning, the coffin he'd made with his own hands. They were deadly enemies, but brothers, too. The blood of our father flowed through both of them, still flows through Linc. He's a Masterson; that fact joins him with papa and Drummond as nothing else can. Not legal titles or a different race or people calling him less than a man. None of that matters now." She pulled her gaze away from Linc to look at Victoria. "You don't know our ways yet, so I'll tell you there'll be no changing his mind about going after the Dandridges. You'd be wasting your breath to even try. The most you can do is wait for him and pray, then love him when he comes back to you . . . if he comes back." She put an arm around Victoria's waist. "We'd best leave him alone now."

Victoria felt shaken by Callie's words, yet she knew somehow they were all true. Reluctantly, she walked with her down the path. At the corner of the ranch house, she stopped and turned to look back at Linc. He'd taken off his black coat and white shirt and put them on the ground. He lifted his hands and looked to the heavens, beginning to move his feet in the shuffling steps she'd seen him do with Two Eagles. Bending slightly and with head bowed again, he did a slow Indian dance around first Drummond's grave, and then the one next to it. She guessed that one must be his father's final resting place. She stood too far away to hear him clearly, but she felt the sound vibrations of the chant—the low, droning song of farewell.

She watched him a long time, aching deeply for him.

After a while she let her eyes drift around her to see i
anyone else was paying attention to Linc. To her sur
prise, she glimpsed young Patrick standing alone at th
edge of the porch, watching silently.

Victoria knew she shouldn't be eavesdropping outsid
the parlor door, but she couldn't help herself. Sh
longed to be with Linc, if only to stand by him, to giv
him some of her strength. Any amount of time awa
from him felt empty and meaningless. Only when sh
was with him did she feel content, complete. This in
tense need for someone was so new and puzzling to her
Thoughts of Linc filled her mind constantly, especiall
now, when he had his half-brother's murder and th
probable loss of owning the Diamond M to conten
with, she wanted to be by his side. But she knew th
reading of Drummond Masterson's will would be for th
family only. Abby Masterson certainly wouldn't welcom
her intrusion at a time like this. So she hung back in
the shadows of the stairwell, hoping to hear Linc's voic
through the open door.

Almost all the neighbors and friends who had come t
pay their last respects to Drummond Masterson and th
family had left the ranch. Taft Denton was one who'
remained. He was with Linc and Abby now in th
parlor, along with Callie and her husband, Brad Mor
row. The parson had also stayed to console the family in
this time of bereavement.

Victoria remembered Denton from the night of th
dinner party. She didn't like the tall, stoop-shouldere
lawyer. His black, beady eyes always seemed to be shift
ing nervously. More than once during that dinner, she'
felt his flicking gaze stop on her, and it had caused

quick shudder of apprehension to run up her spine. She couldn't really explain her dislike of him. She only knew she didn't trust him. She had the feeling he could be ruthless.

" 'I, Drummond Masterson,' " Denton said aloud, " 'being of sound body and clear mind, declare this to be my last will and testament. To my wife, Abigail Masterson, I give and bequeath all my worldly possessions, including the house, out-buildings, and land known as the Diamond M ranch, and all livestock which may be a part of said ranch at the time of my death.

" 'In the event that my wife, Abigail Masterson, should die within twenty-four hours of my death, or become unable or unwilling to accept this bequest for any reason, then I give and bequeath all of the above to my son, Patrick Holden Masterson. If Patrick should not be of legal age at that time, then it is my wish that N. K. Boswell, Sheriff of Laramie, Wyoming Territory, be appointed his legal guardian and executor of this estate, until such time as Patrick reaches the age of maturity and can take over the ranch on his own. N. K. Boswell has already agreed to these terms.

" 'To my sister, Callamae Masterson Morrow, I give and bequeath . . ."

Denton's voice droned on for a short time more, but Victoria barely listened. No mention was made of Linc in Drummond's will. Abby did get everything. She would surely sell out to Clinton Dandridge.

If only I could have arranged to get my inheritance sooner, Victoria thought sadly. But there hadn't been time. Drummond had been murdered by Zeke Dandridge before she and Linc could do anything about claiming her inheritance because of her marriage. Perhaps Clint Dandridge would sell the Diamond M to Linc if the price were high enough.

Victoria hung her head, knowing that wasn't likely to happen. Clinton Dandridge was so like Giles Spencer in his unrelenting drive for power. And here in Wyoming, land meant power. Linc's dream was lost . . .

"Madre de Dios."

Victoria whirled around at the sound of the whispered Spanish words and nearly collided with Anita, the pretty young Mexican servant who'd been so kind to her and Deborah.

"Oh, I—I didn't see you standing there, Anita," she stammered in a low voice, embarrassed to be caught eavesdropping.

Anita lowered her eyes shyly, looking troubled. She motioned for Victoria to follow her farther down the hall, away from the parlor.

"It is all right, senora," she replied softly in heavily accented English when they were far enough away not to be heard. "I, too, listen. I only want to hear my Patrick in there—if he cry or call for me. My English, it not so good. The words I hear, they from Señor Drummond before he . . . he . . ."

Anita's voice cracked with emotion. Victoria saw her velvety brown eyes fill with tears. She put an arm around her shoulders.

"Yes, Mr. Drummond had them written down in what is called a will," she explained, "so his wishes would be carried out after his death."

Anita stared past Victoria to the open parlor door, still looking uncertain.

"Then what I hear, that will be? Señora Masterson have ranch? The words, they will not be changed?"

"Yes, she owns the Diamond M now. The words must

stand as Mr. Denton said them just now." Victoria disliked the thought almost as much as Anita seemed to. The young servant woman, who appeared to be about her own age, looked crestfallen. She wondered what kind of life Anita had here at the ranch, always at the beck and call of the pampered and snobbish Abigail Masterson. There was no doubting Anita's feelings for little Patrick. Love spun through her voice when she mentioned him, something that was quite lacking when Abigail spoke of her son.

Anita put her hand to her temple, looking as if she were thinking hard.

"Please to excuse me, señora. I must think. I am much sad when Señor Drummond die."

"I understand. Come and talk to me later if you'd like."

Anita nodded and turned toward the kitchen, an absent look on her pretty, dark-complexioned face. Victoria wished she could have helped her more. Sighing with a deep sadness of her own, she walked to the stairway at the end of the hall, and went up to check on Deborah.

Chapter Thirty

Victoria hurried out of the house to the stable yard where Linc was mounting his horse with the other Diamond M ranch hands. She wanted to ask him to send the doctor out to the ranch for Deborah. When she saw him checking the bullet chamber of his Colt, the harsh reality of what he and these other men were about to do hit her like a crushing blow.

"Do you have to join the posse?" she asked worriedly.

Linc had changed from the dress clothes he'd worn for the funeral and the reading of the will to tan duck work pants and a light blue cotton shirt. He looked at her now, but his hard gaze seemed to pass right through her.

"Yes," he answered, forcefully pulling the brim of his leather hat down to shield his face from the scorching sun.

"But if it comes to gunplay, how will you shoot with your shoulder injured?" She grabbed the bridle of his roan to prevent him from reining away.

"Let me worry about that, Victoria. This has to be finished. Let go of the harness."

The icy command in his deep voice sliced through her like one of the lances Two Eagles kept mounted on his cabin wall. Unwillingly, she let her hand drop away from the worn leather. Linc's dark gaze locked with hers a moment longer, but he said nothing more, instead turning his attention to the men around him.

"You boys swing by the line shack at the east forty pasture and pick up the hands who're rounding up strays. Then head into Laramie. I'm going to ride up to Como Bluff to see if Bill Reed can spare some of his boys from the scientific digging he's doing up there. Meet you at the sheriff's office. You know what we have to do. Let's get to it!"

Kicking spurs to horses, all the men galloped away, leaving Victoria in the dust, staring after Linc. He'd said no words of farewell or encouragement. How she wished she could go with him, but he'd closed her out, determined to face all his enemies on his own terms, as he always did. But what could she do to help him anyway? She couldn't use a gun. She'd only be a burden to him, even a danger, if she somehow diverted his attention for even an instant in a life-threatening circumstance. But not knowing what would be happening to him felt like brutal torture. A terrible fist of relentless fear gripped her insides. It told every fiber of her being that this could be the end. Linc might not return from his mission of retribution, the range battle he was riding into. Clinton Dandridge would never give up his son for Drummond's murder, not without a bloody fight. His ranch was an armed camp. They'd seen that last night when they'd rescued Deborah. Men would die on both sides. Linc could die . . . she hated the horrible, crushing thought! No! She couldn't lose him! If only she could've stopped him, prevented this showdown. But how?

"Señora!"

Victoria turned to see Anita hike up her colorful red print skirt in her hands and hurry down the front porch steps toward her. When she reached her, she raised her fingers to shade her eyes and looked toward the cloud of dust kicked up by Linc and the others' mounts as they rode away.

"Oh, no, Señor Masterson is gone! But there is something I think is great in importance I am having to tell him!"

Anita sounded frantic. Her dark brown eyes were wide and beseeching when they shifted to Victoria.

"What is it, Anita? Please tell me."

Anita wrung her hands nervously, looking uncertain.

"I am afraid to speak this before, Señora, because I listen. I not mean to, but I pass by door in the hall one day, like today. I hear Señor Drummond and the señora have mucho bad words together. He say he is make new words on paper so the señora no get ranch."

"What?" Victoria grabbed Anita by the shoulders with both hands. "Are you saying Drummond Masterson was going to make a new will and leave his wife out of it?"

"Will, *sí.* That is what he call it."

"But who would get the ranch? Think, Anita. This is very important!"

Anita looked wary, as if she feared she'd said too much already.

"Please, you must trust me!" Victoria coaxed, letting go of the other woman's shoulders, but still keeping one hand on her arm to show her earnestness. "Did he mention Señor Linc?"

Anita shook her head.

"Only my little *niño,* Patrick. The land, he should have it, Señor Drummond say. I run away then from the door. I am frightened to be caught."

"When did this happen? Was it long ago?"

"Only two weeks ago he say this. They fight very loud."

"Are you sure of all this, Anita? You must be certain."

"*Si,* I hear."

"This could change everything." Victoria darted a glance toward the distant riders. "Señor Linc must know about this. Swear to me that when he comes back, you'll tell him exactly what you told me just now. Swear it, Anita!"

"*Si, si,* I swear!" the other woman exclaimed, shrinking back.

Victoria's mind began to whirl. What if, in a fit of anger at Abigail, Drummond had changed his will and left everything to Patrick or perhaps even Linc? That way he'd know the Diamond M would stay in Masterson hands. But if there was a more recent will than the one that had been read this morning, where was it? Somehow she and Linc must find it!

She tried to think hard back to the gruesome scene when Drummond lay dying in the parlor. She'd been so overcome by his mutilated body and certain death, that she'd barely concentrated on the words he'd struggled to say to Linc. Forcing herself to see the terrible picture in her mind again, she suddenly remembered he *had* mentioned Patrick and wanting the ranch to belong only to Mastersons. Did he say something about papers? Papers in a desk somewhere. *Pa's desk,* he'd said. Yes, those were Drummond's words!

"Anita, did Mr. Drummond's father have a desk where he kept important papers?"

"Desk?" Anita looked puzzled.

"Yes, a desk with drawers, like the one in the parlor."

"*Si,* that is a desk for papers of much importance!" Anita answered eagerly.

Victoria wanted to run into the house and ransack the desk in the parlor, but she made herself hold back. Abigail Masterson and Taft Denton were still in there. And besides, she couldn't help wondering if Abigail might have suspected Drummond's plan and been on her guard for a new will. Surely she would have searched Drummond's desk and anywhere she could think of before today's reading. Who would Drummond have trusted to script the new will? Taft Denton? But the man had made no mention of one today during the reading. Had Drummond changed his mind when his temper cooled and not made a new document?

So many questions—and no answers. She must talk to Linc about all this. If there had been a new will, then she and Linc had to find it before Abby could sign over the deed to the Diamond M to Clinton Dandridge or anyone else. But Linc had just ridden off to recruit a posse for a showdown with Dandridge!

She didn't know a way to prevent two armies of hostile and violent men from shedding blood all over the range. She only knew she couldn't stay standing here in the yard watching their dust!

Whirling around, she spied the minister's horse tied to the hitching rail in front of the house. He must still be here. Well, God forgive her, she was going to steal his horse! The Lord would understand that she wanted to do His work by preventing a range war!

A gun. She might need a gun. She ran over to the preacher's mount, but saw that there was no saddle holster holding a rifle such as Linc carried.

"What you doin', ma'am?" The question came from old Pete Foster sitting in a straight-backed wooden chair on the porch. Pete couldn't ride because of a foot swollen by gout, so Linc had left him behind to keep guard in case any Dandridge men showed up. Holding a Winchester rifle across his legs, he leaned forward to talk to Victoria, then winced and glanced down at his foot.

"I need a gun, Mr. Foster!" Victoria exclaimed, skipping up the three steps to the front porch.

"What in tarnation for?" His merry blue eyes, deep-creased and sun-weathered at the edges, widened in surprise.

"I don't have time to explain, but it's very important. Please give me your pistol!" She darted a look at his gunbelt hanging on the back of the chair.

"Why, no, ma'am, I ain't agoin' to!"

But before the elderly man could protest further, Victoria rushed at him and grabbed the revolver out of the holster. Jamming the barrel into the waistband of her skirt, she spun around and dashed down the steps to the reverend's horse.

"No, ma'am, you come back here with that there six shooter, you hear!" Old Pete hollered, but she paid no attention to him. He couldn't catch her, crippled like he was, and she didn't think he'd shoot her to stop her!

It was a high step to reach the horse's stirrup without someone to help, but Victoria grabbed hold of the saddle horn and mustered her stubborn will to propel herself up with quick speed. Shooting a glance toward the northern horizon, she couldn't make out Linc on his horse. The ranch hands had forked off in an easterly direction. She could still see the cloud of dust from their horses.

"Don't fly off half-loco, ma'am!" Old Pete shouted. *"Come back here!"*

"I can't, Mr. Foster! I have to do this!"

Yanking on the reins to turn the horse to the north, she dug the heels of her boots into the animal's sides and hung on for dear life when it plunged forward with a burst of speed. Only one thought possessed her whole being as she rode away—she must catch up with Linc!

A shot exploded in the silent desert air. Victoria pulled back hard on the reins, skidding her mount to a halt. She swung around in the saddle, unable to determine the direction of the gunshot. Heart pounding in her chest, she darted her eyes around the parched, nearly barren landscape, waiting for another firing. Fear gripped her as she expected to be hit by a deadly bullet at any moment, yet she could see no assailant in view. There were no trees and very little else to serve as any kind of cover, either for her to use, or for someone who might be waiting in ambush. Only low rocks, odd shaped cactus, and scattered tufts of scrub grass surrounded her, except to her left where the fingers of foothills from the Laramie mountain range gouged into the edge of the desert. Those hills could easily conceal men and horses, and Linc had been headed for Como Bluff in the mountains.

Victoria swallowed hard, not know what to do next. She felt beads of sweat trickle along her throat and down between her breasts under her clinging blouse. The afternoon sun beat down mercilessly, spreading shimmering waves of heat along the gently rolling ground. She wished she'd brought a hat to protect her head. The oppressive heat felt consuming and dangerous, as if it sought to sap the life out of her to fuel its intensity.

She must find Linc. Had he fired the single shot

she'd heard at an enemy? Or had the bullet found its mark in him? That terrible thought spurred her to action. She kicked her lathered horse into a gallop once more toward the hills.

The rocks at the base of the mountains grew larger as she approached them. Skirting an out-jutting, high pile of them, she pulled her horse up short. Garbled voices carried to her on the gusting hot breeze. Jumping down from the saddle, she bent low and scrambled up over the rocks to a higher vantage point. Taking the gun out of her skirt waistband, she lay down on her stomach and peeked over the boulders. A shallow, three-sided rock canyon was just below her. What she saw made her gasp. Linc stood alone surrounded by eight men on horseback. His horse lay sprawled on the ground, unmoving. Linc's arms were pinned to his sides by a lariat. The end of the rope holding him was tied to the saddlehorn of a horse ridden by Zeke Dandridge!

"Keep strugglin', Masterson!" Zeke exclaimed with a nasty laugh as Linc dug his heels in and twisted against the rope. "It won't do you no good. You're caught, you black-hearted, half-breed bastard, an' I'm gonna take real pleasure in killin' you. Draggin's the best way for the low-life likes of you to die!"

He laughed again and pulled his horse around, digging his spurs into the animal's sides. The roan screamed a neigh and plunged forward. Linc was jerked off his feet to his belly. He hung onto the outstretched rope, but was rolled and bounced from side to side by the galloping horse.

"NO!" Victoria cried, springing to her feet. Linc would be killed if she didn't do something to stop Dandridge!

She was shaking violently as she raised the pistol with

both hands. Desperately, her mind whirled, trying to remember all Linc had told her about firing a gun when he'd shown her how to use the rifle at Two Eagles's ranch. But she had no experience in using a gun like this. Her chances of hitting even a still target were slim at best. Hitting a man on a racing horse would be impossible! Could she fire at a man, perhaps kill him? She hated the thought, but knew she had to try or Linc would die.

Clenching her teeth together, she struggled to pull back the resisting hammer until it clicked into the set place. Then she closed her left eye and squinted down the length of the barrel with her other, using the small raised metal sight at the end to find her target—Zeke Dandridge. He was riding right toward her, looking back over his shoulder at Linc. The seven cowboys with him followed behind, whooping and hollering and firing their guns in the air.

Taking a deep breath, she held it, gripping the gun with all her might. Willing her hands to stop trembling, she took aim with deadly, controlled calm. Her jaws ached from clenching them together. Steadily, she pulled the trigger. The gun discharged with a loud crack, kicking back in her hands. Dandridge's horse dropped like a stone, its front legs collapsing under it. Zeke pitched violently forward, hitting the ground face-first.

The other cowboys whirled their horses around in confusion. Five more times Victoria pulled back on the trigger, emptying the gun into the ring of men. One of them yelped and fell from his horse.

The diversion and chaos caused by the gunfire allowed Linc time to gain his senses. Fighting the sharp pain shooting through his arm and bruised ribs, he spit grit from his mouth and swiftly rolled over to get to his knees. The rope binding him had gone slack when Zeke's horse went down. He easily whipped it off and rose to his knees, staggering for balance. His hand dropped for his Colt with lightning speed. Pivoting on one knee, he fanned the hammer, firing off five shots. Each found its mark in a cowboy. Only one man got away, riding hell bent for leather out of range into the open desert.

When the dust settled, Zeke Dandridge and four of his gunmen lay moaning and writhing on the ground. Two others lay still, dead where they'd fallen from their horses.

Victoria awkwardly scurried down the rock pile, nearly falling on the loose stones. Frantically, she ran into the circle of carnage she'd helped wreck on Dandridge and the ranch hands. Her eyes sought only one man—Linc. Gripped with fear, she dashed to where he was struggling to his feet, still holding his smoldering gun in his hand. He was covered with sand and grass. His shirt was torn in front from the dragging and blood stained it at his injured shoulder.

His scratched, dirt-smudged face registered surprise when he saw her coming toward him.

"Victoria, what—?"

"Oh, God, Linc, are you all right?" she cried, falling into his arms.

"*You* fired those shots?" His voice sounded disbelieving, even when he saw the sixgun in her hand.

She clung to him, looking up into his face.

"Yes. I didn't know what I was doing. I tried to hit Zeke Dandridge, but I shot his horse instead. Then I just kept firing until the gun was empty, hoping to give you time to do something! Dear God, I thought they were going to kill you!" Her words tumbled out in a rush, and she had to stop for a gasp of breath.

"Damnation, you saved my life, woman!" A quirk of a smile curled up the corner of his mouth. He hugged his free left arm around her, then swayed and winced when the effort tormented his ribs. But he still kept one eye on the men on the ground and his gun ready.

"You can barely stand, can you?" She looked at him worriedly. "And your shoulder's bleeding again." She touched the bloody wet spot spreading down his shirt. "The stitches—"

He brushed off her concern.

"I'll be all right. A lot better off than if you hadn't shown up. Why in hell are you here anyway?"

"I had to find you," she explained quickly. "Anita told me she heard Drummond say he was going to make another will and leave everything to Patrick, cutting Abby out completely. If he did, we have to find that will before Abby can sell out to Clinton Dandridge!"

Linc frowned.

"Anita's sure of this? She doesn't speak the best English."

"Yes, she's certain. She overheard Abby and Drummond arguing one day two weeks ago. Could Drummond have hidden a new will in a desk in the ranch house? Remember he said something about papers just before he died."

Linc's earth-brown eyes shone.

"It'll sure be worth a hard look around to find out, after I get Zeke and these other boys in to Boswell."

"You'll need help. I'll come with you." She started to walk toward the rocks where she'd left her horse, but Linc caught her by the arm.

"No, it could be dangerous. You've taken enough chances. When Clint hears his son's in jail on a murder charge, he's going to ride in to take the town apart. I don't want you anywhere around. Go back to the ranch. You'll be safe there."

"But—"

"Don't argue with me, Victoria." He frowned and tried to sound stern, but it was mighty hard with those big green eyes of hers staring up at him. "I can't concentrate on Clint if I'm worrying about you. Where's your horse?"

Reluctantly, she pointed toward the out-jutting of boulders.

"High-tail it back to the Diamond M. I'll round up these boys and head into town. If you can get by Abby, start looking for that possible new will. I'll be back to the ranch as soon as I can."

Impulsively, she swallowed back tears of worry and reached up to hug him hard around the neck.

"Please be careful, Linc. I love you."

He pulled back a little and raised her small chin with his fingertips.

"Don't fret, English. You'll see me again." He bent and gave her a quick kiss, then turned toward Zeke Dandridge, who was wobbling to his feet holding his bloody head with his hands.

Victoria hurried away to find her horse, feeling a myriad of emotions churning inside her. Her great love for Linc filled every sense of her being, giving her an exhilarating feeling of joy that she'd been able to help him. But she worried despairingly about his injuries and the danger he'd be riding into. He was badly hurt, but he stubbornly insisted on seeing Drummond's killers punished. So many futures hung on such a fragile thread now—hers, Linc's, Deborah's, the Dandridges's, her uncle's, Alden's, Abby's. She felt a terrible fore-

boding. They all stood poised on the precipice. Wh
would remain standing, and who would fall?

With a shudder of dread, Victoria mounted her hors
and reined it toward the ranch.

Chapter Thirty-one

"Hey, you there! What's going on?" Linc called, reining in his mount in the middle of Laramie's main street to block the path of a running Chinese man wearing a storekeeper's full white apron. The man skidded to a halt to avoid colliding with the horse. Other people zigzagged around them hurrying toward the east end of town.

"Big trouble Sheriff office," the Oriental blurted in broken English, casting a curious look toward the five battered men and two corpses on horseback that Linc held in tow.

Linc glanced up the street toward the jail.

"What happened?"

"Not know. Big shootout. Go see now." The man ducked around Linc's horse and broke into a run again, following the other townspeople.

Linc did the same. Guiding the horses through the pedestrians, he soon reached the sheriff's office. A crowd stood around it, talking excitedly. Two men and a boy peered in the barred window. Linc spied Clete Duggins from the Diamond M standing in the doorway, keeping curious spectators out of the jail office.

Linc dismounted and tied the horses bearing the two dead cowhands to the hitching rail. Then he pulled his five prisoners off their horses in turn and set them on their feet. He'd tied their hands securely behind their backs at the canyon, so they could give no resistance. Drawing his gun, he prodded Zeke in the back to hurry him along.

"Move! Make way there!" he ordered, yanking on the lead rope holding them together to pull them with him through the crowd along the sidewalk.

"What happened here, Duggins?" he asked when he reached the office.

The young man seemed glad to see him.

"There was a jail break, Mr. Masterson. That feller Giles Spencer got away. The sheriff's shot an' so's one of the masked men who broke Spencer out. I sent for the doc. He should be here any minute."

"Good man. Keep these people out here. Where are the rest of the Diamond M hands?"

"I sent 'em after Spencer and the others, but they had a head start. Don't know if our boys can catch 'em. They'll be back if they lose the trail."

Linc nodded and gestured for Zeke Dandridge and the others to file into the office ahead of him. Inside, he took a sharp look around the ransacked room and saw N. K. Boswell lying on his back on the floor near the overturned desk. Blood flowed from a wound on the left side of his head. A man wearing the striped white shirt, green visor, and sleeve garters of a telegraph operator knelt beside the sheriff, dabbing at the wound with a handkerchief. Another man with a brown kerchief pulled up a mask over the lower half of his face sat sprawled in the corner, unmoving, shot in the stomach.

Linc spied the ring of keys to the jail cells lying on the floor near the door. Going to them, he tossed them to the telegraph man.

"Lock up these boys pronto. I'll have a look at the sheriff," he ordered. He knelt next to Boswell while the telegraph operator herded Zeke and the others into the cells.

Boswell groaned and reached for his holster, which was empty. His gun lay on the floor a little distance away.

"Easy, N. K. It's Linc Masterson. The doc's coming. Don't try to move."

"Linc?" Boswell's eyes fluttered open and he struggled to raise himself. Linc swung an arm under the lawman's shoulders to support him as he stammered to speak. "Tarnation, I . . . could've used . . . you here sooner." He groaned once more and touched his head wound. "Six of em . . . busted in here . . . for Spencer. Wore masks. Got that there . . . evidence letter, too. I . . . shot one of em . . ." His hand shook as he raised it a little and pointed toward the corner, then he fell back unconscious again.

Linc eased him down to the floor, feeling his neck for a pulse. Boswell was still alive, but he couldn't say the same for the man in the corner. Gut-shot at close range.

Squatting down in front of the cowboy dressed in ranch-hand denims and tan cotton shirt, he reached out to lower the kerchief.

"Alden Cummings," he murmured in surprise. He didn't think the foreign tinhorn had the savvy to pull off something like this. He sure wasn't dressed in his usual dandy garb.

"They're all locked up," the telegraph man said, coming to stand next to Linc. "This one won't be doin' no jail breaks from now on."

"Nope." Linc got to his feet. "Much obliged for your help with those men."

"You know you got Zeke Dandridge in that bunch, don't you, mister? He's a bad one. His pa'll be in here after him in no time with a passel of ranch hands who're good with guns. I don't reckon to be around when he does!"

"Well, I do. Clint and I got a score to settle once an for all."

"You know Clint Dandridge? Who are you, mister Don't just anybody take on the Dandridge clan." H squinted hard at Linc. "Wait a minute. I do know you Ain't seen you around town in quite a spell. You're Lin Masterson, ain't you? I heard what happened to Drum mond. Mighty sorry. I reckon you won't have no troubl standin' up to Clint Dandridge, not the way your reputa tion goes for handlin' a shootin' iron."

There was respect in the older man's tone, a respec Linc had worked hard to earn with his gun over the pas few years. But now the telegraph operator's praise had hollow ring to it.

A heavy cloud of gloom seemed to settle on his shoul ders. He'd made his living with his gun for five years But now he wanted something else, and Victoria was big part of it. He wanted to build a place out of the lan with her, something he could look upon with pride, an leave as a legacy to his sons and daughters. But righ now that all seemed like a distant dream. He shouldn' drag Victoria into all this, his ambitions, his revenge hatreds and deceptions that went back way before she' ever come into his life. She had no business being in thi territory at all. Not the likes of her. This country wa hard on a woman. Look what it had done to Callie Made her old and haggard before her time. He didn' want that to happen to Victoria.

Damnation! He shouldn't even be thinking about he at a time like this! Doing so could take the edge off hi concentration. As long as he never thought of anybod else but himself, he had the upper hand. Self-preservatio always made his gun hand move just a split second faste than any opponent's—at least till now.

He knew the showdown with Clint Dandridge was in

evitable. It had been destined between them since the first day Clint showed him how to handle a gun. He knew Clint would someday have to know who was faster—the teacher or the pupil. Clint always had to be the best, own the best. Drumm's murder and the clash over the ownership of the Diamond M had only hastened their final confrontation.

He went back over to the sheriff and tied the man's red checkered neckerchief around his head to try to slow the bleeding until the doctor arrived. Boswell's breathing was shallow but steady. Linc had seen worse wounds. He reckoned Boswell would survive this one. But he wouldn't be of any use today in going after Spencer and Clint Dandridge.

"What you got Zeke an' them boys locked up for?" the telegraph man asked.

"Charge of murder on Zeke, for Drumm's death," Linc answered sternly. "I don't know yet what other Lazy River Fork boys were involved in doing in my brother, but I aim to find out. Did you see the jail break? Was anybody else shot?"

"I heard the commotion an' come runnin' out of the telegraph office into the street. Near got run over by the masked men who broke that there English fella out of here. I was so busy jumpin' out of the way, I didn't see if any of 'em was shot or not. Couldn't believe somebody'd have the hide to do this is broad daylight. You reckon it was more Dandridge boys who done it? Clint Dandridge's been real thick with that Englishman." He snapped his fingers and looked startled. "Why, I remember now. One of the riders was on a Lazy River Fork ranch horse. I saw the brand!"

"Makes sense," Linc answered thoughtfully.

Doc Westcott arrived in the jail office just then, and Linc stepped back to give the older man room to work on the sheriff.

"Well now, you got yourself a real problem, don't you, Masterson?" Zeke spouted cock-surely from his cell. "This here fella's right about my pa gettin' me out of here. No jail cell can hold a Dandridge or anybody sidin' with us. Boswell won't be no law for some time, I'd say. My pa's sure to own this whole territory soon enough. Nobody can stop him. He's got the money and the hired guns. That's all it takes. Nobody'll stand in his way. Any fool who tries won't last long. And that really goes for you, you red-skinned bastard."

Showing no emotion, Linc stepped over in front of the jail cell and stood facing Zeke Dandridge with legs apart. Slowly and deliberately, he drew his Colt Peacemaker, raised it to shoulder level, and cocked back the hammer, aiming the gun right at Zeke's head.

"I've heard just about all I want to from you, Zeke. One more word and I'll save the good taxpayers of this territory the trouble of a trial and a hanging for you."

Linc's tone was deadly serious. Zeke's Adam's apple in his throat bobbed up and down as he swallowed and stared hard at the barrel of the Colt. For a long moment, no one moved or said a word. Only the flies buzzing around the office broke the tense stillness in the stifling hot room. Finally, Linc released the hammer and slid the gun smoothly back into his holster.

"Fetch the undertaker for Cummings there and for the two outside I brought in with me," Linc said to the telegraph man. "Duggins," he called through the door. The young ranch hand ducked his head and came into the room. "Keep a close watch on Zeke and his boys. I'll be back as soon as I can round up some more help. If the rest of the Diamond M boys show up, keep them here at the jail with you."

"Right, Mr. Masterson," Duggins answered, casting a

owning glance toward the prisoners.

Linc left the sheriff's office and went to get his horse at ne hitching rail. His right shoulder had stopped bleed-ng, but it was throbbing badly. And with every step, his ibs reminded him that they'd taken mighty hard treat-nent. Drawing down on Zeke Dandridge the way he'd one just now hadn't helped the pain. But at least he new he could hold a gun. He could block pain out of is mind if he had to. He'd had a lot of practice doing hat.

God, he felt like he'd been stomped by a two-ton bull! weaty, dirty, aching all over. Stepping to the watering rough, he took off his hat and leaned down, dunking in is head up to his shoulders. Coming up, he threw his ead back and wiped his hand over his wet face, then aked his fingers through his hair, relishing the feel of the vater dripping down his neck and chest. Getting dragged ehind Zeke's horse had about scraped off his hide. If 'ictoria hadn't shown up . . . he shook his head, still mazed by the way she'd blasted the canyon and taken eke's horse down. No doubt about it, Victoria was quite gal. He'd never met another woman like her, that was or sure!

Putting on his hat again, he gingerly mounted up, aking care to brace his bruised ribs with his arm. He eeded Bill Reed and his men from Como Bluff more han ever now, since Boswell wouldn't be up to going gainst Clint or swearing in a posse. He'd ride hard up hat way soon enough. It would take a while for Clint to et the word about Zeke and make a plan to come after im. He had a little time to pay a visit to Taft Denton's ffice just down the street.

He skirted the crowd of people still lingering around he jail. No one was on the wooden sidewalk outside Denton's office. He was careful to look around as he tied his horse's reins to the hitching post. He figured Denton would still be out at the ranch with Abby, and that was just fine. It wasn't Denton he wanted to see.

Entering the lawyer's office, he blinked against the dimmer surroundings after coming in from the bright sunlight.

"Yes? May I help you?" asked a balding man of slight build who glanced up from where he was working at a desk cluttered with papers. In his late thirties, he wore a worn brown suit and a crisp white shirt with a high starched collar.

" 'Afternoon, Howell," Linc greeted in a friendly voice, then waited for the other man's reaction. It came immediately.

"You!" His wire, pinch-nose spectacles popped off his bridge and clattered against the desk before being caught up by the thin black ribbon attached to them. Fumbling with the ribbon, the man hurriedly replaced the glasses on his nose and jumped to his feet. "What are *you* doing here? My Lord, you look atrocious!"

"Now what kind of a greeting is that, Griswold? Doesn't sound very neighborly." Linc swung a leg over the edge of the desk and rested against it.

Howell Griswold frowned, which made his glasses tilt slightly on his nose.

"I heard you were back in town, but I'd hoped to avoid any contact with you!" He hurried to the front door and looked up and down the street through the window. Then he locked the door and swiftly pulled down the shade that showed the word, "CLOSED" on the side facing out.

"That'll be bad for business. Taft won't be happy."

"Then get out so I can open again!" Looking very nervous, he wiped his brow with a handkerchief that he'd drawn out of his coat pocket.

"All in good time. Just tell me what I want to know, and I'll be gone. I'm collecting on the favor you owe me. Remember?"

"How could I forget? I've feared Matilda would find out about my . . . indelicate experience every day since it happened six years ago! I've more than suffered for that little bout of indiscretion."

" 'Little bout?' " Linc crossed his arms over his chest. "Sure your memory serves you right, Howell? Seems I remember *three* gals from that fancy saloon in Cheyenne claiming you were the best man they'd ever been with. You recall that jealous barkeep, don't you?"

"Yes, yes!" Griswold threw up his hands and paced in front of Linc. "And I'll always be grateful that you helped me out of that terrible situation and never revealed anything about it to Matilda. You've kept your word."

"That I have. I said I might need a favor for it someday, and now's the time."

Griswold looked as if he expected Linc to ask for his soul.

"Just tell me about my brother's will, and we'll call everything even." Linc sobered his expression now and stood up, hooking his thumbs in the top of his gunbelt.

"Drummond Masterson's will?" Griswold looked wary. "What do you want to know? Weren't you at the reading after the funeral today? Mr. Denton surely—"

"I heard a will read all right," Linc cut in. "What I want to know is was that one Drumm's *last* will? The one I heard gave everything to his wife, Abby."

Griswold lowered his eyes as if he didn't want to meet Linc's demanding gaze.

"Please, I can't reveal that confidence. My position here would be jeopardized." He turned toward the window, wringing his hands.

Linc was pressed for time. He lost patience with the

man. Striding forward, he clamped a hand on Griswold's shoulder and swung him around to face him, grabbing him by the coat lapels.

"Damnation, Griswold, tell me what I want to know! Taft Denton's a crook. His services go to the highest bidder! I've been told Drumm wrote another will just a couple of weeks ago, leaving everything to his boy, Patrick. What do you know about that document? Did Abby pay off Denton to keep him quiet about it?"

Howell Griswold looked genuinely frightened by Linc's anger, and the fact that Linc had lifted him off his feet and shaken him soundly.

"Yes, yes, there was another will!" he cried. "Mr. Masterson sat right there in that chair and refused to leave until I notarized it. Mr. Denton wasn't here at the time. Your brother didn't want him to know about the new will. He made me swear that I wouldn't tell Mr. Denton anything about it, on peril that he would do bodily harm to me if I did! You Mastersons are all alike in your violent ways!"

"And don't ever forget that fact," Linc warned, scowling as he let go of the clerk. "Did you tell Denton?" Linc still towered over the smaller man, letting his gaze look fierce.

"No, oh no, Mr. Masterson. I was afraid Mr. Denton would be angry that I'd provided services behind his back. I can't afford to lose this position. Your brother threatened to break my neck with his bare hands if I said anything, and I believed he would!"

Linc snorted. Drumm was of sound mind when he made that move.

"What did the new will say? Who was supposed to get the ranch?"

"I don't know what it said, I swear!" Griswold protested. "Your brother kept the paper folded so I couldn't see. He said it was for my own good that I not know the contents of it. I just signed at the bottom of the page."

"Is the new will legal? You're not a lawyer like Denton."

"Legal? Oh, yes, quite legal. Anyone can write a last will and testament, even the person himself. The important thing is to have it witnessed and notarized that the person is of sound mind when it's written. It must be signed by a person who is authorized to authenticate documents. I qualify in that regard. I could show you my official certificate signed by the territorial governor."

"No need for that. I believe you. Do you know what might have happened to the new will?"

"No. Mr. Masterson took it with him. I don't know what he did with it, and I don't *want* to know! Now please, Mr. Masterson, leave the office. Mr. Denton could return at any time!"

"All right, Griswold. Don't look so rabbit-skittish. The favor's met. Your Matilda will never know about Cheyenne. You won't be hearing from me about it again."

Howell Griswold appeared visibly relieved as he stepped aside to let Linc walk by him to the door.

Out on the street again, Linc saw a dozen men riding into town. They were laughing when they pulled up their horses in front of the Last Call Saloon.

"The first round's on me, boys!" the tall man in the lead shouted, dismounting. That raised a chorus of cheers from the men with him.

A smile curled up one corner of Linc's mouth as he recognized the big man with the coal-black hair and thick muttonchop sideburns. His luck was holding. Instead of heading for Como Bluff to find Bill Reed, he just needed to walk up the street. His old railroad friend had come to him!

The round of whiskey had already been poured by the

time Linc entered the saloon. The bartender had a wide grin on his face as he tilted the liquor bottle again and again to refill glasses. No other customers were in the big open room. Gaudily dressed women flocked around the men, hanging on their arms, wanting drinks. Bill Reed's eyes sparkled with recognition when he spotted Linc.

"Tarnation, Lincoln Masterson!" He swung a powerful arm around Linc's shoulders and pulled him closer to the bar. "Barkeep! A snort for my friend here!" he ordered, then he turned around. "How in blazes are you, you dadburn rattlesnake? Must be two years since we laid eyes on each other! I'm surprised you're not pushing up daisies in some Boot Hill somewhere!" He laughed heartily at the joke.

"Good to see you, Bill," Linc replied, taking the shotglass of whiskey the bartender handed him and downing it in one gulp. The strong liquor burned a fiery trail down his throat, but he welcomed the sting of it, knowing the aftereffect would ease some of the ache in his muscles. Motioning for the bartender to fill the glass again, he continued the conversation with Reed. "What're you boys doing down from the bluff? I was just heading that way to have a talk with you."

"That so? Well, we came in to celebrate. Found a real stash of fossil bones this time. Othniel Marsh, our boss back East, is going to be right happy, I'll tell you. Looks like we found a full skeleton. It'll mean a bonus for all of us for sure. Put Marsh ahead of this fella name of Ed Cope. The two of them have had this rivalry going on about who can find the most dinosaur bones and get them put together. I tell you, I never saw anything like it. You'd think these fossils we find were gold or something, the way Cope and Marsh act. Nothing else to do with all their money, I reckon. Makes me a good living, though, so who am I to complain?" He laughed heartily again. "Now, what were you coming to see me about? Just a neighborly visit?"

"No, I got trouble, Bill. You haven't forgotten how to use a gun since you took up with a shovel, have you?"

"Hell, no!" He slapped the leather holster on his right hip. "It's always ready. We have to run off Cope's spies from time to time. 'Sides, I'd feel naked without it, just like you would. These firearms got us out of a heap of trouble when we worked for the railroad." His bushy black eyebrows dipped into a frown as his expression became serious. "What's up, Linc? You know I'm your man for help. Lordy, you pulled my neck out of scrapes enough times."

"Thanks, Bill. I'm going up against Clint Dandridge and an Englishman name of Giles Spencer. They've got men, money, and guns. Think they're above the law. They were involved in my brother's murder. Clint's trying to own the whole territory, and he doesn't care how he gets it."

The big man nodded.

"I've heard Dandridge's been moving in on the little ranchers, squeezing them out. Didn't know Drummond hit the last trail. Sorry to hear that. I know the two of you didn't get on none too well, but murder's got to be paid for. My boys here and I'll be glad to throw in with you. What's the plan?"

Chapter Thirty-two

Victoria breathed a sigh of relief when she arrived back at the Diamond M. She was still stunned by what had happened back at the canyon. She felt shaken to the core. Zeke Dandridge and his hired gunmen had cruelly and ruthlessly tried to kill Linc. They'd ambushed a lone man. It was a brutal, cowardly thing to do, the action of jackels, not honorable men.

She couldn't believe the part she'd played in that life and death drama. As she reined in her horse at the watering trough near the side of the ranch house, she glanced down at the gun stuck in the waistband of her skirt. It held no bullets now. She'd emptied it trying to help Linc. She'd shot it at men, something she never dreamed she could do. How often she'd berated Linc for being a gunman, yet when she was desperate to save him, she'd turned to the same violent means. She hadn't thought; she'd just opened fire. Linc's bullets had killed the two men, but hers could've just as easily found those fatal marks. The thought sickened her now, made her stomach reel in revulsion and despair. Yet, in her heart she knew that faced with the same circumstances, she'd act the same way. She'd done what was necessary. Linc meant everything in the world to her. She couldn't have just watched him die at the hands of vicious Zeke Dandridge. Not while she had breath in her body.

How she'd changed since coming to this American frontier. The innocent, naive young woman who'd boarded the train with Deborah and Sir Giles in New York City no longer existed. Nor did she want to be that woman again. While the violence of this land still shocked and disturbed her, she knew she'd been tested to the extreme by it and survived. The pride and strength she felt from that realization were new and exciting feelings.

She dismounted, then stood still beside her horse. Something was wrong; she could sense it. A strange quiver inched down her spine giving her the unsettling feeling that someone was watching her. She shot a look toward the bunkhouse, then to the partially rebuilt barn, and finally to the ranch house. Nothing seemed any different from when she'd left to find Linc, except that old Pete Foster was no longer keeping guard on the porch. Perhaps the heat had gotten to him, and he'd gone into the house.

Suddenly the front door opened and Clinton Dandridge walked out to the porch, accompanied by two cowboys.

"So good of you to join us, Miss Spencer," Dandridge said smoothly. "Or I should say Mrs. Masterson. We were just talking about you. Get her!"

The two gunmen quickly stepped off the porch and came at Victoria. Thinking fast, she grabbed the gun out of her skirt and brandished it toward them with two hands.

"Stop right there! Don't come any closer!" she shouted. She knew the gun was empty, but they didn't know that fact. Both men stopped in their tracks.

"She's bluffing!" Dandridge called. "She doesn't know how to use a gun!"

"I wouldn't count on that, gentlemen," she warned, trying hard to sound threatening as she cocked back the hammer on the gun. "At this range, it would be very hard to miss! Now, throw your guns on the ground."

Neither man moved. Victoria saw the taller one's gaze flick past her for a split second, but she didn't have time to think about what that action might mean. Clint Dandridge had a sly smile on his face as he stepped off the porch and came toward her.

"Don't come any closer, Mr. Dandridge! I said throw—oh!"

Suddenly, the gun was yanked out of her hand from behind. Whirling around, Victoria saw that another one of Dandridge's men had stolen up behind her. He must have been hiding in the barn. She recognized him as the cowboy who'd gotten away at the canyon. He swiftly grabbed her by the wrist before she could think about trying to run away.

"Let me go!" she demanded, struggling hard to twist out of his iron grasp. The other two men with Dandridge were quickly on her as well, pinning her arms behind her and holding her around the waist to subdue her. Then they half-dragged, half-carried her to the porch.

"Take her inside," Dandridge ordered, sneering at her helplessness.

Struggling against her captors, Victoria shoved the tallest man with all her might, then lost her balance and fell across the threshold of the door into the entry hall. When she tried to scurry to her feet to escape, she was quickly subdued by Clinton Dandridge.

"You're a spunky one, aren't you?" he noted, pulling her hard against him by the waist and by one arm.

Victoria hated the close contact with him, but she couldn't do anything to get away. He was too strong for her.

"Here, Jacobs, keep a rein on this one." Dandridge shoved her toward the burly cowboy who'd taken the gun away from her. He laughed as he swung his hairy arms around her and pinned her arms to her sides.

"Giles, you're just in time!" Dandridge called. "Look who just rode in. Now we'll have a hostage to bargain with for my son. Masterson won't want to lose this lovely little filly." He ran a hand over Victoria's cheek.

She whipped her head out of his reach. Glancing to the top of the stairs, she saw her uncle coming out of a bedroom. He frowned menacingly, pulling Deborah after him with one hand and Hannah Perkins with the other.

"Victoria!" Deborah cried, looking frightened. Her lovely face was white, her large blue eyes wide with confusion and alarm. "What's happening?"

Victoria couldn't answer her. She felt just as bewildered as her sister looked.

"How can you be here when you're supposed to be in jail in Laramie?" Victoria asked.

"An excellent question, niece," Giles Spencer answered, looking smug as he forced Deborah and Hannah down the staircase ahead of him.

Victoria had never seen Hannah Perkins look so frightened in all the years she'd known her.

"My good friend Clint here," Spencer continued, "sent some of his men to town to put an end to my untimely incarceration. I've no intention of spending any term in a hellish prison either here or in England. I intend to disappear for a while, travel abroad in Europe until your ridiculous accusations are forgotten. Then I'll return to claim my rightful place with Dandridge in his cattle empire. I'm certain you'll be distressed to learn that your would-be fiance, Alden, poor devil, went into town with my liberators and caught a bullet for his trouble. Shot dead on the spot."

"As was Sheriff Boswell," Clint Dandridge added with satisfaction. "And it's good riddance to that dyed-in-the-wool lawman. After I kill Linc Masterson, nothing will stand in my way for owning this town and then moving on to pluck every ripe plum in Wyoming! I aim to be governor of this territory someday, at the very least."

"You'll never escape justice, Giles Spencer, not while I still have a voice!" Victoria cried, straining against Jacobs' hold.

"It will soon be stilled," Giles stated levelly, giving her a malevolent look.

Victoria shrank back from the terrible implications of his words.

At that moment, Abby Masterson and Taft Denton entered the hall from the parlor. Denton carried several papers in his hand.

"You!" Abby exclaimed fiercely, scowling at Victoria. She waved a fist holding a small piece of paper at her. "You tried to ruin everything! You and your wicked schemes!"

"My schemes?" Victoria shot back, using her anger to overcome her fear. *"You* were the one trying to make secret plans to run away with Linc behind your husband's back, using little Patrick to get him to do what you wanted!"

"That's a lie!" Abby denied, looking quickly toward Clint Dandridge. "Don't listen to her!"

Dandridge's expression darkened. He grabbed Abby by the arm.

"You and Linc? You told me everything with him was over long ago! You lying harlot!" He snatched the small paper out of her hand. "What were you going to do with this bank draft for the ranch? Head East with him the first chance you got?"

"No, Clint, I swear I wasn't!" Abby denied frantically. "I was going to deposit it back into your account and then marry you just as we planned." She softened her tone as she lifted her free hand to touch his face. "You know I love only you. We've wanted this for so long. I must be with you, my darling."

He slapped her hard across the cheek. She cried out and reeled back from the force of the blow. He let go of her at the same time so she fell to the floor. His face reddened with rage.

"I was a fool to believe you! You tried to use Linc and when he shunned you, you lied to me so I'd get rid of Drummond for you. He was a burden to your plans, wasn't he? And how were you going to get rid of me, you conniving bitch?" He drew his gun. "Shoot me in my bed?"

"No, Clint!" Abby screamed, reaching up to grab the weapon. She yanked on it hard, pulling Dandridge off balance. He pitched forward on top of her. There was a struggle as Abby twisted and kicked, still keeping her hand locked on the gun. Dandridge grunted and scrambled to control her. They rolled together on the floor. The gun was lost from view. Then a muffled explosion came from beneath them.

For a long, tense moment, no one moved. Victoria stared in shock at the man and woman on the floor. She gasp in horror when Dandridge suddenly rolled off of Abby and got to his feet. Blood covered his right hand, which still held the smoking pistol. Abby Masterson lay face-down on the inlaid wood floor, unmoving. Dandridge bent and roughly pushed her over onto her side. A bright red stain soaked the bodice of her yellow dress. Abby groaned and opened her eyes.

"Clint . . ." she gasped.

"Mama!" A child's anguished cry shattered the air.

Victoria shot a look toward the hallway to the kitchen. Little Patrick twisted out of Anita's grasp to run to his mother. He dropped to his knees at her side, sobbing.

"Clint . . ." Abby repeated, her voice weaker now. She paid no heed to her little boy. "My money . . ." She lifted her fingers to clutch at Dandridge's left fist, which still held the crumpled bank draft. He jerked his hand out of her reach. Her arm fell back to the floor. "No, it's mine . . . mine . . ."

Her last words. Abby Masterson's face twisted with a look of pain, then her eyes closed and her body went limp.

Patrick screamed and threw himself across his mother. Dandridge reached down and pulled him away.

"Take him out of here!" he ordered fiercely, nearly throwing the boy at Anita. She hugged him in her arms and hurried away toward the kitchen. Dandridge turned to Taft Denton. His voice was emotionless when he spoke again. "She signed the deed papers over to me, didn't she? This ranch is mine?"

"Yes, everything's in order," Denton answered, gesturing with the papers he held. Even he looked shaken by what had happened. His hand shook slightly as he held out the deed to Dandridge.

"She served her purpose then," Dandridge said coldly, taking the document.

The approach of horses sounded from outside. Dandridge stepped to the window.

"Good, the rest of the boys are here. We can head into town for Zeke. Jacobs, stay here with the girl and the Perkins woman. I might need them later. Tie them up and keep your eyes open." He grabbed Victoria by the arm. "Let's go, my English beauty. Your *husband* will be mighty glad to see you, I'm sure. Too bad you're soon going to be a widow!"

"And then a corpse," Spencer added evilly. "I'm coming with you, Dandridge. I wouldn't miss this showdown."

Dandridge pulled Victoria with him toward the front door.

"Suit yourself. You could get a chance to use that new

Colt you've been practicing with." He nodded toward the weapon Spencer wore in a waist holster that put the gun within easy reach. It was a variation of the hip holster most men wore.

"Let's ride, boys!" Dandridge ordered.

"Victoria!" Deborah cried.

Victoria barely had a chance to glance back at her younger sister before Clint Dandridge dragged her out the door.

Chapter Thirty-three

Clint Dandridge lifted Victoria onto a horse, then took the length of rope one of his men gave him and tied her hands to the pommel of her saddle. After he'd mounted his own horse, he took the reins of hers himself and spurred ahead, leading the group of twenty gunmen and Giles Spencer toward Laramie.

The sun had begun its descent toward evening when the town loomed into sight. Soon it would be dusk, Victoria knew, with its twilight making objects difficult to distinguish. Her heart filled with fearful apprehension. Still in shock at seeing Abigail Masterson shot and killed so brutally, she could only imagine what further horror lay just ahead. She looked at the choppy line of distant buildings against the clear blue sky. Was Linc there somewhere? At the jail with Zeke Dandridge? If what she'd heard back at the ranch house about Sheriff Boswell's death was true, then who would help him against Clinton Dandridge and this band of vicious gunmen who rode with him now?

Victoria knew she should be concerned for her own life and Deborah's and even Hannah Perkins'. But she could only think of Linc now. These men who held all of their fates in their hands were brutal and ruthless, taking little heed of a single life or many lives, if anyone dared to stand in the way of whatever they wanted. Giles Spencer had, indeed, found a heartless, mercenary breed of cohorts very akin to himself!

Clint Dandridge reined in their horses, and the other men closed in around him.

"We're going in together, nice and easy-like," he explained, "like we were heading for a Sunday church picnic. Maybe if Masterson sees us riding in in large force, with his pretty little gal an easy target right out in front, he might give up Zeke without a fight. The Linc Masterson I used to know wouldn't go down that easy, but there's no telling what the sight of this woman in my control will do to him. Could be he's changed, gone soft." He turned to a lanky cowboy next to Spencer. "Horner, you keep your gun out and aimed at her at all times, you hear? I don't want her trying to make a run for it. Shoot her if Masterson even looks like he's going for his gun. We'll take that town apart and get my boy out of jail one way or the other!"

"But Zeke might get hit if we go in shootin'!" exclaimed one of the cowboys.

"I hope to hell he's got sense enough to keep his head down if lead starts flying!" Dandridge lashed back.

"We're going to a bloody lot of trouble for that boy of yours," Giles Spencer noted. "He better not get himself shot!"

Clint Dandridge cast Spencer a sharp glance, then he masked it with a mean look of determination.

"There's more at stake here than just Zeke's life, Spencer. Linc Masterson could still stand in the way of our plans. We're going to get rid of him once and for all." He gazed off toward Laramie. "This showdown between the two of us has been a long time coming—We've both known it would happen one day."

"Are you faster on the draw than he is?" Spencer asked.

Dandridge turned toward him slowly, a smile on his face as he gave the simple answer.

"Yes."

* * *

Linc stood in the doorway of the jail office and took count. Each time he raised a hand and pointed, a man positioned on a rooftop or at the corner of a building or behind a watering trough raised a rifle in return. Some were the ranch hands from the Diamond M, who had returned to town when they lost the trail of the men they'd been chasing. There were ten of them in all. The others were Bill Reed and his boys from Como Bluff. That made twenty-two in all, plus himself. Only a few of these men were real handy with their shooting irons, but all of them knew how to use their weapons. That's why he hadn't recruited any of the local citizens. Storekeepers, blacksmiths, bankers, and livery stable owners didn't make for dependable gunmen when serious shooting started.

"We're all ready, Mr. Masterson," Clete Duggins reported, stepping onto the sidewalk from the street. "Want me to head out to the edge of town to keep a lookout?"

"Good idea, Clete. Do it."

The young cowboy headed for his horse at the nearby hitching rail.

"You reckon Mr. Dandridge'll just come ridin' in here big as Sunday in broad daylight?" he asked, untying the reins.

"That's his style. Come in or go out in a cloud of glory, guns blazing, he always told me. Clint Dandridge isn't one to do anything in a small way. We're going to have one damned fight on our hands. You up to it? You could keep right on riding when you get to the end of town." He saw the younger man swallow hard.

"No, sir, Mr. Masterson," he replied, throwing his shoulders back. "I'll see this through with you just like I said I would. You can count on me."

"I will, Clete. Thanks. Mount up."

He watched Duggins ride out, hoping he wouldn't have to bury the young wrangler or any other cowboys who were standing with him, but he had a bad feeling that men were going to die today before the sun set.

He pulled out his Colt and slowly rotated the bullet cylinder, checking to see that each chamber held a full brass casing. The movement caused a piercing pain to shoot through his shoulder, making him grit his teeth. He focused hard on the bullets instead, counting them, one, two, three, four, five, six. Staring at the fancy Colt, he let his eyes slide over the gold etched detailing on the black barrel. The pearl handle fit smoothly, familiarly into his hand. He took a moment to weigh the perfect balance of it in his palm. The sun, sitting low on the horizon now, glinted off the barrel. He smiled seeing it. It was almost like a sign, a shot of light, like a small lightning bolt. Whether it meant a good or bad omen, he'd find out soon enough.

He twirled the Colt once and slid it flawlessly into the holster at his hip. Again, a pain streaked down his arm from his shoulder. Frowning, he clenched and unclenched his right hand several times. More pain. But now there was something else, something that worried him more than the hurt. A slight numbness formed at the ends of his fingers. He dropped his arm down to his side and flexed his hand again hard, wanting the sharp surge of pain to shoot right down to his fingertips. It did. The numbness disappeared for the time being.

He felt tense, edgy, hating this waiting. But he relished the feeling of raw excitement that pulsed over him as well. The threat of death. Risking it all. Putting everything on the line—instincts, skills, luck, the drive to survive. He'd taken the risk before, many times. But he'd never had as much at stake as he did now.

He thought of Victoria, glad that she was safely away from town at the ranch. He'd never had a gal he wanted to come back to so much, never thought of the future like he did with her. The edge . . . he couldn't think about Victoria, the ranch, anything too much. He'd lose his edge—the advantage of a clear, keenly focused mind and controlled reflexes targeted on his adversary.

At the sound of a footfall on the wooden sidewalk, he turned to see Doc Westcott coming toward him.

"How's Boswell, Doc?" he asked.

"Stubborn as ever and madder than a rattlesnake that I'm making him stay in bed!" The old physician shook his head, looking disgusted. "Man wants to kill himself! He's hollering to see you. Said he'd crawl down here to the jail on his hands and knees if I didn't fetch you for him."

"It wouldn't be a good idea for me to leave now, Doc. Clint Dandridge and his boys might ride in any time."

"I know. Told the sheriff that. But he says he wants to swear all of you in as deputies."

Linc mulled over the thought. Wouldn't hurt to have the law officially on his side. After all, he and his men were defending the town, even though that protection stemmed from his personal vengeance against Clint Dandridge.

"All right, Doc. Let's go see Boswell."

The sheriff's head was wrapped in a big wad of bandage. He winced when he tried to sit up in the bed located against one wall in the doctor's office.

"Take it easy, N. K.," Linc cautioned. "Anything you need to do, you can do on your back."

"Hell's bells, I hate bein' laid up!" Boswell spouted angrily, but he slumped back against the pillows just the same. "Why, I declare, you look worse'n I do. What happened to you?"

"Zeke Dandridge figured to have a dragging party with me as the guest of honor," Linc explained.

"Then you should be in this here bed, not me!"

"Lie still, you stubborn coot. You're lucky to still be breathing."

"Damn it, I'm too mad to go boots up! Those varmints stole my prisoner right out of my dadburn jail in broad daylight! And here I'm layin' when Doc says that no-good polecat Clint Dandridge could be on his way right now to shoot up my town! Get me my gun, Linc. I'm comin' to defend my jail!"

He started to get up again, but Linc stepped over to the bed and put a hand on his shoulder.

"There's no need. I have plenty of men with me. Just swear me in as a deputy and then do what Doc here says. And I won't take an argument!" Linc made his tone firm and unyielding. Boswell blew out his breath in defeat.

"Fetch me a Bible, Doc!" he thundered with obvious annoyance. Westcott left the room and quickly returned with a leather bound volume, which he handed to the sheriff. "Put your hand here on the Good Book!" Boswell ordered Linc. "Raise your other one. By the power I got from the Governor of this here Territory of Wyoming, I swear you in as my deputy. And that includes all your boys, too. There're badges somewheres in my desk drawer at the office."

"Thanks, N. K." Linc went to the door. "Take care of that head."

"Take care of yours, Linc. An' try an' keep my jail in one piece, you hear?"

Linc was back at the sheriff's office less than a half hour when Clete Duggins thundered up on his horse.

"Mr. Masterson! They're comin'! They're comin'!" He jumped off his mount before the animal had a chance to prance to a halt.

"I told you my pa wouldn't let me rot here long!" Zeke called from his cell, laughing. "You're a dead man, Masterson—a dead man!"

"Shut up, you yellow-tailed coyote!" Bill Reed growled, banging a fist against the bars, rattling them with the force of his blow. Zeke flinched back a step, eyeing the big man with a hate-filled glare.

"Stay with him, Bill," Linc said. "You know the plan."

"Right, Linc," Reed replied with a nod.

"Plan? What plan, Masterson?" Zeke demanded. But Linc ignored him, walking outside to Duggins.

"How many, Clete?" he asked, glancing up and down the

street to check the number of citizens still about.

"Must be twenty at least! I didn't wait around to count 'em close."

"All right, pass the word to the others, and tell them they're all officially deputized by Sheriff Boswell. Then get to your post. And keep your head down."

"Yes, sir, Mr. Masterson, I will!" Jamming his hat down lower on his head, the young wrangler dashed around the corner of the General Store, out of sight.

Linc stepped off the sidewalk, out in plain view. Drawing his gun, he fired it once in the air.

"Clear the street, folks!" he shouted to the people who turned his way. "There's going to be trouble. Get inside pronto!"

No one stopped to ask questions. In a matter of two minutes, the main street of Laramie was cleared of citizens and horses. Linc nodded toward each of his men, motioning them out of sight as well. Hooking his thumbs in the top of his gunbelt, he waited for Clint Dandridge to arrive.

Victoria was forced to ride just behind Dandridge's horse. She was careful not to make any conspicuous moves as she pulled and worked at loosening the rope binding her hands to the saddle. The rough hemp cut into her wrists, but she just gritted her teeth and felt the pain, taking heart when the rope slackened some around the horn. She felt hot, tired, dirty, and so frightened that her hands shook as she rubbed them over the raised pommel, hoping the sweat on them might make the leather slippery enough for her to yank the rope off of it if she got the chance. Every few moments she cast a sideways glance at the man called Horner, who rode next to her, keeping guard. He always met her gaze, but didn't seem to be aware that she was trying to loosen her bonds.

Finally, they reached the edge of Laramie. Victoria's

heart sank into further despair when she spied Linc in front of the sheriff's office at the far end of the main street. The excitement she always felt at seeing him surged through her, but swiftly turned to terrible dread. Linc could be shot down in cold blood right before her eyes. He stood alone in front of the jail. No other men were in sight to help him defend the jail and the town. The sidewalks were glaringly empty; storefront doors were shut up tight.

Clint Dandridge's face held an arrogant smile, but Victoria noticed he gripped the reins of his mount hard, so his knuckles whitened at the edges. For a moment, she thought about trying to kick her horse into a quick getaway, but Dandridge had her reins wound snugly around his saddlehorn. And Horner had his gun out in full view, pointed right at her. What could she do to help Linc?

Linc's smoldering dark eyes locked onto hers as they rode in closer. One black brow arched slightly for a split second, then returned to place, leaving his handsome face an emotionless mask. But Victoria knew he hadn't been expecting to see her with Dandridge and Giles Spencer. She sensed his keen mind racing to calculate this new complication. His stance looked casual enough—broad shoulders back, easy hold on his gunbelt at the buckle, hat brim cocked up just enough to give him a clear view. As Dandridge pulled up their horses, halting his men in the middle of the street directly in front of the jail, she stared hard at Linc's face. A small muscle twitched at the edge of his chiseled jaw, revealing that his teeth were clenched.

Linc would have sworn mightily if he hadn't known doing so would give Clint Dandridge enormous pleasure. Instead, he cursed himself for not figuring Clint would come up with something like this—capturing Victoria and using her as a hostage to trade for Zeke. He hated having her dragged into this deadly showdown. She looked plenty scared, and with good reason!

Giles Spencer pulled his horse up next to Victoria.

Horner did the same on her other side. Linc felt his blood turn to ice in his veins. A twitch of readiness jolted through his right hand, but he crushed his fingers harder into his belt to resist the reflex response to it. No gunplay yet; he had to think!

"We both know why I'm here, Linc," Clint said, adjusting his hat against the streaking glare of the setting sun. "That a law badge you're wearing on your chest?" He spat the words in a derisive tone, flicking his cold gray eyes swiftly around the street before he slid them to Linc again.

"Yeah," Linc replied. "And there are men hidden around on the street who're each wearing one just like it. That's not counting the deputy inside name of Bill Reed, who has a gun cocked and pointed at Zeke's head. You recollect Bill, don't you, Clint? Used to be a sharpshooter for the railroad in the old buffalo days. I reckon he'll find Zeke a lot easier target to hit than a stampeding bull buffalo."

Clint snorted a laugh and cast a disparaging look over his shoulder at his men, as if Linc had just said something humorous. But his eyes again darted around to rooftops, to the edges of buildings. Victoria followed his gaze and sank into further despair when she couldn't see anyone.

"Sheriff Boswell swore us in," Linc continued confidently, "so we could officially guard his murdering prisoner."

Clint's head shot around. His face lost its look of amusement.

"You're bluffing! Boswell's dead!"

It was Linc's turn to snicker a laugh.

"Nope. N. K.'s kicking up a fuss right now over at Doc Westcott's. Doc had to threaten to calf-rope him to keep him from being here right now. Seems Boswell got a scratch to the head in a jail break fracas. But he'll be back on his feet in no time." Linc looked pointedly at Giles Spencer, then back to Dandridge. "You ought to take care to send boys who can shoot better when you're going to break the law, Clint."

Victoria's wide-eyed stare darted from Linc to Dandridge. Neither man moved, but she could almost see the tightening of muscles getting ready to react. Suffocating heat radiated off the sun-baked street. A highly charged tension jammed the air as the standoff built to an electrifying climax.

"Get my boy out here, Masterson, or your wife here dies!" Clint demanded, shifting to a straighter position in his saddle. "Horner!"

Victoria heard the hammer of Horner's gun cock back. She swallowed hard, feeling a shiver streak down her spine despite the stiffling heat.

Linc stared Dandridge down without blinking. Victoria longed to have him look at her, but knew doing so could cost him his life. The power in each man's piercing glare was as potent as a blow.

"Bill!" Linc called finally.

Bill Reed pushed Zeke Dandridge through the office door ahead of him. Zeke's wrists were secured in front by handcuffs. He stumbled under Reed's shove, but kept his feet, righting himself and walking ahead with an arrogant jaunt. He was beside Linc when Reed's big paw of a hand clamped down on his shoulder, stopping him.

"That's far enough unless Linc says so, runt!" Reed exclaimed, holding his gun to Zeke's head while he kept the hold on him. "You'd be smart not to make any moves real sudden-like. This here gun's got a hair trigger." He glanced toward Dandridge. "Howdy, Clint. Long time, no see. Nice party you're havin' here."

"I reckon it's time the rest of the boys joined us, wouldn't you say, Bill?" Linc asked as casually as if he were offering to buy a round of whiskey at the saloon. "Show yourselves, men!" he shouted in a louder voice.

Suddenly, cowboys became visible all around them. Some stood on the surrounding rooftops with rifles aimed toward the street. Others stepped out from corners of buildings and away from stacks of merchandise in front of the General Store with guns cocked and ready.

"Jesus, Dandridge!" Horner swore. Other murmurs sounded from the rest of the men on horseback.

"Shut up!" Dandridge ordered fiercely. "Hold your positions! We got as many guns as he has, and we still have the woman!"

"And I still have Zeke, Clint," Linc remarked with deadly calm. "Anything happens to Victoria, he dies. You know I'm not bluffing."

Linc let his words sink in. He saw Clint's eyes dart around to the men against him and knew his one-time mentor was ripe for the picking. The air crackled with deadly tension. Any sudden move now by anyone would bring a lot of bloodshed. He prayed Victoria would keep her head.

Holding his hands unmoving at his gunbelt, he gave only a rapid thought to the numbness he again felt inching into the tips of the fingers of his right hand. His shoulder throbbed hard now, but the sharp pain kept his head clear, quickened his reflexes. He chose his words carefully.

"Seems like we could avoid having a lot of lead fly if you and I just settled this between the two of us, Clint. That's if you still got the guts to stand up against a man alone."

Dandridge glared at Linc.

"You calling yourself a man, half-breed?" he spewed viciously. "You reckon you're good enough to come up against me?"

"Dandridge," Giles Spencer started to caution.

"Shut up, Englishman! And the rest of you, back off! This is between you and me, Linc! Always has been. You're the closest any man's come to giving me some kind of a contest, and that's because I taught you everything you know, you bastard!"

"Not everything, Clint! Make your move!"

Hands whipped down faster than lightning strikes. Clint

Dandridge's gun exploded almost at the same instant Linc's did. But Linc's went off a split-second quicker. Fanning the hammer twice, Linc brought down Dandridge and then Horner. Victoria screamed as Horner toppled to the ground. His horse pranced and shied, riling her mount. Hanging onto the saddlehorn to keep her seat on her nervous horse, she heard Zeke Dandridge shout.

"Pa! You shot my pa!"

Terrified, she looked past Sir Giles to the front of the jail. Bill Reed still held Zeke in check in front of him like a shield, pointing his gun out toward the street. Linc stood slightly crouched, gun ready to fire again at anyone who might make a move. Dandridge's men all held their hands in the air in surrender, trying to keep their frightened horses in control. It was then she saw Sir Giles reach for his waist holster.

"No! Look out!" she screamed to Linc, kicking out with her leg.

The toe of her shoe caught her uncle hard in the thigh, making him jerk just when he pointed his gun at Linc and pulled the trigger.

"Linc!" Victoria cried in horror, seeing him spun around by the force of the bullet. He clutched at his left side and fell on his back on the wooden sidewalk. Her eyes widened in panic when Sir Giles next turned the gun on her!

His nostrils flared and his face twisted in an ugly grimace of rage as he roared, "Now you die!"

Victoria reacted swiftly. Finding a strength she didn't know she had, she yanked hard on the rope binding her hands to the saddlehorn. At the same time she pitched forward, diving for the ground. She landed hard on her side on top of Horner's body, losing her breath. Through her mount's side-stepping legs she saw Sir Giles dig his heels into his horse. The animal screamed a neigh and plunged forward up the street. Victoria saw Linc roll over and struggle up to one knee as Spencer rode past him. His gun hand whipped out. The Colt exploded. Giles Spencer stiffened from the bullet's impact and fell backward off his horse to land face down in the dirt of the street. He didn't move again.

Linc collapsed, still clutching his bleeding side. Gasping for breath, Victoria struggled off Horner's dead body and scrambled to him on her hands and knees.

"Linc! Dear God, Linc, please be alive!" she cried, pulling him into her arms. Her heart jumped into her throat, cutting off any more words. Her pulse raced frantically as she tried to will her strong spirit for living into his battered body. Blood showed everywhere, at his shoulder, down his shirt, on his gunbelt, all over his hands. Weeping, she touched his bruised, dirty face. "Oh, please, my love, open your eyes! Breathe! Say something!"

At last she saw his eyelids slowly lift. The piercing earth-brown eyes that could see into her very soul focused on her face.

"Take it easy, English," he rasped out, coughing from the effort, then adding, "I don't reckon to make you a widow yet."

"You better not, Linc Masterson!" she exclaimed, hugging him to her. "You just better *never!*"

Chapter Thirty-four

"Damn, but I wish I coulda been there!" Sheriff Boswell exclaimed, slapping his knee. "Clint bit the dust an' that Spencer feller, too! Horner won't be missed much either, I reckon. The hand of justice'll come down hard on Zeke for Drumm's murder an' practically murderin' you. Tarnation, you sure do know how to clean up a town, Linc!"

"Next time I'll leave the job to you, N. K.," Linc replied tiredly, turning his head with an effort toward the sheriff's bed in the corner.

"Hold still!" Doc Westcott ordered, bending over Linc's prone length lying on the examining table in his office. "Or I'll never get this bandaging finished! I declare, you lawmen sure are keeping me and the undertaker busy today! You're mighty lucky that bullet went clean through your side and didn't hit any vital organs, or we'd be burying you now alongside Clint Dandridge and those English fellas. How do your ribs feel?"

"Like hell, along with the rest of my body, but I'll live, I reckon."

"If you hang up that gun of yours now you just might," the doctor noted with a sharp nod. "Keep wearing it, and you'll be boots up on cemetery hill one of these days."

"Just get the bandages on and don't lecture me, Doc," Linc replied, wincing when the physician pressed a wad of white bandage over his newest wound.

Victoria watched from the window, aching to go to the

table and help. But her hands had just now stopped shaking, and her breathing still swept heavily through her, as if she'd run a long distance without rest. The shock and horror of what had happened out on the street left her unspeakably weak, drained of all energy. But Linc was alive and that was all that mattered. She couldn't even speak to him, because her throat felt tight with the welling of tears of joy she fought to hold back. She didn't want to cry or give in to her great need to cling to him in front of the sheriff or the doctor. She wanted to appear strong, as one of the survivors of that slaughter in the street must be. She wrapped her arms around her, feeling a shiver despite the heat the evening still held. The chill of death seemed to hang over her. Yet she knew that the way Linc had challenged Clint Dandridge had saved lives. If he hadn't carried that through, the men on both sides would have opened fire against one another, and many more would be lying dead in the street right now, awaiting the undertaker's gruesome chore. How cold and brutal the killing had been. For a long time to come, in her mind she'd hear the guns exploding, see the smoke spew from the barrels, watch the men pitch from their horses in death. But she couldn't help thinking that her murderous uncle and Clinton Dandridge had received swift and righteous judgment for the cruel killings they'd committed. Justice here on the American frontier was quick and harsh, but it did seem to get the job done.

Perhaps her terrible nightmares about her father's death would end, now that the truth was known and the punishment executed.

Finally, she felt calm enough to step from the window. She couldn't stay away from Linc's side any longer. The love she felt for him coursed through her as she silently said another prayer of gratitude for his life. She wanted nothing more than to love him back to health, take care of him, watch his magnificent body mend and become whole again. But three dark clouds cast mean shadows over that idea—Deborah, Hannah Perkins, and the Diamond M ranch.

Coming to the examining table, she swept her hand over Linc's forehead, brushing back his wavy black hair.

"Will he be all right, doctor?" she asked quietly, feeling that powerful surge of love wash over her again as Linc's eyes shifted to her.

"Don't ask him," Linc answered. "Ask me. I've had worse hits, and I'm still kicking."

"All at the same time?" she teased, feeling her insides knot up recalling once more how close Linc had come to dying.

The doctor snorted, turning to wash his bloody hands in a shallow basin of water.

"Not hardly. Just pure mule stubbornness keeping him going right now," he said.

Victoria nodded, knowing the gruff old doctor's words were true. Linc looked bone-weary. The creases at the edges of his eyes and around his mouth were deepened with exhaustion and pain. How could she ask more of him? And yet, she must. She bit her lip, hating to say the words.

"Deborah must be rescued again."

"What?" Linc's dark eyes locked with hers. "Where is she?"

"She's at the Diamond M," she hurried to explain, wringing her hands with dismay, "but Clint Dandridge left her there with a guard, a man called Jacobs. He was the one who got away at the canyon. Hannah Perkins is with my sister. We must help them." She lowered her eyes, feeling a new kind of fear—for Deborah. Then she remembered something else Linc should know. She put her hand on his arm. "Abby Masterson is dead. Clint Dandridge shot her in a struggle for a gun before coming to town. She used him to have Drummond killed. She tried to steal money from Dandridge to go back East."

Linc's handsome face registered surprise, then his black, sharply arched brows dipped down in a harsh frown.

"Looks like more than one score's been settled this day," he murmured levelly. "What about Patrick?"

Victoria tried to swallowed the lump that rose in her throat at remembering the little boy's terrible anguish.

"He saw his mother die. She didn't raise a hand of love or farewell to him. To the last, she sought only the money she wanted so desperately. She'd signed the deed to the ranch over to Dandridge before she died."

She saw that tiny muscle twitch at the base of Linc's square jaw which always showed when he clenched his teeth.

"Then Clint's money belongs to Patrick." He turned to the sheriff. "N. K., Drumm named you guardian of his boy."

"I know, Linc. We talked about it a while ago, before you came back to town," the lawman replied. "But now that you're here, you bein' the boy's kin an' all . . ."

"That won't make any difference under the law, if Drumm's will holds up. And if we don't find the last will he made a couple of weeks ago."

"Then what Anita said about another will is true?" Victoria asked hopefully.

Linc nodded.

"According to Taft Denton's clerk, Howell Griswold, there was. He didn't know what it said, though, or what Drumm did with it. Could be Abby got her hands on it and destroyed it. Right now, Clint's money is owed to Patrick. The ranch'll go to Clint's wife, I suppose, since Zeke'll be swinging from a rope soon enough."

"His wife?" Victoria questioned, surprised.

Linc nodded, making himself sit up. It was a painful process, but he waved away any help from her or Doc Westcott. He was sweating and breathing hard when he finally stood on his own two feet next to the examining table.

"Most of Clint's money came from his wife, Louise," he managed to explain, taking time to breathe slowly to favor his bruised ribs. "She was a lot like Abby. Hated the ranch. As soon as she gave Clint a son—Zeke—he let her go to Boston to live with some relatives. I don't think he ever divorced her though, because of the money. He didn't want to lose that."

"Then if she doesn't like Wyoming, perhaps she'll sell the Diamond M back to us," Victoria offered. "When I get back to England to obtain my inheritance—"

"Whoa, Victoria," Linc cut in, holding up a hand. "First things first. We'd best get to the ranch and see to Deborah and Hannah Perkins. That gunman guarding them might be getting mighty itchy to know what happened here in town by now."

Too much was happening at once. Victoria's mind whirled with a myriad of thoughts. Deborah, Hannah, Sir Giles, Alden, Clint Dandridge, his son Zeke, little Patrick . . . and Linc. Always at the fore was Linc. Handsome, brave, strong-willed, risking his life for what was right and good. She reached out to touch his arm again. How she loved him. Completely, deeply, tenderly, passionately . . . With the doctor and sheriff in the same room, she could only try to show him her heart-felt feelings with her eyes, with the press of her fingertips against his flesh. He raised his eyes to hers, and his compelling gaze told her he understood.

"I left my horse tied behind the sheriff's office," he said, reaching for his gunbelt where the doctor had hooked it over the back of a chair.

"But you can't ride in this condition," Victoria protested. "You'll hurt yourself more."

"Listen to her, Linc," Doc Westcott chimed in. "Those stitches holding you together won't stand up to too much abuse."

"They'll have to, Doc. I have a sister to rescue and a will to find, if it still exists. Let's ride, Victoria."

Linc and Victoria crouched behind the watering trough by the half-finished barn back at the Diamond M. Darkness helped conceal them. Everything was quiet, except for the usual night sounds of insects and small creatures scurrying along the ground.

"You sure Jacobs is the only Dandridge gun in there?" Linc whispered, peering around the end of the wooden trough toward the ranch house. Lights appeared in the parlor and kitchen windows. "What happened to old Pete?"

"I—I don't know," Victoria answered in a low voice, worrying now about the elderly wrangler with the bad foot. "He wasn't at his post on the porch when I returned from the canyon. I hope Clint Dandridge didn't—"

"Maybe he's just laid up somewhere. We'll find him." *Alive, I hope,* Linc added to himself. He liked the crusty old cowboy, had known him since he was a kid. Pete had worked for Mastersons since the Diamond M was started.

He shifted positions and let out a grunt of pain, grabbing his midsection. His breath came in gasps.

Victoria squatted beside him, putting an arm around his shoulders. She couldn't see his face clearly because of the darkness, but she knew it would be tight with stubborn determination to keep the pain at bay.

"Oh, Linc, you shouldn't be here. You're hurt so badly." Tears stung her eyes, but she blinked hard to hold them back. She hated to see him hurting. If she could've taken it

rom him and felt it herself, she would've done it in a min-
te. "Are you bleeding again?"

"Don't think so."

"Can you go on?"

"Yeah."

He sounded brave, willing, in control, but Victoria
new by his clipped words and the sharp intakes of breath
hat he was suffering.

Linc drew his gun. With stealthy movements, he and
'ictoria crept around the house to the open window of the
arlor. He motioned for her to squat down beside him
ext to the sill, then quickly pushed her back against the
vall of the ranch house when a shadow blocked the lamp-
ght coming from the window. A man looked out, then
urned back into the room. They heard his nervous, agi-
ated voice.

"Clint shoulda got back by now. Somethin' musta gone
rong. I'm not stickin' around here. You're comin' with
e, sweetie. Git up!"

"No!" Deborah cried.

Victoria gasped and started to stand up, but Linc
rabbed her arm and yanked her down again.

"Wait!" he whispered fiercely. Reluctantly, Victoria
beyed.

"Don't hurt her, you brute!" Hannah Perkins shouted.

"Git outta my way, you old hag!"

"Oh!"

Linc and Victoria heard a loud thud as if someone had
llen.

"Hannah!" Deborah gasped. "You've killed her! Look at
er neck. Hannah! Hannah!"

"Git away from her! She hit her head. It was her own
ult. Stupid old woman, comin' at me like that. I told her
ot to git in my way! Now you do what I want, or you'll
e gittin' the same thing. You're comin' with me as a hos-

tage, in case we meet up with the law." His savage voic lowered, but sounded even more cruel when he added " 'Sides, you're a pretty one. You an' me 're gonna have u some fun once we're clear of this place."

"Damn!" Linc swore under his breath.

"My God . . ." Victoria gripped his arm. Her heart bea frantically. She wanted to dash into the house to save he sister, but her knees shook so hard, she wasn't sure they' hold her. Jacobs seemed edgy and brutal enough to com mit any heinous act against Deborah, especially if he wer surprised or attacked. He was a good-sized man, close t Linc's height of just over six feet, if she remembered right He'd be a treacherous adversary under any circumstances let alone when Linc was so weakened by his wounds.

"What are we going to do?" she whispered to him des perately.

"Don't touch me, you vile creature!" Deborah cried ou just then.

"Shut up!" Jacobs ordered angrily. "I'll do what I want Here's a taste of what you'll be gittin'!"

"No!"

With Deborah's cry came the sound of cloth tearing then in the next instant, Jacobs gave a yelp. A loud crac followed, like a slap. Deborah started to whimper.

"Let that be a lesson to you!" Jacobs taunted. "Bite m again an' I'll shoot you dead! Let's git to the barn *now!*"

"Linc . . ." Victoria pleaded in the dark.

"Follow me," Linc rasped out, holding his arm agains his ribcage. Crouching with an effort, he ducked under th window sill and headed toward the front of the house.

Reaching the porch with Victoria close behind him Linc threw a leg over the railing. Victoria lifted her skir and quickly did the same. They stood up, pressing thei backs against the wall of the house.

"Do exactly what I tell you," Linc murmured, wiping th

back of his hand over his sweaty forehead. Breathing hard, he could feel a warm wetness oozing down his side from his gunshot wound.

"What should I do?" Victoria asked in a worried whisper when he didn't speak.

Linc shook his head to try to clear the dizziness creeping across his senses. Damnation, he cursed to himself, he'd have to get this done pronto, before he passed out.

"S-stay here," he stammered, "close to the front door. When they come out, if Deborah's first, grab her and yank her out of the way. I'll take care of Jacobs."

Without saying anything else, he stepped in front of the door to wait on the other side.

Suddenly the door was pulled open from the inside, and the shadow of a man and woman in close contact cut into the beam of lamplight cascading from the doorway.

"Stop fightin', I said. Move!" Jacobs ordered.

Deborah stumbled over the threshold, nearly falling. Victoria reached out and clamped a hand on her sister's arm, pulling with all her might. Deborah gave a cry of alarm and fell fully on top of Victoria.

"What the—" Jacobs began, stepping through the door with his gun pointed.

Linc brought the stock of his Colt smashing down hard on the other man's wrist. Caught off guard, Jacobs grunted from the pain and dropped his pistol. At the same time, Linc swung his left arm and smashed Jacobs in the jaw with a powerful left cross. The cowboy reeled around from the force of the blow and landed on his belly with arms and legs sprawled out on the floor in the entrance hall. He didn't move.

Linc groaned and clutched his side. Pointing his gun at Jacobs in case he might still be a threat, he leaned against the wall for support, then slowly sank down to the floor of the porch when his legs wouldn't hold him any longer.

"Linc!" he heard Victoria call, but she sounded so fa away. He tried to focus his eyes on her. He thought he sav her scrambling out from under Deborah, but it was to dark. Everything was too dark and closing in on him Finally the blackness consumed him, sweeping him int oblivion.

Chapter Thirty-five

Victoria lay on her side next to Linc on the big double bed. She felt exhausted from worry, yet sleep wouldn't come. With loving care, she had bathed her husband, changed the dressings on his wounds, spoken to him in hushed tones of her love and devotion to him. And throughout the time, Linc remained unconscious, moving little, saying nothing.

He'd lost so much blood. She knew that even in his quietness now, he still fought a battle. His iron will and his strong body struggled for survival against the battering they'd taken in overcoming the evil that had been Giles Spencer and Clinton Dandridge.

She snuggled her naked body closer against the length of his side, needing to touch him as much as possible, to have the intimate contact with him. His flesh felt hot where it met hers, making her fret that he might be feverish from infections in his wounds. But when she slid her fingertips over his forehead, it seemed to be warm from the heat in the bedroom and not from fever.

She let her fingers trail down the side of his handsome face over the short stubble of black beard growing there. She ran one fingertip over his lips with a light touch. How she longed to have him awaken and draw her into his arms, have his soft, sensuous lips cover hers so lovingly and possessively as they had before. The aching need she felt inside to have his mouth and hands caress her was almost more than she could bear. Her throat tightened with a threatening sob. Tears brimmed in her eyes.

She lifted her hand and laid it gently on his broad, muscular chest. The thin layer of dark hair on it felt coarse beneath her palm as she gently stroked him.

"You must live, my love," she murmured, taking heart in seeing the shallow rise and fall of his chest with his even breathing. "We have so many plans to make, so much to live for. I love you . . ."

She brushed away the tear that had fallen on her cheek and raised up on one elbow. Leaning over, she kissed him gently, tenderly—his mouth, his cheek, his eyes. The exquisite taste of him brought flashes of memory of the great passion they had known together and the great love. What was one without the other? Passion was of the body, love so much a part of the soul. To know the two together with one man was the most wondrous, overwhelming, and fulfilling feeling she'd ever known. With all her heart, she yearned for Linc to be vibrant with strength and power and need for her again.

She lay down beside him once more, resting an arm over his chest. Closing her eyes, she willed her own strength to be in him, just as she had out on the street when she thought he'd been killed by her uncle's bullet. Down his whole length she sent the heat and energy of her body to him, calling on God, the Great Spirit, and any other deity that might listen to her pleas to heal him.

"If this is some kind of new cure for gunshot wounds that Doc's trying, I'm all in favor of it."

Victoria's eyes flew open. Startled, she quickly sat up.

"Linc! Dear God, you're awake!" She hugged him and let the tears come at last.

He gathered her in his arms and stroked her hair.

"Whoa, take it easy, English. I'm not dead."

"N-no, I know that. I'm crying because I'm so happy you're alive and finally awake. I was so afraid . . ." She couldn't finish the terrible words, wouldn't think of them. He was conscious. His handsome face held its rugged color again. His arms around her felt strong once more.

"How long have I been out?" he asked, rubbing a hand over the whiskers on his chin.

"Two days—the longest two days of my life! After you lost consciousness, Deborah and I found Pete Foster tied up in the cellar. He took Jacobs into town, with Hannah's body and Abby's. Hannah had hit her head on the bricks of the fireplace when Jacobs pushed her. The blow broke her neck. She really did try to help Deborah. It cost her her life. Perhaps that's some sort of redemption for her." She sighed heavily. "So much has happened. Giles paid the ultimate price for my father's murder. Clinton Dandridge can no longer be a threat to anyone.

"I was so worried about you, my love," she went on. "Dr. Westcott's been here twice to tend you. He said we just had to wait and see, that whether you lived or died was out of our hands. But I wouldn't accept that. I wouldn't let you die, Lincoln Masterson!"

"Oh, you wouldn't, huh? And why was that, Mrs. Masterson?"

He smiled at her. His voice, coming low and easy, caressed her, making her spirit soar with joy and gratitude. She gently stroked his chest and returned his smile.

"Because I love you and need you too much. I couldn't live without you. Our life together has only begun. We have a cattle empire to build, remember? I can't do that without you." The look of love he gave her melted her heart.

"Are you sure, Victoria? It won't be easy. Ranching's a hard life, and you're not used—"

"Hush." She put a finger over his lips. "Say no more. I took a vow to be your wife. I may not have meant the words at the time—I know neither of us did. But I mean them now . . ." She looked deeply into his dark brown eyes and spoke with the strength of love that filled her heart and all of her being. "I'll be your wife, Linc, and love you till the end of our days, if you'll have me."

"Then it looks like I'm a husband with a wife, because I want you, Victoria." He tenderly brushed a stray strand of blond hair away from the side of her face. "When I was unconscious, I knew you were near me. I heard your words deep in my mind, felt your touch. There's something strong and good that unites us. With you at my side, I feel anything's possible. Even if we don't find Drumm's last will, there'll be some way to build a ranch of our own." He looked at her levelly. "I'd like to raise Patrick, if I can get the court to let me. Boswell can still have control of Drumm's estate for the boy. That doesn't matter. One way or the other, Patrick's kin to me, and a Masterson. Could you see your way clear to raise him with me?"

"Yes, of course, my love," she answered without hesitation. "The poor child will need all the love we can give him. He's been through so much, losing his mother and . . . father." She lowered her eyes, dreading to tell him her discovery.

He saw the change in her expression.

"What is it, Victoria?" He raised her chin.

"There is no other will, Linc. I've searched and searched for it. I've all but torn apart the desk in the parlor and another small writing desk in Drummond and Abby's bedroom, but I haven't found anything. I'm afraid Abby must have found it and destroyed it."

Linc looked thoughtful for a moment, then he spoke.

"Or Drumm might have hidden it someplace where he was sure she wouldn't find it. I just have this gut feeling . . ."

"Then we'll search for it more when you're stronger. You must be starved. I'll get you something to eat." She started to swing her legs off the bed, but he pulled her back.

"I am hungry—for you, my English beauty. I want you.

Stay here with me."

"And I want you, my savage, gunfighter husband. My God, I must be insane to love you, but I do, with all my heart." She kissed him, long and lingeringly. His arms pressed her to him. His hand began to stroke her back. To catch her breath, she raised her head away for a moment and smiled down at him. "You're tormenting me, Linc. You should be still, to get your strength back and heal. We should wait, my love. Be patient. There'll be so much time later to be together, I promise."

"Not later, Victoria. Now . . . I need you now."

She couldn't argue any more, for her body was already coming to life as he took her hand and drew her over on top of him. She kissed him, consuming his mouth with her lips and tongue. He returned her ardor, matching her kiss for kiss. His hands held the sides of her face, then stroked down her throat and over her shoulders. She raised up so he could caress first one breast and then the other. His fingers glided over her nipples until both were taut and tingling. His touch sent fire through her veins. The exquisite pleasure made her mind whirl and sing. Nothing else mattered. The rest of the world disappeared. Only Linc existed, his hands, his lips, his splendid, demanding body. Her senses came alive with demand for him, to feel him, taste him, hear him murmur her name and words of love and need. When he drew her up so he could follow the same searing path over her breasts with his mouth, she thought she would die from sheer ecstasy.

Breathing hard, she kissed his face, his eyes, his mouth, relishing the rough feel of his whiskers on her cheek. The cords of muscles in his arms twitched in response to her nipping caresses. She rubbed her palms over his chest, then bent to kiss every part of it. She heard his quickened breathing and moved her kisses down his belly, carefully avoiding his wounded side. She ran her hands down his hips, along the outside of his thighs, and then the insides.

His readiness for her excited her to a frenzy of feeling. Desire burned through her, snatching her breath away. She murmured his name, her aching need for him. She knew only that she must have him, must feel him within her, totally possessing and consuming her.

Linc rolled with her then, turning her on her back. The pain the movement caused meant nothing to him compared to the great intensity of feeling Victoria ignited within him. A multitude of overwhelming sensations shot through him as he kissed and stroked her straining breasts, then found her lips again and devoured them. He couldn't get enough of her. Tasting, touching her, seeing the heated desire in her emerald eyes, beckoning him into her. On and on he caressed her, loved her, until her legs parted to receive him, and he hesitated no longer.

She clung to him, entwining her fingers in his hair, arching her hips to receive his penetrating thrusts, and crying out with fevered pleasure when unending waves of pulsating feeling crashed through her.

Only moments later, Linc's own climax overwhelmed him, coming in glorious, swift throbs of pure rapture. Feeling a wild tension race through his body, he stiffened and held until his passion was spent within her.

When at last he lay down beside her, he gathered her in his arms to caress her. Slowly, tenderly, he kissed her, stroked her breasts, until her breathing was even again, and the look of love in her eyes told him she was fulfilled. That feeling of complete contentment matched his own. Yet he knew he would soon hunger for Victoria again. Victoria, his wife. The thought left him with a happiness he'd never known before.

Chapter Thirty-six

Dawn was just breaking over the distant jagged mountain peaks, sending crimson rays inching through the open window of the bedroom when Victoria slowly awakened in Linc's arms. Opening her sleep-heavy eyes, she found him looking at her.

"You sure are one beautiful sight," he murmured softly, kissing her forehead. "This is the way I'm going to wake up every morning, with you naked beside me, your pale yellow hair all tangled up around you." He slid his hand tenderly over her breast.

"And this is the way I intend to wake up every morning with you, my love." A tingle of delight whisked over her at his intimate touch. She snuggled closer against his side, smiling. How she loved his tousled, bewhiskered look, and having his strong arms around her.

"You know," Linc went on, "a good ranch wife would be up by now, fixing her man a hearty breakfast of beefsteak, eggs, potatoes, fresh-baked bread, and coffee so strong it could eat through a branding iron."

Victoria cocked an eyebrow at him.

"And what, pray tell, is her man doing all this time while the good ranch wife is slaving away in the kitchen?" She raised up on one elbow and eyed him suspiciously.

He grinned, pulling her over on top of him.

"He's wishing she was right here, making love with him." He kissed her hard, possessively.

When she could finally pull away a little to catch her breath, she laughed softly, happy about his eagerness for her, for it matched her own for him.

"But you must eat, my love, to keep up your strength," she said. "I'll bring you some food."

"No, I'll come downstairs with you."

"But you shouldn't be getting up yet, Linc," she scolded, looking worried as she sat up next to him.

"Don't nag me, woman," he replied with mock severity, dipping a dark eyebrow at her as he sat up. He winced with the movement, but still let the beginning of a smile curl up one corner of his mouth. "If I'm strong enough for loving like we did last night, then I reckon I'm strong enough to get out of this bed. There's a lot to do. And the first thing's to clear up this mystery about Drumm's last will. Hand me my clothes."

To her relief, he did seem to have his usual vigor back again. The deep creases of fatigue that had ringed his eyes and mouth before were all but gone, leaving only the tiny lines of a ruddy complexion weathered some by sun and wind. His handsomeness struck her senses as always, making her want to drink in as much of him as she could with her eyes. His back, with its deeply tanned expanse of broad shoulders and rippling cords of muscles trimming down to his narrow waist, was turned to her. Her fingers longed to touch him, stroke over him.

She leaned forward and hugged her arms around him, pressing her naked breasts against his strong back and leaning her head on his uninjured shoulder.

"I love you, Linc," she murmured. "No matter what happens with Drummond's will or the ranch or anything else, I love you with all my heart. I just want to be wherever you are."

He took hold of her hand, glancing over his shoulder at her. His voice was low and full of sincerity when he spoke.

"I know, Victoria, and I'm mighty grateful for that. I've

never had feelings as strong as I have for you. It's everything—knowing you're at my side."

Her heart swelled as she hugged him again and kissed his back. She knew how hard it was for him to show his feelings, let alone speak them. Already she'd learned that that wasn't the Indian way, nor Linc's. But he was changing. They'd both changed. She was no longer afraid of the future or this rough and rugged territory that was so like a block of granite just waiting for the sculptor's chisel and mallet. Some cuts already had been made, smoothing a few of the edges, but the bulk of the stone still remained, its promise yet to be realized. She welcomed the chance to meet the challenge of this land, to help create something worthwhile and lasting out of it.

Linc wouldn't let her help with his clothes. Exasperated, she quickly got dressed herself in the white cotton blouse and many-colored skirt Anita had given her and watched while Linc labored to pull on the tan shirt and blue denim pants that she'd found in his saddlebags. His other clothes had been too bloody, grimy, and torn from the dragging and his wounds to salvage. He pressed his lips together and didn't utter a sound as he carefully added each piece of clothing, but she saw the beads of perspiration on his forehead and noticed how often he paused to take it easy. Finally, he pulled on his boots and stood up. Before he left the side of the bed, he reached for his gunbelt, which Victoria had hung on the end of the headboard. A small twinge of regret crossed her mind when he buckled the Colt Peacemaker in place, but she now knew that the gun was as much a part of Linc as his boots or anything else he wore. He had taken lives with that weapon, but also had saved others, including her own and Deborah's, more than once. Perhaps the time would come someday when he wouldn't feel the need to wear a gun, for having it so close at hand seemed to invite the need to use it. She longed for that day, so danger wouldn't always be a real presence, but now she knew she had to take Linc on his terms. She couldn't do otherwise. She loved him too much.

The stairway was an object to be reckoned with, but Linc finally managed to negotiate each step with a minimum of jostling to his battered body.

"Please let me help you," Victoria begged, reaching for his arm. But he waved her away, shaking his head.

"I can do it," he insisted.

She pursed her lips and put her hands on her hips, frustrated by his stubborn attitude. But at the same time, she admired his determination.

"I'm going to the parlor to take a look at that desk," he said when he'd reached the last step.

"I'll bring the food in there then," she replied. "Are you certain you're all right? You're looking a little pale again."

"Change in altitude, that's all," he quipped, though he continued to grip the wood bannister at the bottom of the stairs with both hands.

Reluctantly, she left him and headed to the kitchen.

Linc ate heartily of the steak and eggs and fried potatoes. Anita had had the breakfast ready in the kitchen. Victoria ate more than a fair portion of the delicious food herself, washing it all down with the strong black coffee, as Linc did.

"I remember now," Linc said suddenly. He'd been staring at the big desk in the corner of the room without saying anything for some time.

"Remember what?" Victoria asked, following his gaze.

"That's not the right desk."

"What do you mean? Anita said the only other desk in the house was the small one in the master bedroom. I searched that, too."

"Drumm said 'pa's old desk' just before he died. Can you go and find Pete for me, Victoria?" Linc flinched as he sat forward on the sofa. The urgency in his voice moved her to rise to her feet.

"Yes, of course. But why—?"

"Just get him!"

She returned a short time later with the old wrangler hobbling on his gout-ridden foot.

"You wanted to see me, Linc?" Pete asked. "Good to see you up an' around. You give us all a real scare there for a spell. Thought we was gonna have to bury you, too."

"Thanks for your concern, Pete. I'll be all right," Linc replied matter-of-factly. "You've been around here a lot longer than Anita. Do you know anything about my pa's old desk, the one that used to be in this room? Drumm and I carved our initials in the top of it when we were kids, remember?"

The wrangler's blue eyes lighted with memory.

"Shore, I recollect that time." He gave a short laugh. "Your pa near tanned the hides off the both of you for that mischief. I told him you was just bein' boys, but he was madder'n all git out at you."

"What happened to that desk, Pete? Did Drumm get rid of it?"

"Hmm, let's see now." The old cowboy squinted one eye and stroked the growth of gray whiskers on his chin. "Was Miz Masterson wanted a new desk in here. She shore did change a lot of things after she hitched up with Drumm. Said your pa's desk didn't fit with the de-cor—that's what she called all them new chairs an' that there sofa she bought, along with them fancy pictures on the walls. Drumm couldn't bring hisself to git rid of the desk though. Let's see, where'd we store it?" He looked thoughtful again. Then he snapped his fingers. "I recollect we was gonna put it in one of the empty stalls in the barn. Wouldn't be in nobody's way there."

"Then the fire got it," Linc said flatly.

Victoria looked at him. Her heart sank, feeling his

disappointment.

"Well now, let me think here a might longer," Pete continued, scratching his head. "Must be four or five years since we moved that big thing. Near throwed my back out of place totin' it . . ." He stopped, looking surprised. "Why, I remember now. We didn't take it out to the barn. Had a full herd of stock in there then. Weren't no empty stalls. So we toted that confounded desk downstairs to the storm cellar. I reckon it's still there."

Linc was on his feet, grabbing the glass-globed lamp and the small box of matches from the end table next to the sofa. His eyes met Victoria's. A spark of excitement glistened in their deep brown depths.

"Show us where, Pete," he said, nodding for Victoria to come with him to the parlor door. He hobbled through the house almost as clumsily as Pete. Victoria noticed he kept his arm bent and pressed against his wounded side, but he didn't say a word of complaint or give any exclamation of pain, so she kept still beside him, knowing there would be no stopping him to rest now.

They had to go outside to reach the storm cellar, which was underground at the back of the ranch house. Victoria helped Pete pull back the heavy wood plank doors. Linc lit the lamp and led the way down the steep stone steps, taking care to go slowly. It was cooler in the cellar than outside. Dust and stale air made Victoria sneeze several times. Shelves built along the left-hand wall held canned foods. A coating of dust and cobwebs kept her from being able to tell what was stored in the glass jars.

"I think it's over there." Pete pointed toward the farthest end of the narrow room.

Linc moved ahead with the lamp. In the corner was something bulky and square-shaped, covered by a piece of canvas.

"Here, give me the light," Victoria offered, taking the lamp from him so he could pull back the canvas.

Another cloud of stirred-up dust made her cough and blink. She waved her free hand in front of her face to try o clear her view. Excitement swelled through her when he saw an old roll-top desk.

"This is the one, pa's desk," Linc murmured, carefully pushing back the slatted cover. It rolled out of sight into he back of the desk. He ran his fingers over the dusty initials carved so long ago on the front edge. A faraway look came briefly into his eyes, then disappeared. He cleared his throat. "Well, let's have a look. Victoria, check these side drawers."

She nodded and handed the lamp to Pete to hold. While Linc examined the small drawers and cubbyholes at the top back of the desk, she drew out each of the three drawers on the right side one by one. When they showed nothing inside, she removed them completely so she could examine the sides and bottom of each one.

"Nothing here," she hated to report. With a sudden hought, she carefully ran her hand along the inside of the desk where the drawers had been. Still she found nothing.

"Same here," Linc replied. The excitement of before had left his voice. He hung his head, leaning over with both palms resting on the desk's writing surface. "Come on, Drumm, where'd you put it?" he mumbled under his breath.

Victoria put her hand on his shoulder, trying to think hard about where to look next. Her heart ached for Linc, knowing how high his hopes had been of finding Drummond's last will here.

"Perhaps we should move it away from the wall," she uggested. "Something could be wedged along the back or he bottom. Or, often these old desks have a secret drawer hidden someplace."

Linc's head shot around toward her.

"Of course!" he exclaimed. Then he grabbed her and gave her a quick kiss on the mouth. "You're wonderful,

Victoria!" Just as abruptly, he released her and turned back to the desk. "I should've remembered this, but it's been so long. Hold the lamp closer, Pete. Yes! Look at this company nameplate, Victoria." He pointed at a tarnished brass strip two inches wide and about five inches long that was screwed into the wood above a row of six letter slots. Part of it was covered with dust, but the name "Brentdennis Supply Company of New York" could be read through the film. "See this left edge where the dirt's a little wiped away?"

Victoria squinted to locate the place he meant.

"But why does that matter?" she asked.

"Drumm must have wiped that spot clean when he did this." Using two fingers, he pressed gently on the edge of the nameplate. Instantly, the brass nameplate popped out, revealing that it was attached to a small hidden drawer. Something rolled to the front of the drawer, hitting the end with two sharp thuds. Linc reached in and took out the contents—two large marbles, one made of amber-colored glass and the other green, and a white vellum envelope.

Victoria's eyes lifted to Linc's. Her heart began to race with excited anticipation, and she knew his must be doing the same.

"Drumm and I each put one of our prized marbles in this drawer when we were just boys. This one was mine." He held up the small amber globe of glass. "This was his." He looked down at the green one resting in his palm. "We did it to seal a pledge we made that we'd always stand up for each other, no matter what." He rolled both marbles around in his hand. "That sure changed when we grew up. God, how we hated each other . . ." He paused, sighing heavily as he looked up at Victoria. "Except at the end. I came back to Laramie because Drumm asked me to. He said he was afraid of losing the ranch to Clint Dandridge and he needed my help to stop it from happening. I could only think about besting Drumm and getting the ranch for nyself. A lot sure has happened since then."

He looked down at the envelope in his other hand. Vicoria touched his arm, trying to offer support. This was ery hard for him, she knew. So many memories and emoions must be swirling around inside him, things he probaly wished he could forget. And now the final testament bout his brother, his family, the ranch lay in his hand in he plain white envelope.

"Let's go outside to read this," he said. "Come on, Pete, ou're a witness, too." He led the way back up the stone teps.

They all blinked against the bright sunlight. Linc moioned for them to follow him to the back porch of the ouse where an overhang of roof provided some shade. Then he opened the envelope and unfolded the single heet of paper inside, reading aloud.

" 'Today is June twenty-first, in the year eighteen-eighty. , Drummond Masterson, am making this new will for the urpose of disposing of my property and possessions in ase anything happens to me. I'm of sound mind and body ight now, and I know exactly what I'm doing, so I don't vant anybody saying otherwise when this will is read.

" 'I'm going to make this simple and easy to understand. When I'm dead, I want the ranch—the Diamond M—to o to my brother, Lincoln Masterson. That includes everyhing that's part of the ranch—the house, stock, and equipnent. That also means the debts go with it, but I know Linc will find a way to take care of them. Only Masterons are ever going to own this piece of land. Linc undertands this. We've had our differences in the past. God nows, we near killed each other more than once. But the anch means the same to both of us. Always has.' "

Linc stopped reading and wrapped an arm around Vicoria. He glanced at her and smiled slightly, not looking riumphant, but relieved, vindicated. Her heart filled with ladness as she watched him gaze out at what was now his heritage. Finally, he could truly call this place home. And so would she.

"There's more," he said, lifting the paper to read on.

" 'To my wife, Abigail Masterson, I give the sum of one thousand dollars. Linc is to take out another loan at the bank if need be to get this amount. Abby is to leave the ranch as soon as she gets the money. She can go back East like she's always wanted. I want Abby to know I loved her more than any man should love a woman who can't be faithful to him.

" 'This brings me to the boy, Patrick Holden Masterson. I've loved this boy like my own son since the day he was born. He's a Masterson by blood, but I know I'm not his father. That responsibility goes to Linc, too. I knew Abby was going to have a child by Linc when I married her. It was a secret we both agreed to keep. But now, I think Linc deserves to know. Abby isn't much close to the boy. Patrick needs to be here at the ranch with his father. It's where he belongs, where his roots are, and where his future will be.

" 'Here ends this will. The rest is up to Linc. He gets all this with my blessing. He's going to need it.' "

Victoria saw that the paper was duly signed and dated by Drummond, and notarized by Howell Griswold.

"Oh, Linc, I'm so glad," Victoria whispered, hugging him. "The ranch is yours, and now you know Patrick really is your son."

"Well, I'll be!" Pete declared, scratching his whiskered chin. "Looks like I'll be workin' for you now, Linc, that is, if'n you still want me around the place with this here bum foot of mine."

"Of course you're staying, Pete," Linc assured him, "along with all the other boys, too. We got a lot of work ahead of us. I'll need good men I can depend on."

"That's me, all right." The old wrangler grinned. "Reckon I kin go tell the rest of the boys about you bein the boss now?"

"Well, it's not exactly official yet," Linc said, folding the paper and putting it back in the envelope. "But it will be as soon as the circuit judge comes around and takes a look at this will. Go tell the boys I'll do the best I can by them. They'll be getting their back wages, too. That's a promise."

Pete almost did a dance off the end of the porch. Then he remembered his foot and grabbed a roof post for support just before he fell.

"Lordy, the boys'll shore be glad to hear all this! It'll be jus' like old times! See you later, Linc. Excuse me, ma'am." He gave Victoria a nod and hobbled off toward the bunkhouse.

Linc smiled and slipped an arm around Victoria's waist to draw her to him.

"Life is good, Mrs. Masterson. Do you know that?"

She returned his smile, feeling full of love for him.

"Yes, Mr. Masterson, I do."

"You'll be staying then?"

"Just try to get rid of me! I think Deborah will be staying, too, if you don't mind. Her health really has been better in this climate than it was in England."

"Looks like we'll be having a houseful starting off our marriage," Linc noted, grinning. "Should be mighty interesting." He guided her to the end of the porch. His expression became serious again as he looked out toward the distant mountains. "You know, I lost something important to me when I left this place five years ago—a sense of belonging, being part of the land that I had here. I traveled all over trying to find it somewhere else, but I didn't feel it again until I came back. This is where I belong."

"And I belong wherever you are, my love." She slipped her arms around his neck and drew his head down to kiss him.

"You won't miss England?" he asked when they'd pulled away a little.

She shook her head.

"I'll probably need to return there for a time, to settl
my father's estate. Will you go with me? I remember Gile
talking about a hearty breed of cattle being developed o
some of the back Yorkshire farms. He had the idea t
bring some of them here to America for possible cross
breeding. You could investigate them while we're there."

Linc raised an eyebrow at her in surprise.

"You have a good head on these beautiful shoulders c
yours, wife of mine. I think I picked the right gal."

"You *think?*" She gave him a mockingly stern frown.

He raised his hand to touch the side of her face.

"I *know* I did, Victoria, and I love you with all m
heart." He leaned down to kiss her again.

"And I love you, my husband," she murmured agains
his lips, so happy to be in his arms now, and always.